THE CONSPIRACY WITHIN

The Conspiracy Within

Sean Mackie

The Conspiracy Within

A Novel by Sean Mackie

The Conspiracy Within

ISBN: 979-8-9934717-1-6
Cover design by Will Phillips Hallewell
Published by Phillips and Dunn Publishing

Phillips & Dunn and Sean Mackie would like to thank the following donors who helped get this book and Phillips & Dunn Publishing off the ground:

- Sean Mackie
- Karis Benner
- Tim Mackie
- Nathan Benner
- Kim Ogden
- Will Phillips Hallewell
- Stephen Bialik
- Donna Monks
- Christina Miller

It's an honor to have such great friends!

We truly appreciate you!

Dedication:

To my wife, Sue -

You're the reason why I'm the man I am today. Our many adventures, laughs, silliness, and love have led me to a life far beyond anything I've ever dreamed of.

And we have many more adventures to come. I love you!

Acknowledgment -

I'd like to thank my brother-in-law, William Phillips Hallewell (The Commander).

He's my editor, publisher, and mentor, helping guide me through my first book. He's an accomplished writer in his own right, and none of this would be possible without him.

Thank you so very much for helping me get to the stars, Commander.

Prologue

"Quiet, please," the RT Gen 6 bot spoke sternly to the classroom of noisy second graders, its head smoothly scanning the room with fluid, almost hypnotic precision. The seamless motion, six generations in the making, glided from left to right like a camera on a silent gimbal; so graceful, it barely registered as mechanical. The second graders, slouched in their ergonomic learning pods, didn't understand how significant that improvement was. But to engineers and observers who'd seen the stiff, jerky movements of the GEN1 bots, it marked a monumental leap forward in robotic mobility.

"If you don't want your education credits to get taxed for misbehavior and your parents to find out about it, I would suggest that you close your mouths and turn your attention toward the front." The bot's voice, though smooth, carried a sharp mechanical edge — unwavering, emotionless. "Ever since 2032, changes have been made to our society to benefit us. Not just you, but all of us; humans, bots, and… the Norn. They have been made to advance our cumulative society, to make it better than your ancestors could ever have imagined. So," the Gen 6 bot looked around with impassive eyes, "I suggest you pay attention."

The overhead fluorescents dimmed with a slow whine, casting the room in a muted half-light that made the children shift in their seats. Brian Mackey Jr., tousle-haired and always toeing the line of rebellion, leaned sideways and jabbed his best friend in the ribs. "Pay attention, Zeke, or your credits will be taxed," he intoned, mimicking the droning cadence of a bot, his arms stiffly raised like an old tin soldier. The robotic impression was crude, exaggerated, and outdated, like something from a retro museum exhibit.

The real Gen 6 bot, all subtle precision and machine authority, snapped its head toward Brian in a single, whip-like motion. No gears clicked, no servos whirred, only silence and that ever-present, deadpan stare. Zeke, wide-eyed, jolted upright in his seat like he'd touched a live wire.

"Shut up, man. You're gonna get us in trouble," Zeke whispered, his words barely brushing the air, just low enough to dodge the bot's auditory sensors.

From above, a white projection screen descended with a soft electronic hum, like the ghost of a forgotten slideshow. It snapped into place with a mechanical finality, and within seconds, flickering images began to appear. The film projector's simulated whirr filled the room; not a real projector, of course, but a sound file designed to mimic the nostalgic churn of old reels.

The kids groaned in unison, a quiet chorus of disappointment that seemed almost ceremonial. They knew what was coming. Brian, still sulking, dropped his head to his desk with a theatrical sigh. "Ugh. Not another Movietone," he mumbled into the crook of his arm.

The GEN 6 bot moved. One second it stood in still surveillance, and the next, it was beside Brian's desk, swifter than any adult could have crossed the room. A ruler cracked across the tops of Brian's hands. He gasped, biting down the yelp, his knuckles flaring red beneath the harsh classroom lighting. That was enough to silence him.

Since the beginning, May 8th, 2032, the day the Norn arrived, Earth had changed in ways both wondrous and chilling. Chief among the Norn's peculiar preferences was their obsession with Movietone newsreels, a medium dead and buried since 1963. These grainy black-and-white shorts had once narrated the world's triumphs and tragedies with bombast and orchestra, serving as cinematic snapshots of history. Now, inexplicably, they had become the official voice of alien enlightenment.

To the Norn, the Movietone format offered clarity, authority, and emotional distance. It was news told like myth; dramatic, digestible, and unarguable. The dramatic voiceovers once delivered by Lowell Thomas had been resurrected by AI, the vocal patterns painstakingly restored to sound just like the original - soothing, iconic, and eerily disembodied. The Norn believed it was the most non-threatening way to teach humans.

The screen flickered, then flared to life in shades of smoky gray. A title card floated on a soft gradient, surrounded by curling shadows. The whole presentation was designed to cast a nostalgic, reverent glow - sacred history repackaged as retro film.

Title Card: The date, May 8th, 2032, 12:15 EST.

PATRIOTIC MUSIC FILLS THE ROOM AS THE NARRATOR BEGINS

NARRATOR:
After decades of speculation and conspiracy theories, the residents of Earth finally have the answer to the question that has been eluding us for years. ARE WE ALONE IN THE UNIVERSE?
On May 8th, twenty thirty-two, we were answered with a resounding No!

ON-SCREEN:
Cloud-streaked skies. A pill-shaped spacecraft drifts into view, its metallic hull glowing in the midday sun. Each of its four corners pulses with radiant, alien light. In the streets below, people freeze. Cell phones drop. Groceries spill. All eyes lift skyward in a moment of collective astonishment.

NARRATOR:
We were introduced to an alien civilization. They called themselves the Norn. Not the three women from Norse mythology Norn. Not the ones who spun, measured, and cut the threads of fate. These Norn were much more than that...
Their name, in their language, was a storm of clicks and guttural sounds no human could hope to reproduce. "Norn" was simply the label they offered for human convenience. It was not their name, not really. Just a placeholder.

ON-SCREEN:
Chaos erupts. Military vehicles roll in. Tanks pivot their turrets skyward. Fighter jets roar overhead, trailing smoke. Bullets and missiles streak toward

the craft, but none make impact. The ships hang motionless, untouched, and unbothered.

NARRATOR:

On that fateful day, the Norn arrived and quickly took hold of all the governments of the world. Some saw it as a hostile takeover. But most saw it for what it was: progress.

ON-SCREEN:

All across the globe, Norn ships descend like thunderclouds. In harbors, warships fire futilely at the alien vessels. The Norn crew, unarmed, stands on deck with hands raised in something between surrender and superiority.

NARRATOR:

In total, five hundred ninety-five ships landed that day.
The human race began to panic and ready themselves for a nuclear attack on the Norn, but they quickly realized that even their nuclear capabilities had been rendered useless.
The Norn had taken over the world without firing a single retaliatory shot, and the human race could do nothing except stand and watch.

ON-SCREEN:

A single ship, larger than the rest, looms over Washington, D.C. A hush falls over the crowd. Then: static. All screens go black, then shimmer back to life with a soft blue glow.

NARRATOR:

On May 8th, 2032, 6 p.m. EST, the Norn took over worldwide communication. All television, internet, and military communication had been interrupted and replaced by the soft, albeit alien, voice of the Norn's representative.

Back in the classroom, the RT Gen 6 bot stood watch over its flock. Its tablet-like clipboard blinked softly in its hand, a screen of checkboxes and forms. It tapped gently at the "OBSERVATIONAL LOG – SEGMENT A." One field read, *"DOES THE CLASS SEEM ENGAGED BY THE FILM?"* Another, more ominous, *"DO YOU SEE ANY POTENTIAL DISSENSION? IF SO, INCLUDE THE STUDENT'S NAME AND HUMAN NUMBER IN THE SPACE PROVIDED: ___________________."*

The bot's visual sensors glided over the class, pausing momentarily on Brian Mackey Jr.

NORN REPRESENTATIVE (VOICEOVER):

We're here to help you.

We mean no harm to your people. This isn't a takeover. It's an intervention.

For centuries, we've been watching and waiting for you to come to us. We have had minimal contact with your world's governments for some time, but instead of being honest with all of you, they chose to withhold information about us for decades. They'd rather keep you in the dark and control you than further advance your species. We're here to change that. We're here to take you to unprecedented heights. It's now time to go far beyond what you thought you were capable of. We'll lead you to the stars, and we will grant you true free will.

The RT Gen 6 bot's eyes narrowed as it looked at Brian again. It raised its pencil, paused... then lowered it, folding its arms in quiet judgment.

The film pressed on.

NORN REPRESENTATIVE – CONTINUED:

We have two gifts to bestow upon you.

The first is an energy source. It was created from elements from our planet, but it is sustainable here on Earth. It is shaped like a diamond and can power your planet for ten thousand years. Homes, cars, and power plants can all benefit from this source.

ON-SCREEN:

A diamond-shaped crystal rotates slowly in space, surrounded by glowing tendrils of animated energy. The halo of power pulses outward, illuminating cities, charging vehicles, turning night into day.

NORN REPRESENTATIVE – CONTINUED:

We have created six hundred of these power sources, plenty for many lifetimes if your governments will allow them to be shared.

Our second gift to your planet and its inhabitants is the Reverie Halo, a device that allows its wearer to find out who they were in a previous...

ON-SCREEN:

A serene human model reclines in a padded chair. A smooth metallic ring hovers just above his scalp, emitting faint pulses of light. The model's eyes are closed. His lips curl in a faint, knowing smile.

NARRATOR:

The Reverie Halo, despite its popularity, was labeled dangerous and locked away from public use. No one has seen or used the Reverie Halo since its initial display.

In the meantime, the dramatic reshaping of society began.

Around the world, people eventually began to learn and to change. A new, better way of living began. And, although it took a couple of generations, the human race bettered itself and began to reach new heights.

Despite the attempts of tyrants who tried to fill the vacuum that the lack of government control left, the lifestyle that the Norn introduced took hold, and the human race began to flourish.

ON-SCREEN:

A grayscale panorama unfolds, a meadow bathed in soft light, with wildflowers swaying in the breeze like nature's applause. Families gather beneath a wide sky, holding hands and laughing as children race between them. The image is static, like a photograph frozen in time, but its serenity speaks volumes.

NARRATOR:

The early twenty-second century saw innovation like never before!
In the year twenty-one-hundred, medicine, science, food production, engineering, and education achieved boundless potential.

Cities rose with graceful, curved architecture; crops grew faster and stronger in climate-stabilized zones. The air was cleaner. The diseases of the past became distant memories.

A new credit system was developed, replacing the need for money and creating a deterrent for thievery and government control. In every walk of life, on every corner of the planet, everyone had their own wealth, and no one ever went without. Poverty became a thing of the past.

ON-SCREEN:

A vibrant logo spins slowly into view, the letters "NU" surrounded by a ring of clasped hands, each one a different hue. The hands rotate together in perfect sync, symbolizing unity, inclusion, and global cooperation.

NARRATOR:

With the new order, the NU was born – Nations United. One representative from each country would be appointed by order of election, put in place simply to share new ideas, breakthroughs, and developments in all lines of work.

A new cure for disease? It was reported to the NU.
A new advance in technology? It was reported to the NU.
Their mission statement? Ensure a Better Future for all of the world.

THE PATRIOTIC MUSIC GROWS SOMBER

ON-SCREEN:

Two men engage in a carefully choreographed battle. Each punch was exaggerated, every motion a spectacle. Behind them, banners wave. Spectators cheer. It's a staged performance, but the tension feels all too real.

As anyone from that era will tell you, not everything was perfect in the utopia that the Norn tried to create here on Earth.
Crime, on the whole, decreased throughout the years, but those crimes that were committed became more heinous. Human trafficking began to increase at levels not seen before.

Eventually, a new experiment was undertaken. Tracking chips were embedded in every newborn baby. And even though it was met with some controversy, it was agreed that something had to be done to protect the human race. People were disappearing at alarming levels, and the tracking chips would keep track of everyone everywhere.

Back in the classroom, Brian leaned close to Zeke, eyes darting to the front of the room. The Gen 6 bot stood motionless, as if in deep standby or lost in the rhythmic cadence of the film. Its posture was rigid, arms folded, face unreadable.

"More like spy on everyone, everywhere," Brian whispered, barely parting his lips, like a ventriloquist testing the limits of silence.

The RT Gen 6 bot didn't move, at least not immediately. But as soon as Brian turned back toward the screen, the bot's arm subtly twitched. Its pencil made a faint scratch against its clipboard.

NARRATOR CONTINUES:

In the end, the microchipping was deemed an overwhelming success! Information was stored at all times regarding every person's movements, and safeguards were put into place to deter the removal or reprogramming of the chips.

Humane prisons were built in every country to house microchipped offenders, where they could be visually monitored twenty-four hours a day.

THE BACKGROUND MUSIC BECOMES MORE UPBEAT

On the lighter side, while there was less governmental control, there was also an increase in governmental departments being created.

New departments were created in Space Exploration, Infrastructure & Architecture, Agriculture, Medicine, Defense, Paranormal, Transportation, Food Services, Accounting, Archaeology, Academia, Emergency Services, Arts & Entertainment, Athletics, and AI.

Of those Departments, Space Exploration quickly became the desired career for all those willing to strive for success. Only the absolute best, the top one percent, became Space Explorers, able to join the Exploration Department.

A streamlined rocket, white with deep blue accents, launches into the sky with a roaring trail of flame. Behind it, a bold insignia: the logo for the Space Explorers - an upward-pointing triangle encircling a starburst.

This sought-after position would drive the human race to explore other planets, travel through space, and establish our place in the universe.

Along with a new, stronger metal that allowed not only space travel but the use of bullet trains that ran along a series of magnetic tracks, automobiles slowly began to dwindle in number in favor of the sleeker and more exciting mode of transportation.

The future was becoming exciting, and it was being led by the four new spaceships created to lead the way:
the Elevation, the Evolution, the Intervention, and the Innovation.

Space travel was just a leap away, and thanks to the Norn, the future of the human race looked bright.

The film reel ended with a final crescendo of patriotic music: brass horns blaring, strings swelling with emotion. The image faded to white, then to black, and the lights in the room slowly brightened, lifting the shadows from every desk and face.

The RT Gen 6 bot moved with practiced calm to the front of the room, resuming its sentinel stance.

Brian Mackey lifted his head, blinking against the light. He leaned once more toward Zeke and whispered, "Yeah, but then what?"

Chapter 1: Coronation

The summer of 2199 was in full bloom as Alexander Belle sat patiently in Horseshoe Park, Columbus, Ohio. Once home to the Ohio State Buckeyes football team, the stadium had been transformed into a stunning garden, its horseshoe shape filled with vibrant plants and flowers of red and somehow gray, engineered to bloom in those exact shades as a tribute to OSU's legacy. The old bleachers were gone, replaced by terraced planting beds and winding walking paths. Ivy twisted up the concrete remnants of support columns, and fragrant bursts of honeysuckle drifted through the air. Ohioans, nostalgic as ever, had preserved the iconic landmark in a new form, and today it served as the backdrop to a moment that could change Alex's life forever.

It wasn't that football no longer existed; it had simply outgrown such humble spaces. The sport had evolved exponentially, drawing crowds in the hundreds of thousands. Stadiums now spanned cities, not blocks, and the "Shoe" had become a sacred relic of a simpler time. Still, its presence carried weight, especially today.

For his part, Alex was waiting to find out if he would be chosen as the successor to Dayo Emem, the liaison to the Norn. Dayo had recently retired, leaving the role open for a new representative, someone uniquely gifted in diplomacy and understanding.

At just 26 years old, Alex's accomplishments were staggering. He had joined the Space Explorers at 18, becoming the youngest ever to do so. By 24, he was nominated as the NU Representative for the United States. Now, he was on the brink of what could be his most significant achievement yet: becoming humanity's voice to the Norn. It was a large undertaking for sure, but Alex knew he was ready for the challenge.

Nicknamed "Alexander the Great," a moniker he accepted with good humor, Alex's very name carried weight. His mother, Alexandrea, hailed from Scotland, and his father, Marco Belle, from Italy. Both were celebrated scientists who had moved to Columbus, Ohio, to further their research in what was considered one of the top programs in the world. Their faith in Alex's extraordinary potential had been unwavering, and their decision to retire and return to Italy six years ago had been a selfless one: to allow their son to grow independently.

As Alex waited and watched the Gen 6 robots performing their various tasks around the park, trimming hedges with microscopic precision, replenishing hydration stations, and gently guiding visitors along the flower paths, his thoughts flickered to the immense expectations placed on him. Was it too much, too soon? He was so young, after all. Yet his natural charisma and humility reassured him. Standing at six-foot-one with a fit frame, light-brown hair, blue eyes, and a warm demeanor, Alex had a gift for making people feel seen and valued. It was why so many believed he was destined for this role.

A bot approached him with a tray of drinks, its movement silent, seamless. Alex was about to take one off of the tray when, out of nowhere, the Norn appeared.

They always moved with such uncanny speed and grace that it was impossible to detect their approach. Most people figured the Norn knew how to travel in and out of different dimensions, phasing between realms of matter and thought, but it didn't lessen the jolt that came with their sudden presence. It was like turning around and realizing a statue had moved.

Known as N1 and N2, their true names still unpronounceable even after decades of contact, they were an imposing pair, each standing seven feet tall. Though humanoid in shape, their features were undeniably other: elongated torsos, more pronounced jawlines, slightly wider and darker eyes with no visible whites, and hairless heads that reflected light with a faint silvery shimmer. Their skin held a grayish hue, mottled slightly in patches that pulsed with bioluminescence depending on their emotional state.

Late-night talk show conspiracy theorists often compared them to the mythical alien race known as "The Grays," a theory fueled by their appearance and reclusive nature. The chatter only grew louder when viewers zoomed in on their pupils, black and endless, like portals to some otherworldly realm. Despite their unsettling aesthetic, their aura exuded kindness and restraint, almost too much, as if overcompensating. This paradox only deepened public suspicion.

The Norn had left Earth in 2156, after 124 years of involvement with humanity. Their intervention had begun during the global crisis of 2032, when their technology and insight stabilized a planet on the brink. Over time, they stepped back, remaining observers more than rulers, intervening only when a nudge was needed. Their legacy was one of strange but steady guidance, and their philosophy was clear: success must be earned, not given.

When they departed, they left behind two ambassadors, N1 and N2, to shepherd humanity in their absence. These ambassadors, it was said, chose only one human at a time to serve as liaison between Earth and the Norn. The first had been Wei Qi Lai of China, a calm visionary who held the post for forty years. After him came Dayo Emem of Africa, a brilliant negotiator and diplomat whose presence still lingered in global memory.

Now, it was Alex's turn.

His palms were damp with nervous sweat as N2 approached, his gait as fluid as molten metal — fast, deliberate. N1, meanwhile, drifted away toward a thicket of metallic orchids, flowers engineered by gene-splicers to shimmer like chrome in the sun. N1 was always the quieter of the two. His silence had become a matter of speculation. Why didn't he speak? What did he know? What did he see?

"Hello, my friend. How are you today?" N2's voice was smooth, almost human, with just the faintest undercurrent of electronic modulation. It resonated somewhere between a diplomat and a machine. Alex, startled but composed, shifted from one foot to the other.

"I'm well… and nervous," he admitted, a sheepish smile tugging at the corners of his mouth. "I appreciate you calling me here, and I don't want to be presumptuous, but… am I the one?"

N2 responded quickly, with a warm but inscrutable smile. "It's OK to be nervous and a bit presumptuous, Alex. You are deserving, after all. If it makes it any easier for you to feel justified in taking the role, please note that we took great care in our decision. We have followed your accomplishments for many years and determined that you are the perfect heir to Dayo."

Alex exhaled sharply, running his hands over his face. A tide of emotion rushed through him — relief, joy, awe.

"She's extraordinary. I hope, at the very least, I can live up to her legacy. It's truly an honor to succeed her. I won't let you down."

N2's smile widened. "We're counting on it. Do not worry; our expectations are simple. Continue on as you have been. Our role is to observe and assist only when necessary. It is our goal and our main objective to offer advice sparingly and interfere even less."

Alex nodded, absorbing the weight of those words. His gaze shifted across the park toward N1, who now appeared to be in conversation with a Gen 6 bot, though no sound came from his lips. The exchange was silent, like a chess match played with eyes.

"Does N1 ever speak?" Alex asked, his curiosity piqued.

N2 chuckled softly, the sound like silk brushed across glass. "Sometimes. Only when he feels it is absolutely necessary. He is my superior and believes that fewer words carry more weight, so he leaves the speech to me. He means no disrespect; he simply wants you to learn on your own, as has always been the goal of the intervention."

Then, with a gentle pivot, N2 changed the subject. "Now, tell me, where are we on the Elevation testing?"

Alex blinked. That was fast.

It had taken nearly the entire 22nd century to design and build the first four interstellar shuttles capable of deep-space travel. Blueprints were passed through generations like heirlooms. Failures became teachings. Solutions were precious. And now, Alex stood as the chosen voice overseeing that legacy.

"We're ready," Alex said, confidence sharpening his tone. "The unmanned test run is scheduled for December 15th. Commander Will Phillips will pilot the drone. Representatives from the NU and Space Explorers from around the world will be present. The launch will take place at Cape Canaveral, as it is only fitting to do so, and so far, the forecast is sunny and 68 degrees that day. Speaking in space program terms, everything is a go. Will you be attending?"

"No," N2 said, his head tilting slightly. "But we will observe from our realm. After the launch, we will meet with you privately and discuss the results. In the meantime, should there ever be a need for us to contact you or for you to get in contact with us, here is a special communication device."

From seemingly nowhere, perhaps from an invisible fold in his suit, N2 produced a small, sleek object. It was the size of a credit chip, glinting slightly like polished obsidian.

"It's compact and easy to lose," N2 added with a chuckle. "So be careful with it, but it will allow direct communication with us."

"There are no buttons," Alex noted, turning the device over in his hand. It felt impossibly light.

"Simply hold it up to your face," N2 replied, miming the action with his long fingers. "Now, we must go."

As if on cue, N1 returned, his long strides slow and deliberate. It was unclear whether he had overheard the entire conversation or simply knew when it was time.

N2 raised a hand in parting. "Congratulations, Alex. We look forward to working with you, as we did with your predecessors."

"Thank you! I won't let you down," Alex said, his voice rising in urgency as if afraid the opportunity to speak was closing.

N2 nodded. "Good. We are certain of your abilities. Now, go see your friends. They're waiting for you in the parking lot."

And just like that, they were gone - no shimmer, no sound, only absence.

Alex stood still for a moment, breathing in the garden's scent, grounding himself. Then he turned and jogged toward the parking lot, where two familiar figures awaited him.

Lisa and Brian Mackey stood beside a sleek black transport, practically bouncing with anticipation.

"Well?" Brian shouted as Alex approached. "What happened?"

"They picked me!" Alex called, breaking into a full sprint.

The three collided in a joyful embrace, laughter echoing into the warm air. It was the sound of friendship, of triumph, of new chapters beginning.

Lisa, a brilliant scientist of Asian descent, and Brian, an African-American astrophysicist with an infectious grin and quick wit, had been by Alex's side since their teen years. Both now 28, they were integral to the Elevation flight crew and proud parents to young Brian Jr.

"I'm so happy for you!" Lisa beamed. Her eyes sparkled with genuine delight.

"How are you feeling?" Brian asked, half-laughing, half-tearing up.

"Nervous! Excited! Fantastic!" Alex said, and then quickly deflected. "But enough about me, are you finally going to tell me what you've been hiding?" He raised a suspicious brow. "You two have been like giddy children around the office. Is there another Junior on the way?"

Lisa began to play coy, but Brian rolled his eyes. "Let's just tell him. He'll hound us until we do."

Lisa sighed dramatically. "Fine. You do it."

Brian turned, grinning. "You're right. We're having another baby!"

Alex lit up. His hands landed gently on both of their shoulders. "That's amazing! I'm so happy for you both! Why didn't you tell me sooner?"

"We didn't want to distract you during the selection process," Lisa said.

"Nonsense! You both mean the world to me. It would've been a pleasant distraction from having to endure that torture." He grinned widely. "Have you picked a guardian for the baby?"

"We were hoping it would be you," Brian said. "That is, if you don't mind having another one like Brian Jr. around. Did you know we have to go to the office again for his interruptions at school…"

"Of course!" Alex interrupted. "Do you know the sex yet?"

"A girl," Lisa said, smiling softly. "She's due in January."

"So see, no junior. What's the name? Have you picked out a…" Alex asked, already excited.

Lisa answered before he could finish. "Her name will be Grayle."

Chapter 2: History on a Hard Drive

The nine months following the announcement of Grayle's impending birth had passed in a blur, and now Alex sat in the control room, lost in thought. The towering silhouette of the ship, the Elevation, loomed just beyond the reinforced glass, bathed in warm twilight. Its sleek lines shimmered in the floodlights like a slumbering giant, poised for tomorrow's ascent.

To his right, a television played a Movietone newsreel in soft black-and-white, its old-timey grain crackling against the ambient hum of the control room. The tick-tick-tick of the faux projector filled the silence like a ghost from another era.

ON-SCREEN: Movietone News Title Card
Patriotic music swells as the title fades to black-and-white footage of bustling activity at Cape Canaveral.

NARRATOR (Voiceover):
December 14th, the world holds its breath as Cape Canaveral becomes the epicenter of humanity's most ambitious leap into the cosmos. Tomorrow, the Elevation will undergo its first test launch, a moment that could redefine the boundaries of human exploration!

ON-SCREEN:
Engineers in crisp uniforms swarm around the massive shuttle, inspecting every rivet and panel with surgical precision. Their movements are orchestrated, near-silent, as drones hover overhead recording telemetry and sensor data.

NARRATOR:
Last-minute preparations are in full swing, with over six hundred experts from around the globe meticulously inspecting every piece of the Elevation.

These brilliant minds are ensuring nothing is overlooked in this historic endeavor.

ON-SCREEN:
A sleek humanoid figure sits upright in a test chamber, monitored by a team of scientists in white lab coats. The figure blinks, its synthetic skin almost indistinguishable from real flesh.

NARRATOR:
Leading the charge is the Artificial Intelligence Department, unveiling its crowning achievement: a first-of-its-kind AI. This revolutionary creation mimics the vital components of a human being, from skin tissue to internal organs. Its mission? To test the limits of deep-space travel and assess how the unprecedented speeds of the Elevation will affect the human body.

ON-SCREEN:
The Elevation stands proud on the launch pad, its advanced propulsion system glinting under the golden sun. Wind rolls across the metal hull like a sigh.

NARRATOR:
Thanks to propulsion technology reverse-engineered from power sources gifted by the Norn, the Elevation can achieve speeds of up to one hundred Gs, a feat once dismissed as the stuff of science fiction.

ON-SCREEN:
Quick-cut montage: early shuttles erupting in flame, disintegrating midair, split-second failures; then, sparks fly as new alloys are forged in containment labs.

NARRATOR:
The journey to this moment has not been without setbacks. Numerous prototypes were pushed to their breaking points. Yet, with every failure, humanity forged ahead, creating stronger metals and more resilient alloys. Now, the

Elevation stands as a testament to perseverance — a ship believed capable of surviving these extraordinary forces while keeping its crew safe.

ON-SCREEN:

A camera drone soars high above the Earth's curvature. Then, darkness... starfields blinking into view, infinite and waiting.

NARRATOR:

If successful, tomorrow's launch will propel humanity beyond the pale, opening the door to the stars and possibilities yet unimagined.

ON-SCREEN:

The final frame: the Elevation gleaming against a deep-orange sunset. Across the screen, the words: "Tomorrow: Humanity's Leap to the Stars."

Alex blinked, the screen's reflection still dancing across his eyes. *He wondered if tomorrow would be the day,* just as the familiar click of boots and a boisterous voice shattered the reverie.

"Hey! Are you going to keep staring at that monolith all evening?" Tim Stevens called out, stepping through the control room doors with his usual swagger. "It isn't going anywhere until tomorrow, and I'd like to get dinner soon."

Tim's compact, wiry frame moved with restless energy. His intense presence and blunt delivery were a perfect foil to Alex's calm, contemplative nature. At just 22, he'd been plucked straight out of Florida State University for his sheer intellectual firepower. In another lifetime, they might've been brothers or rivals.

"Aren't you even the least bit concerned or worried?" Alex asked, eyes still locked on the distant bulk of the ship.

Tim crossed the room, hands clasped behind his back like a soldier observing a war monument. His voice dropped to a thoughtful murmur. "Nope! Not at all. We're not sending real people up there, so what's there to worry about, Al? Don't tell the AI Department I said that, though. They'd probably blow a gasket." He turned and grinned wickedly. "The way they act, you'd think they touch that thing inappropriately when no one's around." With a laugh, he smacked Alex playfully on the shoulder.

"C'mon, Tim," Alex muttered, shaking his head. "Aren't you ever serious?"

Before Tim could answer, Alex pivoted. "Where's Richard? Have you seen him?"

"He should be here soon. I think he's vetting that reporter kid you're about to interview," Tim said, now peering out the window at the Elevation. "How long is that interview going to take? I'm gonna leave. Richard can hang out with you for that."

"Okay, okay." Alex waved him off with a chuckle. "I'll see you later for a drink. Go. Eat. You're a real pain in my…" He trailed off, trying to be the responsible one. "You know, for an apprentice, you'd think you'd care a little more."

Tim grinned. "Yeah, you'd think. But… no." He left with a shrug just as Richard entered.

"Not sticking around, Tim?" Richard asked with a knowing smirk.

"Nah," Tim replied over his shoulder. "I have better things to do. Like, catch a meal."

Richard chuckled, shaking his head as the younger man vanished. "Better things to do than watch history be made?"

He stepped fully into the control room and looked toward Alex, raising his voice just slightly. "Of all the people you could've brought on as your apprentice, why that asshole?"

"Because he's great at what he does," Alex replied, grinning as he stood and shook Richard's hand. "There are plenty of people in the SE Department who are strange. But we look for brilliance, and, like it or not, Tim fits right in."

Richard returned the grin, but his tone shifted.

"Anyway, I know you're about to talk to that reporter from *Look* in a minute, but there's something I need to tell you."

Alex tilted his head. The mood shift was subtle but real. "Are you okay? Something wrong?"

"No, no. I'm fine," Richard said, though the hesitation lingered. "I just wanted you to know that after the new year, the first week of February, I'll be leaving the SE Department. I've, um, accepted a position with the Defense Department. I'll be Assistant Director under Director Mathews."

Richard smiled, lifting both arms like he was accepting applause. "He's tapped me to be his replacement. I'll take over as Director of the Eastern Division in 2204."

Alex's jaw dropped slightly before snapping into a congratulatory smile. He grasped Richard's hand again, this time with firmer enthusiasm. "Wow! I didn't even know you were considering a move. Why now? Are you unhappy here?"

"No, it's not that," Richard said, waving off the thought. "The stars have always been your passion, not mine. I'm more interested in what's happening down here. I'm a detective at heart. That's where I feel I'm best utilized."

Alex smiled, nodding in understanding. "Well, maybe now that we're not coworkers, we can finally grab a drink after work sometime."

"Maybe," Richard replied with a grin, giving Alex a friendly slap on the shoulder. He gestured toward the door. "Okay, the *Look* magazine kid is ready for you. I'll be next door if you need me."

"Great!" Alex nodded. "Send him in. Director."

Richard flashed a thumbs-up before slipping out. The door closed, leaving Alex alone, just long enough to gather himself, when the reporter walked in, extending a hand with youthful eagerness.

"Mike Wilson, *Look* magazine."

Alex returned the handshake, then motioned toward a table.

"*Look* magazine. That's a bit crazy, isn't it? I mean, it was a great magazine in its day, but didn't it fold back in the nineteen-seventies?"

Mike shrugged, already unpacking a laptop and a sleek digital recorder. "Well, you know the Norn and their nostalgia. First, it was Movietone. Now *Look*. This interview is one of our first articles.

We're doing a print version in the same style as the original, but we'll also publish the video interviews online."

Alex smiled. "No worries. I'm glad you're here. We like transparency. Makes people think everything is the way they expect it to be. No surprises."

He stepped over to a cabinet, pulled out a bottle of aged Scotch, and dropped two clinking ice cubes into a pair of glasses. "Do you want a drink? Might help calm your nerves."

Mike, pleasantly surprised, accepted the offer and followed Alex back to the table, placing his drink beside his equipment.

"Thank you," he said, visibly more relaxed.

Alex nodded toward the camera. "Are we ready to go?"

"I'm ready whenever you are," Mike said, flipping on the recorder and adjusting the lens.

Alex took a sip of Scotch, glanced at the two-way mirror, and raised his glass in a silent toast. He knew Richard was watching.

Richard mimed a toast in return, grinning behind the glass. But before the interview could begin, footsteps approached from the hallway.

Lisa and Brian arrived quietly, Lisa glowing and nearing the end of her pregnancy. She gave Richard a gentle hug.

"Hey, Richard!" she said softly, sliding into a chair by the speaker monitor. "Did they start the interview yet?"

"Not yet," Richard said. "Just about."

He motioned to Brian, who leaned in and gave him a shoulder pat. "How's that baby girl doing?"

Lisa chuckled, rubbing her belly. "Ready to jump out of me! She might come early, but she's healthy and raring to go. I just hope it's not *right now.*"

Richard laughed. Brian leaned closer and grinned. "Yeah, she's going to be a force to be reckoned with."

Then he lowered his voice, still smiling. "I hear congratulations are in order. It's cool that you're becoming the Assistant Director in the East."

Richard nodded sheepishly. "I'm guessing it's hit the news broadcasts?"

Both Lisa and Brian nodded as Lisa replied, "Did you at least get a chance to tell Alex before the news broke?"

"I did," Richard said, a faint smile tugging at one corner of his mouth. "I was just with him when…" He glanced toward the mirror, where Alex and Mike were settling in. "Oh, looks like they're about to start the interview."

Brian, always warm but never long-winded, quickly leaned in with a grin. "We'll talk after this is over? Maybe over dinner?"

Richard shrugged, the corners of his eyes creasing slightly. "Maybe. We'll see. I'll check my schedule."

Now that he was settled in, Mike began the interview, his voice crisp and clear as the camera started recording.

"Good day, I'm Mike Wilson, and welcome to *Look*. I'm coming to you live from inside the control room for tomorrow's highly anticipated big event: the launch of the Elevation. Joining me is none other than Mr. Alexander Belle, space explorer, NU Representative, and liaison to the Norn. Thank you for having me, Alex. My first question is on the lighter side, if I may. When do you find time to do all of these things?"

Alex chuckled, flashing a polished grin, fully aware of the camera's gaze. He had always possessed an effortless poise when the spotlight was on.

"Oh, good. A softball question to start with. Honestly, it is a lot to juggle. Sometimes, I wonder how I do it myself. I have no idea. I just move from one thing to another, and I rely heavily on my digital assistant."

He gestured toward the small earpiece nestled comfortably in his right ear. With the meteoric rise of AI back in the twenty-first century, personal digital assistants had become as indispensable as shoes. Now, most people wouldn't dream of leaving home without one.

Alex paused briefly, then continued.

"I guess the Norn mostly staying away is very helpful in my time management. Over the past six months, I think I've briefed them only on our progress and launch preparations. After that, they usually leave us alone. I think they're just looking forward to seeing how it goes. Perhaps we'll speak afterward. As for everything else on my plate, I have a fantastic team behind me. Lisa and Brian Mackey both do outstanding work. Tim Stevens has excelled since joining us. Richard Douglas' contributions are immeasurable. And the entire world... man, the countless hours and hard work everyone on the planet has put in toward reaching our goal is incredible. These are exciting times, for sure."

He lifted his glass in a small toast and took another sip of his Scotch, the clink of ice a soft punctuation.

Mike smiled in approval and moved on.

"Next question: if something happens and this doesn't go well, or as we all hope, will it be a disappointment to you?"

Alex leaned back slightly, the lights from the control board casting a soft glow over his face as he considered the question.

"I'll be disappointed for sure. I mean, who wouldn't be? But we learn from our mistakes, right? Besides, we still have the Evolution, Intervention, and Innovation projects. Win, lose, or draw, we're completely satisfied with what we've achieved together so far. If tomorrow's not the day? It's okay. We're under no restraints or deadlines."

"I'm sorry if that sounded like a negative question," Mike said quickly, eyes darting down as if hoping to erase the words. "I don't mean to sound negative. I want you to succeed."

"*Us*," Alex corrected with a warm smile. "This is a worldwide project."

"Right! *Us!*" Mike echoed, visibly relieved to be let off the hook.

Alex shook his head with a chuckle.

"Besides, I didn't think you were being negative. Not to wonder about things would mean that you are nothing more than... a Gen 6. Am I right?"

The jab landed with gentle humor, and Mike visibly relaxed again. Just as he was about to move to the next question, Alex leaned over and gave him a playful slap on the leg.

"But..." he raised one finger theatrically, "if tomorrow *is* the day... holy shit!"

Both men burst out laughing, the sound genuine and unfiltered. In the adjacent room, the laughter was contagious.

"That's why he's so loved and revered," Lisa said, her voice soft and admiring. "He has this easy way about him. The man never gets upset about anything. In all the time we've spent with him, we've never seen him angry."

"He wouldn't hurt a fly," Brian added with a fond smile.

Back in the control room, Mike continued.

"Are you still single?"

Alex erupted in laughter, clapping his hands. "Wow! You go right for the jugular."

He leaned into the camera, his grin widening.

"Yeah, still single. Eventually, I'll strike up a relationship. It just might be a little while."

Then, with mock seriousness, he added, "Sorry, Mom and Dad, no grandchildren just yet."

Mike let the moment breathe, then moved into deeper waters.

"May I ask about Project Rewind?"

Alex shrugged. "Sure. I don't see why not."

Mike took a breath and read from his notes.

"As you know, Project Rewind won't be up for another World Vote for two years. What are your thoughts on it? It's still the most controversial topic of discussion out there, and no one seems interested in bringing it back. The last vote by the NU saw a staggering 97% rejection. What's your stance on the project?"

Alex leaned forward slightly, elbows resting on his knees. His posture tightened, no longer casual, but deeply invested.

"I'm glad you asked, Mike. I think, ultimately, we're going to end up giving the Reverie Halo back to the Norn."

His voice took on a weight rarely heard.

"Since 2032, we've made stunning discoveries for sure. We've learned that we're not alone in the universe and that there is an afterlife. Ghosts, demons, things that go bump in the night… those things? They're real. Bigfoot, underwater cities, the list goes on. We've made progress on those topics. But the experiments with the Reverie Halo? They've all failed."

Mike looked puzzled. "I have to tell you, Alex, I have no idea how any of that works."

"Every single one failed," Alex said solemnly. "For one reason. The microchips implanted in us at birth, the tracking devices, are recording devices. They store data. Now, when you put on the Reverie Halo, you're transported back in time *mentally,* not physically. Yet for some reason, the tracking chip records everything you're seeing. That's not supposed to happen, and we have no idea why it does."

Mike interrupted, his brow furrowed. "But hasn't the Halo been around longer than the microchips?"

Alex nodded. "Good question. Before the tracking chips, early test results were mixed at best. Out of fifty participants, all complained of severe déjà vu and hangover-like symptoms. Now? It's all that plus vivid memories lasting ten to fifteen days. The tracking chip overloads, shuts down, and reboots, which takes time to recover from."

He paused, and his voice dropped; lower, quieter, filled with the weight of hard truths.

"It's all incredibly harmful. Out of thirty participants, post-tracking chip implantation, sixteen committed suicide, ten never recovered and had to be institutionalized, and four disappeared entirely. Their chips were permanently damaged."

Mike blinked. "Can we improve the tech?" He raised a hopeful hand. "Can't we find a way to make both the Reverie Halo and the tracking chips work in tandem?"

"You would think," Alex said gently. "The ongoing assumption is that the last experiment, thirty-five years ago, used less advanced chips. Some believe we might yield better results today, but nobody's in a rush to find out... nor should they be."

"Wow," Mike whispered, genuinely stunned. "All this is above my understanding."

"Mine too," Alex replied. "But you seem to have a grasp. At least somewhat... or maybe more than we do."

He laughed lightly, letting the tension ease.

"Still, as far as we've come, that piece of technology reminds us we're outclassed by the universe, and probably will be for a while. It begs the question: do we need to know everything? I don't think so, and I'll leave it at that."

Mike nodded solemnly. He glanced at his notes, then looked back up at Alex.

"May I ask one last question?"

"Of course," Alex said.

"Tomorrow is one of the most significant days in the history of the world! If we achieve our goal, we can start sending people deep into space to explore the galaxy! That's a lot to take in! We know what this means to the world, but... what does this mean to *you* personally?"

Alex leaned forward, a quiet joy spreading across his face. His smile turned inward.

"When I was a boy, eleven years old to be exact, I would tinker around with building my own shuttle in the backyard. While my neighborhood friends were out running around and playing, I was hard at work building a spaceship."

Mike raised his eyebrows. "Wait. What? This was just some cardboard ship with a lot of duct tape, correct?"

Alex shook his head, his expression mock-serious. "No. I... actually built a ship. Well... what I *thought* was a ship."

Mike laughed, lowering his notepad to his lap.

"It obviously wasn't space-worthy," Alex continued. "Still, at the time, I thought it was. I was, and am, a dreamer. My parents were scientists, and we lived near a lot of research labs. Being the deviant that I was, I was always sneaking into their storage areas, looking at old blueprints, and studying whatever decommissioned tech I could get my hands on. I started collecting scrap metal, pipes, and parts from old aerospace projects. I even managed to get my hands on a retired experimental drone shell. It was the closest thing to a real cockpit I could find. It took a lot of doing to get that thing home, but you can bribe a lot of unsuspecting teenagers into helping you if you just use pizza."

Mike laughed harder. "So, once you got it all home, you put it together? *How?*"

"I rigged up a basic control panel using salvaged flight simulator parts and an old AR interface. It didn't do much, but I felt like I was in command of a real ship. I even tried building a propulsion system. At first, I experimented with compressed air and electromagnetics, but then I got my hands on a small hybrid rocket engine. It wasn't powerful, at least, that's what I *thought*, but it was enough to cause some real trouble."

Mike leaned in. "Let me guess. You tested it, and the results were beyond what you had ever imagined."

Alex sighed, rubbing his temples. "More than you know. I had been tinkering with the setup for weeks, getting ready to simulate a launch. My dog, Lou, a big, beautiful black Lab, was my co-pilot. Or at least, my test subject. I strapped him into the cockpit just to see how the harness fit. I wasn't planning on actually launching anything, but..."

Mike's jaw dropped. "No! Don't tell me you launched your dog into the sky!"

Alex groaned. "Yeah... I hit the wrong button on my makeshift control panel, and before I knew it, Lou was airborne. The rocket ignited, and my good boy was lifted straight up into the sky. He was only up there for about twenty seconds, but those were the longest twenty seconds of my life."

Mike was in tears from laughter now, nearly breathless. "Oh my! What did you do?"

"I panicked! Obviously!" Alex cried. "I scrambled to shut everything down and used what little control I had to bring him back safely. He landed a little rough, but he was fine. My parents ran out to the yard, screaming, thinking I had just blown up half the neighborhood."

Mike gasped for breath, still laughing. "And Lou? Was he okay?"

Alex rubbed his face with both hands. "Oh, he was fine. Physically. Mentally? Not so much. That dog hated me for two months. Every time I tried to pet him, he growled and tried to bite me. I had to bribe him with treats just to get back in his good graces."

Mike wiped a tear from his eye. "That's an incredible story. I can't believe that actually happened."

Alex smirked. "Yeah, well, my parents believed it. They banned me from using anything remotely explosive for a long time after that."

He chuckled, the memory still fresh in his voice. "Still, something good came from it. That was the moment I *knew* that space was where I was meant to be. I've spent my whole life trying to get back to that feeling, launching into the unknown."

He paused, eyes drifting toward the darkening control room windows where the Elevation waited like a myth forged in metal.

"Now, hopefully, tomorrow, we'll do it for real."

Mike grinned and pointed at him. "And this time, no dogs in the cockpit."

Alex raised his glass, meeting the joke with mock solemnity. "No dogs in the cockpit."

The clink of the glass echoed softly in the quiet that followed, a moment that somehow felt both ceremonial and personal. Alex drew in a breath, the air seeming heavier now, not oppressive, just charged with meaning.

Then he leaned forward again, a gesture Mike had come to recognize. When Alex leaned in, it wasn't just for emphasis. It was a cue: *this matters.*

"Mike," he began, his voice low but electric with hope, "we've been to the Moon, to Mars, and places within our reach. But if we're successful tomorrow... we can push beyond our limitations. We could travel to planets that are hundreds, even millions, of light-years away."

His eyes sparkled as he stood, unable to stay seated through the gravity of his own words. He swept his arm in a wide arc, encompassing the glowing consoles, the cameras, the very air of the room.

"We could meet new races. We might inhabit other worlds. All of that, *all of that,* would make the Moon landing in 1969 look like a casual drive around the neighborhood."

He paused, then lowered his voice to a confident hush.

"We can do this. I have the utmost confidence."

Mike sat back, stunned by the conviction in Alex's voice. He wasn't just a diplomat or a face for the cameras. He was a dreamer. A believer. And it was contagious.

"Well," Mike said with sincerity, "I can certainly understand why the Norn chose you to be their liaison."

Alex's expression softened. "Thank you for that," he said, sitting back down slowly, the emotional swell ebbing into a thoughtful stillness. He looked almost spent, not from fatigue, but from the emotional outpouring of a man standing on the edge of something greater than himself.

Mike glanced back at his notes, then looked up, his tone shifting toward finality.

"Okay. I think we'll stop here for now. I want to thank you for your time, sir. It was an honor and a privilege being here with you."

He extended his hand across the table.

Alex took it with both hands, warm and steady. "Absolutely," he said with an easy smile. "We're looking forward to tomorrow, and the days to come."

As they stood, Alex added, "And as for the interview, you did an excellent job, Mike. Anytime you want to talk, feel free to reach out to me. I mean that. We'll see you tomorrow."

Chapter 3: Are We There Yet?

Launch day had finally arrived, the moment the world had been waiting for. All of the prep work, all of the interviews, everything leading up to this day was now behind them. The weight of the moment pressed on everyone involved, and anticipation filled the air like static before a storm.

On the ground, the Space Explorers conducted the final inspections on the Elevation. The ship wasn't massive, standing at only 42 feet tall and 10 feet wide. Compared to the space shuttle from the twenty-first century, which measured 122 feet tall and 78 feet wide, the Elevation was as thin as a needle, ready to thread the fabric of the universe.

Its sleek, metallic black exterior shimmered in the sun, giving it a classic rocket silhouette with a single forward-facing window near the top. Inside, there was just enough room for seven crew members, though its streamlined design and advanced systems put older shuttles to shame.

The cockpit was tight and efficient, built only for two. It featured a central navigation column, multi-layered radar panels, and holographic readouts that floated inches from the operator's eyes. This was no luxury cruiser; it was a test craft, built with purpose and precision.

Unlike the roaring engines of Earth's past, the Elevation's single-engine design was powered by the diamond-shaped energy source gifted by the Norn. Despite decades of study, scientists still had no clear understanding of how the device worked. The core glowed with a low hum, and though it had no discernible fuel source or moving parts, it provided limitless power. With minimal guidance from the Norn, Earth's best minds had reverse-engineered an engine to house it. The power may be alien, but the framework, the controls, and the systems were entirely human. Whether they were cut out for deep space or not, the Norn had made it clear: the journey must be theirs.

At noon, under clear blue skies and a gentle sixty-four-degree breeze, Commander Will Phillips emerged from a sea of scientists and engineers. He paused in front of the ship, taking in the final form of what humanity had built. The crowd behind him buzzed, but for a moment he heard only the wind.

Turning to the ground crew captain beside him, Will asked, "Well, what do you think, Joe? Is she ready?"

Joe grinned, white teeth bright against sun-tanned skin. His solid build, squared shoulders, and regulation buzz cut marked him as a launch pad veteran. His eyes were alert and sharp, the kind of eyes that didn't miss a detail.

"She's one hundred percent ready, Commander!" Joe gave a sharp salute, not out of obligation, but instinct. Will returned it with equal respect.

Military protocol wasn't strictly necessary anymore, but in moments like these, tradition still felt right.

"Perfect," Will replied, his thinning gray hair ruffled by the wind. "Let's get her fired up and see what she's got. Evacuate the ground crew and get to your stations. I'm heading to the control room to run diagnostics. Wheels up in one hour."

He clapped Joe on the shoulder with a warm grin and climbed into his transport. As he drove the mile to the control center, crowds lined the road on both sides, waving, cheering, throwing confetti, and holding signs. The excitement was overwhelming. It felt like a parade. It felt like history.

When he stepped out of the transport, the sound hit him like a tidal wave. Tens of thousands of voices roared in celebration. He could feel the vibrations through the concrete. It was electrifying.

Alex waited at the entrance, beaming with pride. He grasped Will's hand with both of his and shouted over the roar, "I know you always wanted to be a rockstar, Will! What do you think of all this?"

Will laughed loudly, the sound nearly lost in the crowd. "It's overwhelming! I can't believe this many people showed up. It's just remarkable!"

He turned toward the building, eyes wide with excitement. "Well, I'd love to stay and chat, Alex, but I've got a job to do."

"Go get 'em, Commander! I'm heading next door to the stadium." Alex gave him a final pat on the back before they parted.

The special indoor stadium adjacent to the launch site was packed to capacity. With room for two hundred thousand people, and even more gathered outside on massive Jumbotrons, it had become the global viewing hub for the launch. All 195 NU Representatives were seated at the center of the floor, dressed in formal attire, ready to witness history.

With just twenty minutes remaining, Alex was asked to say a few words.

He approached the podium with his usual calm confidence, raising both hands to greet the thunderous applause. Cameras zoomed in as his face filled the massive screens overhead. The crowd slowly quieted.

"Ladies and gentlemen of the world," he began with a knowing grin, "you already know what today is. There's no reason for me to stand up here and flap my gums."

A ripple of laughter broke out. Alex continued, shifting to a tone of gravitas.

"When humanity landed on the Moon in 1969, it was one small step."

He paused, letting the weight of his next words build.

"Today, we take a giant leap in human evolution."

The arena erupted. Cheers bounced off the dome. Flashing lights danced across the stands.

Alex waited for the wave of sound to subside before continuing. "Now, I could sit here and continue to bore you with useless information, but I'm not going to do that. So, without further ado, I give you Commander Will Phillips."

He gestured toward the large screens as they cut to the live feed inside the control room.

Commander Phillips sat in a simulated cockpit, joined by Captains Lisa and Brian Mackey. The trio was calm, composed, and focused. Everything inside the control room mirrored the Elevation's cockpit exactly, right down to the chairs and console layout.

Will flashed a warm smile to the camera. "Look alive, crew, cameras are rolling. Good afternoon, everyone. We're fifteen minutes from launch. I'm joined by Captains Lisa and Brian Mackey."

Lisa and Brian waved, their nerves masked behind practiced smiles.

Will continued, "For you rocket geeks out there, we'll be pulling fifteen Gs until we exit the atmosphere. Once we pass the first space station, about two hundred and fifty miles from Earth, we'll accelerate to seventy-five Gs for twelve minutes, then flip and decelerate to lunar approach. At that speed, we should reach the Moon within an hour. Today's unscrewed test lets us push fifteen to one-hundred G profiles safely."

Gasps rippled through the stadium.

Will smirked. "Well, that's actually not true."

A pause.

"We'll reach the Moon in about twenty-five minutes."

The crowd exploded again.

"But we'll need to throttle back to get ready for the big show. That's when we gradually push to the full one hundred G limit, hold for twenty minutes, then slow down and return home."

Alex raised his hands to calm the crowd, eyes returning to the screens as silence took over once more.

Ten minutes passed.

Every second stretched like a lifetime.

"Captain, begin the final countdown," Will said.

Lisa responded smoothly, "Ten… nine… eight… seven… six… five… four… three… two… one. Ignition."

"Radar is clear, all systems intact," Brian added, scanning his console.

"Captain, we're a go. Send it," Will commanded.

Lisa pressed the launch command.

The Elevation vanished from its launch pad in a burst of silent brilliance. There was no thunder, no flame — the nozzleless field-drive shimmered as it pierced the sky. The world watched in awe.

"Commander, you have control," Brian said, voice calm as the ship passed the space station ahead of schedule.

"Approaching seventy-five Gs. How's our trajectory?" Will asked.

"Still on course," Brian replied, nodding with a smile.

Then Lisa's expression changed.

"We've got a sensor alert! Rear section! Rear sensor alert!" she said, voice sharp.

Will's jaw tightened. "Throttling down. What's the issue?"

"There's a breach in the rear hull. One point nine. If we push her any further, the ship could break apart."

"Understood." Will focused, hands steady. "Throttling down to minimum thrust. Deploy the AI repair unit, Brian."

Brian activated the onboard repair system. A moment later, the ship's internal AI welded a patch over the breach with precision arcs of cold plasma. The warning light faded. Tension lifted.

Will turned to the camera. "Everything is under control. The hull breach is sealed, the ship is stabilized, and all safety protocols are engaged."

He spoke with clarity and confidence.

"The ship has been designed to section itself off in case of a breach such as this. The cockpit, midsection, and lower half can separate and operate independently. If necessary, we can eject the entire damaged section and return with the remaining two-thirds. It's a bit slower, but it can be done."

The audience exhaled. Relief rippled across the planet.

Will continued, his tone that of a seasoned leader. "For the next several hours, we'll carefully guide the Elevation home. Once it's grounded, we'll assess the issue and try to figure out what went wrong. Seventy-five Gs is no small feat. Still, I'd call this mission a success."

He paused, letting the moment breathe.

"Thank you, world, for your devotion to this project. Until then, this is the Elevation crew, signing off."

He gave a crisp salute. The feed ended.

Back in the stadium, Alex jumped to his feet, energized. He turned to the NU members nearby.

"I'm heading to the control room to relieve Lisa and check in with Commander Phillips. Anyone want to join me?"

Max Huber laughed. "Whew! No thanks. That's enough excitement for one day. Go check on your crew. Let Commander Mackey take leave. Let us know what you find out later."

Alex nodded. "I'll set up a conference call."

As he made his way to the control center, he passed through crowds slowly filing out, their faces still glowing with amazement.

When Alex arrived, he entered with a smile. "Hey, gang. How are we holding up?"

Lisa let out a groan. "Whoa. My baby girl is kicking the hell out of me. I think she's had enough for today."

"No worries, Lisa," Alex said gently. "I can only guess at the stress we're placing on you and Grayle. You're relieved. Stanowski's on his way up to take your place."

"I'm taking my leave, then," Lisa said, rising with effort. "Brian can stay and troubleshoot. I don't need him to help me sleep."

Brian stood, hesitating. "You sure, love?"

She kissed his cheek. "I'm fine, babe."

She turned and left, and Alex moved to sit beside Commander Phillips, ready for the next phase of what had already become a monumental day.

"Alright, Will, Brian, what do you think happened up there?" Alex asked, his voice shedding the warmth of ceremony. Now that the crowd was gone and the cameras were off, the formality faded. It was just the core team, focused and honest.

Will exhaled, leaning back in his chair. He rubbed his chin thoughtfully, his eyes scanning the ceiling as if trying to recall every detail. "My best guess? As the ship was accelerating, it probably struck a piece of space debris. It was a small hole. If we had a human crew onboard, no one would've been harmed. Scared shitless, maybe, but not harmed." A faint grin tugged at the corner of his mouth. "The safety protocols worked perfectly, so I'd say this was a solid first run. The fact that the ship held together is promising. We've got work to do, but this was a success. We're on the right path."

Brian leaned forward with his hands pressed together, energized by the debrief. "Will is right. The fact that the ship didn't completely break into pieces is really promising! That was a nice test run. I can't wait to dissect the AI from the cockpit and see what kind of, if any, impact it had on the spacesuit. I'd like to check its replica vitals and organs, tissue samples." His eyes gleamed at the thought, like a scientist on the verge of discovery.

Alex rose from his chair and began pacing slowly across the room, each step deliberate. His fingers tapped rhythmically against his thigh as he thought aloud. "There's a lot to do for sure, but hearing you two talk so positively is reassuring." He turned, eyes now glowing with renewed hope. "I'd even go so far as to say it's exhilarating."

Both men chuckled in unison, the camaraderie between them tangible. "It is!" Will agreed, his voice carrying the confidence of a man who had just stared down the unknown and lived to tell the tale.

With a satisfied smile, Alex gave a nod. "Okay, I'll leave you two to it then. Lots to do, little time, and all that." He gave them a final glance before walking out, the faint echo of his footsteps trailing behind him.

Brian and Will exchanged a knowing look, then turned back toward the control panels and data streams now filling their screens. The adrenaline of launch day hadn't worn off; it had simply transformed into determination.

"Well, here we go," Will said with a quiet smile, already scanning through the diagnostic logs as their post-mission work began in earnest.

Chapter 4: New Year, New Me

Title Card: December 31, 2199

PATRIOTIC MUSIC FILLS THE ROOM AS THE NARRATOR BEGINS

NARRATOR:

It's been sixteen days since the test launch of the Elevation, and the world is abuzz, united in its efforts to analyze the mission and uncover the cause of the small breach in the ship's hull. New, stronger, more durable alloys are being developed by the day, and while the hype has grown to a frenzied height, the first launch was deemed a success by most. Still, not everyone shares that sentiment.

"That was absolute dog shit," the apprentice Tim Stevens blurted out, seated at the conference table in a boardroom in Alex's headquarters in Columbus. Alex, Will, and Richard sat with him, discussing the December 15th launch, and Tim's arrogance and intelligence were on full display.

"Care to elaborate, Tim?" Alex asked, rolling his eyes with a sarcastic tone to his voice. "Or maybe you can offer something... more scientific?"

Tim leaned forward, undeterred. His wired intensity sometimes reminded Alex of a younger version of himself. "We failed. I know the NU and other SE Departments around the world are patting themselves on the back, and I get that, but we didn't get the job done. We got lucky the ship was even salvaged, thanks to Commander Phillips here. If it had been... what's his name... the guy from Spain?"

"Santos?" Commander Phillips interjected. "He's a wonderful pilot."

"Whatever," Tim scoffed. "If Santos were behind the controls, that thing would be in pieces, floating in outer fucking space."

The room fell silent. Alex and Will exchanged glances with Richard, who finally raised his hand.

"Okay, okay, okay," Richard said, trying to defuse the tension. "Look, this went better than you think. The cockpit AI suffered no damage, the flight suits held up beautifully, and we didn't lose the bird. Plus, we managed to haul some serious ass. We're not there yet, but we're… as you might say… pretty friggin' close."

Tim shot back, his frustration boiling over, his comments and his eyes directed at Richard. "What's with the 'we' shit? You're leaving at the end of this month… Dick. Have fun blowing Mathews."

"Fuck, Tim!" Alex snapped, jumping from his chair. "I swear to God, you're like dealing with a small child sometimes. You do realize that you're just an apprentice, right? The rest of the men in this room have a lot more experience…"

Alex took a deep breath, then turned to Richard. "I'm sorry for Tim, Rich. He's just…"

"It's fine," Richard replied with a chuckle. "I know he means well. We've all had that youthful angst in our lives."

Will joined in the laughter, while Tim sat with a thud and sulked in his chair.

Alex sighed. "It's clear we're not getting anywhere today. It's three p.m. That's a wrap. Tonight's New Year's party kicks off at seven on the Ohio State campus. We're expecting over five thousand people. It's gonna be a blast!"

"Tim, will you be there?"

"Sure. I've got nothing better to do," Tim muttered, pushing back from the table. "I'll see you later." Dejected, he stomped out like a childish ten-year-old. The three remaining men simply waved as he left, chuckling as he went out of sight.

"Commander?" Alex turned to Will.

"Yep, my wife and I will be there," Will replied. "But not too late. I'm not much for late nights." He shook hands with Alex and Richard and started to leave. "Well, it is New Year's Eve. Maybe I'll make an exception." Will left the remaining two men alone at the table.

"Will's the nicest man," Richard said with a respectful nod.

"He really is genuine. I'm happy he's on our team," Alex agreed.

"His call sign… 'Butch,'" Richard asked with a quizzical look on his face. "Why doesn't he use it anymore? And where did he get it?"

Alex laughed. "He got it because his dad took him to a barber when he was two, and had the barber give him a butch haircut. Nobody had seen that style in one hundred and fifty years, so the novelty kind of stuck. I don't know why he doesn't use it anymore. Maybe he just outgrew it.

Fun fact," Alex continued. "Our good commander is a multi-talented musician and singer. He's one of those… what do you call them… polymaths? He can do so many things. Still, he chose flying, so I guess we should be grateful."

Alex kicked back a bit in his chair. "Will is so principled," Alex added with a grin, ready to add more to the legend. "Once, when he was a teenager, he got drunk and apologized to his parents."

Richard laughed, but not too loudly. "I guess that's not too bad, considering who it is."

"For three weeks?" Alex laughed.

Richard smiled and shook his head, letting the silence between the two men grow. He tried to renew the conversation. "I didn't know any of this," he said, leaning forward in his chair. "I've been here five years and still don't know much about… anyone."

Alex leaned back toward the table, his voice a bit more serious. "You would if you hung out with us sometime. How about tonight? You coming to the party?" Alex asked genuinely.

"No," Richard replied quickly.

"Oh, c'mon. It would mean a lot to everyone if you did. We never get to spend much time together outside of work." Alex gave him a look that usually melted people's resolve.

Richard grinned. "Oh no. I see what you're doing. You know my deal, Alex."

"Yeah, I do, but tell me again just for the hell of it," Alex pushed.

Releasing a pent-up breath, Richard responded slowly and methodically. His hands were closed, and he moved them forward and back for emphasis as he spoke. "Developing close bonds and relationships, there's nothing wrong with that. It's just that, for me, I couldn't push you or any of the others if I didn't stay impartial. Please, it's not personal. I'll cherish the five years I spent here."

"Yeah, I get it. You did push me hard, and I appreciate that," Alex replied sincerely. "But hey, I know you're building that old-style den in your house, so I expect an invite sometime."

"Maybe. We'll see," Richard said, standing up to shake Alex's hand. "I'm gonna call it a day. Have fun tonight."

The music was thumping as the New Year's party at Ohio State University was in full swing. The energy was electric. People were drinking, dancing, and celebrating the dawn of a new century. The twenty-third century was at hand.

At approximately eleven-thirty, Alex jumped on stage and grabbed the mic. "Hello, everyone! You having a good time tonight?!"

The crowd roared in response, their excitement and intoxication blending into a euphoric buzz.

"Alright," Alex continued, "we're thirty minutes from midnight! And right now, I'd like to call Commander Phillips to the stage... maybe play us a song or two?" He grinned down at Will, catching him off guard. "Listen, I have to get him up here now because, by twelve-o-one, he'll be out the door. It's now or never!"

Will shook his head, feigning anger, but agreed. Everyone could tell that he wasn't that put out by the invitation. Once on stage, the normally reserved commander transformed. He turned to the band, called out his song, and, like flipping a switch, became a rock star.

Meanwhile, Alex returned to his table, where Lisa and Brian were waiting.

"Hey, you two lovebirds! Having a good time? Got enough to eat?" Alex was gleeful, maybe a bit too much spirit in his veins.

"We're great," Lisa replied with a smile. "You and food. Always with the food."

Brian leaned in. "Everything's been awesome tonight, Alex. But the commander isn't the only one splitting at twelve-o-one."

"Yeah, yeah, I know you've got to go soon," Alex waved them off. "But before you do, there's something I want to tell you both. I wasn't sure when the right time would be, but..." He paused, taking a breath. "I've been thinking... I'm going to resign as the NU Representative. Being the sole liaison to the Norn is all-encompassing. I know I haven't been doing the job long, but it feels right to step down."

Lisa and Brian exchanged a glance, unsurprised and visibly relieved.

"This is good," Lisa said warmly. "It's too much. We can see the stress it causes you, and we love and worry about you."

"Yeah, man," Brian added. "That's a lot of responsibility. We don't want you to burn out. We're thrilled you made this decision. When are you announcing it?"

"In the next couple of days. I even have my replacement in mind, Doctor Susan Hallewell. She's brilliant and will do a great job. She's already beloved in the Medical Department, and I'm confident her nomination will easily pass any vote anywhere."

"Great! That's awesome! She's a solid choice," Lisa exclaimed, but her attention was drawn across the room. She scrunched her eyes. "On a side note... holy shit! Is that Tim over there talking to a girl?!"

Alex gasped in mock surprise. "Small wonders." He smiled, and the three of them settled in to enjoy Will's superb vocals, singing them into the New Year.

Three a.m. The dawn of 2200 - the turn of the century.

Alex returned to his office, expecting it to be empty. But when he opened the door and flicked on the lights, he found Tim sitting alone in the dark, hunched over his monitor.

Startled, Alex jumped back. "Damn it! You scared the shit out of me! What are you doing here? Last I saw, you were talking to a woman."

"True, but she wasn't as interesting as this," Tim replied, not looking up from his screen.

"What are *you* doing here?" Tim asked, finally stopping his work and glancing at Alex.

"I don't know," Alex admitted. "Just milling around. Everyone went home, and I'm not tired."

Tim cut him off. "Stop. You don't have to explain. I'm just as obsessed with the failure as you are."

"I'm not," Alex said, incredulous. "What are you talking about?"

Tim turned fully to face him, his chair offering a small squeak as he spun. "You can try that bullshit charm, but it doesn't affect me. I saw how bitterly disappointed you were sixteen days ago during the broadcast."

"You weren't even there," Alex tried to defend his position, but he was failing.

"It's alright, Al. I saw it on your face. You think because I haven't worked with you for long and I don't know you as well as the others do, I'm immune to your shit. No, I just don't think you're being honest about how you feel. It's okay to be upset, you know? I don't think anyone would be disappointed in you. You put a lot into this program."

Alex sighed, his defenses dropping. As if he were suddenly granted permission to change his mood, he flipped the switch on his emotions. "I am mad, Tim. I am disappointed. You want to know how I feel? I want this. I want it bad. This is what I'm good at. This is the one thing that I'm the best in the world at. So yeah, I wanted it to go right. And I wanted it the first time." He exhaled and sank into his chair. "Shit, we still haven't figured out what went wrong up there. That's why I'm here after..." he glanced at the time. "After three in the morning... maybe a little drunk." Alex raised his head to the ceiling, eyes glassy.

"Cool," Tim said, turning back to his monitor. He tried to carry on the conversation to avoid the silence. "Wasn't there anything else you wanted to try for a career? Ever?"

"Nah, what's there to do?" Alex shrugged. "You can take a bullet train from New York to LA in two hours. Fly to Japan from anywhere in three. Our transportation is flawless. Medicine's so advanced there's no sickness, and life expectancy is one hundred and ten. The food we eat, the air we breathe… never better. It's all perfect." He sighed again, running a hand through his hair, the weight of the world pressing down on him. "So, what does it mean to be dubbed the smartest man alive? Alexander the Great? When the world's already brilliant? It means nothing. That's why I push myself here, because what the hell else is there?"

"Wow! That's some riveting shit," Tim said, his tone light, trying to ease the tension. He continued to tap on the keyboard. Finally, Tim spun around and faced Alex. "Well, if it's a challenge you need, Al, you have one now. Because I don't have a clue what the hell happened up there. I see nothing."

"Yeah, that's what I saw too. Nothing. I thought that alloy was stronger. I thought the engineering was sound. It's just… whatever." Alex waved dismissively, frustrated. "Hey, what do you say we get out of here and have a quick nightcap? We've got plenty of time to look this over. And, by the way, we're on vacation for the week. That's non-negotiable. You need time off, I need time off, so I don't want to see you in here until next Monday."

Tim stood up, closing the laptop on his desk with a soft click. "Fine by me. I'm cool with some time off. Might even go out with that girl or something." He gave a wry smile, eyebrows arched.

Alex shook his head knowingly. The two gathered their belongings, jackets slung over their arms, and made their way to the door.

As they stepped into the dim hallway, Tim glanced at Alex. "Hey! Have you heard from our alien ambassadors lately? Seems like they've been silent for a pretty long time. What's up with that?"

"Not sure," Alex replied. "I haven't heard from them since the test run." His tone changed to one of acceptance. "If I don't hear from them in a couple of days, I'll reach out."

Out of nowhere, a voice echoed from the shadows.

"We've been around. Observing."

N2 emerged from the dim corner of the room, his tall frame slowly revealing itself under the low lighting. Both men jumped, startled by the sudden presence.

"Holy crap!" Tim and Alex shouted in unison.

Alex narrowed his eyes at N2. "What the hell are you doing over there? And how long have you been listening?"

"For a while. Since Tim arrived," N2 replied calmly, as if nothing was wrong with him lurking unseen.

Tim turned in a slow circle, clearly agitated. "This is creeping me out. Bad," he muttered. He raised his hands in a defensive motion. "Wait! I'm not even supposed to be talking to you, am I? And how the hell do you get in and out like that?!"

"It's fine. Nobody needs to know," N2 assured them, raising a hand in a disarming gesture. "Your flight didn't go accordingly. We were disappointed in the result, for you, of course. We know that you want to achieve this. So, tell me what we can do to help."

Alex took a breath, trying to steady himself. "I don't know. We're going over everything right now and doing what we can, but I'm afraid we may have exhausted all of our avenues. The alloy just isn't strong enough to hold up. That's the conclusion we keep coming back to, and we don't have anything stronger. It might take years to invent a new metal alloy."

"What if I told you there was a faster way to get this done?" N2 asked, his voice measured and composed, as if offering a suggestion about the weather.

"Are you going to build it for us? Because that would be much easier," Tim joked, glancing at Alex and then back to N2, immediately realizing he may have spoken out of turn. He looked relieved when Alex backed him up.

"Yeah, do you want us to cheat?" Alex grinned, offering Tim a knowing look before turning back to N2.

"No. We gave you the tools to make something like this possible," N2 said.

Alex frowned, trying to piece together the implication. "The power sources? We still have no comprehension of how that works. We're doing our best to figure it out, but we…"

"The Reverie Halo," N2 clarified.

Alex stiffened, a sharp edge of anger rising in his tone. This wasn't what he expected. "Okay, what about it? We've had disastrous results and haven't used it. We were going to shelve that thing."

"I know," N2 nodded. "Your minds can't handle that much. We understand that. But look at it this way. It is a device that moves you through time and space. The wearer's brain operates at full capacity, one hundred percent."

"Sure," Alex countered. "But what about the side effects? Out of fifty participants, all complained of severe déjà vu and…"

"I know the statistics you told that reporter, and I'm sure they are true, but if you want, I can implant a new chip inside you. It'll be a better chip, more equipped to handle the trauma you'd endure." N2 paused, scanning their faces. "Think of all the knowledge you'd have, all the things you could do."

"No, no, no, no!" Alex shouted, backing away, frightened. "Would I remember every life I've ever lived? Every feeling I've ever felt? Pain, sorrow, misery? And for how long? I don't know. This sounds like an awful idea!"

"It's only for this life. You won't remember it in the next one. And you need to do this more than you know."

Alex's face contorted with frustration. "Now what does that mean? It sounds like an ultimatum."

N2 raised his hands in a placating gesture. "As always, it's your choice, Alex. You have free will."

"I'll do it!" Tim blurted out, eyes wide with excitement.

"No! No, you won't," Alex snapped, rounding on Tim with a pointed finger. "What are you thinking?"

"The offer is to both of you," N2 interjected, his calmness unwavering.

"Well, it's not going to be Tim. I'm not going to subject anyone else to this... this nonsense." Alex's voice softened to a whisper. His mind was spinning with the gravity of what was being asked.

"If I didn't think that success with this mission mattered to you, I wouldn't even tell you. I can't say anything more," N2 said cryptically.

Alex sighed heavily, pressing his palms into his eyes. "Okay, let's say I consider this. What then? After... after I succeed or get torn to a zillion pieces, or go fucking crazy, what then? Do you take the Halo back?"

"No. It's yours. It belongs to planet Earth."

"If I survive, and there's no guarantee that I do, can I give it to someone for safekeeping? Maybe have it locked away for, let's say, ever? So no one else can use it?" Alex asked, his voice cautious.

"You can do with it as you wish."

"I can't believe I'm... ugh. When do you want to try this?" Alex asked, his heart pounding in his chest.

"Soon. Are you in agreement?" N2 asked, his tone unchanged.

Alex swallowed hard, looking at Tim. "Can Tim and I talk it over?"

"Contact me when you have an answer," N2 said before vanishing as silently as he had arrived.

"I still don't know how he does that," Tim muttered, staring at the now-empty space N2 had just occupied.

Chapter 5: Dreamers

Movietone Newsreel – March 2205

Triumphant orchestral music swells as the black-and-white footage flickers to life, casting a nostalgic glow over a futuristic tale.

NARRATOR:

From Great Britain, we bring you the next great leap in human space exploration! Five years after the historic, though troubled, test flight of the Elevation, the world now turns its eyes to the Intervention, a vessel unlike any seen before!

ON-SCREEN:

A sweeping aerial shot of the Intervention dominates the screen. Its massive, box-like frame contrasts sharply with the rocket-shaped Elevation. The craft looms like a floating fortress, vast and resolute. Engineers in white coats and smart uniforms scurry around the final stages of assembly while robotic arms glide overhead, fitting each segment into place with mechanical perfection.

NARRATOR:

At an impressive four hundred feet in both length and width, the Intervention is a behemoth of human ingenuity. Designed to house up to two hundred crew members, it represents the next crucial step toward sustainable deep-space travel. Gone are the days of compact, single-purpose shuttles. This vessel is built for longevity, equipped with cutting-edge technology and state-of-the-art living quarters to support crew safety and mission success!

ON-SCREEN:

Inside a bustling mission control center, planners huddle around a star map glowing with trajectories and planetary bodies. Fingers trace lines across space, plotting each phase of the mission with care and precision.

NARRATOR:

Unlike the Elevation, which pushed the limits of acceleration and structural endurance, the Intervention will take a more methodical approach. This mission, set to last three weeks, will test the ship's ability to sustain prolonged deep-space travel. The crew will conduct planetary flybys and make a close pass around the Sun to evaluate a new heat-resistant coating developed by Alex Belle in association with the world's leading engineers. If successful, this test could pave the way for longer missions beyond our solar system!

ON-SCREEN:

Commander Will Phillips stands before a cluster of reporters, his sharp eyes and furrowed brow suggesting cautious wisdom. His solemn tone underscores the gravity of his words.

NARRATOR:

Yet not everyone is convinced the time is right. Veteran astronaut and former test pilot Will Phillips, who led the mission of the Elevation, has opted out of this journey, stating his belief that humanity is 'not quite ready' to take this next step. Others, including former crew members Lisa and Brian Mackey, remain on the fence, weighing the risks against the call of duty.

ON-SCREEN:

The focus shifts to Alex Belle, mid-speech, animated and fervent. His eyes sparkle with vision as he gestures enthusiastically to his team.

NARRATOR:

However, Alexander Belle, the brilliant mind behind the SE Department, remains undeterred. A firm believer in the Norn's gifts and humanity's place among the stars, Belle continues to push for progress. He has recruited top minds from around the world, hoping to bring trusted allies, like the Mackeys, on board for the mission. Whether they will accept remains to be seen.

The music swelled to a crescendo, and the screen faded to black.

March 27, 2205 – 7:00 a.m.

A child's cry pierced the early morning silence like a siren in the stillness. Grayle Mackey bolted upright in bed, her small frame shaking, her face streaked with tears and flushed with fear. Lisa rushed into the room, abandoning her steaming cup of morning coffee in the kitchen. She scooped Grayle into her arms without hesitation, her maternal instincts on high alert.

"Oh, sweetheart, Mommy's here. I've got you," she whispered, rocking back and forth as she stroked Grayle's hair. Her voice was a gentle balm, a practiced comfort that came from countless similar moments.

Brian appeared in the doorway, silhouetted by the soft hallway light. His features were drawn with worry. "Is everything okay?" he asked, scanning both faces.

Lisa nodded, continuing to rock their daughter. "You're okay, baby. It's all right. Take a breath in and out like I showed you." She inhaled and exhaled deliberately, and Grayle mirrored her. Slowly, the panic began to melt from the little girl's expression.

"Did you have another bad dream?" Lisa's voice remained calm but probing.

Grayle lifted her head, nodding slightly.

Lisa swallowed, steeling herself. "Was it the glowing lady in white again?"

Another reluctant nod, more fearful this time. Lisa felt her stomach twist.

She looked at Brian. "Tash will be up in a minute. Could you get her?"

Brian nodded and disappeared down the hallway.

Two years after Grayle was born, the Mackeys had received an unexpected blessing: another daughter. They named her Natasha, affectionately called Tash. The joy had doubled, and so had the challenges. Lisa and Brian had stepped away from their work at the SE Department to focus on raising their young girls. Now, years later, that peaceful sabbatical was ending.

Alex Belle personally reached out to request their return, this time to assist with the monumental launch of the Intervention.

Brian returned with a groggy Tash nestled in his arms, her curls tousled, eyes still half-shut.

"Do you want me to postpone this afternoon's meeting in New York with Richard?" he asked, watching Lisa cradle Grayle as they headed to the kitchen.

Lisa shook her head. "No, your parents will be over soon. It's nice enough outside for the park."

She hesitated, then stopped Brian at the threshold of the kitchen while the girls settled in for breakfast. Her voice dropped to a whisper.

"I think we need to revisit our conversation about Grayle. Maybe we should contact the Paranormal Department. Let them monitor her. Just to see what's going on."

Brian's jaw tightened. "I don't know, Lisa. Don't you think she'll grow out of it? I mean, kids have dreams, and she seems fine most of the time."

Lisa's expression darkened. "Why do you hate the Paranormal Department so much? What happened? Every time I bring them up, it's like I insulted your whole career."

Brian pinched the bridge of his nose. "What can they do for her, Lisa? Hold a séance? Ask the ghosts to leave?" He tried to chuckle, but the tension killed the humor.

Lisa wasn't laughing. "She's four, Brian. And she says things no four-year-old should say. She talks like someone else entirely. Just this morning, she whispered, 'There goes my baby,' and 'I love you, Bridge.' How do you explain that?"

She opened the cabinet with force, pulling out cereal boxes as if they were to blame. "Dr. Hallewell doesn't think it would hurt. Neither do I." The cupboard slammed shut, nearly swallowing her last words.

Brian sighed and rubbed the back of his neck. "Okay, love. I'll talk to Richard today, and then we'll figure it out. I promise. I love you, and I do want what's best."

Lisa melted into him, resting her head against his chest. She sighed, comfortably. "I know you do. We'll figure it out."

New York City – Later That Afternoon

Brian stepped off the sleek high-speed train, greeted by the electric buzz of the city. Horns honked in the distance, and the rhythmic stomp of a thousand footsteps filled the air. The skyline, both familiar and futuristic, towered around him like guardians of progress.

Instead of calling a cab, he chose to walk, weaving through the flow of people with practiced ease. He passed neon-lit cafés, outdoor art installations, and digital billboards the size of buildings. Despite the passage of time, New York's pulse hadn't changed; it had only quickened.

His destination was the Empire State Building. Though renovated and technologically enhanced, its Art Deco bones remained. Of sixteen departments within the Eastern Defense Division, ten were housed within this architectural icon.

Brian entered the marble lobby, awash in a warm amber glow from chandeliers that hung like floating stars. Polished stone gleamed beneath his boots as he approached the curved reception desk.

Behind it sat a woman of quiet efficiency, her dark eyes met his with composed alertness. A nameplate read "Elena Wu – Administrative Liaison."

She glanced up from her holographic display, her fingers pausing mid-air. "Captain Brian Mackey, SE Department. I have a three p.m. with Director Douglas," he said.

Her expression warmed. "Welcome, Captain. I'm Elena Wu. The director left instructions to send you up the moment you arrived. He's expecting you."

Brian raised an eyebrow. "I'm an hour and a half early," he said cautiously.

The receptionist chuckled. "He knew you would be. He's looking forward to catching up with you beforehand, and he has to leave after your vetting session to go to a meeting in the Midwest. His instructions were to send you up as soon as you arrived. Trust me, he knew you would be very early." She pointed toward the opposite side of the lobby. "The elevators are just there, Mister Mackey. Head up to the one hundred and second floor. The director's office will be on the right just outside of the elevator."

Brian shook his head, amused, thanked Elena, and turned to head toward the elevators.

When the doors opened on the 102nd floor, Richard stood waiting at the entrance to his office, as polished and commanding as Brian remembered. His short black hair was immaculately combed, his gray suit crisply pressed, his director's insignia gleaming on his shoulder.

"Brian," Richard greeted him with a firm handshake and a deep, booming voice that exuded confidence. "Good to see you, old friend. Thank you for coming in today."

"You're welcome, sir. It's good to see you as well," Brian replied. "I have to say that I was surprised that I got an invite to come to the main office. I didn't expect to do this in person. We usually handle these remotely."

Richard smirked. "Well, this is worlds better than a hologram; it's more personal when I have the chance." Richard started to turn. "At least when we meet face to face, I can tell if you're wearing pants!"

Brian laughed at the well-worn hologram quip as they walked together into Richard's office, a sprawling, modern space that overlooked the city with floor-to-ceiling windows stretching across the north and east walls. "Unfortunately," Richard added, "everyone's always so busy it isn't practical to meet face to face."

Brian took it all in as he listened to the Director. The room, 400 square feet of luxury on the corner of the building, afforded Richard a perpetual view of the city's skyline and bustling movement below. The walls were lined with shelves of books and framed artwork, each piece strategically placed. Two black leather couches in the center of the room sat opposite each other with a lengthy glass table between them. Still, despite the grandiose furnishings, what caught Brian's eye were the two statues in opposite corners. One depicted a seven-foot-tall Norn, vibrant and imposing, with an inscription at the base that read 'Friends', and the other was a replica of Neil Armstrong's first step on the Moon, inscribed with the iconic words: 'One Giant Leap.'

Brian whistled. "This is stunning."

Richard grinned. "Not what you were expecting?"

"Not at all. I didn't know you were into this kind of stuff." Brian continued to walk the room, scanning the various paintings on the wall: surreal space vistas, historic NASA moments, and abstract depictions of the human spirit.

"You've seen Alex's office back in Columbus," Richard chuckled. "Still bare and gloomy?"

"Worse," Brian laughed. "Still the same off-white walls, dim lights, and uncomfortable chairs. He had the walls repainted, but he chose the same dull color."

Richard grimaced. "That man, for all his brilliance, has zero creativity when it comes to anything beyond space." He held his hands out to encompass the room. "I spend so much time here that I want to make this place feel as warm as possible."

"I get that," Brian replied, still gawking at his surroundings.

Richard nodded and winked. "Here, Brian. Grab a seat. Let's catch up for a minute."

The two men dropped onto the couch opposite each other, and Brian rubbed his hands over the upholstery in amazement.

"How are Lisa and the children?" Richard asked, breaking the ice.

"Everyone is doing well," Brian nodded enthusiastically. "We are both looking forward to the upcoming test launch. It has been our dream to participate, and we are pleased to be involved in any capacity. You could say that we are... over the Moon!"

Brian laughed a little too heartily at his own joke, but it didn't seem to faze Richard.

"I'm glad! You two are designated as emergency team number four. You will be located directly in the back near the propulsion system, which, unfortunately for you, is the noisy part of the ship. Still, I'm sure it will be an interesting experience. I am pleased for the two of you."

"Thank you," Brian replied. "I am really anticipating launch day."

Richard nodded and then leaned forward, placing his elbow on his knee and resting his chin in his hand. Brian became aware of the quick change in the tone of the conversation.

"I want to ask you something... off the record."

Brian's amusement faded. "Okay..."

Richard leaned back then, studying Brian with a curious expression. "Now, off the record," he began, his tone measured but laced with intrigue, "what are your thoughts on Alex's new alloy? Stronger than anything ever made. It's one of, if not the, most impressive things he's ever done. I'm in awe of it. Truly remarkable. And he managed to pull it off in such a short amount of time." He paused, tapping a finger against the armrest of the sofa. Brian could tell that this was the crux of the question. "How did he do it? Do you think he had help from the two Norn ambassadors?"

Brian exhaled, shaking his head slightly. "Well, that's been the general consensus," he admitted. "But if that's the case, Alex isn't saying a word. We've tested it in every way possible, and it holds up. It starts as a liquid and solidifies in about thirty minutes. Our first test was applying it to a piece of paper, just to see what would happen." He leaned forward, eyes glinting with amazement. "Richard, that paper was so damn strong, you could've thrown it through a building. I've never seen anything like it."

Richard grinned, his amusement clear, but Brian could read that there were many more questions. "Outstanding." He shook his head in disbelief. "Look, I don't give a shit how it was made. It's been scrutinized and put through the wringer by every major research team on the planet, and no one's found a flaw. So, from a scientific standpoint, we're all in agreement. This coating might just be the last piece of the puzzle for deep-space travel." His grin faded slightly as he considered his next words. "But that brings me to another question."

Brian arched a brow. "Go on."

Richard hesitated, then leaned in. "Have you noticed anything… different about Alex?" His voice lowered as if the question itself carried weight. "A shift in his attitude, his demeanor?" He gestured vaguely. "Anything off?"

Brian frowned. "How do you mean?"

Richard rubbed his chin. "We've had anonymous reports from the Columbus office. People say Alex has been behaving strangely. Staying in the office for days at a time, barely sleeping, wearing the same clothes. And Tim… apparently, he's been making disturbing comments. Gruesome things. Even hinting at personal experiences with death."

Brian's stomach twisted. He stammered his reply. "I… I haven't noticed anything like that. I just spent some time with Alex the other day and didn't notice anything unusual. I thought he was his usual, charismatic self. As for Tim," Brian said, waving his hand dismissively, smiling while he did so. "No one's ever really liked the guy or liked being around him, so I'm sure that has something to do with it. But no, I've never heard of anything like that come out of him."

Richard held out his hands to his sides. "I don't like asking these questions, Brian, but it's a part of the job. It would have been interesting to be there as Alex was developing this concept, however. The scientific challenges involved are significant. A discovery of this magnitude requires substantial effort, so maybe it's just stress. I mean, the amount of work Alex has done is… staggering."

Brian leaned back in his chair, chuckling. "I don't know if you realize this, but you're greatly missed in Columbus. You always provided the perfect counterbalance to Alex. The two of you are so different, yet equally determined. You pushed him and made him earn everything. The staff loved watching you two spar every day. It was great fun."

Richard smirked, nodding. "Yeah… those were great times. Honestly. Some of the best years of my life. Experiences I'll always cherish."

Brian shifted slightly forward, his tone growing more inquisitive. "My turn. Can I ask you a few questions?"

"Feel free." Richard waved a hand and crossed his legs, settling in comfortably.

Brian didn't hesitate. "Alex turned the Reverie Halo device over to you in 2201. Do you think that has anything to do with his attitude, his shift, whatever it is you've been hinting at? And why did you leave five years ago? You seem to still have a deep affection for the SE Department and space, judging by all the memorabilia you've got in here. So, why walk away from it?"

Richard exhaled, rubbing his chin thoughtfully. "Fair questions." He met Brian's gaze. "As for the first one, I don't think there's any direct correlation between Alex's performance and the Halo. He never wanted anything to do with it. Not even a little curiosity. Still, I wasn't surprised when he turned it over to me. He knew I'd keep it safe, and frankly, it belongs in my hands rather than his."

Brian studied him. "And the second?"

Richard leaned forward slightly. "Truth is, I loved what I did there. But my most important work is here, working defense. People don't like to admit it, but even in a society as advanced as ours, with all the supposed harmony, there's still a criminal element. An underworld that wants nothing more than to disrupt the system, no matter how advanced our tracking is."

Brian scoffed. "They're chipped, just like the rest of us. So why even bother trying?"

Richard's expression darkened. "Because there's no such thing as a perfect system. Someone is always thinking of ways to beat the system. It starts small — an idea, bad intentions. Then, before you know it, people start buying in, and suddenly you have a problem that no one saw coming because they were too arrogant to pay attention." He paused, inhaling deeply. "I'm paying attention."

Brian tilted his head, intrigued. "Like your trip later. You're seeing the Midwestern Director, right?"

Richard nodded. "He reported some suspicious activity in Kansas. One of the Defenders picked up on an informant's tip. It seems like a possible weapons deal."

Brian's brow furrowed. "Weapons? Who the hell needs weapons anymore? And how do they think they're gonna get past an elite group such as the Defenders?"

Richard's lips pressed into a thin line. "Exactly my point." His voice was edged with steel. "I take these matters seriously, Brian. We've had tyrants and tyranny throughout history. I'll be damned if I let everything the Norn have done to help us go to waste because some lunatics want to pull us back into chaos. The universe is watching. I refuse to let us fall into the same divisive traps and violence that plagued us for centuries." He leaned back again, but the fire in his eyes didn't dim. "I love space, Brian. I can't wait for the day I finally step onto another planet and experience it firsthand." He let out a slow breath. "But as much as I love space, I hate crime even more. And I will stop at nothing until I crush it."

Brian sat in stunned silence, his jaw slightly slack. "Damn," he finally said. "I don't even know how to follow that. I just learned more about you in five minutes than I did working with you for years."

Richard chuckled. "Sorry about that. It's just how I operate." He waved a hand toward the desk. "Alright, let's get this procedure out of the way. It'll only take a few minutes."

Brian nodded. "Let's do it."

Richard turned toward his computer and spoke a command. "Start recording log. The time is two p.m., Eastern Standard Time. Date, March twenty-seventh, twenty-two-oh-five. This is Eastern Defense Director Richard Douglas, joined today by Captain Brian Mackey of the Space Explorers, United States Division."

The recording indicator continued to flutter, its light blinking in a steady rhythm as Richard leaned forward again.

"I've reviewed your most recent test results. Your physical exam shows you're in peak health, and your flight simulation scores are nearly perfect," he said, scrolling through the data on his screen. "As you're aware, we're once again launching from Cape Canaveral. Your official designation is Team Four, emergency pilots. Three teams of two will be ahead of you, with ten AI repair bots rounding out the crew. Great Britain's ship, *the Intervention*, will be taking center stage."

He glanced at Brian over the edge of the display, his expression firm. "Have you been fully briefed by the British SE team on your flight path?"

Brian nodded, his posture straightening. "Yes. We'll be taking off at approximately two p.m. Eastern Standard Time, January twenty-first, next year. It's a three-week mission designed to test *the Intervention's* durability. We'll fly to Mars, complete two revolutions around the planet, and then pass by the Sun. The whole trip is roughly two point two billion miles. A staggering number, to be sure, but all of this is designed to test the endurance of the ship's hull and our spacesuits."

Richard typed a few quick notes, his fingers tapping against the glassy surface of the desk. "Very good. I realize it's a staggering distance, as you say, but do you have any concerns or issues with the mission parameters?"

"None," Brian replied without hesitation.

"Alright then. End recording log." Richard leaned back in his chair as the recording indicator dimmed and stopped. "I'll send this along with your test results to the British Director and SE team. You should be cleared soon."

Brian rose from his chair and stretched slightly, the hours of travel and sitting finally catching up with his back. "Well, if there's nothing else, I'll let you get to that pressing matter in Kansas."

The two men stood and shook hands.

"Great seeing you again, Brian," Richard said with a warm smile. "Best of luck on the mission. I'll be vetting Lisa next week."

Brian gave a short nod but paused when Richard didn't immediately return to his desk. The Director's expression shifted subtly, more hesitant now, more personal.

"There's one last thing I wanted to talk about," Richard said.

Brian's brow furrowed. "What is it?" He had assumed the meeting was over.

Richard hesitated, as though weighing whether or not to bring it up at all. "Lisa mentioned something when I set up her appointment. She told me Grayle's been having nightmares. Lucid dreams. I know it's none of my business, but... why haven't you contacted the Paranormal Department?"

Brian let out a long sigh and rubbed his face. "Shit. She told you that, huh?"

Richard nodded.

"She said you were cold on the idea. Why?"

Brian let out a dry, humorless laugh. "You're really killing a lot of birds in this conversation, you know that?" He shook his head. "Alright. My honest opinion? That department is old hat. Outdated. People stopped giving a damn about that stuff a long time ago. It's the lowest-priority division in the world. Hell, I'd argue the laziest people end up there just to waste time. They haven't done anything relevant since, what, twenty-fifty?" He smirked bitterly. "I can't even say this to Lisa. She'd kill me. And I'm not stupid enough to piss her off."

Richard smirked. "Smart man." He gave Brian a friendly pat on the shoulder. "That department used to be the number one field in the world, you know. Everyone wanted to be there."

"Yeah. A long time ago," Brian muttered.

"Well," Richard continued, straightening slightly, "I already took the liberty of contacting someone. A man named Phil Wells. He's brilliant. Came out of Michigan three years ago..."

Brian groaned, his face twisting. "Michigan? Fuck no."

Richard burst into laughter. "What is it with you, Ohio-Michigan people?" He raised a hand to stop the protest. "Let me finish. Phil's phenomenal. I tried recruiting him for Defense, but he turned me down. Still, he said he'd be happy to help. I think you'd like him. And no, his office isn't in Michigan. It's in Philadelphia."

Richard reached into a drawer and pulled out a slim business card, handing it to Brian. "Here's his contact info. I think he can help. Give him a chance. And..."

He leaned back again and dug into a small wooden box on the side of his desk. From within, he pulled out an object and extended it toward Brian.

Brian peered at it. "Is that a... dream catcher?"

He took a half-step closer, then shook his head with a crooked smile as he accepted it. The piece was delicate and well-made, the center web woven tightly with beads along the edges.

"Really?"

"Just take the damn thing," Richard said with a grin. "Hang it over Grayle's bed. It'll buy you some time with Lisa, and more importantly, it'll keep her from killing you in your sleep."

Brian chuckled as he took the small token and tucked it under his arm. "Alright, alright. Thanks, man. I appreciate it."

Richard gave him a firm pat on the back. "Good. Now, I should get going. I have a flight to Kansas to deal with this situation, but I'll keep you posted."

Brian nodded. "Sounds good. And thanks for setting up that consultation, even if I'm still skeptical."

Richard smirked. "That's what I do."

They shook hands one last time, and Brian turned toward the door. As he stepped into the hallway, he glanced down at the dream catcher, its delicate threads swaying gently as he walked.

He exhaled slowly, the weight of the conversation lingering. He wasn't sure if he believed in any of this paranormal nonsense, but something deep down gnawed at him.

What if Lisa was right?

What if Grayle's dreams meant something?

Brian stepped into the elevator and let the doors close behind him. He tucked the dream catcher securely under his arm.

One thing at a time.

Chapter 6: The Most Wonderful Timing

Lisa stood in the hallway, watching her little girls play in their room. Toys were strewn everywhere, as though a cataclysmic event had just occurred. A small Christmas tree on their dresser gave any newcomer insight as to the time of year, and the lights twinkled as Grayle and Tash laughed and tumbled through the debris field. Their giggles echoed like the sweetest melody ever composed. Lisa's heart swelled with joy at the sight, for it had been months since Grayle's nightmares, and it seemed like they were finally behind her.

Brian appeared beside her, wrapping his arms around his wife. He gently pushed aside the long, sleek strands of her black hair to kiss the back of her neck. His hands drifted near other spots on her body that he found particularly attractive, though he never probed further with the girls just feet away. He didn't want to risk the embarrassment should they detect their parents in the doorway.

"Look at those two," he murmured. "So happy."

"I think the dream catcher worked," Lisa said with quiet confidence.

Brian sighed and nodded, kissing her neck again. "Yeah... it certainly seems so."

Lisa turned in his arms, her dark eyes sparkling with amusement. "Captain, did you just admit to being wrong?"

Since she had finally turned to face him, Brian took the opportunity to kiss her lips softly. He whispered almost as softly, "Yes."

Lisa grinned, savoring the rare moment of victory. She returned the kiss with one of her own that made it clear she had gotten the better of him this time. "What time will your parents be here?" she asked, pulling him closer.

"They'll be here at one," Brian said. "And Brian Jr. should be back from his friend's house around three."

Lisa slid her arms around Brian's shoulders, leaning in so her voice was just above a whisper. "Well, Captain... that means we have an opening."

Brian arched an eyebrow, intrigued.

She smirked, her voice sultry and inviting. "Why don't I turn on the Nanny AI, and we... sneak off for a minute?"

A grin spread across Brian's face as he eagerly nodded. They turned to slip away, moving quietly toward their bedroom, when an interruption shattered their plan.

A chime rang through the house, followed by the synthesized voice of their security system. "A transporter pod has entered the driveway."

Brian groaned, pressing his forehead to Lisa's. "Arrgh. Whoever this is, I'll get rid of them quickly. Don't go anywhere." He turned and jogged downstairs.

When he opened the front door and stepped outside, a tall, broad-shouldered man stood at the edge of the driveway. He looked about six-foot-three, with an athletic frame, wearing a sleek black coat over his crisp dress attire. He had a commanding presence, his eyes sharp and observant.

"Hello. Merry Christmas," the man greeted with a polite smile. "My name is Phil Wells, from the Paranormal Department. I was wondering if I could have a quick chat with you. You're Brian Mackey, correct?"

Brian frowned, confused by the unexpected visit. "Yeah... What can I do for you, Mr. Wells?"

"I was just on my way to Portland, Oregon, and I happened to be passing through. I hope I'm not interrupting anything," Wells said smoothly. "I just wanted to stop by for a minute and see how your daughter, Grayle, was doing, if that's alright?"

Before Brian could respond, Lisa appeared behind him, her voice warm and welcoming.

"Yes, please, come in, Mr. Wells. We'd be happy to talk to you." She threw Brian a wink, muttering under her breath, "The sooner we get this done, the sooner we can get back to what we were going to do."

Brian sighed, but couldn't help smiling as Lisa led their guest inside.

They entered the living room, standing awkwardly for a moment before Lisa gestured toward the seating area.

"Take your hat and jacket off, grab a seat," she said. "Would you like something to drink?"

"No, thank you," Wells replied, settling onto the couch. "Like I said, this will only take a minute. I apologize for the unannounced visit. It's not a habit of mine. I was just curious how things were going... and if you used that dream catcher I sent to Director Douglas." He smiled knowingly. "He mentioned you took it rather reluctantly."

Lisa beamed. "It's working great! After we hung it over her bed in March, it's been almost nine months, and nothing."

Brian, ever the skeptic, added dryly, "Or maybe she just grew out of it."

Phil chuckled, shrugging as if he were quietly trying to appease Brian. "That's very possible. Both things can be true."

Brian leaned against the armrest, a smirk creeping onto his face. "By the way, how'd you like that game a few weeks ago? Looked like your Wolverines sleepwalked right into a beatdown."

Phil grinned, unfazed. "That didn't happen when I was there three years ago. I caught ten balls for two hundred eighty-one yards and three touchdowns when we blew your doors off."

Lisa rolled her eyes, trying to get the conversation back on track. "Boys..." she dragged out the word, already tired of the imminent sparring. "Can we just get down to business?"

Both men chuckled but relented, trading a quick glance. On some level, sports was a sacred language neither of them would abandon.

Phil leaned forward. "I'm glad to hear Grayle's nightmares stopped. Can you tell me what she was seeing? What did she say to you?"

Brian exhaled. "She'd say odd things, like 'I love you, Bridge' and 'There goes my baby.' She also mentioned a woman in white, with long, flowing red hair, who spoke to her. But she was always too far away to understand what she was saying." He hesitated, then added, "She always seemed so sad."

"Like she was missing someone?" Phil asked.

"Yes, something like that," Lisa said, her voice laced with concern. "Why would that happen?"

Phil folded his hands together. "It's said that when you're young, you still have some attachment to your past life. If you had a fulfilling, satisfying previous life, you're less likely to carry baggage into the next one. But if you had a terrible end... some of that trauma lingers."

Brian's skepticism flickered. "So... you think she's remembering another life?"

"In a way. But the good news is that the older she gets, the less she'll remember. Her mind will fill with new memories, and the past will fade."

Lisa looked on, fascinated. Brian quickly replied, "The soul and the brain aren't intertwined?"

"Yes and no," Phil explained. "The soul, once it enters a new body, begins adapting. There's no prior information in the brain, so it starts fresh. We've discovered that when you die, you jump from one life to the next pretty quickly. Reincarnation usually happens within a day or two."

Lisa was immediately intrigued. "What happens in that time, between lives? I guess that's the mystery." She sighed, giving Brian a pat on the leg. "I'd love to know what's on the other side."

Phil's eyes widened as he gave Lisa a nod. "So would I," he admitted.

Brian smirked, giving a quick wave of his hand. "Richard has the Reverie Halo. Have you ever asked to experiment with it?"

"Oh, I've begged him to let me look it over," Phil said, laughing. "But he won't let me near it. Says it's too dangerous because of the side effects." He sighed. "That tech could unlock so much. It could take my work to a whole new level. I'd even go so far as to say that it could change everything."

Lisa interjected. "But what about the woman in Grayle's dreams? Why would she be seeing her?"

Phil's expression softened. "When two souls form a deep bond, it doesn't end in one lifetime. Love is eternal. It's what binds us all." He paused and held out his hand. "Ever heard of quantum entanglement? When two electrons are entangled, you can change one and instantly change the other, no matter the distance. Somehow bonds like that are created so that when that bond, or that entanglement, is severed devastatingly — like in an accident, or something..." He hesitated, then continued, "...dare I say it, something more sinister... the soul can't rest. It becomes inconsolable. The departed may wait in the afterlife for their lost love until they're reunited. They never transition back."

There was a brief silence while they all took in Phil's words, then he finished a bit flustered. "Well, that's what I was wondering... if maybe that's what was happening to Grayle. But if she's happy now, then that's a good thing and something not to be interrupted. We always have to be mindful of those moments as well."

Lisa's eyes shimmered with unshed tears. "That's... beautiful."

Even Brian, as skeptical as he was, found himself moved.

"Well, that's all I was wondering about with Grayle."

Lisa glanced at the stairs. "Would you like to meet her?"

Brian hesitated, then nodded. Even he was ready to accept what was happening after Phil's speech. "I'll go get the girls."

A moment later, he returned with Grayle and Tash, who giggled as they played, oblivious to the weight of the conversation.

Lisa looked at Phil. "Would you like to ask her anything?"

Phil watched Grayle for a moment. She waved at him, smiling brightly, then went back to entertaining her little sister.

Phil appeared to want to say something but then changed his mind and shook his head. "No... She looks like a happy soul." He started to head toward the front door. "Well, I should get going. I have some tough work ahead today."

Brian showed the way to the door. "So, what's in Portland?"

Phil grinned. "Meeting a Catholic priest. We're performing an exorcism later. Believe it or not, it's my third one."

Brian blinked. "Hmm. Okay then."

Phil chuckled at the odd exchange. "Merry Christmas, you two. Call me if you need anything."

They saw him off, and as the transporter pod disappeared, Lisa turned to Brian. "Well?" she asked. "What do you think of the whole paranormal thing now?"

Brian exhaled. "I don't know. But he's a nice guy... even if he is from Michigan."

Lisa laughed, shaking her head and playfully slapping his shoulder. "Ugh, please stop."

Brian grinned at her, but she pushed forward. "Alright, we've got a Christmas get-together to prepare for tonight. Your parents will be here before too long."

Brian sighed dramatically. "But... but... we're not doing the other thing we were about to do?" His voice dripped with mock sadness.

Lisa smirked. "Good things come to those who wait."

"Ugh! C'mon, Phil!" He raised his hands in mock anger to the sky.

Later that evening, the Mackeys hosted a small holiday gathering with family and close friends before the Christmas rush set in. The house was filled with warmth, laughter echoing through the rooms, glasses clinking, stories being told. That familiar holiday spirit wrapped comfortably around them, a reminder of what truly mattered.

As the evening settled, Lisa stepped into the kitchen to put a few things away. She was greeted by Brian's mother, Rose, who stood near the counter with a knowing smile.

"How are you doing, darling?" Rose asked, her voice filled with motherly warmth.

Lisa returned the smile, setting a dish down before walking over to embrace her. "Oh, I love this. I love this time of year. And I'm grateful for my wonderful mother-in-law."

Rose chuckled, hugging her tightly. "Oh, sweetness, we love you too."

Lisa pulled back slightly, her expression growing thoughtful. She was lost in thought for just a few seconds as she remembered her parents and yearned for them to still be alive. As it was, she had to hold on to the feeling that they were pioneers when they tragically passed in that pod accident twenty years ago. And, as for her and Brian, sometimes pioneering comes with consequences — malfunctions, and crashes.

Realizing that she had drifted away from the conversation, Lisa quickly wiped away the beginning of a tear and smiled back at Rose. "And thank you again for watching the kids while we're gone. I know you always say we don't have to thank you, but it means a lot to us. We get to live out our dreams." Her voice softened as another tear came. This time she spoke it out loud. "I just wish my parents were here to see all of this."

A shadow passed over Rose's features. "Oh, dear." She reached for Lisa's hands. "Are you feeling any worries or trepidation about the flight?"

Lisa shook her head. "No. We have the utmost confidence that everything will go smoothly. Alex wouldn't put us in harm's way if he didn't believe one hundred percent that we'd be safe."

Rose studied her for a moment, then nodded. "Speaking of Alex... where is he? Why doesn't he show his face as much anymore?"

Lisa hesitated. "He's busy," she said at last. "As much as we're looking forward to this, he's looking forward to it even more. He's a little obsessive about it, but I think after we're successful and the dust settles, he'll be happy. He'll get back to normal."

Rose sighed. "I certainly hope so. Last I saw him, he looked worse for wear."

Before Lisa could respond, Brian entered the kitchen, stretching his arms above his head. "I'm going to take the kids to bed. It's getting late."

Lisa nodded. "Okay, I'll be up in a minute."

Hugs and kisses were exchanged around the room as Brian scooped both girls into his arms. He turned to his son, who sat at the table, still wide awake. "Brian Jr., you coming?"

The ten-year-old grinned. "Nope. Grandpa Art said I can stay up. I'm old enough to hang out a little later."

Brian smirked. "Alright, big guy. One more hour, then you're off to bed."

With that, he carried Grayle and Tash upstairs, their small arms wrapped around his neck. He laid them down gently, covering them with their blankets, and kissed each on the forehead. Already exhausted from the night's festivities, they fell asleep almost instantly.

As Brian turned to leave the room, his gaze landed on the dream catcher still hanging above Grayle's bed. He stared at it for a moment, let his pride get the best of him, then reached up and carefully took it down.

"I don't think you need this anymore, sweetheart," he murmured, his voice filled with reassurance.

With a final glance at his sleeping daughters, he quietly stepped out of the room, feeling a sense of peace settle over him.

Chapter 7: Infamy

Christmas and New Year's passed in a blur as the Mackeys prepared for their mission. Before they knew it, the big launch was upon them. It was January 21, 2206. At 8:00 a.m., Brian and Lisa were heading down to Cape Canaveral.

The previous week had been spent in Great Britain, running preflight preparations, equipment tests, and final checks. Now they were back home in the US, their bags packed and set neatly by their front door. Rose, Arthur, and the children stood by, watching as Brian and Lisa prepared to leave. It was all Lisa could do to say goodbye.

"Well," Lisa said, exhaling sharply, fighting back tears. "We're all set and ready to go."

Arthur nodded, pride and concern etched into his face. "Be careful up there, you two."

"The kids will be fine with us," Rose assured them.

"Yes, they will," Arthur agreed.

"Thank you for everything, Mom and Dad," Brian said, hugging both of them as he prepared his final goodbyes. "We'll check in once we're down there. We land in Florida at nine-ten, briefing at eleven, luncheon at one-thirty, and then we should be back in our room by three." He spoke in his usual military fashion, ticking off each event in a precise, practiced cadence.

Lisa rolled her eyes playfully. "Always precise. And serious." She turned to the children, her arms out wide. "Alright, guys, come give us big hugs."

Brian Jr. and Tash ran over, wrapping their parents in tight embraces and peppering them with kisses, but Grayle didn't move. She sat on the floor, facing away from them, her small figure still and silent.

Lisa walked over and knelt beside her. "Grayle? You gonna come over, baby?"

Grayle didn't respond.

Lisa smoothed her daughter's hair back gently. "Sweetheart, why do you look so sad? We'll be back before you know it. And when we do, we're gonna have the biggest sixth birthday party ever."

Grayle lifted her head, her big, solemn eyes locking onto her mother's. "Mommy?"

"Yes, baby?" Lisa answered, leaning in.

Grayle inched closer and whispered in her ear, "Why do you and Daddy have to die?"

A chill shot down Lisa's spine. Her mouth went dry as horror gripped her. For a long moment, she struggled to find words. Finally, she forced a gentle smile. "Sweetheart, Daddy and I are going to be just fine. Nothing's going to happen to us. Why would you say that?"

"The lady came close to me while I was sleeping," Grayle murmured sadly. "She said so."

Lisa swallowed hard and forced herself to stay calm. "Well..., that's just not true." She cupped her daughter's face and kissed her forehead. "Come on, hugs."

Brian scooped Grayle into his arms, rocking her slightly. "We're going to be back before you know it," he assured her. "Mommy and Daddy are the best ever. Nothing can hurt us." He flashed her a big, silly grin.

As he set her down, Brian turned to his parents and indicated that they should follow them outside. Alone. "Hey, you know, maybe it's best if they don't watch tomorrow. At least not Grayle. I think this is giving her anxiety."

Lisa's expression darkened unexpectedly. "You think that's anxiety?" she snapped. "You took the dream catcher down, and now she's having weird dreams again."

Brian sighed. "Come on, one doesn't have anything to do with the other."

Lisa's jaw tightened, and her eyes flared with a touch of anger. "Okay. If you say so."

Arthur raised a hand between them. "Listen, you two. You need to focus on the task at hand. Arguing won't do any good right now. When you get back, you can deal with this. Just be safe. Please."

Rose nodded. "Your father's right. Go do your thing and be safe. We'll talk to her, see what's wrong. Maybe she is just anxious, but we'll take care of it. You two have bigger things to focus on; you can't be mad at each other now."

Lisa and Brian both exhaled deeply, nodding in agreement. They embraced their family one last time before stepping outside to their transport. As they turned to look at their home, their hands instinctively found each other's.

Lisa squeezed Brian's hand. "We're going to be fine," she said, though her voice carried a slight tremor.

"You're goddamn right we are," Brian replied, his voice steady and self-assured. They climbed into the transport and departed.

***

Much like the test launch of the Elevation in 2199, the day had all the pomp and circumstance one would expect. The streets were packed with parades, banners, and throngs of excited people waving flags, all anticipating great success.

Richard Douglas stood alongside his assistant director, Stan Collins, surveying the massive turnout. "Wow," Richard breathed. "What an unbelievable sight."

Collins nodded. "Yes, sir. I'm pretty sure there are more folks here than last time."

"Maybe," Richard said, smiling.

A group of reporters approached with microphones and cameras in hand, descending on Richard like a swarm of worker bees on the queen.

"Director Douglas! Can we get a few comments, sir?" one asked eagerly.

Richard obliged. "Of course."

"Sir, with Great Britain leading this mission, where will you be stationed during the launch? With the NU? Down at the site?"

"We'll be in the West Tower," Richard replied, pointing toward the sleek observation structure. "Over there, overseeing the activities."

The West Tower stood as one of the most secure and technologically advanced observation structures at Cape Canaveral, positioned for optimal viewing of the launch site. Designed with a sleek, futuristic aesthetic, the tower was a multi-level command and observation facility, constructed from reinforced alloy and glass, giving it an imposing yet functional appearance.

Similar to a control tower at an airport, the 300-foot monolith offered an unobstructed panoramic view of the launch pad and surrounding areas. It was strategically placed a distance from the launch site, providing a safe yet immersive vantage point.

"Who else will be with you?" another reporter inquired almost timidly.

"A small group: myself, Collins, Commander Phillips, Alex Belle, Tim Stevens, and a handful of SE members from different divisions. It's a distance away, and since we're mostly spectators today, we figured we'd stay out of the way."

Before they could ask more questions, Richard gestured toward the tower. "I'm sorry, but we have to get moving. We'll be happy to talk to you after the launch."

Some of the reporters kept shouting out questions, hoping that Richard would take the time to turn and answer one of them, but instead, he and Collins made their way toward the tower.

Richard always liked being in the tower because it was one of the best places he had ever worked. Everything in the tower screamed the retro-futurism that the Norn appreciated. From the clean lines of the furniture to the warm colors of the walls, the tower was very retro 1960s-70s. The dark wood paneling on the walls was a stark contrast to the white, leather chairs that surrounded the consoles, looking out to the launch pad. And, even though the displays on the consoles were modern, digital displays, the consoles themselves leaned toward being from a day and age when spaceflight was in its infancy.

Richard's love of the room and its decor was short-lived as Commander Phillips greeted them with his normal enthusiasm. "Gentlemen, good to see you," he said, reaching out and shaking their hands.

"Will!" Richard grinned. "It's been too long. How the hell are you?"

"All good," Commander Phillips replied. "Just enjoying the day."

Collins tilted his head. "How come you didn't want to fly today, Will? This was a big deal for you. I thought you would be champing at the bit to go."

Phillips exhaled, a small smile forming. "I don't know. I've been feeling pulled in a different direction recently. Writing, music... I think it's time to start focusing on other things. I've kind of lost the drive to do this full-time."

"Are those the only reasons?" Richard pressed, his expression a bit more serious now. "There were rumors that you and Alex haven't been seeing eye to eye."

Commander Phillips chuckled. "You're always on, aren't you? Always detecting. Always directing."

"Always," Richard admitted with a smile.

Commander Phillips smirked. "Well, my friend, there's no truth to that. We're fine."

A deafening cheer erupted from the crowd outside, and the men all turned their attention in that direction.

"I think that's them," Richard said, nodding toward the commotion.

They all looked toward the video feed just outside of the tower, and they saw Alex Belle and Tim Stevens emerging from a transport, waving at the crowd with calculated smiles. They continued to watch the video feed as someone approached Alex from behind.

A familiar voice called out from behind the two men. "Alex! Alex!"

Mike Wilson, the journalist from Look magazine, pushed through the crowd, grabbing Alex's arm. "Hey, Alex. Sorry if I'm overstepping, but do you think I can get a quick quote?" he asked excitedly.

"I'm sorry. I'm in a hurry," Alex said curtly. He genuinely liked Mike and didn't want to upset him, but then Mike kept pressing, and Alex felt his blood pressure rise.

"Oh, come on! Just a second, Alex. I just wanted a quick..."

Without warning, Alex whirled around, seized Mike by the arm, and pulled him close. His voice turned ice-cold, and his eyes grew narrow. Alex could feel Mike trying to back away as if he realized that he had made a mistake, but Alex wouldn't relent.

"Look, do you think I have the fucking time to dumb myself down for you, you stupid fucking imp?"

Alex released him with a shove, leaving Mike standing there, stunned and humiliated.

Alex started to march away angrily, but then Tim grabbed his arm and pulled him tight. "Hey! What was that? Get yourself together, turn on your bullshit charm, and go make it right."

Alex sighed, plastered on a fake grin, and turned back, retracing his steps to the reporter. "Mike! Come here, buddy."

Mike hesitated, shaking his head. He seemed very reluctant.

"No, no, it's okay," Alex coaxed. "I'm sorry. Stressful morning. I didn't mean it."

After a few minutes of forced pleasantries and a short interview, Alex rejoined Tim.

"There. Better?" he asked smugly.

"Yep," Tim replied flatly, somewhat taken aback by Alex's behavior.

Even though he wasn't able to hear what was being said, Alex's behavior set an alarm off inside Richard. Something was off. Something wasn't right at all. And for the first time that morning, he felt the weight of dread settle in his chest.

When the two men walked further inside the tower, they greeted the staff they passed with all the warmth and sincerity of used car salesmen. Their eyes were heavy with exhaustion, their movements sluggish, as if they were running on fumes.

Richard had left the control room and met them in the hallway, his sharp gaze assessing their demeanor. Once more, he had the eerie feeling that something was not right.

"Gents," he greeted, his voice laced with casual familiarity. "How are you doing? Long time, no see."

Alex barely looked at him. "Good. Good to see you," he replied in an indifferent tone as if he were offended by being talked to.

Tim, on the other hand, barely made the effort. "Hey, Dick," he muttered, his voice carrying all the enthusiasm of a man being forced to make small talk.

Richard raised an eyebrow in question and concern. "Big moment for you two," he said, puzzled by their lack of excitement. "I thought you'd be a little more... Excited?"

"Yeah, yes," Alex answered, his tone flat. "It's great."

Alex, as if suddenly remembering something, turned to Tim. "We're just a couple of hours away from takeoff. I think I'm going down to the shuttle to see Lisa and Brian off."

Richard frowned. "I don't think they'll let you down there. It's a heavily restricted area."

Alex smirked, his arrogance palpable. "Yeah? Well, I'm Alex Belle," he said, his voice dripping with self-importance as he stormed away. "I can do whatever the fuck I want."

Collins, who had been listening from a few feet away, exchanged a look with Richard. He could sense the same thing that Richard was sensing. Something wasn't right.

"I think we should keep an eye on them," Collins murmured under his breath.

Richard nodded, his expression hardening. "I think so too."

MOVIETONE NEWSREEL

Presented in glorious monochrome with the crackle of old film, complete with an upbeat orchestral score underscoring the grandeur of the moment.

ON-SCREEN:

A grand aerial shot sweeps over Cape Canaveral, capturing the massive crowds gathered around the launch site. Fireworks burst overhead as thousands wave banners and flags. The grand spectacle of human achievement is on full display.

NARRATOR:

And now, ladies and gentlemen, a moment for the ages! The eyes of the world turn to Cape Canaveral as eight brave pioneers prepare to take humanity's greatest leap forward! Science, courage, and determination have brought us to this threshold, a coronation of human ingenuity.

ON-SCREEN:

The camera zooms in as the eight pilots step out of their private headquarters, clad in gleaming, pressurized flight suits. They march forward in perfect unison, their expressions a mix of excitement and unwavering focus. Behind them, streamers cascade from above, filling the air with color.

NARRATOR:

One by one, the brave men and women of the Intervention emerge! These are the finest among us, trained, tested, and ready to etch their names into history! Their mission: to take us farther than we have ever dared, beyond the cradle of our world, into the great cosmic beyond!

ON-SCREEN:

The crowd roars in unison, an ocean of hands reaching out from behind barricades, waving flags, cheering, and calling the astronauts' names. There isn't a dry eye in the crowd. The pilots wave in return, offering reassuring smiles as they board the sleek transport pod.

NARRATOR:

Listen to them, folks! The voice of the people, of an entire planet, rising in one chorus of celebration and pride! It is a sound that will echo through the ages! No one may cross the barriers, but their spirits soar alongside these heroes as they embark on this, the next great chapter of exploration!

ON-SCREEN:

The transport pod glides smoothly along the track, carrying the crew toward the final security checkpoint. The camera follows their journey, capturing the shimmering hull of the Intervention in the background, her sleek, box-like form standing proudly against the backdrop of Earth's brilliant blue sky.

NARRATOR:

There she is, ladies and gentlemen! The Intervention, our finest vessel yet! Designed to house and protect, to push the boundaries of what we once believed possible! She stands ready, waiting for the signal, as her crew approaches the moment of truth!

ON-SCREEN:

The pilots exit the pod, offering one final wave to the gathered masses before stepping into the security checkpoint. The camera shifts to a close-up as each astronaut undergoes a full-body scan, ensuring absolute precision in protocol.

NARRATOR:

One last wave, one final salute! And now, the most critical of procedures, the final security scan! Every detail accounted for, every precaution taken! Nothing is left to chance on this momentous day!

ON-SCREEN:

Inside the staging area, the pilots don their helmets, making final adjustments to their suits. A technician fastens the last straps, offering a firm handshake to each as they prepare for the mission ahead. The camera lingers on their faces, smiling, confident, ready.

NARRATOR:

And so, the final moments before history unfolds! No hesitation, no fear, only the steady hands and focused minds of those who have trained their entire lives for this very moment! For them, this is not an ending, but a beginning!

A moment that will pave the way for future generations!
This is not just another test; this is the defining moment of an era, the turning point in human destiny, the dawn of a new frontier!

Alex's transport pod pulled up to the scene. Initially, security moved to intercept him, but the moment they recognized him, they stepped aside. No one questioned Alex Belle. He strode through the checkpoint, was scanned, and then cleared.

As Alex spotted Lisa and Brian preparing to board at the rear of the ship, his pace quickened. The Intervention featured three designated entry points: lead pilots boarded at the front, the core four in the middle, and the emergency crew at the rear. This mirrored the ship's engine configuration, designed to stabilize its hover before tilting into a perfect 90-degree ascent.

Lisa and Brian, both surprised and suspicious, turned as they saw Alex sprinting toward them.

Brian raised his voice over the noise of the crowd. "What the hell are you doing here?! You're not supposed to be here!"

"I know! I know!" Alex called back, waving a dismissive hand. "Get in! I'll be right behind you."

The three of them stepped inside, sealing the door behind them.

Lisa, arms crossed, narrowed her eyes. "The fuck is wrong with you?" she demanded. "I know you think security protocols don't apply to you, but they exist for a reason."

Alex raised his hands in mock surrender. "Hey, hey, hey. Don't be mad. When you're me, you can get away with these things." He grinned. "I just wanted to see you guys off. Is that such a crime?"

"No," Brian said with a chuckle, relaxing a bit. "No, no, it's not. But since you're here, you might as well come up with us."

"You know I would if I could," Alex smirked.

Lisa shook her head. "Well, it's not our fault you're a shitty pilot."

Alex feigned offense. "I have other talents, I'll have you know. I'm... an excellent dancer."

Lisa rolled her eyes. "That isn't true either. I've seen you."

The three laughed, but the moment soon passed, and Alex's expression grew serious.

"I just wanted to tell you two that I love you," he said, his voice unusually soft. "Have fun up there. Be safe. If anything goes wrong, don't hesitate to eject. Just get back down here safely."

Lisa and Brian exchanged a glance before stepping forward to embrace him.

"Thanks, Alex," Brian said sincerely.

"Go," Lisa added. "Get out of here before security drags you out."

Alex stepped back, placing a hand over his heart. "Alright, I'm going." He pointed at them. "Godspeed, you two. Enjoy the ride."

He turned toward the exit but stopped abruptly. His gaze flickered toward the propulsion system.

Without a word, he slipped toward the rear of the ship.

A moment later, he reappeared, catching the wary eyes of Captain Costa, one of the core pilots.

"You can't be back there, sir," Costa said, his voice tinged with suspicion. "You need to leave." He looked back toward the ship. "What were you doing back there?"

Alex met his gaze, his face unreadable. "Nothing," he said quickly. "It looked like the AI system running the propulsion was glitching. Check on it, will ya? It's probably nothing, but take a look anyway."

Then, without another word, he exited the ship.

He returned to his transport pod and headed back toward the West Tower.

Inside Intervention, the ship sealed shut. The pilots ran their last checks.

Back in the West Tower, the party swelled with energy. The atmosphere was electric, champagne flowed, laughter filled the space, and large screens displayed a panoramic view of the launch. The NU sat in the stadium, joined by a staggering crowd of 100,000. Beyond that, nearly four million people flooded the surrounding streets, and 20,000 people stood at the closest permitted distance near the launch site itself.

Collins nudged Richard as they looked out the window toward the launch site. "Is that a smile? Are you actually excited?"

"Shush it," Richard said, but the grin on his face betrayed his amusement.

Collins' expression darkened. "So weird," he murmured.

"What's weird?" Richard asked.

Collins nodded toward Alex and Tim, who stood apart from the others, stiff and emotionless.

"They helped make this happen," Collins muttered. "Biggest moment in history, and they're just... standing there. Like statues."

Richard followed his gaze. He hadn't noticed before, but now that he was looking, something felt deeply wrong. He stepped toward them. "Enjoying yourselves?" he asked lightly, though his gut churned with the turmoil welling up inside of him.

Neither man responded.

Richard frowned. "Hello?"

Alex and Tim remained utterly still, their eyes fixed on the launch pad.

Over the loudspeaker, the final countdown commenced.

"T-minus one minute."

Richard's heartbeat quickened. An uneasy feeling settled over him, an anxiety he couldn't shake.

"You okay?" he asked, his voice carefully measured.

Tim turned his head slightly, just enough to make eye contact. His voice was eerily calm.

"Sure," he said. Then, after a beat, "Are you?"

Richard's stomach dropped as the crowd in the tower all called out together, the air pulsating as if it were alive. "Thirty seconds!"

Richard briefly took his eyes off Alex and Tim and watched the ship.

"10... 9... 8... 7... 6... 5... 4... 3... 2... 1... We are go for liftoff! Intervention, you are clear."

A return call from the ship filled the tower. "Roger that! Raising the landing gear. We're on our way."

The onboard cameras showed all of the pilots smiling as the ship began its ascent.

The shuttle slowly ascended, fire and smoke billowing from its engines. The crowd erupted in deafening cheers, and the West Tower shook with the force of it all.

Richard glanced back at Alex and Tim again, but the two of them still looked on emotionless, as if they weren't even there.

Collins tapped Richard on the arm, and Richard turned to look at him. Collins was smiling and trying to say something, but Richard couldn't hear a word over the noise. He pointed to his ears and shook his head.

The shuttle stopped in midair as if it were posing for pictures, then seconds later, the nose of the ship tilted up and the commander came over the comm one last time. "We are now starting our ascent out of Earth's atmosphere! Throttle up!"

Throttle up. Words that would live on in infamy.

A small pop. Sparks shot out from the rear engine. The crowd in the tower released a collective gasp. The rear engine fired up and ignited...

...a moment of silence.

A MASSIVE EXPLOSION TORE THROUGH THE SHIP.

In an instant, the Intervention disintegrated in a blinding flash of fire and shrapnel. A deafening blast rippled through the sky, sending shockwaves for miles.

The crowd fell into chaos. Screams and confusion were rampant as everyone began to run in a myriad of directions. Hundreds, if not thousands, of people were knocked to the ground and trampled as the debris from the explosion began to fall onto the crowd.

Richard turned, his breath stolen from his lungs, but Alex and Tim remained frozen, untouched by the horror around them. He moved in closer to them as the screaming in the tower began to take shape and grow in magnitude.

Tim tilted his head. "Hmm. That alloy is really something," he mused.

Alex nodded. "Held up beautifully."

Richard's hands clenched into fists. His face contorted with fury.

Now, he knew.

He knew the face of his enemy.

Chapter 8: Fallout

ON-SCREEN:
Grainy, high-contrast black-and-white film flickers to life. A triumphant orchestra swells.

NARRATOR (calm, commanding):
From Cape Canaveral, the next great leap forward! The Intervention, humankind's crowning achievement, ascends toward the stars - a masterpiece in engineering; bold, brilliant, and unshackled from the limits of Earth!

ON-SCREEN:
The towering ship lifts off in slow motion. Its engines blaze white-hot, the roar swallowed by the swelling cheers of millions. Confetti rains from the sky. Global unity flags wave. Faces shine with pride, gazing upward at destiny unfolding before them.

NARRATOR (exhilarated):
This is a moment for the ages! Eight pioneers! Eight heroes! A mission to pave the way for our children's children!

ON-SCREEN:
The Intervention tilts gracefully, preparing for its ascent. The ground trembles. The people rejoice. Hope incarnate streaks toward the heavens.

CUT TO:
The sky. A distant pop. Then... fire.

NARRATOR (voice falters slightly):
But something is wrong...

ON-SCREEN:

A blinding explosion rips through the ship's rear. A fireball expands outward in a violent burst. Debris sprays across the sky like shattered stars.

NARRATOR (tone shifts, heavy with dread):

Disaster! An unspeakable tragedy unfolds before our very eyes!

ON-SCREEN:

The Intervention disintegrates in a heartbeat. The mighty roar of engines is replaced by horrified screams. Charred wreckage plummets. A woman shields her child. A man collapses to his knees, clutching his face in grief. The crowd surges; some people are trampled. Scattering in all directions in chaos, fleeing from the fiery rain, humanity is in a state of collective shock from which they may never recover.
The sky, once filled with triumph, is now a burning debris field that is falling onto the masses below.

NARRATOR (somber, disbelieving):

What was meant to be a new dawn... has become a dark, dark day.

ON-SCREEN:

The footage slows. Smoke billows upward in unnatural spirals. Confetti meant for celebration drifts through the air, now tainted with ash and sorrow. A global unity flag, torn and burning, flutters weakly before crumbling to embers.

NARRATOR (hushed, grieving):

A moment that was meant to define a generation... instead leaves a scar upon history itself.

Richard awoke with a snap from the slumber he'd slipped into on his chair. He wiped his hands over his face, ran through his breathing exercises to regain his composure, then began pacing his office.

The last three weeks had been brutal. A lack of sleep and a lot of extracurricular drinking had him on edge, and the now infamous Movietone newsreel footage of the ship exploding played over and over again in his mind. The horror of the people scrambling and trampling each other, the women and the children falling to the ground in a tangled mass of humanity, tore at his mind almost continuously.

He looked at the time. His call with Dr. Matto was finally at hand, and he treasured it for the respite he anticipated. At least he hoped it would be respite. He barked out a directive, the first one in a few weeks, and realized that it felt good.

"Collins! Get in my office. I want you on the call with Director Matto."

"On my way!" Collins replied.

A few moments later, Collins entered the room, his expression expectant and filled with relief. The entire staff had grown fearful of Richard in this state, so any movement toward normalcy was welcome.

"That was faster than I expected," Richard said, mildly surprised.

"I was just next door when you called," Collins indicated with a wave of his thumb over his shoulder. "What do you need me for?" Collins asked hopefully.

Richard sat down and leaned back in his chair. He steepled his fingers and took a deep breath. "I just want you to sit back and observe. Let me know if you pick up on anything. I'm still being haunted by the aftershock of the explosion, and I'm looking for answers." Richard gestured to the seating area that was adjacent to his desk, but out of video range, and Collins nodded and headed in that direction. Adjusting his screen to make certain Collins was not visible, Richard initiated the call. The screen flickered to life, and Director Michael Matto's face appeared.

"Director Matto here. Richard, how are you?"

"Fine, fine," Richard replied, keeping his tone neutral, even though he was boiling with rage and anxiety on the inside. He tried to be professional and authoritative, but at times his voice betrayed him, and he appeared nothing more than needy, as if he were looking for someone to hold his hand and get him through this horrible scenario that was playing out in front of him. "Just checking in to see if you have any leads yet on what happened three weeks ago."

Matto exhaled, rubbing his temple. "Nothing yet, sir. We've replayed the footage and salvaged whatever we could from the explosion... nothing. Nothing has changed. If nothing else shows up, we're prepared to officially rule this as a faulty AI malfunction. Somehow, it must have infiltrated the propulsion system. That's the only explanation we've come up with so far. What about you? Anything?"

Richard sighed, the images of those women and children haunting him. "How are we going to explain this to those who lost loved ones?" He paused to regain his composure before he lost it. "Still, we've come to the same conclusions. I'm sure the AI Departments worldwide hate our guts at the moment."

Matto let out a dry chuckle. "Yes. They vehemently disagree with our assertion and are still protesting. I understand where they're coming from. I wouldn't want something this big on my hands either."

Richard raised his hands in a calming gesture. "We're all working together. We'll get through this together." The words seemed weak to him, so he got to the thrust of the call: the reason he had called Collins to sit in. "But I do have to ask a question. A more serious question."

Matto raised a brow, surprised by Richard's change in direction. "Go on."

Richard hesitated for a fraction of a second before pressing forward. "How thoroughly was Alex Belle checked before he boarded the Intervention? I mean, he would've been the only one who could've brought something on board."

In the seating area, Collins threw his hands up in the air in disbelief. He mouthed the words, "What are you doing," in Richard's direction, but the director pressed on.

Matto's expression darkened, his posture stiffening. Both Richard and Collins could hear the leather of his chair creak as he leaned forward toward the camera. The pleasantries were all gone. "First off, sir, our safety protocols that day were flawless. Are you implying that we weren't up to par?"

Richard gave Matto a haunting smile. "No, of course not. It's just a question, Michael. Don't be defensive."

"Fuck you, Richard!" Matto snapped like a wire. "Look, this was an unfortunate accident. My heart aches for all who lost their lives, but you have no damn right, sir, to question our security measures! And are you seriously pointing the finger at Alex Belle? You'd better watch yourself."

Richard held up his hands in a placating gesture once again. "Michael, my apologies. I didn't mean to offend. Look, let's end this call now. We'll talk later in the week. Again, I'm truly sorry. I meant nothing by it."

Matto's glare softened slightly, though his jaw remained tight. "Good day, sir." He cut the connection. The silence was palpable.

When he was certain that the call had been completed, Collins jumped up from the couch, storming toward Richard's desk. "Just... what... the... fuck... was... that?" he demanded, utterly astounded.

Richard met his glare evenly. "I had to ask."

"Did you?" Collins snapped. "Alex was checked. He had nothing on him. You know this. Why would you ask such a provocative question? You're too smart to throw out Alex's name like that. He's Alex fucking Belle! If you're going to go after him, you need more than innuendo, Richard. Come on, man! You're better than this."

Richard exhaled sharply. He reached forward and pressed a button on the control panel in front of him, and the Movietone newsreel of the explosion played once again. "You see this? This plays in my head in a loop. I understand what you're saying, but I just needed to see if Matto suspected Alex of any wrongdoing. Clearly, he doesn't. Now we can move on. Simple as that."

Collins shook his head in disbelief, reaching over and shutting off the video before it reached its completion. "Look, I know you're tormented. We all are. Those images," he gestured toward the video screen, "They're everywhere. No one can escape them. But the truth is, we're in peaceful times - no FBI, no CIA, no MI6 bullshit from centuries ago. Transparency, that's what we have now; no secrets, no lies. This isn't some covert op. I get the feeling you forget that sometimes. You'd better kiss Matto's ass on the next call. I'd be offended too." Collins shut down his tirade before it went on any longer, and he sighed. His voice softened. "You have to be smarter than this."

Richard sighed, running a hand over his face. "You're right. I went about this the wrong way. Maybe I should've been more careful."

Collins spoke almost in a whisper, his lips betraying a smirk. "Yeah, I think so, friend."

Richard leaned forward, changing gears. "I don't know why I'm worrying about it so much. The global vote should be finished by the end of today, and so far, discontinuing space travel is leading by seventy-nine percent. It's over anyway."

Collins crossed his arms. "You're worried because we appear to have a problem and only we can solve it." He lowered his voice to a whisper. "So what do we do about our Alex and Tim problem?"

Richard stared straight ahead. "Simple. We wait. We watch them and see what they do in the coming months, maybe years if it takes that long. And we wait and see how the Norn responds. For now, we control the narrative, and I'd like to keep it that way."

Richard tapped his fingers on his desk. "I want to find out what they've done to themselves. Back in twenty-two-oh-one, when Alex handed off the Halo, something was off. He didn't seem like himself. He and Tim have altered themselves, somehow, and I want to know how. I've heard Alex is putting together a small team. Maybe we should do the same. Find me some trustworthy people for a special covert operation. We have the Halo, let's experiment. Let's find the truth."

Collins looked at Richard with a grin, rubbing his chin. "The game is afoot."

Meanwhile, in Columbus, Alex and Tim were emptying their office space. Computers, testing equipment, and even the desks. Everything was stripped away and was being packed for a move.

Dr. Susan Hallewell of the NU arrived at the office, stepping into the eerily vacant reception area. A janitor, the only person in sight, looked up from his cleaning.

As she scanned the remains of the reception area that once bustled with activity, she addressed the man. "Excuse me, have you seen Alex or Tim?"

"Boardroom, three doors down on the right, Doctor."

"Thank you." She proceeded down the hall and entered the boardroom, where Alex greeted her at the door. The surveillance cameras were clearly still connected.

"Hey, Sue," he intercepted her, a bit frazzled by her appearance. "Why are you here?"

Susan folded her arms in anger. "We just heard a few days ago that you were shutting this office down and moving operations to Cleveland. We also heard you won't be joining them. What's going on?"

"That's correct," Alex confirmed. "I'm sending everyone north. I'm moving south to Dayton. It has an eight-hundred-thousand-square-foot warehouse. That's where I'll be doing my primary work."

She was taken aback by his confirmation. "Just you?" She glanced through the door at Tim. "What's going on with you? Isolating yourself isn't going to help you cope with the loss."

"Coping? Oh, no, no. I've concluded that I can't trust anyone to do their job properly, so I've handpicked eight top scientists, engineers, and AI professionals to join me and Tim. Just the ten of us. No one else."

Susan's eyes filled with sadness. "Alex, what happened to you?"

"Nothing! I just... I just don't need all of you in my way." Alex's tone was sharp.

Sue reacted as if she had been slapped, and her tone softened a bit. "Does this little project of yours have a name? And where are the Norn?"

Alex lowered his head, this time taking a verbal smack of his own from Sue. "Gone," Alex muttered. "Don't know if they'll come back. We failed. And no, the project has no name."

Susan shook her head in disgust, no longer swayed by Alex and his theatrics. "You know what, Alex? You're an arrogant asshole. The whole world mourns, and all you care about is yourself. I can't stand this whining and this holier-than-thou attitude of yours. You know what," she poked him in the chest with her finger. "Fuck you, Belle. Fuck you and the Norn."

She stormed out, leaving Alex standing there, unflinching.

Back in Columbus, Arthur and Rose continued packing up the Mackey home. The house felt hollow now, its warmth drained along with the life that had once filled its walls. Moving the children out West, they decided, would give them as normal a childhood as possible. It was the least they could do. They wanted them to have a future where Brian and Lisa's memory would be cherished but not overshadowed by grief.

Arthur sat heavily in Brian's favorite chair, his fingers tracing the worn armrests with sad memories. It had been his son's place of quiet contemplation, a spot where he would sit and unwind after long days. Now, it felt like a relic, a haunting reminder of what had been lost.

Rose, standing in the kitchen sorting through the last of their things, noticed him sitting there, shoulders hunched, staring into nothing. She stepped into the room, her voice gentle.

"Art, can I get you anything to drink, love?"

Arthur lifted his head, meeting her eyes with a small, sad smile. He did his best to be the jovial old self he had always been. "No, thank you, my lady," he murmured, his voice thick with emotion.

Before Rose could say anything more, the house's alert system chimed, its synthetic yet soothing tone breaking the heavy silence.

"A transport has entered the driveway. ID check?"

Arthur sighed, pushing himself up from the chair with a light groan that matched his age and his mood. "No, I'll go out and look."

He walked to the front door, pausing briefly before stepping outside and shutting it behind him.

A sleek black transport sat in the driveway. As the door slid open, a man stepped out. He was tall and composed, but with an urgency in his expression.

"Hello, Mr. Mackey," he said with a polite nod.

Arthur eyed him warily. "Can I help you?"

"My name is Phil Wells. I'm with the Paranormal Department," the man explained, stepping forward. "Lisa and Brian contacted me just before they left for Cape Canaveral. Before the..." He hesitated, choosing his words carefully. "Before the accident. Listen, sir, I know this isn't an ideal time, but it's imperative that I see Grayle. I heard about the troubling comment she made before they left, and I'd like to ask her..." Phil paused and looked away, clearly troubled, then sighed and turned his attention back to Art. "Well, you see, sir, a child's memory can fade quickly. And, if I'm to gather any meaningful information, I need to do so now."

Arthur stiffened, his protective instincts flaring. His grief, still raw and unyielding, boiled into a quiet but firm resolve.

"No," he said sharply.

Phil held up his hands in a calming gesture. "Sir, please. This is important."

"The answer is no," Arthur repeated, his voice unwavering. "Go away, Mr. Wells. You're not needed here."

Phil called out pleading after Art as he started away. "Sir, your wife called..."

But it was too late. Art walked back inside, leaving Phil standing alone in the driveway.

Rose looked up as Arthur entered, her brow furrowed. "Who was that?" she asked. "Was that Phil Wells?"

Arthur exhaled through his nose, his frustration evident. "Yes. Why?" He gave his wife a sideways, questioning glance.

"Because I called him," Rose admitted.

Arthur's jaw clenched. "No," he said again, his voice final. "We're not doing this. We're not allowing our girl to be prodded. She's been through enough. They all have."

"You're being close-minded, Art," Rose countered, her voice steady but firm.

"Maybe," Arthur conceded, running a hand over his face. "Look, I don't know how to handle this. But down the line, if Grayle wants to look into this, then it'll be up to her to find answers. Until then, we need to figure out what to do without all of that..." Art waved the matter off and ended it without another word.

They didn't speak about the matter any further. Instead, they continued their preparations in silence, the weight of their choices pressing down on them like a storm cloud that refused to pass. Finally, hours later, the packing was complete. Arthur and Rose stepped outside, suitcases loaded, the house empty behind them. They turned for one last look, standing side by side as the reality of their departure settled in.

Arthur's shoulders shook as he finally broke down. "I can't believe it came to this," he sobbed. "I don't want to say goodbye. This wasn't how it was supposed to be."

Rose didn't answer. Tears streamed down her face as she simply stared at the house, her grief swallowing any words she might have offered.

As they stood in sorrowful silence, another transport pulled up. It slowed to a stop, and a figure emerged from within.

Alex.

His usual arrogance was absent, replaced by a pang of quiet, heavy guilt. He approached slowly, his hands in his pockets, his expression haunted.

"Hi," he said, his voice barely above a whisper.

Arthur and Rose offered polite nods, but the air between them remained heavy with unspoken pain.

Alex swallowed hard, forcing himself to continue. "I'm sorry," he said. "For everything. I promise I'll do my best to help you take care of the children. I'll make sure they have everything they need."

Arthur, still looking at the ground, lifted his head slightly. His voice was soft but carried a sharp edge. "Let's hope so," he said. "It's the very least you can do."

Alex's throat tightened as Art stared him down with cold, blackened eyes, but he said nothing more. He simply nodded, his guilt far too heavy to convey with empty words.

Back in New York, Richard Douglas stood in his office, gazing out at the vast cityscape, his arms crossed defiantly in front of him. The view, typically a source of clarity, did little to settle the storm raging in his mind. Assistant Director Collins sat across from him, waiting.

"So," Collins said at last, "what are we going to do about Belle and Stevens?"

Richard didn't turn away from the window. "We watch them," he said. "See what they're up to, where they're going, and what their intentions are." He turned away from the window. "Do we even know the names of the eight specialists they've enlisted?"

"No," Collins admitted. "They've kept that completely under wraps. Stevens isn't even in Dayton right now. He's in Dallas." He matched Richard's cold gaze, his jaw tight. "Listen, if we're going to keep an eye on them and their team, we need to do it off-book. Unofficial."

Richard nodded, but his expression remained uneasy. He turned back to the city. "You know what that means, right?"

"I do," Collins replied.

Turning back once more, but now with the demeanor of a man who has seen the worst in his old friends and wants swift retribution, he faced Collins with an expression of dark fury. Through gritted teeth and a guttural voice restrained by anger, he spoke. "We're going to get those bastards. No matter how long it takes. No matter the cost."

Chapter 9: The Kids Are Alright

Brian Jr. opened his laptop with care, and the screen blinked to life. With dexterity, he typed in his passcode and reopened the video editing software that he had left running before getting his morning cup of tea. He adjusted himself in his chair, took a sip of the tea, and pressed PLAY.

ON-SCREEN:

A grainy black-and-white video flickers to life. The recording appears homemade, edited with care but carrying the nostalgic Movietone aesthetic that the Norn had introduced to the world. A title appears on the screen:

The Mackey Chronicles: A Family in Motion.

A faint hum of vintage projector noise crackles in the background. The scene transitions to an old photo - Grayle and Tash as children, playing in a wide Wyoming field, their laughter caught in time. The voice of Brian Jr., deep and steady, narrates.

NARRATOR (Brian Jr.):

Seventeen years have passed since the Mackey children were brought under the loving care of their grandparents, Arthur and Rose Mackey. What began as a chapter born of tragedy soon became a story of resilience, strength, and unwavering family bonds. Against the backdrop of Wyoming's endless skies, the three siblings found something resembling a normal life — at least, as normal as life could be for the children of heroes.

ON-SCREEN:

A montage of home videos plays. Tash, as a small child, riding on Art's shoulders, pointing excitedly at the horizon. Grayle, no older than eight, standing alone in the field at dusk, staring at the vast sky, lost in thought. The footage glitches briefly. A static interference flickers in and out.

The screen flashes forward in time. Brian, now a teenager, practices hand-to-hand combat under Richard's supervision, his youthful grin showing both determination and uncertainty.

TITLE CARD:

And yet - some things never fade away.

NARRATOR (Brian Jr.):

But even time cannot erase the echoes of the past. For some of us, the past is a training ground, a lesson in vigilance, a chance to learn and to grow from our experiences. For others... it is a whisper in the night, calling them back to something unfinished.

ON-SCREEN:

A distorted dream sequence... Grayle, older now, tossing and turning in bed. The video is taken from a slightly opened doorway leading into her bedroom, where shadows stretch unnaturally across her walls. A faint whisper from the sleeping Grayle echoes:

"Let go... let go... let go..."

Her eyes snap open - she gasps - sweat beads along her forehead, and the camera deftly vanishes as the door closes without a sound.

The screen flashes with static again before cutting to Brian Jr., now 27, sitting at his desk in his Defender uniform, staring at the camera, narrating from his desk. His expression is thoughtful and troubled.

NARRATOR (Brian Jr.):

We grow up. We move forward. We forge our own paths. But some of us never stop looking over our shoulders. Not because we fear what's behind us, but because we know that whatever is waiting back there...

(Brian Jr. wipes his hand over his face slowly as he measures his next words)

"isn't finished with us."

ON-SCREEN:

The video ends abruptly. The screen freezes on an image of Grayle standing at the edge of the Wyoming field at sunset, looking toward the unknown. A new title card hovers over her image:

TITLE CARD:
THE MYSTERY OF GRAYLE MACKEY – UNRESOLVED.

A faint reflection of Brian Jr. is visible in the screen's glow. He exhales sharply, rubbing his temple before closing the file. He leans back in his chair, staring at the ceiling, lost in thought, contemplating his life, the life of his sisters, and the future.

With a deep sigh, Brian Jr. places his hand on his laptop, closes it gently, and stands. Straightening his uniform, he grabs his laptop, places it into his case, and heads toward the door.

Outside, the sun is rising over Wyoming. Today is a big day.

*** ***

Saturday, May 6th. 8:30 A.M. The Year 2223

A girl lying in bed suddenly woke with a gasp. Her eyes shot open, sweat beading along her forehead as she tried to shake off the nervous disorientation of not knowing where she was. She lifted her head slowly, attempting to get her bearings. Her eyes remained wide with what appeared to be fright.

With a slightly frantic motion, she reached for her electronic notepad on the nightstand and activated it.

"Record," she said in a sleepy but urgent tone.

The words escaped her lips instinctively: "Let go."

She took a deep breath, releasing a sigh of relief as she let her head sink back into the pillow, still struggling to fully awaken. Before she could process the strange moment any further, a knock sounded at her door.

"What?" she asked groggily, if not somewhat angrily.

"Hey, Grayle! You awake yet?" came the familiar voice.

"Yeah, Tash," she sighed, a bit upset at her sister's intrusion. "Come on in."

Tash pushed open the door and flopped onto the bed beside Grayle, nestling up close. "Hey, hey, college grad! Today's the day, babe. Why aren't you up and about yet?"

Grayle smiled at her little sister, wrapping an arm around her. "Oh, Tashy," she said with warmth. Then, with a slight furrow of her brow, she continued, "I had another weird dream. I can't remember most of it. Just blurred faces speaking softly in the distance. I could barely hear what they were saying, but they were there. For a second, I thought it might be Mom and Dad, but I can't say for certain." Her face dropped in what appeared to be disappointment.

Tash propped herself up on one elbow, suddenly serious. "What did you hear?" She was always eager for news from what she deemed was the other side, with hopes that they might glean a message from her parents.

"Just two words. Let go."

Tash frowned. "Not sure what that means, but... whatever." She smiled, trying to shake off the eerie feeling. "I think they'd be proud of us."

"They absolutely would." From the doorway, Rose watched the girls with a soft expression. Her voice was warm.

"Hey, Gram!" the sisters chimed in unison.

Rose gestured behind her. "C'mon, it's time to get going. Your brother's on his way. He'll be here shortly."

Grayle groaned and sat up. These late-night visions always made her very tired, but still, somehow, she managed to fight her way through them. "Alright, Gram. Ugh! Let's get this over with."

Tash gasped dramatically. "I can't believe how blasé you are about this!" She bounced out of bed, brimming with excitement. "If it were me graduating from college, I'd be all... aaarrgh!" She waved her hands wildly in the air and made an equally wild face.

Grayle shuffled to the window and pulled back the shades, letting the golden Wyoming sunlight flood the room. Outside, the rolling hills stretched endlessly beneath a perfect blue sky. She stared out at the peaceful scene before speaking. "I'm just not that excited about a career in the Infrastructure & Architecture Department. It's not where I'm meant to be."

Tash tilted her head inquisitively. "So what do you really want to do?"

Grayle turned to her sister, leaned in, and whispered, "Keep this between us."

Tash's eyes widened. "Tell me more!" she practically squealed with exuberance.

"Keep your voice down, you nut!" Grayle hissed, stifling a laugh. She continued speaking, this time in a lower voice as she took hold of Tash's hands. "I'm still going to Florida for the interview with the I & A Department. But before I come back to Wyoming... I'm going north to Philadelphia. To see Phil Wells, Head of the Paranormal Department."

Tash blinked. "Huh? Why? We already know ghosts and goblins exist. Why do you need to go find them?" She burst into laughter.

"Tash!" Grayle scolded. "I have questions that need answers. Something is gnawing at me, something I can't explain. A problem I can't solve. Remember, I told Mom and Dad before they died that they were going to. Or did you forget that?"

Tash's laughter faded. "I'm sorry," she said softly. "I didn't mean to upset you."

Grayle pulled her into a hug, stroking her hair gently. "It's fine, sweetness. I'm just scared, and I need to know why. Wells might be the one to help. He visited us when I was five and was never allowed to come back. Gram and Gramps always tried to shield us from what happened seventeen years ago, but we're older now. They can't keep us safe forever." She dropped Tash's hands and turned, heading back to the bed to sit on the edge of the mattress. "Look, B.J.'s a Defender, you're heading abroad, and I'm off to find my path. I have to figure this out."

Tash nodded, her playful demeanor replaced with solemn understanding. She walked over to the bed and gave Grayle one more hug, which lasted until it grew uncomfortable. "Okay. You're right. I know you're right."

"Alright," Grayle said, shaking off the heavy mood, standing, and breaking off the embrace. "Let's eat. I'm starving."

At breakfast, Arthur, Rose, Grayle, and Tash gathered around the table, chatting about the day ahead.

"Ceremony starts at what time again?" Arthur asked.

"Three p.m., Gramps," Grayle replied. "I have to be there a couple of hours ahead of time."

"Good, good," Arthur said, nodding. Then, with a sly grin, he added, "By the way, young lady..."

Grayle raised an eyebrow. "What?"

"You never did mention how that date with that Matt fella went last week."

Grayle smirked, twirling a strand of her long brown hair. "Fine," she said with a shrug and a wink.

Arthur leaned forward. "That's it? That's all you've got for us?"

"I don't know. I might see him again." She acted shyly toward her grandfather.

Tash, ever the instigator, piped up. "Did ya hit it?"

Rose groaned, putting her head in her hands. "Ugh! Okay, I'm leaving the table now."

Tash doubled over laughing while Grayle reached over and patted her on the back. "Oh my, you're so tactful, babe - and in front of our grandparents. Nice."

As they finished eating and began to clear their dishes away, the familiar rumble of a transport pulling into the driveway signaled Brian Jr.'s arrival. The girls were out of the house and down the driveway before he could even step out of the vehicle. They almost tackled the much bigger Brian Jr. as they hugged him. At twenty-seven, Brian Jr. was tall, broad-shouldered, and exuded the natural confidence of a leader, much like his parents.

Through the years, the three siblings had used tragedy to forge an unbreakable bond. No matter where they were or what they were doing, they would drop everything to help each other. Nothing could ever get between the Mackey children's love for each other. Part of the reason Brian had become a Defender was to protect those he loved.

"Hi!" he said, squishing his sisters in a bear hug, his smile wide and sincere.

"Lighten up, man!" Tash gasped, laughing as she tried to wriggle free.

"Sorry, sorry." He released them from his grasp. "I'm just excited to see you guys."

Brian had spent the last several months abroad in New Zealand, accompanying Richard on security summits. Richard had taken Brian under his wing once he had joined the Defenders, molding him into a future leader. One day, Brian hoped to become a Director himself.

"Hey, real quick," Brian said, releasing his sisters and reaching into his transport for his bag. "I talked to Damon on my way home. He said you two haven't taken your most recent tactical training classes yet. How come?"

Tash groaned. "B.J.! We'll get around to it. I'm not interested in learning how to use ancient firearms from two hundred years ago."

Brian frowned. "Those guns are still out there, Tash. Small numbers, but still dangerous. I just want you both to be prepared."

Grayle waved him off. "Not today, big guy. No work talk. It's a celebration day! Besides," she grabbed Brian's bag from his hand. "Only underworld people mess around with that primitive bullshit. I can learn how to dismantle that stuff in two seconds, so it's not worth my time." Grayle started away, but Brian stopped her.

"Come on, guys," B.J. said in a semi-serious tone, his arms crossed. "I'm not trying to be a jerk. I just think you should know these kinds of things, that's all."

Grayle raised her eyebrows and grinned, nudging his arm. "We know. We love you. And you're paranoid."

Tash, ever the curious one and possibly trying to redirect the conversation, leaned forward. "Hey, how was New Zealand?"

B.J.'s expression shifted, his face lighting up with admiration and memories. "It was incredible. The people, the tradition — it's all so rich. And the countryside? Absolutely breathtaking. Can't say enough about my time there."

Grayle tilted her head, somewhat taken aback by being pushed aside by her sister. "Uncle Richard is on his way back, too, right, Bri? Is he coming today?"

"Yeah," B.J. nodded. "He landed early this morning and is boarding a shuttle in New York soon. He'll be here in about an hour or so. The man never sleeps. It's astonishing."

Over the last seventeen years, Commander Will, Richard, and, to a lesser degree, Alex, had all played a role in watching over the Mackey siblings. Richard and Alex, however, maintained an adversarial relationship; their tension undeniable. With both men set to be in the same place for the first time in nearly a decade, an unspoken apprehension settled over the Mackey household. They wanted things to go off without a hitch, so they readied themselves against all eventualities.

The outdoor conversation now over, B.J. walked inside with his sisters, greeting his grandparents with warm embraces as they met them at the door. "Hey, it's so good to see you two. Love you," he said, hugging them tightly.

Grayle and Tash headed upstairs to start getting ready for the graduation. "We're going to go get ready. You three can catch up."

Rose followed quickly behind them. "Make that two. I'm not ready either, and this reunion has made me fall way behind."

***

As the Mackey women all left the room, B.J. stood alone with his grandfather in the quiet of the living room. He motioned toward the steps. "Do you...?"

Art smiled, giving B.J. a pat on the back. "Nope. I'm ready. It doesn't take much for me." He reached in and hugged B.J. "It's so good to see you, kid."

B.J. sighed. "Yeah, I know. I'm sorry I haven't been around much, Grandpa. Working with Richard doesn't leave much time for family or a social life."

Art waved off the apology. "Oh, geeze, it's fine. It's not like we haven't talked."

"I know," B.J. admitted, rubbing the back of his neck. "But I like being here in person. I hate communicating over comms, and being a hologram at Sunday dinners just doesn't feel right. I miss too much these days."

Art's gaze softened. "Listen, if you want to be a leader, you have to do what leaders do. It's about discipline. I'm glad Richard's showing you the ropes. He's one of the finest men I've ever met. Your parents had a great deal of respect for him. They were saddened when he left the Space Explorers."

"Yeah," B.J. said thoughtfully. "He's definitely a disciplined man."

Art clapped him on the shoulder. "Come on. Let's take a walk. Feels like you need it."

They stepped outside, walking across the porch and down toward the open fields. The Mackey cabin, a two-story, four-thousand-square-foot home, sat against the countryside, backed by towering mountains and untouched landscapes. It was a deliberate choice, made by Arthur and Rose when they took the siblings in, to remove them from the chaos of the world and provide them with a simple, peaceful upbringing, just as Brian Sr. had been raised.

As they strolled, Art glanced at his grandson. "What's troubling you? And don't say anything. I can read you like a book. I know when something's amiss."

B.J. exhaled, looking out at the endless stretch of land. "I don't know. I feel like there's always danger around the corner, Grandpa. There are only one or two crimes a year worldwide, and yet...I don't feel safe. I wish Grayle and Tash would join me and become Defenders. They're more than capable, but they have no interest."

Art shook his head with a small chuckle. "They're capable, but that's not their path, B.J.. Tash is on her way to Italy soon, and Grayle...Florida, maybe? She's strong like your mother, but they both have to find their own way."

Art sighed deeply and looked out over the landscape. "It's crazy how the three of you have gravitated toward separate mentors. Tash toward Will because of his musical and artistic side, and you, Richard, because of your interest in becoming a defender and moving up into a leadership role. And Grayle... Grayle, God bless her, latched onto Alex because of her nature and determination to find solutions to problems and achieve the impossible." Art looked a bit more concerned and turned back toward Brian. "Still, you seem to want them with you. Why, B.J.? Do you feel lonely?"

B.J. hesitated, then nodded. "Yeah. A little."

Art sighed. "I'm just happy none of you wanted to do space stuff. I don't know that I could go through that again." He paused before adding, "On a side note, not that I want you to think about work, but did you see that news story a couple of days ago about the scientist who was missing for fifteen years and suddenly turned up out of nowhere?"

B.J.'s brow furrowed. "Yeah. Owen Stipe. Popped up in North Carolina. We're still trying to figure out what happened to his chip tracker. Strange thing, there was no reading at all. And where did Michael Wilson even get that picture of Stipe in the first place? Plus, I think it's odd that he ran it as a headline instead of notifying the Defenders or Richard first."

"Twenty-eight people missing over seventeen years," Art mused. "And Stipe is the first to come back. Any theories?"

B.J. let out a frustrated breath. "None. Nothing. We don't know if the Norn are secretly working with these people or if it's another alien civilization. These people have disappeared without a trace, and we can't solve it. It's infuriating."

Art hummed in thought. "I'd be surprised if it were the Norn. They haven't been heard from since the Evolution's demise. Maybe they gave up on us."

"Only one man knows for sure," B.J. muttered. "And he says very little." He hesitated and let out a deep sigh of frustration. "Speaking of Alex…is he showing up this time?"

Art scoffed. "Nobody knows with that asshole. I don't know why Grayle even bothers with him. *We* gave up on him a long time ago. I think it's a disaster inviting him here, but it's Grayle…"

"Me too. Disaster waiting to happen," B.J. muttered.

Art clapped his hands together. "Alright, let's get back inside and have a quick nip before we go. I just bottled a nice batch of whiskey I've been waiting for you to try."

B.J. smirked. "Isn't it a little… early for that?"

"Never," Art said with a wink.

Hours later, the graduation ceremony was in full swing, a tradition upheld through the centuries. The caps and gowns, the glow of youthful ambition, the cheers of loved ones… it all remained unchanged, even in this era of peace and technological progress.

Grayle stood among her classmates, the weight of the moment pressing on her. She was happy. She was proud. And yet, something still felt…off. Missing her parents, lingering questions she couldn't quite piece together… she tried to push it all aside as her name was called.

"Grayle Mackey!"

She stepped forward, and a cheer erupted from her family. She spotted them standing, beaming with pride: her grandparents, B.J., Tash, Commander Phillips, and Richard. Still, no Alex Belle.

She barely reacted, simply shaking her head before turning her attention back to her professor.

"Congratulations!" The professor handed her the diploma.

"Thank you, Professor," she replied with a bright smile, returning to her seat.

After the final names were called, caps soared into the sky and fireworks exploded overhead. The crowd erupted in applause, but as the first firework cracked, Grayle flinched. The sudden noise took her back to 2206, to another explosion, another moment where cheers had been drowned by destruction. For just a second, panic crept in, but she forced herself to breathe, to mask her reaction, and she hugged her classmates.

When the ceremony officially ended, Grayle made her way to her family. They greeted her with a chorus of cheers. "Woo-hoo! Yes! That's our girl!"

Grayle hugged her grandparents first, the three of them sharing a tearful moment. No matter the past, the love they had built was unwavering. This day, at least, was filled with hope. It was a chance to escape the past and to build for tomorrow.

After greeting her family, Grayle turned to Richard, who stood watching her with glassy eyes. "So very proud of you," he said, his deep voice thick with emotion. "I'm not sentimental, never have been, but you three have been like my own kids."

Tears welled in Grayle's eyes as she buried her face into his shoulder. "We love you too, Richard."

As the celebration continued, Grayle pulled Richard aside. "Hey, I need your opinion on something."

"Sure," he said. "What's up?"

She hesitated, then confessed, "I mentioned this to Tash earlier, but I'm going to go to Florida in a couple of weeks, and then I'm heading to Philadelphia to see Phil Wells. He's eager to talk to me and, well... I'm thinking about joining the Paranormal Department."

Richard grinned. "I think that's a great idea."

Grayle blinked with surprise. "Really? You do?"

"Of course. You'll learn a lot. Phil doesn't get the credit he deserves. He's a wonderful investigator! Everyone disses the Paranormal Department, but it's still important research, and you can learn a lot from Phil! And, if you should happen to satisfy that curiosity with him, maybe you can move on up North with me in New York." He started laughing, but Grayle could tell he was pretty serious.

She smirked. "Always an angle with you."

Richard winked. "On a side note, I'm sorry Alex isn't here. I may have my differences with him, but I know what he means to you."

Grayle replied quickly, if not a bit angrily, giving a wave of displeasure. "Meh, screw him. He's always been unreliable, so I'm not bothered by his absence. Let's go celebrate."

She took Richard's arm and they rejoined the party.

Chapter 10: Whiter Shade of Pale

A whirring. A soft, mechanical click. The slow, methodical shift of servo motors woke the man from his unconsciousness. His breath hitched, and his pulse spiked before he could even open his eyes, and the sound stirred something inside of him again. It was so familiar. Far too familiar.

The memory arose like a dead man bobbing to the surface of a lake after the ropes that anchored him finally eroded and set him free. The memory was an article. His own words:

"Despite the Norn's assurances of safety and progress, the implementation of the Gen4 bots in schools has sparked widespread concern. Originally intended to foster a nurturing and disciplined learning environment, these AI-driven educators have instead become a source of fear among students. Children as young as six have described them as 'cold,' 'unfeeling,' and in some cases, 'downright cruel.'"

"One parent, who requested anonymity, reported that her son came home crying after a Gen4 bot methodically humiliated him in front of the entire class for struggling with fractions. Another parent described the eerie precision of the bots; the way they moved just slightly too smoothly, the way their heads tilted just a fraction too slowly when observing a student, as if calculating something beyond just learning potential."

"If the Norn truly seek unity with humankind, why do they create machines that terrify our children, and by extension — us?"

The one good thing that the memory accomplished was that it re-fired the synapses in his brain, and he remembered his name. Michael. His name was Michael. He may not have known much else right then; his brain was moving slowly, but he knew that.

As he awoke, he felt as if his consciousness were clawing its way out of a suffocating fog. Panic gripped him as he struggled against what appeared to be restraints. They cut into his skin as he thrashed about, and he knew that there was no escape. Head pounding. Heart racing. Breathing heavy. Mind swimming.

He opened his eyes but met only darkness. Confusion again. His eyes were open; he knew it, but still, there was no light. On the back of his head, he sensed something. Perhaps he was blindfolded. He shook his head, trying to rid himself of the suffocating fog, but then he had a thought... perhaps he had been sedated. Perhaps he had been drugged, and this is what waking up felt like.

"Where am I?" he screamed, his voice cracking with panic, barely holding steady.

A low-pitched, menacing voice answered back from the darkness, a voice Michael recognized. At least he thought he recognized it. "You're nowhere."

Michael thrashed against the restraints, his pulse racing. "I don't know who you are, but I'll be found soon. You know that, right?! Right?!"

A door creaked open in the distance, and right then, Michael heard something other than his own uneven breathing. The sound of servo motors shifting entered the room and terrified him once again. So, he *hadn't* been dreaming. He recognized that metallic sound as coming from a bot, and his years in prep school immediately came to the forefront. The generation four and five bots that he had to live with in school were always terrifying at best; the way they snuck around and seemed to be nefarious agents for someone, somewhere unseen. That fear was what had prompted him to write the article after all. But those unnerving motors with their slimy, serpent-like sounds were nothing compared to when he heard human footfalls. Calm... deliberate... footfalls.

Michael swallowed hard, forcing himself to stay still, though his body shook with fear. He feared that he might not be able to control his bodily functions, but then found that he didn't really care.

"Prop him up," a second voice commanded.

Recognition struck like a jolt of electricity through his veins. He knew that voice.

"Alex? Alex Belle?" his voice cracked as his stomach twisted into knots, and his brain ached from the lightning bolts that shot through it as he spoke.

A series of mechanical clicks followed. The table beneath him whirred, shifting from a horizontal position to an upright one, and his restraints tightened like a steel vise to keep him pinned in place. The sudden movement sent his stomach lurching once again.

The blindfold was ripped away.

Blinding light flooded his vision, and he squinted against the harshness, his eyes adjusting to the dim, gray-lit room. The walls were cold, unyielding concrete. The floor, solid cement. No windows. No escape. Positioned in the center of the space, he faced the single entrance. To his right, standing still as a statue, was Tim Stevens. And directly in front of him, only three feet away, sat Alex Belle in a folding chair, watching him with a casual, unnerving smile. Behind him, as cold as gray steel, was what he had feared. The Gen 6 bot. He tried to block out the nightmares from prep school, but the bot stood there - glassy, soulless, eyeing him as if he were a specimen under a microscope. His mind went back to that torturous time, the Gen4 bot taunting him for the simplest of mistakes.

"A right triangle has a hypotenuse of ten centimeters and one leg that measures six centimeters. Using trigonometric functions, calculate the angle opposite the six-centimeter leg. Show your work."

Michael began to sweat now at that horrific memory, not to mention the twisted version of Alex Belle who stood before him, and his mind raced in different directions trying to reconcile it all.

The once-energetic Explorer, once trim and immaculate in appearance, now looked like a shell of his former self. Though only forty-nine, his face bore the deep-set wrinkles of a man at least twenty years older. His hairline had receded significantly, and his once-athletic frame had given way to a paunch.

Tim, though still fit, exhibited the same unnaturally aged complexion. At forty-six, he stood only 5'8", yet his presence was no less imposing. His expression remained blank, unreadable.

Alex tilted his head, his smile widening, his arms crossed in front of him. "Michael Wilson. It's been a while, old friend." He glanced at the bot and then back at Michael, realizing that there was a sense of fear in Michael's darting eyes. "I see you don't like our bot friends." He chuckled as he stood and began to come closer to Michael.

Michael swallowed hard, trying to keep his throat from tightening up. "Why am I here? Where am I?" His voice wavered with fear.

Alex sighed, almost in disappointment. "Oh, come on, Mikey. You know why you're here."

Michael's mind was racing as he glanced one more time at the Gen 6 bot, and once more his fear caught Alex's attention.

"Interesting, your fear of the bot. Still, a little over a day ago, you reported a story about a missing scientist, Owen Stipe. You remember, Owen, right? He was presumed dead after being missing for fifteen years. You even published a picture of him with his family in North Carolina."

Alex snapped his fingers, and the bot raised its hand and displayed the picture from the article on the Vapor Display between its index finger and its thumb.

Michael stiffened.

Alex's smile didn't waver; he simply gestured toward the picture as he paced and looked closer at Michael. "That's troublesome, Michael," he continued. "You see, I've gone to great lengths to conceal the identities of the people working with me. And I know you didn't get that picture on your own. You want my guess, Mikey? My guess is that Richard and his lackey, Collins, handed it to you. Right? Am I right?"

Michael could only stare at Alex. Something felt very wrong here, and from out of the blue, the answer to the trig problem crossed his mind with robotic clarity. "Thirty-six point eight seven." Michael shook his head and looked fearfully at the bot. As if it knew what was going through his mind, the photo of Owen Stipe changed to a diabolical, red 36.87! It flashed and danced in circles, and Michael closed his eyes to shut it away, to bury it.

"Open your eyes!" Alex screamed, and Michael's eyes snapped open. The picture was back, and he let out a sigh of relief, but it was short-lived. Quickly, the picture was replaced by a hologram of himself and Richard. Richard was speaking. "If we can confirm Stipe is still alive, it blows open everything. The Norn, the disappearances... it all points back to Belle. You can do this, Michael. We just need more time to dig deeper."

Alex was upon him now, and Michael could feel his breath. "Aw, see there? All nice and neat." He crouched a bit to look Michael in the eyes. "What I'd like to know is — who else is working with them? What else have they told you? Any information, my dear friend, Michael, would be... beneficial to you."

Michael forced himself to breathe. "I'll be found," he whimpered, the words lacking conviction. "They'll track my location." He took a gamble. "We're in your warehouse in Dayton, right? It's only a matter of time before you're caught. Just let me go! I won't say anything!" His voice cracked in desperation.

Alex smirked and reached into his pocket, pulling out a small, sleek device and waving it around lazily. It was shaped like one might expect an old TV remote to look, with three distinct buttons.

"You see this?" Alex asked. "This little gadget was given to us by the Norn. It's quite interesting, Mikey. You see, with just one click," he snapped his fingers for emphasis. "I can disable the chip tracker in your body." He switched his voice to a sinister whisper. "In fact, Mikey, I already have. The moment we took you, you... went... offline."

Michael's blood ran cold.

"You're not in Dayton," Alex continued. "You're actually in Kansas City, Missouri." Alex laughed. "Funny thing, Missouri, misery. You're in both places at once!" Alex returned to his sinister voice. "Anyway, the interesting thing about this place, if you like history, Mikey, is that two centuries ago, some real estate developers took an abandoned missile hangar and fallout shelter that the U.S. government had forgotten about. They turned it into luxury housing. Condos. Lavish apartments. Very posh. Very comfortable. And then, it was abandoned, lost to time. Until… we stumbled across it." He leaned forward, his voice darkening. "We restored it. Made it one of our many bases of operation."

Alex placed his hands on Michael's shoulders and drew close to him. "So, no, Michael. You will not be found."

Alex leaned back and exhaled sharply, moving slightly away from Michael. "So, let's cut to the chase, Michael. Your little… what do I call it? Faux pas? Screw up? Brave attempt by a little man to shake the bushes? You made me miss my niece's graduation. Her party is happening right now, and instead of being there, I'm here, dealing with you. So, your cooperation would be greatly appreciated."

Michael's breath hitched and he tried to find a way into Alex's psyche. "Grayle? Your niece?" He glared at Alex with disbelief. "You talk about her like she's family, Alex. Still? After what you did to her parents? What the hell happened to you?"

Alex turned slightly, shaking his head. Then, in an exasperated voice, he spoke directly to Tim, who was still standing motionless. He wore a fake smile. "They always say that, don't they, Timmy?"

His smile quickly vanished, his expression turning sharp, and he hurried back to Michael. "You're testing my patience, Michael," he growled. "Here's how this is going to go down. Tell us what we need to know, and I'll return you home, unharmed. You see, we have a special drug for situations like this. It induces complete memory loss. You'll have permanent amnesia about this - well, most events - but you'll be alive."

He paused, his eyes darkening.

"Or," he added, his voice turning cold, "we can do this the old-fashioned way. That's what Timmy prefers."

Tim shifted, his lips curling into a small, humorless smirk.

Alex let out a chuckle. "Tim is an OG kinda guy. To him, the old-fashioned way is the way to go. To me, it's quite… unpleasant. Messy. See, nobody knows where the AI plants your tracking chip. So, Tim here… he starts at the bottom. He takes a scalpel, makes an incision at your feet, and then digs around in the tissue with forceps. Those chips are hard to find, you know, Mike? You really gotta get in there." Alex made the motion of digging with forceps to reinforce his words. He laughed softly. "FYI, Mikey… Nobody has ever made it past the ankles before giving in."

Michael felt his stomach turn, and despite Alex's words, he still glanced fearfully at the Gen 6 bot.

Alex leaned closer and patted Mike's cheek. "I don't want to do that to you. I just need to know what you know."

Michael stared at him, horror creeping into his eyes, but he couldn't help the feeling that no matter what he said, he wasn't going to get out of this… alive. "You're a sick son of a bitch, Belle," he breathed.

Alex exhaled and sat back down in his chair. "Yeah, well… anyway, Mikey, typically this process would take weeks," he admitted. "We'd strap you up, dig a little, wait until you passed out, do it again and again… yada yada, you know the drill. But I don't have that luxury. So I'm giving you… ten seconds. Tell me what I want to know, and I'll give you the pill. Otherwise, we start cutting."

Michael broke at that point. Maybe he could tell them something and still wrangle his way out of whatever that pill would bring. "Okay, okay, okay! I'll tell you what I know!" he blurted, his whole body trembling. He realized that he was beginning to drool slightly.

He sucked in a breath, trying to retract the drool, his voice barely above a whisper. "Richard gave me the family picture. He wanted it published. He said it was just a feel-good story. That's it. That's all he told me."

Alex tilted his head. "So… are you feeling good right now?"

Michael openly sobbed.

Alex sighed and turned to Tim. "What do you think, Tim? Believe him?"

Tim gave a single, slow nod.

"Alright," Alex said, standing and sighing. He opened his palm, revealing the pill. He held it close to Michael and then he stopped. He turned back to the Gen 6 bot. "You know what? You know what might be better for you?" A twisted look came upon his face and he walked over to the shadows. He handed the pill to the Gen 6 bot. "You do it."

Michael felt his heart slow. What was happening? He looked to his right and the Gen 6 bot appeared, carrying the pill in its open hand as if inviting him to take it. Its look was cold. Calculating. Michael screamed, "No, no, no," and he felt his bowels release.

The bot placed its hand on Michael's jaw and began to pull it downward as Michael did all he could to resist. He tried to turn his head, to wrangle away, but it was impossible. The bot had his jaw in a grip so tight that, if it tightened any further, he feared it would crush his jaw. "Why are you doing this?" he screamed the best he could. "I can do anything you want. I can help you!"

Alex smiled. "One last story for you, Michael. Let me know what you see."

Michael was confused. "You... You told me this would wipe my memory clean. You... You were never going to let me leave?"

Alex met his gaze. "No." He stood before him, calm, almost amused, like a man delivering a speech he had rehearsed a thousand times.

"You were always my favorite reporter," Alex said, voice smooth, measured. Too casual. Too final. "So I saved one last story for you on your way out." He let out a soft chuckle. "Not that you'll remember it."

Michael's pulse hammered against his ribs. He pulled at his restraints again, a useless, desperate motion. Somewhere behind him, the quiet whir of servo motors filled the silence, the mechanical shifting of the Gen 6 bot gripping his jaw tighter and pulling his mouth open. There was no more resistance. He could feel the pill in his mouth, could feel it dissolving, and then he could hear the bot's motors whirring again as it stood at attention. Its duty was done and Michael could only wonder when the end would come.

A shadow moved at the edge of Michael's vision. Tim Stevens. Silent. Watching. Waiting.

Alex sighed and folded his arms. "I'm kind of jealous of the journey you're about to go on, Mikey." He shook his head in mock jealousy. "That pill, it's something far different than the Halo."

Michael felt tears drop down his cheek as his mind began to lose focus.

"You see, we've both used the Halo," Alex went on, pacing now, his eyes distant, lost in his own narrative. "And, well… we had rather horrible results. As you and I have talked about before, it made us completely unstable. The brain wasn't meant to handle what it unlocked. "

He turned back to Michael, lips curling slightly. A shark's smile.

"So, the Norn had a solution."

Michael swallowed hard, his throat dry as dust, the pill now fully dissolved. He could feel its effects even greater now.

"They came up with new chips, ones that would help us retain knowledge from our past lives." Alex tapped his temple for effect. "They also helped us focus more. They… took the psychotic edge off, if you will."

Michael's skin prickled as he began to feel the full effects kick in.

"Of course," Alex continued, with a mock sigh, "since the human mind can only take so much, we've only been able to hold onto about four hundred years of knowledge." His eyes gleamed. "Turns out, that's plenty, by the way."

Michael began to slump down as he could feel something happening. Something horrible. Consciousness was a fleeting memory. Alex crouched down, bringing himself to eye level with Michael as he continued.

"It allows us to tap into our fullest potential. We think faster. Move faster. Process information beyond anything any human could ever comprehend."

Michael's stomach turned and he vomited on himself. One last memory.

Still, it didn't faze Alex.

"Side effects, you ask, Mikey?" Alex smirked, standing again. "We age faster. As you can see." He spread his arms, gesturing to his own wrinkled, worn-down form. His face, once that of a brilliant young Explorer, now looked decades older than his true age, skin stretched too thin over his bones, his once-sharp features eroded by time. "We probably can't sustain this for too much longer." His expression darkened. "But the reason for all this? I'm glad you asked." Alex looked at the now quivering, convulsing Michael, his voice rising, turning bitter. "The Norn."

Alex moved away to the chair and kicked it, sending a metallic echo through the room. He raised his hands in angry defiance. "They left! They left, Mikey!" The words ripped through the air like a curse. "They betrayed us! They turned their backs on us and left shortly before the Evolution test launch. They left us to fend for ourselves!"

Alex grabbed Michael by his chin and lifted his messy face, then let it slump back again. He exhaled sharply, running a hand through his graying hair. "But you know what, Mikey?" He laughed, a low, humorless sound. "I say… FUCK THEM! We don't need them anymore. We can do things and advance our civilization without them." His eyes burned with something feverish inside as he continued. "Tim and I are all our people need. We'll drag you all into the future or take you all down to hell with us. Nothing and no one can stop us."

Alex breathed heavily as he looked at Michael who was somewhere else. "I know what you're thinking, Mikey. You're thinking that we're psychotic and delusional." Alex laughed. "I know it. I know how you think." He wagged a finger at Michael. "But… are we?" he asked, voice soft, almost mocking. "I don't think so. In fact, Mikey… I'd say… we're Earth's saviors."

Alex looked again at Michael, this time changing his voice so that he was speaking in a mocking tone. "Richard will stop you, Alex. Richard will…." He changed his voice back to himself. "No. We're too advanced. Even for someone as savvy as Richard." He chuckled, pacing again. "You see, in one of my other lives, I was… still an astronaut, Mikey. Fun fact," Alex mused. "I was one of the seven people aboard the space shuttle Challenger mission. That ship broke apart 73 seconds after launch. January 28th, 1986." He spread his arms, smirking. "Do you see the irony of the Challenger and Evolution missions, Mikey? Do you?"

Michael's breathing was becoming labored.

Alex's gaze drifted to Tim, who still stood by the door, silent.

"Tim, over there?" Alex motioned toward him. "He was a soldier. A General. He fought and died in a lot of wars. World War I. World War II. Vietnam. Iraq... just to name a few." Alex's smile wavered, just slightly. "All that fighting. All that violence." He shook his head. "Something in his soul broke. He had seen and done so many bad things in those lifetimes that it carried over with him. From the years 2014 to 2029, he became one of the most prolific serial killers ever. He was never caught. He died in some ridiculous accident. Fell off of something. I can't remember, but it was quite funny, really, when you think about it."

Alex paused and breathed in and out for a few seconds. "Now, why am I telling you all of this? Why am I making you think that I'm a crazy, insane, rat bastard? Well, because I wanted you to know that Tim and I are two of the most dangerous men walking around today."

Alex paused. He lifted and let Michael's head drop again. "Ah, fuck it. You won't remember anyway."

As the pill was kicking in, Michael heard Alex begin his diatribe, up to where he said, "Four hundred years of knowledge..." and then the darkness began to creep into his mind. A voice emerged from that growing void, clear and cold: "Would you like to try again, Michael?"

A problem appeared before him, swirling and pulsing like a living entity. "A right triangle has a hypotenuse of ten centimeters and one leg that measures six centimeters. Using trigonometric functions, calculate the angle opposite the six-centimeter leg. Show your work."

Michael responded reflexively. "Thirty-six point eight seven."

"Show your work!"

"Thirty-six point eight seven," he repeated, his younger voice trembling with fear.

Flashes of light erupted in his mind - random images, data streams, and cryptic symbols he couldn't comprehend. They struck him like waves, relentless and overwhelming. History, languages, mathematical equations, and cosmic secrets poured in, flooding every corner of his awareness. It was too much.

He heard voices layered atop one another, rising in a dissonant chorus. Were they echoes of a past life? His own lives? Someone else's? Time lost all meaning. His thoughts fractured under the strain. The symbols and images began to distort, stretching and shrinking as though reality itself were unraveling.

A classroom blinked into existence. He was young again, a frightened boy seated at a desk. In front of him hovered a Gen 4 bot, its metallic form towering, emotionless. "Show your work! Show your work!" it demanded.

Sweat streamed down his child's face. He screamed one final word: "No!" Then the numbers returned - 36.87! 36.87! 36.87! - blinking in and out of existence, floating through darkness and bursts of vivid light until, at last, there was only a void.

From deep within that void, Michael heard his own breath, faint and labored. A mechanical hum echoed in the distance: the servo motors. He felt a prick in his arm. Tim's voice pierced the silence. "It's done."

Tim pulled the needle from Michael's arm after administering the lethal dose and turned to Alex. "We need to get rid of Owen now."

"Agreed," Alex replied with a firm nod.

Tim continued, his face unreadable. "Take Owen north to Minnesota and put him on a bullet train heading west to Seattle. Tell him we're using Green Option Five in our evacuation protocol. Before he boards, turn his chip tracker back on. He'll draw the Defenders' attention. Be careful not to be seen with him. You know what to do."

Alex nodded, calculating.

"As for me," Tim said, "I'm going to melt down Michael's body and extract the chip. Then I'll head to the Florida swamps and feed it to the alligators. They'll be looking for Michael, so I can't waste any time."

He rubbed a hand down his weathered face. "Once I'm in position and you're in Minnesota, we'll turn both trackers back on at the same time. It should throw them off long enough to give us the edge."

"And the others?" Alex asked.

"Notify the other seven," Tim instructed. "Tell them we're at Red Option Three. Get there and stay put. We'll meet on the island in a couple of days."

Tim exhaled slowly. "We'll return to Dayton tomorrow. I'm sure Richard will be by."

A slow smile curled on Alex's face. "Yes," he murmured. "I'm sure he will."

With that, he rolled his shoulders and shook off the moment. "Alright."

Tim gave the place one last look. "Get Owen and wait for my signal. I'll handle Michael's body, set the charges, and blow this place once I'm clear."

Alex let his eyes sweep the shadowy room. "This was my favorite hideout, ya know," he said softly. "Shame we have to waste it."

"I know. Mine too," Tim agreed, rare emotion in his voice. "But Owen's been spotted around town. Richard will find this place soon."

A quiet understanding passed between them. Without another word, Tim walked toward the exit.

Alex watched him leave, cracked his neck, and muttered to himself, "Time to get to work." He took a deep breath. "Alright. Let's get going."

Chapter 11: Run!

Owen Stipe sat in his luxury suite in the converted missile hangar, waiting patiently for his next orders, but the fact that he was in an abandoned missile hangar wasn't lost on him. There was some eeriness here as if ghosts of the past had never left —and had brought all of their baggage with them. The stillness of the room settled around him like a heavy fog, but he had learned to accept the waiting, even though it was very difficult. He kept reminding himself that it was all part of the process. He closed his eyes to rest, but almost immediately a sharp knock sounded from the door. He exhaled, stood up, and opened it.

Alex stepped inside without hesitation, catching Owen a bit off guard.

"Owen," Alex greeted him, barely glancing around the room. Owen could sense that something was wrong or… possibly something had changed. The change in Alex notwithstanding. He could never get over that.

"Come in," Owen said, stepping aside uncomfortably. "Are you finished down in the… basement? Doing… whatever you were doing?"

"Yes," Alex replied curtly. Again, that feeling that something in Owen and Alex's world had just shifted.

Owen frowned. "Okay. Good. Can you tell me what it was?"

Alex shrugged, his tone devoid of emotion, his gaunt face silent and more uncomfortable than before. "Just some minor trash removal."

Owen narrowed his eyes but didn't push any further. He didn't want to find out what that 'whatever had changed between them' was.

"Fine," he muttered, ready to move on and get out of this place filled with its eerie silences and ghosts with baggage. "What's the next move?" he rubbed his hands together, eager to get going. "What's the plan?"

"Green Option Five," Alex said, devoid of emotion.

Owen exhaled through his nose, surprised at this move. "So, I'm going to Seattle."

"Yes," Alex confirmed, his voice cold. "Per our emergency protocols, I'll be dropping you in St. Paul, Minnesota, where you'll catch a bullet train. There's only one stop on that route - in Fargo. From there, you'll go straight through to Seattle and be dropped directly at the harbor." Alex fixed him with a sharp look. "You... remember where the boat's docked?"

"I do," Owen replied, wanting to move along as quickly as possible and get away from Alex even quicker.

"Good." Alex's voice remained clipped, impatient. "The boat's fully stocked. Once you're on board, make your way up to Alaska. The directions to the safe house are already loaded into the boat's onboard computer. Do your facial recognition scan, and the autopilot will take you directly to the Alaskan coast. From there, you're looking at a six-mile hike, but that'll be easy for you, I would think. And there's nothing around for miles. You should go undetected."

Owen hesitated, then spoke quietly. "I'm sorry, Alex. I never meant for any of this to happen. I just wanted to see my family."

Alex's face twisted with fury; the ways that he had changed made it look like something from a horror film. "If you were sorry, you wouldn't have let this fucking happen!"

Owen flinched. Not a good move. No. He wanted to apologize again but thought better of it.

"We leave in an hour. Get your things ready. We need to move quickly." Alex snapped his fingers three times in succession and spun on his heels, exiting the room.

Owen ran his hand through his hair and sighed, turning in the opposite direction to gather his things.

The hour swept by quickly and Alex returned to collect Owen, stopping briefly to call Tim and check in.

"Hey. I'm getting Owen and heading north now," Alex said.

Tim's voice came through crisp and efficient, just like a dutiful soldier accepting orders. "Sounds good. I've retrieved Michael's chip, and I'm on my way to the ship. I'll be taking off for Florida in five minutes. At exactly eleven p.m. your time, turn his tracker on. I'll check with you one last time before that. And… I've set the detonations, so don't take too long. Get moving so you don't get caught in the maelstrom that's coming."

Alex nodded, a brief panic setting in. He had to get Owen and get out before he became a casualty of his own making. Still, he was Alex Belle; that meant he was above mistakes.

"Got it," he said before cutting the comms and knocking loudly on Owen's door. "Owen! Let's go. Time's wasting!"

Owen opened the door, looking hesitant. "Do I have time to call my sister? It's going to be a while before she hears from me again."

Alex clenched his jaw. "Get to the fucking vehicle! We don't have time to mess around, Owen! Come on!"

"Okay, okay! I'm sorry!" Owen stammered, swinging open the door and grabbing his bag. Lugging it as if he were carrying the entirety of his belongings, he hurried after Alex.

The two men made their way to Alex's hovercraft, stopping briefly as Owen had to rearrange his bags on more than one occasion. Once aboard, Alex punched in the coordinates for St. Paul, and they took off.

The trip was silent but unnerving. Owen could tell that something seemed off, and the blast in the distance that lit up the sky confirmed it. Both men looked on in silence as debris swirled in the air and then fell to the ground.

Owen looked at Alex suspiciously, but Alex offered up nothing, his tight, harried face lit by the remains of the explosion.

***

St. Paul, Minnesota – 10:55 p.m.

The hovercraft set down a quarter mile from the bullet train station. Alex powered down the engines, checked his watch, and sighed.

Owen turned to him, speaking for the first time since leaving the hangar. "Look, for what it's worth… I'm…"

"Shut. The. Fuck. Up." Alex's voice cut like a blade.

Owen recoiled.

Alex got closer, seething and Owen slightly turned away, the odor of Alex's breath accosting his face. "Your gross incompetence led me to do something tonight that I didn't want to do. You jeopardized everyone's safety. I'm done with you."

Owen lowered his head. "I… I feel like you're overreacting a bit, Alex. I know you liked the Kansas City location, but isn't this a bit much?"

Alex ignored him and checked the time again: 10:55 p.m. He tapped his comm. "Tim, you in position?"

Tim answered. "Yes. We're a go. I repeat, we're a go."

Alex's lips curled into a thin smile. "Good." He looked at Owen and gave a slight nod. "Train leaves at eleven-fifteen. Get out of the vehicle."

Owen blinked in disbelief. "You… You're not going to drop me at the door?"

"You can run and make it in two minutes and thirty seconds," Alex said flatly.

Owen obeyed, stepping out of the hovercraft. Alex followed, dragging Owen's bag behind him. He checked the time: 10:59 p.m.

Owen started to speak, but Alex clamped a hand over his mouth.

"Shhhhhh," Alex whispered.

The clock struck 11 p.m. Alex activated his tracking chip.

He took a step back and said, "Go. Go now. Run!" He shoved Owen forward and climbed back into the hovercraft.

Owen's eyes widened, and he hesitated, staring at Alex. "Wait. What did you just do?"

Alex glared at him and sneered. "Go!"

Owen suddenly feared for his life more than ever before. He turned and bolted toward the train station.

***

Wyoming, 10:22 p.m.

Back at the Mackey ranch, Grayle's graduation party was still in full swing. Richard was sitting with the guests when his comm buzzed. It was Stan Collins. He stood and excused himself. Stepping into a quieter room, Richard answered. "Stan, what's up?"

Collins' voice was urgent. "We've got a situation."

Richard stepped outside toward the tree line. "Okay. What's going on?"

"At eleven o'clock Central Time, both Owen Stipe and Michael Wilson's trackers went online. Just before that, an explosion was reported in Kansas City. I'm not saying they're connected, but…"

"They are," Richard replied coldly — confidently.

"Yeah, well," Collins said. "Owen's on a bullet train heading west. Michael's tracker shows Florida. I'm airborne and heading south. The Defenders are en route."

Richard sighed. "Holy shit." He headed for his transport. "Where's it stopping - the bullet train?"

"Directly at the Seattle pier."

Richard sighed. "Alright. I'm going to intercept; with any luck, I'll get there before it stops."

"Hurry, sir."

Richard sprinted to his transport. He didn't notice Brian Jr. stepping outside. "Richard! What's going on? Do you need me?"

Richard never looked back, but his voice was stern. "No. Go back inside. Be with your sister. This isn't your fight." Richard climbed into his transport and headed to his airborne vehicle. He didn't want to be delayed by switching transports, but he had no choice.

Once airborne, Richard tried to catch up with the train. He had wasted thirty minutes getting to his single-passenger air transport, so now it was time to high-tail it. When he was able to finally set the autopilot, he contacted Stan again.

"Okay, I'm airborne. Should overcome that train soon. What's your ETA?"

"I should touch down in Florida in about an hour," Stan replied through static. "You?"

Richard looked out his window, scanning the skyline. "I'm going to fly to the Oregon coast and work my way up from there." He paused and then spoke as he checked his GPS monitor. A red dot indicated Stipe's location. "I'm checking now, Stan. Looks like Stipe's tracker has him just past Billings, Montana. He's got another thirty-five to forty minutes, tops, before he reaches the coast. I already have The Defenders at the station waiting for him, so we should apprehend him easily."

"Roger that. I'll catch you in a few for any further developments." Collins's comm clicked off, and Richard settled in for his longer flight.

Together, yet separate, the two men continued to work their way toward their intended targets.

Owen Stipe sat on the bullet train heading west, completely unaware of what awaited him at his last stop. His mind was reeling with options, none of them good, and he sat tensely in his seat, staring straight ahead, hoping for some sort of entertainment to come by. Perhaps a pretty woman, or some children on a business trip with their father, causing a ruckus that might take him away for a few minutes. Instead, from just to his right, walking down the aisle casually, as if not wanting to cause a stir, Scott Sims approached. This was not the distraction he was hoping for.

Sims, one of the eight people working with Alex and Tim, slid into the seat next to Owen, his presence sending a fresh wave of paranoia through Owen's system. Whatever had been going through Owen's head about his situation at his final stop had suddenly taken a drastic turn. And it wasn't good.

"What are you doing here, Sims?" Owen asked, his voice edged with suspicion as he tried to slide as far from Sims as possible.

"Relax," Sims said smoothly, looking straight ahead. "I'm here to help you."

He reached into his pocket, pulling out a small device; a quiet click occurred. "You're offline again."

Owen's eyes widened in shock. He looked at Sims with fear. "What the... I didn't even know it was on to begin with," he hissed, both surprised and aggravated.

Sims leaned in, lowering his voice. "Look forward, Owen. No one needs to know something is going on. There are eyes everywhere, man."

Owen looked forward, but he couldn't stop the fear in his eyes. He hoped it didn't betray him too much, but then again, how much was too much? With these people, any slight movement might be enough to set them off.

"Look," Sims continued, "I'll get to the point. My main job here is to help you get off this train undetected. The others and I were supposed to meet Alex and Tim in Michigan at Beaver Island. Have you heard of it?" Sims shook his head, preempting a reply. "Doesn't matter if you have or not. It's a remote island on Lake Michigan, small enough to be covert, but large enough not to seem out of place. All kinds of people go there and live there, so it's actually a good place for hiding out. It turns out we're not going, however. Instead, we're heading north of there into Canada. We've got our own safe house up there."

Sims looked back at Owen with anger in his eyes, and Owen was hard-pressed to know if it was genuine. Sims continued. "What I'm saying, Owen, and let me be crystal clear here, is I'm done with Alex. We all are."

Owen blinked, trying to process this sudden revelation. "What?"

Sims exhaled, his tone firm. "Too much secrecy. Too much bullshit. Alex and Tim aren't giving us the full story. We don't trust them anymore. Whatever they're doing, we don't want to be a part of it. We're out, and I'm offering you a chance to come with us."

Owen hesitated, his mind racing. "I don't know..." His voice trailed off, completely distressed.

Sims pressed further. "Look, they've held up their end of the bargain with you, right? Given you access to alien tech? Let you work on things you wouldn't otherwise have gotten your hands on? That's been fulfilling, hasn't it?"

Owen nodded hesitantly. "Yeah, it has." He sighed, rubbing his face. "But you're right. They're holding something back. I've known it for a while now. Like the safe house in Kansas City. Why did they have to level that place? Alex never blinked when that place went up. And what was the 'minor trash removal' Alex had to do in the basement? And why do they look so... so different? Are they messing with things that they..."

"Shh. We're running out of time," Sims whispered.

Owen took a deep breath and then nodded. "Alright. I'll stick to my current plan. I'll make my way to the Alaskan safe house first, lay low for a day or two, and then I'll trek on into Canada to meet up with you." He frowned as a realization struck him. "Wait. Why did Alex turn my tracker on?"

Sims shook his head. "He didn't say."

A sense of unease settled in Owen's gut. "Do you think..."

Sims continued before Owen could speak his suspicions into reality. "Now listen. And this is important. There are going to be Defenders waiting at the last stop, so we're going to move to the back of the train and exit through the rear door. There's a wooded area nearby. We'll cut through there and head north until we hit the shoreline at

Puget Sound. From there, you should be able to make your way to the boat. Move fast. Don't stop for anything."

Owen's frustration boiled over, but he didn't want to raise any alarms, so he leaned down slightly and hissed in Sims's direction. "What I don't understand is why all this covert bullshit! We haven't done anything wrong! We've broken no laws! They need to answer for this. Alex and Tim both!"

Sims gave him a knowing look and a quick raise of his eyebrows. "They will, Owen. In due time, they will."

A short time later, the train hissed to a stop at its destination. Owen and Sims wasted no time in exiting, moving as stealthily as their shadows. Keeping low, they slipped through the rear exit, undetected, and disappeared into the wooded area beyond the tracks.

Inside the train, Defenders halfheartedly canvassed the carriages, now fully aware that Owen's tracker had been deactivated again. Two of them strolled through the train, making small talk.

"Why are we even looking for this guy again, Jesse?" the first Defender, a tall, muscular man in a bulletproof vest, asked as he swept the area with his weapon. He looked as if he had been snatched from inside the pages of an old western magazine- ranches and horses and pretty maidens posing on tractors.

The second Defender, Jesse, shrugged. Opposite the first, Jesse was wiry and muscular as if his workouts consisted of wrestling crocodiles in a back swamp. His long, stringy hair flowed down below his cap, but he seemed as much on the sharp end of the blade as his coworker, Tex. "I don't know. It's stupid, is what it is, Tex. Some guy's chip is malfunctioning. Our only orders were to stop him and make sure he's okay." He paused. "Eastern Director, Douglas, is en route. He was at an event nearby, I guess."

Tex scoffed. "Hmm. Okay. Whatever they want. Director Long can't be bothered with it - if that tells you anything. Said Douglas can handle it."

"Yeah, well, I'm gonna get on the comm and see if anyone has seen or heard anything." Jesse stopped, lifted the mic from its clip on his shoulder, and spoke into it.

Outside, a small group of Defenders lingered on the platform, casually chatting with the handful of passengers disembarking. No one seemed particularly urgent about their search.

Owen and Sims maneuvered through the deep, dense woods, the darkness surrounding them almost swallowing them whole at times. When they reached a quiet stretch of road, Sims stopped.

"Alright, Owen. This is where we part ways," he said. "Head west up this road. It'll take you straight to the pier. It's a pretty short walk." He placed a firm hand on Owen's shoulder. "Good luck. I'll see you soon."

Owen exhaled sharply, still seething over the secrecy surrounding everything, but feeling better now that he had talked things over with Sims. "Thanks, Scott. I'll see you soon."

With that, the two men separated, and Owen trudged toward the pier, his mind still reeling.

The short walk took twenty-five minutes on mostly flat terrain, so it was a fairly easy jaunt to the pier. Once there, Owen ducked behind a small building and scanned the area methodically. Hardly anyone was out. No Defenders. No signs of trouble. Everything was eerily quiet. He rolled his eyes and muttered under his breath, "This is so stupid."

Coming out from behind the building, Owen was finally able to relax. He was fairly confident in his ability to sense danger, so he strolled toward the docks, taking one final look around before proceeding. The air carried the distant sound of laughter from a group of partygoers nearby and the calls from a flock of seagulls, but otherwise, the night was still.

As he reached the assigned dock, he was greeted by a sleek, 55-foot vessel in pristine condition. It looked as if it had just come off the factory floor: white, bold, and amazing. Owen wondered if it had ever been used before as he stepped on the deck and studied his surroundings.

Reaching the entrance to the cabin, Owen stepped inside and whistled in appreciation. The cabin gleamed with luxury furnishings and cutting-edge tech that rivaled anything he had ever seen.

"Zowie! I'm traveling in style," Owen exclaimed a bit too loudly.

Eager to get moving, he retraced his steps and quickly returned to the dock. Crouching down to untie the boat, a voice interrupted him.

"How's it going, friend?"

Owen glanced up as he finished with the ropes and tossed them aside. A man dressed in casual boating attire stood nearby, offering a friendly wave. He even donned a quirky, white captain's hat that looked as if it had been purchased from the local gift shop.

"Fine," Owen replied curtly, waving in return and then stepping back onto the dock. His suspicions got the best of him, so he kept his movements cautious and purposeful.

The stranger tilted his head. "Name's Garman. Gavin Garman. Heading out a little late, aren't you?"

Owen narrowed his eyes, now very suspicious. "Sure. What's it to you?" His tone came out sharper than intended.

"Hey, just being friendly," the man said, holding his hands up in a defensive gesture.

Owen exhaled, feeling ridiculous for snapping. He turned and fully faced the stranger. "Sorry, friend. No offense intended. Just trying to cast off. I like boating at night. It's… peaceful. I never go out far; I just like to sit under the stars. Get to see the occasional shooting star or even the space station if I'm in the right place, right time."

Gavin nodded, his expression understanding. "It certainly is peaceful. I like to go at night too. My boat's right over there." He motioned to a docked vessel behind him before continuing, "I just got in myself. Be careful tonight, though, the water's a little choppy."

Owen offered his hand for a handshake. "Thanks, mate. Take care. Have a good ni…" Owen turned his head slightly as if he had seen something in the shadows. Did he just catch a glint of something reflecting? He squinted in that direction as Gavin Garman opened his mouth to reply, but before either man could get another word out...

A deafening gunshot echoed through the still night. Owen's head exploded in a grotesque spray of blood and bone, his body crumpling instantly. The force sent him toppling into the water, his right foot striking the large ship he had just been aboard. As he began to float on the surface, bobbing with the flotsam as small waves lapped against the shore, the ship began to drift away on its own. No one noticed.

Gavin gasped in horror, his eyes wide with shock and fear. He staggered backward, his face and clothes splattered with Owen's blood and brain matter. His stomach twisted violently, and he dropped to his knees, retching.

Nearby partygoers heard the shot and rushed toward the scene, but they stopped yards away, certain that they didn't want to get involved.

Owen Stipe was dead.

Murdered in cold blood.

Chapter 12: Why?

Richard stood on the dock, surveying the chaotic scene before him. The Defenders, emergency personnel, and local authorities had cordoned off the area, their voices hushed, their movements unsure. It was the first murder in eighty-seven years. In an unprecedented era of peace throughout the world, no one had experience handling an event like this. Instinctively, and hope-filled, all eyes turned to Richard. At that moment in time, in the history of the planet, he was the leader they needed.

He exhaled sharply, muttering under his breath as he began a task that he didn't want to start. "Alright, let's get down to business here."

He turned toward Defender Adams. "How is Mr. Garman?" he asked. The one person who had seen Owen get... well, obliterated... was someone he needed around. The investigation, at least early on, hung on Gavin Garman. Still, Richard smiled at the man's unusual name, trying not to show it.

Adams shook his head, his weapon still by his side and ready at a moment's notice should something else occur. "Sir, he's still in a complete state of shock. We already sent him to the hospital for further evaluation and treatment. We couldn't get a single word out of him."

"That's to be expected," Richard sighed sympathetically, even though he appeared angry. "Do you think he'll be able to be interviewed?"

"Not sure, sir. Perhaps give him some time. Let him get over the shock." Defender Adams hesitated before continuing, watching Richard nod his head. "What kind of weapon do you think was used in this attack, sir? I'm certain that this didn't come from our standard weapons."

Richard's gaze dropped to the blood splatter on the dock, then he turned away, scanning the shoreline. To his right was a set of train tracks that ran along the shore, and beyond that Chambers Bay golf course. The incredible beauty of that scene wasn't lost on him, but he wasn't here to sightsee.

Richard pulled a range finder from his pocket and began measuring the distance from where he stood to various areas that surrounded him. He knew the course: a wicked layout of small hills—perfect for a concealed shooter. But the Chambers Bay Loop seemed the likelier firing point. From there, no one, absolutely no one, could have seen the killer. Richard turned his attention there and gave a small smile. "There," he pointed. "That wooded area right there in the Loop. That's approximately one hundred sixty-seven yards away. Perfect range." He turned toward the Defender. "Adams, take a group and start canvassing the area. If we're lucky, we might find something."

Adams nodded. "What exactly are we looking for?"

"Possibly a shell casing."

"A shell casing? In the woods?" Adams repeated, confused.

"Yes. If we're lucky," Richard confirmed, his voice firm. "In all likelihood, the weapon used was from an older series of guns. This looks like a rifle shot." He raised his arm, pointing toward where he thought the shot may have originated, then paused, considering. "A sniper rifle. This was a precision shooter. Someone who knew exactly what they were doing." His voice grew more measured as he continued. "On the other hand, maybe it's more likely that you won't find anything. I'm guessing whoever did this knew exactly how to cover their tracks. They calculated the perfect distance for the most efficient shot and had the perfect gun, like a Steyr Scout or something similar. Portable, lightweight, and won't eject a shell unless done manually." He sighed. "A gun like a Steyr in those woods? The shooter had the advantage." And given the fact that Owen stopped to talk to Mr. Garman..." Richard looked around again, his gut telling him that he was following a very cold trail. He spoke again, this time with resignation. "Hitting a moving target is tricky, Adams. Someone standing still? Let's just say that I'm not confident you'll find anything."

Adams swallowed hard and nodded. "Okay, sir. Still, we'll cover our bases. I'll lead a team, and we'll begin the search. You never know."

As Defender Adams left to gather his team, Director Long approached. His expression was somber, his body language contrite. "Richard," he greeted the director. "Good to see you, despite the circumstances. I just want to say right off the bat, I'm sorry. I'm sorry my team and I didn't take this more seriously."

Richard held up a hand, stopping him. "No. Don't do that. Don't beat yourself up over something that couldn't have been avoided." His voice was calm, comforting, and steady in a way that made even Director Long pause. "This isn't anyone's fault. Nobody knew things would turn out the way they did. Owen Stipe was in trouble with no one. We simply wanted to talk to him. Nothing more."

Long glanced down at the blood splatter, his face pale. He appeared to be quite shaken. "Who would do such a thing?" he whispered. "We don't live this way. This is barbaric."

"Yes, it is," Richard agreed, his voice cold with determination. "And I'm going to find out who did it." He angled his body away from Director Long, as if to speak in confidence, yet with just enough carelessness to suggest he didn't mind being overheard. "Then I'm going to crush them." He turned completely then, his sharp gaze sweeping across the gathered crowd. He spoke in a cold, calculated tone, gesturing with the confidence and grit that a true leader exhibits in a crisis. "This isn't going to happen again."

Those who heard him looked up, stopping what they were doing, and they joined Richard in freezing that moment in time as his words struck deep.

A train passed. A man on the golf course teed up a ball to hit into the Sound, and the seagulls cawed overhead. No one moved until Richard's comm buzzed, breaking the spell and signaling that it was okay to continue.

Richard looked down at his comm. Collins.

He answered immediately, his heart skipping a beat as he asked his question. "Hey, Stan! Did you find Mike?"

Stan sounded baffled, as if his answer didn't even make sense to him. "Not... exactly."

Richard frowned. "What does that mean?"

Collins let out a humorless laugh. "We found an... alligator. A fucking alligator."

Richard stiffened, "Come again?"

"The chip appears to be inside the gator," Collins explained. "We only stunned it; it's unharmed, but what should we do?"

Richard ran a hand down his face. He was growing more and more uneasy. "Take the reptile. Extract the chip. We'll secure it and return it." Even after he said those words, his mind produced a reply. *Return it to whom?* He couldn't help suspecting the worst for his friend.

Collins sighed and changed the subject. "You know the explosion in Kansas City? It was an old, abandoned bomb shelter and missile testing site. It had been turned into a living headquarters but was abandoned again after the Intervention. The blast appears to have been contained to that area, so no one got hurt, but still..."

Richard absorbed the information quickly, measuring his response. "This was a precision strike, Stan. The tracking signals going off simultaneously, a bomb detonating at the exact moment... Whoever we're dealing with has military training and a technical understanding of old weaponry. Now I'm worried about Michael Wilson. If his chip is inside an alligator and there was a blast in Missouri..." He tried to keep his mind from going down that path.

A Defender standing nearby chimed in. "Do you think it could be criminal underworld involvement?"

"Possibly," Richard admitted, not addressing the Defender directly. "But not likely. They don't have this kind of expertise. No, this is something much different." His words were subdued as he turned his attention back to his comm. "Wrap it up in Florida, Stan. We'll continue investigating here."

"Alright, sir. I'll see you back at headquarters," Collins replied.

The dawn breaking over The Sound wasn't lost on Richard, who watched the sun rise over the water with concern still on his mind.

A young woman had walked down to the beach with her German Shepherds, and they were enjoying the water and the beauty of this place to its fullest, but Richard was having a hard time focusing. The investigation yielded no evidence; no footprints, in all probability no shell casings, no DNA. A perfectly executed crime. Richard stood with his hands behind his back, watching the water, when a Defender approached him, holding a touchscreen device. "Sir, the AI satellite scans are in."

"Oh, good," Richard said. "Why did it take so long? You would think something like that would be faster." He rubbed his temple, exhaustion pressing in on him, but he turned and looked at the Defender's device.

"I'm not sure, sir, but the AI we use for scanning, probed this area multiple times." The Defender flipped the screen around, showing the images. "See? Right here. Exactly where you said a shot would've been fired." He zoomed in using his two thumbs to pinch the display. "A shadowy figure. Cloaked in black. It has no tracking signal and no facial recognition."

Richard squinted. "And?"

The Defender hesitated. "From the spot where our shooter was, this person takes the shot and then heads northeast through the woods. Goes about sixty-two yards, gets back to the main road, and then... completely vanishes."

Richard's eyebrows shot up. "Vanishes? Like in... vanishes? Gone? Completely? Are you sure?"

"Yes, sir," the Defender confirmed. "Gone. No trace."

Richard exhaled through his nose, patting the Defender on the back and sighing. Rubbing his temples again, he tried to offer encouragement in an unencouraging situation. "Good work."

Director Long, who had been taking in all that Richard had been assessing, took a deep breath and faced Richard. "What the hell are we dealing with? How does someone just... vanish?"

Richard's expression darkened. "Perhaps something otherworldly. I don't... know." He checked his watch. "Well, I'm heading back to

New York. I need to report in with my team and see if they found anything with Wilson's tracker."

Director Long nodded. "Alright, Rich. I'll stay here for a while longer and let you know if we stumble across anything. Looks doubtful, though."

"Great. Thanks." He shook Director Long's hand and started toward his transport. Once inside with the door closed, he leaned back in his seat, exhaustion pressing into him like a heavy lead weight. Yet even now, he knew the day was just beginning. Richard closed his eyes and allowed himself to power down for a brief nap. He needed to recharge.

His comm buzzed, waking Richard with a start. "What the..." He glanced at the comm. Collins again. Trying to shake off the residuals from his power nap, he answered. "Hey, Stan. Got anything off Wilson's tracker?"

Collins sighed heavily. "No. We found the spot where his tracker went dead. He was in lower Manhattan at the time. Whoever grabbed him did so while he was using a restroom at a local restaurant. There's a back exit that leads to an alley. The abductor took him through there, into the adjacent building, waited, then exited somewhere else a short time later. Because of all the traffic and congestion, we can't determine, even with AI, exactly where they went. Wilson was likely incapacitated. And with no tracker, he could've gone anywhere. It's genius, I'll give the abductors that. They waited for the perfect window and took him completely undetected. We're dealing with sophisticated criminals, Richard. We're at a complete disadvantage."

Richard exhaled, the weight of the report settling like stone in his chest. "And whoever killed Owen Stipe managed to board a cloaked vehicle and make a clean getaway. No signature. Nothing. According to satellite imagery, he was there one second and gone the next." His voice turned grim. "Quite possibly, we could be dealing with something extraterrestrial." Richard hesitated and then choked out the next sentence, no matter how much it hurt him to admit it. "And the

KC bomb underground had something to do with the whole thing. Sadly..." he choked, voice tightening, "That's likely where Michael Wilson was being held." He paused for a very long time. "I'm not sure he's alive."

Collins hesitated, his voice subdued. "Sad to hear that, sir."

"Yeah, well... anyway, you did great work, Stan. Go home and get some rest."

"What about you?" Collins asked, his voice apprehensive and somewhat despondent. As fearless as he liked to think he was, this investigation was beginning to take a toll on him.

"I'm stopping in Dayton," Richard replied, sighing with resignation and anger. He wiped at a tear on his cheek, not caring who saw. Michael's face kept entering his mind, and although he didn't want to believe what he was thinking, he couldn't help but think it had to be true. Why else...

"You're going to see Belle and Stevens?" Collins interrupted his thoughts, confused.

"Yes," Richard confirmed, anger beginning to well up inside of him. "I just want to see what they have to say."

Collins sighed. "Waste of time, Rich. Their chip signatures have them in Dayton all night."

"You already checked?" Richard seemed surprised.

"Yes, sir. I wanted to rule them out. I figured you'd want that info."

Richard smiled faintly, although it didn't help much. No matter how much he tried to dismiss them as the culprits, he couldn't do it. They left fingerprints behind that only he could sense. "Good work, Stan. Get some rest. That's an order," Richard spoke, offering a small smile.

Stan chuckled dryly. "Alright, sir. See you tomorrow."

Richard cut the comm, looked around sadly one more time at his surroundings, and set his autopilot for the airport. From there, he'd head to Dayton, arrange another transport, and confront the animals he knew were responsible. This would give him plenty of time to rest. He had a feeling he'd need his full strength for what was coming next.

What seemed like a day full of travel later, Richard arrived in Dayton, Ohio. The long trip had allowed him to get just enough rest to be sharp and on point. He knew he would be dealing with two men who were both cunning and, in their way, smarter than he was, so he would have to keep his cool. They were going to try his patience, but he had to be more resilient.

The shuttle that he had procured for this trip to the warehouse wasn't nearly as nice as the one he had when he was in Seattle, but he made do. All a transport had to do was get him from point A to point B, and this one was sufficient.

Arriving just outside of the warehouse he knew he'd find them in, Richard stepped out, gathered himself, and made his way to the door. With a confident stride and a blank, expressionless demeanor, he approached. Before he could take a proper look around, however, the door opened, and a voice called from within. This rattled Richard slightly, but he supposed that was their goal.

"Come in," a voice broke free of the intercom in front of him, and Richard did just that.

Stepping into the warehouse, Richard wasn't sure how much he was going to have to look around to find Tim and Alex, but he was fairly surprised when he saw Tim Stevens sitting at a small desk inside a locked reception room, three monitors in front of him. Tim was absorbed in some type of work and didn't even bother looking up.

"Our sensors detected your landing. I figured I'd roll out the welcome mat for you. What can we do for you..., Dick?" Tim asked with a roll of his eyes.

"I'm sorry. Am I keeping you from something important?" Richard replied, stone-faced, his anger rising. He hated when people called him Dick. He felt it was demeaning and condescending, but again, he figured they knew that. He had to stay ahead of their game, or they would get the best of him. The cat-and-mouse game between them started as soon as the intercom buzzed in anticipation of his arrival. Nothing was lost on these two.

"Nah, nothing pressing," Tim answered, finally swinging around in his chair to face Richard. "Wow! You look like total dogshit! Did you have a late one, Dick?"

"You know I did," Richard responded.

"Do I?" Tim grinned, confident that he had the upper hand.

"Cut it, Tim. You look like crap yourself, and I doubt it's from lack of sleep. Where's Alex?"

"He's taking a shit. Wanna go in there and wipe his ass for him?" Tim quipped, eager to needle him from the outset.

"I'll wait," Richard replied calmly.

The two men remained silent for several minutes. Tim sat still. Richard stood about ten feet away. They stared each other down. Neither moved. Neither blinked. The tension was thick.

When Alex finally walked in from another room, his arrival sliced through the intensity like a knife. He immediately slid out of his slimy, lizard skin and put on his charming persona, no matter how contrived it felt.

"Richard! Oh my! So good to see you, old friend. Been too long! You look a little worse for wear. Can I get you a seat and something to drink?" Alex asked, smiling politely. He reached down and pressed the buzzer to the door that would have led into the warehouse. "Come around, ol' chap."

"No, thank you," Richard ignored the invitation. "I'm not staying long. I just wanted to ask the two of you a few questions," Richard said stoically.

"Fire," Alex responded with a grin and a shrug, letting go of the button.

"Cute," Richard muttered. He sighed, continuing. "A man by the name of Owen Stipe was shot dead last night in Seattle. He's one of eight missing scientists and engineers. One of the eight believed to be working with you two in secret."

"Objection!" Tim called out. "We only work together, by ourselves."

Alex chimed in, looking at Tim in faux shock and disbelief. He crossed his arms in front of himself in mock indignation. "That's right, Dickey! We have no one else working with us. Unless you have evidence to the contrary, you're just baselessly speculating, and I don't appreciate it!"

Richard chuckled, looking skyward and rolling his eyes. "You two are really something. I know it was you. Last night. All three incidents. You covered your tracks well, so I have to give you that much."

"We had nothing to do with anything!" Tim interrupted, throwing his hands up. "We were here all night. I'm no dummy, Dick, so I'm sure you checked our tracking logs. You know I'm not lying." Tim rose slightly, pointing toward the door as his face grew red. If he were acting now, he was doing a good job. "So instead of looking for the real culprits, you chose to come here and harass us? Get the fuck out, Dick." He sat back down in his chair with a thud before adding, "You sure are a real piece of work."

Still unfazed, Richard took in a deep breath and released it, asserting himself again. "It's just a matter of time before I catch you in the act. You may think you are, but you're not better than me at this."

Alex let out a whistle. "Whoo Wee! Check out the ego on you!" Alex bellowed. "Is that what this is? Still feel inferior to me? On your best day, you could never keep up with me. You had to leave the SE Department because you couldn't pull your weight. You helped shut down space exploration, and now you're trying to pin bogus claims on us?" Alex took a step toward the window and leaned in slightly. "Remember this, Dickey. I'm Alex Belle! I'm above you in every way that matters! Don't you forget it."

Richard returned Alex's glare with one of his own. "You're not above this, Alex," Richard replied, staring him down. "And recently? It appears I have the upper hand in looks. You two look so fucking old."

Tim finally sprang completely out of his chair, but Richard didn't flinch. He was just as good at a pissing contest as any other man he had ever met, so he simply shifted his eyes from Alex to Tim.

Finally, Richard broke the trance. "We can dance any time you want," Richard said calmly.

Tim's face lit up at the challenge. He turned to his right. "Alex?"

"Let him in," Alex replied.

Tim pushed the button, and the buzzer sounded once more. This time, Richard opened the door and headed into the entrance to the warehouse, just by the door that led to the reception room, where Alex and Tim were moving out to greet him. This greeting wasn't a pleasant one, however, because before Tim could make a move toward him, Richard turned his body slightly to the right, tapped his hip, and a laser discharge fired from his belt buckle, striking Tim in the abdomen. Tim went down, screaming in pain.

"Fuck!" he yelled, collapsing to his knees and then to the ground, curling up.

Alex stood there, smiling, and gave Richard a salute. "Very nice, sir. Nice gadget, sir."

Tim tried to catch his breath, a nervous laugh coming from his lips. "Hahahahahaha! Shit, Dickey, you got me."

"Yeah," Richard smiled diabolically. "This is one of my favorites." He tapped close to the same area again, and Alex flinched despite himself. "Close-quarters combat belt. Useful when you can't draw on a nearby aggressor."

Alex shook his head, trying not to sweat at the obvious threat on Richard's hip. "Always developing weapons for a war that never comes, aren't you, Dickey? You want something bad to happen so you can flex your military prowess."

Richard looked in Alex's direction, confident that Tim was shut down. "Look..., Al. Let's get to the point, or do you want to keep this going?" Richard asked.

"Your claims are baseless, Dick, and you know it. You have nothing tying us to any events that have transpired. I don't know why you're even... here." He spun slightly with his arms to his sides. "I'm guessing you missed us. Did you miss us, Dick?" Alex said smugly.

Richard just smiled, standing with his hands folded in front of himself as if waiting patiently in line for a buffet. "I just wanted you to know that I know, Al. You won't be able to elude me forever. You'll eventually slip up, and I'll get you," Richard said confidently.

Alex, realizing that he had been bested this time, tried to make the most of it, to get out of the situation he was in. He waved Richard off and started to walk away. "So, if there's nothing more, we have a lot of work to do today. Plus, I have somewhere to be." He winked in Richard's direction. "Please try to do better next time, Dickey. Or don't waste our time at all."

"Yeah, fuck you, Dick," Tim groaned, still on the floor.

"Okay, well..." Richard replied, starting toward the exit. "I'll leave you two to it." Confident that neither man would be coming after him, Richard exited the building.

When the door slammed shut and Richard left, Alex walked over to Tim and nudged his foot with the toe of his boot.

"You good, man?" he asked.

Tim groaned, still curled slightly on the ground. "I think I shit my pants, but other than that, fine."

Alex barked out a laugh. "Well, get cleaned up."

As Tim began to push himself upright, he winced and reached toward his abdomen. "The intensity is starting to ratchet up, Alex. We took a big risk yesterday doing all that we did at once. We likely can't pull off something like that again."

He brushed himself off, pausing as a foul smell hit him. He grimaced. "Ugh. I really might have shit my pants."

Alex chuckled again, but his tone turned more serious. "Yeah, you're probably right. The other seven should be on Beaver Island, safe and secured, so let's wait till nightfall and go see them. I'm sure they have questions."

Tim smirked as he limped toward the back of the warehouse. "I'm sure. At any rate, we need to let them know what happens when you don't follow our guidelines."

"Exactly," Alex said, already halfway to the door. His voice lost any hint of warmth. "After that, I'm going to Wyoming to see Grayle."

Meanwhile, as Richard piloted his shuttle over the darkened Ohio landscape, the city lights far behind him, his comm crackled to life.

"Stan," Richard greeted wearily. "I thought you'd be sleeping by now, man. What's up?"

"You actually did it?" Stan's voice carried disbelief and exasperation. "You went to Dayton? I always knew you were crazy."

"I just wanted to look them in the eyes. Gauge their reaction," Richard replied, his voice laced with fatigue.

"And let me guess…, you got nothing, right?" Stan replied, not hiding his irritation. "I told you it would be a waste of time, Rich!"

Silence lingered for a moment on the line as both men sat with their thoughts.

"Anyway, I'm glad you had your old-fashioned standoff," Stan added, though his tone hadn't softened.

"Stan, I know I messed up," Richard admitted. "But it's over now, so stop busting my…"

Stan didn't let him finish. "Yeah. And it cost Michael Wilson his life! We should've never contacted him to run that story. Doing that set off a chain of events that didn't need to happen! You probably don't know that it's all over the media today!"

"How?" Richard barked back, caught off guard. "What could possibly…"

"It doesn't matter, Richard. They found out about it all. The entire NU wants a conference call with you tomorrow morning at nine a.m. And they said sharp."

Stan paused, then continued with more restraint. "Rich, everyone still loves Alex Belle. They still herald him as one of the greatest heroes of our time. And looking into last night's events, there's absolutely nothing, no evidence whatsoever, that ties him to anything."

"Well, that's just…" Richard began to interject, but Stan cut him off.

"Now listen," Stan warned, his voice harder now. "I know you'll be tempted to implicate him tomorrow, but please don't. I know you have your theories..."

Richard hesitated. "Whoa. Stop there for a second. What do you think, Stan? Am I wrong about this? Do you believe me?" His voice grew quieter. "You don't, do you? You don't believe me."

Stan was quiet for a beat. "Richard... I don't know. There's no proof."

"You're not wrong," Richard sighed, deflated. He leaned back in his seat, letting the stars slide by overhead through the shuttle's canopy. "You know what, Stan? I'm going to go get some rest. I need it. If anything transpires, let me know. I'll be out for the rest of the day, and I'll see you tomorrow."

"I'm sorry, Richard," Stan said gently. "I know how you must feel." He didn't want to push further. "Get some rest, and let's get back to it tomorrow."

Chapter 13: Aurora Borealis

Night had fallen, and Alex and Tim had already departed Dayton and made their way to Charlevoix, Michigan. From there, they'd take a short boat ride northwest across Lake Michigan to Beaver Island.

In its solitude, Beaver Island had become an ideal stronghold, a refuge and emergency meeting point, perfect for disappearing when needed. The homes and properties were lavish, well-appointed with luxurious furnishings and elegant architecture, and were nestled deep in the woods for the most part.

Alex, Tim, and their small circle of followers had snagged up some of the best properties available. There, they lived among the Islanders like royalty.

On the coast of Lake Michigan, in the opulent town of Charlevoix, Alex and Tim stood on the pier watching the boats and ships move in and out of the channel that led to Round Lake. This lake and the drawbridge that had been there for hundreds of years now served both the wealthy residents of Charlevoix as well as those of Beaver Island.

As they stood in the shadowed light of dusk, with party boats bobbing on the water and laughter echoing from the decks, the two men remained unnoticed. Their silhouettes blended into the night, shadows among shadows. It was perfect camouflage for anyone who might be surveilling them.

"How do you want to get across?" Tim asked as a larger vessel passed by on their right. The sun, now low on the horizon, bathed the lake in a rich tapestry of orange and purple.

"How much time do you need?" Alex replied, glancing at him.

"Not much. They'll expect us to fly in, so I'll take the submersible and dock at the lighthouse. It's quick. I'll get in place and begin surveillance. When you arrive, stay on the main pier where I can see you. Let's make it fast," Tim said, voice clipped. "I don't know how much dissension Owen's death has caused, but I'm sure there'll be some."

"We'll see. I'm not sure I agree with your assessment, but I do agree that we can't be too careful, Alex nodded. "So, I'll take the speedboat over. We'll need it anyway once we're there. I'll arrive after you as a diversion. They'll expect me. That should draw attention away from you if there's any trouble."

"Alright." Tim pulled out a tablet and scanned the signals on-screen. "I'm double-checking the chip trackers." He paused. "Hmm. Says we're showing up in Dayton."

"No shit," Alex scoffed. "I activated our alternate trackers." He turned his gaze toward the west and muttered, "Why are you being so paranoid, Tim? We weren't followed."

Tim followed Alex's stare. "We can't be too careful. I still think we should have waited a couple of days."

Alex turned sharply toward him, irritated. "No. The sooner we get this over with, the better. We need to deal with them."

"I know." Tim sounded tense. "But I think this might be more than dissension. We may have made a tactical error. They could be planning something. We might not have the upper hand."

Alex sighed, exasperated. "Look. I'll do the talking. Just get to the lighthouse and watch my back."

Tim nodded, but the anxiety clung to him. Without another word, the two men made their way to the beach and silently split off in different directions.

The waters of Lake Michigan were calm as Alex set off toward the island, a blessing he didn't take lightly. On rough days, the lake could churn with a ferocity that made even seasoned sailors queasy.

The setting sun painted the horizon in hues of fire and wine, and Alex allowed himself a moment of peace. He engaged the boat's autopilot and settled into the captain's chair. "Glad I took this route instead of the submersible," he said to no one. "Even though we're heading into a hornet's nest, at least I get fifteen minutes of beauty. Tim gets nothing but darkness. Sucker."

He leaned back, letting the golden warmth of the sun relax his otherwise guarded mind.

14 minutes left: Alex sighed and closed his eyes. Serenity began to trickle in.

12 minutes left: His thoughts drifted to Mike Wilson. He shook his head. Remorse? No, Alex Belle didn't do remorse.

9 minutes left: A loud "Caw!" from a gull startled him. He jolted awake.

6 minutes left: The vision came again, Mike Wilson and the Gen 6 bot. Mike's jaw pried open, eyes wide with terror. Alex could feel his heartbeat as if it were his own. Gasping, he sat up. "No," he muttered. "I'm Alex fucking Belle. No retreat. No surrender. And definitely no remorse."

A tear betrayed him, slipping from his right eye. He looked at the sun, half-dipped beneath the horizon. Another tear formed; he turned away.

"Mother always said don't look at the sun, dummy. No wonder you're tearing up."

3 minutes left: Tears streamed down his face. Alone, he let them fall. No one could see. No one could judge. He wiped them away and forced himself to breathe slowly, deliberately.

1 minute left: The comm crackled to life.

"I got you in sight, Alex. You copy?"

Tim's voice snapped him back. Alex cleared his throat and pressed the comm. The moment of divine confrontation had passed.

"Suck it," he whispered to the air, to the God he defied. "I'm Alex Belle, and I will not be told who to be or who to worship. I worship me."

He keyed the comm. "I copy. Are you in position?"

"At the lighthouse. All clear so far, except Scott is on the dock waiting for you. Haven't spotted the others. Haven't had the chance to scan the island yet. You're in the clear."

"Very good."

Alex disabled the autopilot and slowed the boat as he neared Saint James Harbor. Scott Sims was already pacing on the dock. Alex could sense his agitation but remained calm.

He docked, secured the boat, and walked toward Scott, arms spread wide.

"Scott! Good to see you!"

"That's far enough!" Scott barked, holding up his hand.

"Relax. I'm here to help." Alex stopped and raised his hands to show he was unarmed. He noticed Scott held a stun gun. Alex sighed and pointed at the weapon. "No need for that."

"Bullshit!" Scott screamed, brandishing the weapon. "Just like Owen didn't need one, huh? You had me meet him and never said a word about killing him!"

"You're anxious. I get it," Alex said, taking a few slow steps forward. "What happened to Owen was tragic, but it was a lesson. There's a reason we have protocols."

"Fuck you, Alex! Where's Tim? I know he's here!"

"He's not, Scott. It's just us."

"You're such a liar! Do you even know when you're telling the truth anymore?"

"Look, Scott. Owen got sloppy. We told you this could be dangerous. Apparently, that part didn't stick."

Scott lowered the stun gun slightly. "Dangerous didn't mean getting killed! We were in this for the tech and the thrill, not to die!"

"Take me to the others," Alex remained calm. "We'll work this out."

"They're not here! It's just me." Scott raised a second object, a chip controller like the one Alex owned. Then he tossed it into the lake.

"Now you can't track us. The other six? Not here. And you won't find them. We're done. All of us."

"Scott. You don't know what you're doing. Have you ever seen the stars from the north side of the island? The Aurora Borealis? That's why we started this: to reach them."

"Yeah. I remember. And we don't need it anymore," Scott's reply was angered.

"Fine," Alex said, turning back to the boat. "Good luck. See you around, Scott," he added as the engine roared to life.

The comm crackled again.

"Do you want me to follow him?"

"No," Alex said. "End it here."

"Copy."

Scott stood at the dock's edge, heart pounding, mind reeling. He turned and darted through the trees toward the safe house, repeating names like a prayer: Quentin Cole, Roland Goff, Paul Lamb, Rachel Dillen, Eddie Shiner, Addison Heinz. He had to reach them.

Inside the safe house, he activated the security system and breathed deeply. Relief washed over him.

He opened the touchscreen and initiated the group call. Their faces appeared almost instantly.

"Scott! You're alright! Thank God!" Quentin exclaimed.

"Q, I... I can't even explain it. Alex was alone, at least that I could tell. Tim's probably around, but I need to get out of here now."

"Paul is on his way from Whiskey Island. He'll be there soon. Get to Donegal Bay, now!"

"I'm checking the cameras. Hang on." Scott clicked through each feed, eyes darting. A few moments later, he spoke again with urgency. "I don't see anything, Q. I think I'm gonna make a run for it. I'll grab my bike. I can be there in a couple of minutes. Signing off."

"Paul's got you. You'll be okay," Quentin assured him.

Scott made a beeline to the back of the house, running as fast as he could. He uncovered his motorcycle, a bit of an old-fashioned dirt bike suited for the rocky terrain, looking around dutifully as he did so. His breathing was rapid and heavy.

Once outside of the garage, Scott realized that it was so dark he could barely see anything in front of him. He could see down over the hill that the lights on Donegal Bay Road were still on, and for that he was grateful. Not all of the sidewalks were rolled up yet. Once he got to the main road, he'd be able to navigate more easily. Starting the bike, he took one last look around and took off, spinning the tires and ripping out of there as fast as he could go.

Making the left around the corner, he almost dropped the bike, but corrected himself and throttled up once he reached the main street. He hoped Paul was close by because he didn't want to be a sitting duck.

Focused and determined to escape, Scott was so focused on the task at hand that he barely saw the shadowy figure emerge from the wooded area to his left. He had just enough time to notice the figure of a man decked from head to toe in black. The man took three steps, stood in the middle of the road in full view, pulled an arrow from a quiver on his back, and fired directly at Scott.

Scott had no time to react. The arrow struck just underneath his neck, hitting his right collarbone. Hitting his brakes with quickness and fright, Scott slid the bike to the ground, toppling over and continuing on five feet past it. He was nearly unconscious.

As he lay there immobile, the man dressed in black - Scott quickly thought that perhaps it was Tim - slowly walked up and stood above him. Scott wanted to say something, perhaps just call out Tim's name, but the shadow figure pulled out a large blade, roughly three feet long, and stabbed Scott. Whatever Scott was thinking was erased with the last beat of his bleeding heart.

The shadow person stood over Scott's lifeless body for a moment, wiped off the blade, sheathed it, and jumped onto Scott's slightly dented bike. He continued down the road until he reached the bay. There, he stopped, looked around, and waited quietly, moving slowly into the shadows. In the distance, Paul Lamb was driving his boat in. The killer waited for Paul to dock.

Paul, armed with a taser and a spotlight, saw the parked dirt bike and called out to Scott.

"Yo, Scott! You out there?! Where are you?" Paul shouted into the night. "Come on, brother! We have to go! We can't be sitting out here like this. We're sitting ducks."

Paul used his spotlight to canvass the area. It was eerily quiet. He saw nothing other than the parked bike and started to fear the worst.

"Come on! Come on! Come on!" Paul muttered under his breath, growing increasingly anxious. Climbing from his boat, he approached the bike, took a quick look around, and turned back. He flashed the light behind him, then turned to face the road again, shining it to catch anything at all.

"Okay, relax," Paul said to himself. "Maybe Scott's being cautious." He tried to steady himself, even though it was the last thing he would ever do.

Another arrow whispered through the dark and struck Paul directly in the throat, lodging there as it passed through. He dropped his light and stun gun, grasping at the arrow and choking, his eyes wide with fright. A second arrow hit him solidly in the chest with a *whoomp* sound, and this one dropped him to the ground. He choked on his own blood as it poured from the wound, and within a short minute, Paul's eyes grew blank.

From the shadows, once again, the man in black walked out, checked on Paul, and vanished once more.

In a hotel in Green Bay, Wisconsin, Quentin paced his room. It had been five hours since he had last heard from Paul and Scott. The plan had been for Paul to extract Scott from Donegal Bay, then boat to Green Bay Harbor, where Quentin would meet them. From there, the three would travel through Wisconsin and Minnesota, cross the Canadian border, and head to Edmonton, where the other four scientists awaited them. But they hadn't arrived. And he hadn't heard anything from either man. He played every scenario out in his head.

Maybe they encountered something unusual, rerouted themselves, and went radio silent until they reached safety. Maybe the boat got stuck on something. "Damn it! What's happening?" Quentin spoke out loud in his room.

He took a few deep breaths, deciding to wait a little longer. Knowing he wasn't in immediate danger, he hoped they'd call and kept watching for any sign.

His pacing of the room was interrupted by a call from Roland Goff. Quentin hastily answered. "Yeah, Roland. What's up?"

"Q! You hear anything from the guys yet?"

"Not a damn thing!" Quentin responded angrily. "I was hoping you were calling to tell me that you had. Paul was supposed to signal me as soon as he picked up Scott, but I've heard nothing. I don't know, maybe they're having trouble with their comms? Or, maybe I'm just hoping. Tell you the truth, I'm scared, Roland! Really fucking scared!"

"Well, maybe… oh hell. I don't know, Q. Do you think Alex and Tim did something to them?" Roland asked, unsure what to say next or even how to approach the topic.

"I hope not! That Tim is a crazy psycho. And Alex isn't far behind! I'm going to wait here until nine in the morning. It's the least I can do. If I hear nothing by then, I'm going to make my way to you and just presume the worst."

"I'm sorry! We should've never gotten ourselves mixed up in all of this," Roland replied somberly.

"Yeah, yeah. The benefit of hindsight. Whatever," Quentin answered, feeling completely deflated. "I'll keep you posted, Roland."

"Alright. Be safe, Q. Please. Don't take any unnecessary risks," Roland said, fearful for his friends.

"I won't! I promise," Quentin replied as he disconnected the call.

A new day dawned.

In Dayton, Alex waited for Tim in their mostly empty warehouse. They didn't even try to hide the fact that they did little to nothing in the space.

When Tim finally arrived, waltzing through the door, he was whistling. "Good morning," he greeted Alex like a man who had no worries and no cares. And, for someone like Tim, he probably didn't. A conscience wasn't high on his list of attributes.

"What kept you?" Alex asked nonchalantly.

"Well, I had to take care of the safe houses. I burned them down and changed clothes. I can't walk around in the daytime, smelling like fire for heaven's sake. People would think I was up to no good," Tim laughed maniacally.

"Did you put out the fires?" Alex asked as if this were their first rodeo.

Tim sighed, disappointed in Alex's trust in him. "Of course. I didn't want to burn down the entire island. Don't worry about it, man. Everything has been disposed of properly. Efficiently," Tim replied, self-assured.

"Okay, I trust you. Good work," Alex replied with a smile and a pat on Tim's shoulder. "I'll be heading to Wyoming soon. Why don't you go ahead and kick back for a bit? The past seventy-two hours have been plenty busy. Kick your feet up and relax."

"Yeah. I can use a little R&R. Maybe go find a girl to hang with," Tim replied with a sneaky smile as if finding girls was something he did with ease.

Alex smirked. "Yeah, sure. Don't get crazy."

Meanwhile, a meeting of the 195 representatives of the NU was commencing, and Richard was preparing to speak. It was a mandatory meeting, so he expected everyone to be in attendance. He sat patiently in his office, waiting for Dr. Susan Hallewell to begin the inquiry. Stan sat across from Richard in his normal spot.

A light flashed on his touchscreen, replacing the words PLEASE STAND BY, and signaled that the conference was ready to begin. When he could see himself on the monitor and his audio feed turned from red to black, Richard greeted the NU, "Good morning, every-one!"

"Good morning, Richard!" Susan replied curtly. Normally cordial, Susan appeared a bit angered and anxious. She jumped right into starting the meeting. "Alright, we all know why we're here, so let's get down to business. Are there any leads in Owen's murder investigation?"

"No," Richard replied. "We've found no evidence. DNA, murder weapon, tracking signatures, motives, nothing! It's as if the crime was committed by a ghost."

"What's the possibility that the assailant was of an extraterrestrial origin?" Susan asked, more businesslike than he had ever seen her.

Richard took in a deep breath and then exhaled, pondering the question. "It's possible and… very likely," he responded with words he presumed were going to shock the representatives.

"Are you saying the Norn were involved somehow?" Susan questioned.

Richard sat back and folded his hands. "We can't rule out anything at the moment. We have no leads, so anything is possible."

"Okay, Richard. We're going to deliberate. If anything changes, notify us immediately," Susan replied, and Richard could feel her coldness toward him.

"That's it?" Richard asked, seemingly puzzled by the brief interview. His mind appeared to be reeling with many possibilities, but to have the interview end that quickly caught him off guard.

Susan shrugged. "You have nothing. So there's nothing to talk about. Call on us when you do. Have a good day, Richard."

"Good day to you all," Richard replied a bit hesitantly. He wasn't sure what the coldness from Susan meant, and he and Stan just looked at each other, sitting silently for a brief second.

"I'm glad you didn't say what you were thinking," Stan said as he exhaled.

"Exactly. Like I know they have something to fucking do with this!" Richard angrily snapped at Stan.

"Conjecture," Stan replied with a coldness that matched Dr. Hallewell's. "If you said that to the NU, they'd have you expelled from your position, and you know it."

Richard sighed and placed his fingers under his chin. He looked at Stan with a look of concern on his face. "Will you do something for me?" Richard asked.

Stan sat back and sympathetically replied, just as eager to let the moment pass as Richard was. He tried to get things back on a normal footing. "Sure. Anything for you, my friend. You know I'm always on your side, right?"

Richard put up his hands. "I know. I know. I didn't mean to snap at you just now. It's just that you're the only one I trust to carry out an assignment. Even when I know you don't agree with what I give you to do, you'll still do it to the best of your abilities."

"What is it?" Stan begrudgingly asked, knowing that Richard was leading up to something.

"I want you to follow Tim Stevens for a bit," Richard began. "Not round-the-clock surveillance, just follow him around here and there. He typically moves a lot at night in the shadows. If we're lucky, maybe we'll stumble onto something," Richard said.

Stan sighed and nodded. "I'll do this because you are the one who is asking. I'll take a few days to follow him around and see what he's up to."

"I know you don't believe they have any involvement in this, so let's make sure, okay? At this point, we need to find some solutions before more people die." Richard gave Stan his instructions, and Stan listened eagerly. He wanted this to end just as much as Richard did.

In Green Bay, Quentin woke up with a start. Tired from staying up all night waiting for Scott and Paul to check in, he had fallen asleep in his chair. His computer and comm device sat idle on the table next to him. A sudden panic gripped him. He checked his equipment to see if he had missed anything, but there were no messages, no updates... nothing. His heart sank deeper into his stomach. Now he could do nothing except anticipate the worst.

He stood from his chair, still rubbing the sleep from his eyes, when a knock echoed from the hotel door. Excitement overtook him.

Maybe it wasn't that bad after all. Maybe, just maybe, they had played it safe and kept radio silence. He rushed to the door, hope rising in his chest, expecting to see either Scott or Paul.

But his face fell when he looked directly into the eyes of Addison Heinz.

"Add, what the… what are you doing here?" Quentin asked, his nerves suddenly on edge again. "You're supposed to be in Edmonton right now! With the others!"

"I'm here to get you and get the hell out of here," Addison said, pushing her way inside. She looked around the room briefly before turning her focus back to Quentin. "I figured you'd be fatigued and I didn't want you to travel alone," she added. "Things are heating up—we need to make tracks."

Quentin tried to steady himself. "Okay, I'm sorry. I just thought for a moment it was the other two… Scott and Paul."

"I hadn't made it to Canada just yet," Addison explained. "I was still on the border of Minnesota when Roland contacted me about what was going on here. We agreed I should return for you."

Her voice carried a sharp edge, worry crackling underneath.

"We need to leave here, Q."

Quentin replied quickly, "Maybe we should wait just a little while longer for them. Maybe they…"

Addison cut him off gently, trying her best to comfort her distressed friend. "I'm afraid they're likely gone, Q. They're probably… gone."

Quentin met her eyes. His own began to water, brimming with the fear and heartbreak he'd been trying to keep at bay. Deep down, he knew she was probably right. He just didn't want to admit it.

"Can we find out for sure? I mean, we can make it to the island fairly quickly from here."

Addison shook her head vehemently. "That's a horrible idea, Q. Nothing good can come of that. Let's regroup with the others. Look! I'm not feeling good about writing them off either, but both Scott and Paul laid the plan out for us and we need to follow it. Scott would talk to Alex, tell him we're done, and then they'd get the hell out of there. If we didn't hear anything within the hour after Paul picked him up, you were to leave immediately."

Quentin sighed and looked one last time at Addison. "I know. I just hoped that maybe we could..."

Addison took Quentin's arm and began to lead him away. "No. It's been hours, and there hasn't been any communication. I don't like it either, but we need to get moving. Rest assured, we're going to get those motherfuckers. We're going to make them pay. It may not be today," she conceded. "But it will happen. Now let's go."

Saddened by these turn of events, Quentin put a hand on Addison's shoulder and gave it a light squeeze. "Okay, Add. Let me get my stuff."

After everything was packed up, the two left the hotel in Green Bay and started making their way to the Canadian border.

Chapter 14: All Apologies

The mountains in the background of the ranch seemed more picturesque than usual on this sunny, 76-degree day. The air carried a soft breeze, just enough to rustle the grass and give the wind chimes on the porch a faint, melodic clatter. Grayle, Tash, and Brian were gathered together in the open field behind the house, enjoying some old-fashioned skeet shooting. It was a bittersweet moment, knowing they would soon be heading off on their own paths.

Brian was preparing to return to his post as a Defender, Tash was departing for Italy to study abroad, and Grayle had finally made up her mind to skip her previously planned Florida trip and go straight to the Paranormal Department in Philadelphia. With the decision now made, she was trying to use this peaceful interlude to share her plans with her siblings.

"Pull!" Grayle called out, raising the shotgun to her shoulder with the ease of someone who had done this a hundred times.

She fired and hit the clay pigeon dead center, splitting it cleanly in two with a satisfying crack.

"Nice," Brian muttered without enthusiasm, lowering his eyes to inspect his gun.

Grayle laughed at him. "You always get so pissed. It's not my fault you're a terrible shot. Honestly, I don't know how you passed the Defender tests with the way you shoot."

"Lasers are easier to fire," Tash added with a grin, stepping up and settling into position. "You don't have to be good with those things. They pretty much shoot themselves."

"Pull," she said, then fired - and missed.

Tash tried to hide her smile as she lowered her weapon. Despite her best efforts to stay composed, the grin betrayed her.

"Ha! You suck too," Grayle crowed, turning to her sister with exaggerated flair. "It's me five, Tash two, and Brian a big fat ZERO!"

She held up her hands to make a mocking circle and laughed. Brian simply rolled his eyes and shook his head. "Whatever."

A moment of quiet passed between them, and Brian's expression softened as he looked from one sister to the other.

"This is the last time the three of us will be together for a while."

"Yeah. I'll miss you two," Tash replied, her voice quiet and wavering. She was grateful for her sunglasses, which concealed the tears pooling in her eyes. "Growing up sucks."

She stepped in to hug Brian, and Grayle joined the embrace. The moment lingered as they held one another, the bond between them palpable.

Grayle, always the outspoken one, managed to choke out, "We can always come here. To this place. We'll always have this, our grandparents, our personal retreat. All the great memories."

"Yeah. Our grandparents deserve a break," Tash added with a soft laugh, gazing back toward the ranch house. It stood warm and welcoming, its large porch a backdrop for countless memories. "Just think of some of the stuff we put them through."

"No kidding," Brian said, chuckling. "Still, thank God for them. Without them... I don't even want to think about what life would've been like."

A comfortable silence followed as they all looked toward the porch, letting their shared history play quietly in their minds. Then Tash stepped back and wiped her face.

"I'm gonna go back to the house and shower. Uncle Will should be here in a couple of hours to fly me out of here."

"Alright, we'll see you up there," Brian said.

As Tash started away, Brian turned to Grayle. "I need a quick word with you."

Grayle nodded and brushed away a stray tear. "What's up?"

"Richard mentioned a couple of days ago at your party that you're heading to the Paranormal Department. Is that true?"

Grayle hesitated, then met Brian's gaze directly. "Yep, B.J.. It's true. I know it's not everybody's first choice for me, but..."

"Oh, no, it's okay," Brian cut in. "It's just... you're my sister, and I want to look out for you. Are you sure this is something you really want to do?"

Grayle smiled softly, touched by his concern. "I do, Bri. I'm skipping the interview in Florida. My heart's not in that. It's in the P.D. Or at least, I think it is. I have to try it out and see if it's where I belong. If it's not, I'll know. But I have to find out."

She looked at him with a flicker of vulnerability, waiting for his response.

"I was going to tell you about it soon enough," she added.

"I know. I'm not judging," Brian said quickly, as if trying to assure her. "I hope you find what you're looking for. But if you don't like it, you should join me with the Defenders."

Grayle raised an eyebrow. "Was that a pitch?"

"No, no," Brian replied with a grin. "I know better than to think you could be swayed that easily."

"You got that right, brother," Grayle said, giving him a light slap on the shoulder.

They were interrupted by the sound of a transport coming up the gravel driveway.

"Welp, that must be Alex," Brian said, glancing toward the road.

"Of course it is," Grayle muttered.

"The man is so unreliable, Gray. I don't know why you bother with him."

"Sometimes, I don't know either," she replied with a shrug. "I'm sure he'll apologize profusely for missing the party. Blah, blah, blah. That's him, all apologies, all the time."

Brian shook his head. "Yeah. I wonder what our parents would've thought about what he's become. Everyone still praises him, but he's just... kind of lost now. Like he's stuck in the past."

"Oh, look!" Grayle pointed skyward.

An Osprey-style aircraft was circling for a landing nearby, the rotors chopping the air as it began to descend. "Must be Will."

She started walking toward Alex's vehicle, and Brian followed.

"I don't think those two have spoken in seventeen years," she added. "Will still blames himself for not being more involved in the Intervention test flight. But at the same time, I think he blames Alex more for rushing the project, for ignoring the warnings. They're oil and water, those two."

"Should we cut them off before they explode?" Brian asked.

"No!" Grayle laughed. "Let them have a moment. It serves Alex right for skipping the ceremony. Let him sweat a little."

Brian looked at his sister and grinned. "I love your thinking."

Alex saw Grayle and Brian Jr. walking toward him as he pulled into the driveway, but his attention was quickly pulled skyward. Will's vehicle was making its descent, its rotor wash stirring up clouds of dust across the open field. His stomach dropped.

"Shit," he muttered under his breath. "Commander Self-Righteous."

Shielding his eyes from the sun and the whipping wind generated by the aircraft's powerful rotors, Alex watched as the sleek Osprey-style vehicle landed with precision. Though such hybrids were now commonplace, this one stood out. Powered by Norn crystals and advanced tech, it could make the trip from the U.S. to Italy in just two hours, four times faster than older planes.

As the aircraft powered down, Will stepped out, spotting Alex almost immediately. Alex noted the weary slump in Will's shoulders and knew that neither of them was looking forward to this reunion. Their steps toward one another were slow and uncertain, tension simmering beneath the surface.

"Commander," Alex offered, aiming for a light tone that barely masked his discomfort. "How are you doing?"

"Fine. You?" Will answered, matching the effort with equal insincerity.

"How's Hollie doing?" Alex asked, trying to smooth over the strain.

"Good. All good," Will said flatly.

"I'm sorry I missed the wedding a couple of years ago," Alex added with a lack of conviction.

"Well, I didn't invite you," Will replied without hesitation, the edge in his voice unmistakable.

"That would explain my absence," Alex said with a smirk.

They stood in silence for a beat, watching Grayle and Brian inch their way toward them.

"They're walking slowly just to torture us," Will said, half-joking.

"No doubt," Alex replied, his foot idly kicking at a rock in the dirt.

"By the way, Alex," Will added with a cutting grin, "you don't look so good. The years haven't been kind. Or, is it something else…"

"Fuck you, Commander," Alex snapped, though a crooked smile tugged at one corner of his mouth, making the insult feel more like an old reflex than real animosity.

From the porch of the ranch house, Rose stepped outside and cupped her hands to her mouth.

"Good God," she called out with a laugh. "You two better be behaving yourselves."

Both men gave sheepish waves.

Alex glanced at Will. "Shall we?"

"Sure. The kids can just meet us there."

They turned and began walking toward the house, making sure Grayle and Brian noticed, shifting course toward the porch.

As they neared, Rose descended the steps and wrapped Alex in a warm hug.

"Always taking 'fashionably late' to another level," she teased.

She turned to Will and embraced him just as warmly. "Will, good to see you. Take care of our Tashy today."

"Will do, Rose. You can still trust some people to come through," Will said, throwing a jab in Alex's direction.

Alex rolled his eyes but held his tongue as Grayle and Brian finally caught up.

Rose gave the men a gentle pat on the shoulder. "Since the kids are here now, I'm going in. I'll catch up with you two later."

She disappeared inside to join Art, who wanted no part of being around Alex and Will at the same time.

Left in the quiet, Alex shifted awkwardly, then spoke. "I'm sorry I didn't make it to your graduation, Grayle."

"I know," she said kindly. "Still, you're here now. That's what matters. I'm going in to help Tash. She's leaving soon."

She gave a faint smile and walked off. Alex watched her go, uncertain if his apology had landed.

Turning to Brian, Alex offered a slight nod. "Brian. How are you?"

"All good here," Brian said curtly, his tone clipped. He looked away, exhaling slowly, then met Alex's eyes. "Look, I know you don't think this, but I am glad you showed up."

"Well, something came up that needed my attention," Alex replied, though he knew it sounded hollow.

Brian laughed once, a short, sharp bark. "Something always does with you."

He turned his gaze to the open land before them, its beauty unspoiled, as if Alex's presence was something to look past.

"You're probably aware of the whole Owen Stipe situation. And the reporter, Michael Wilson - possibly eaten by an alligator?" Brian paused, then glanced at Alex. "Oh, and the K.C. thing. What do you know about that?"

Alex met his gaze. "Are you implying something, Brian? Is this really the best time for an interrogation?"

"No, I'm not implying anything? Why? Feeling a little paranoid?"

Alex tried to diffuse the heat. "Sorry. That whole thing has the entire world on edge."

Brian nodded, his expression sobering. "I'm due back soon. We're on high alert; it could be criminals, it could be something else. Any help you can give would be appreciated. What do you think?"

"You sound like Richard, always digging. I honestly have no idea," Alex's reply was curt.

Brian sighed. "I hope we're not heading back to the darker times. Back before 2032, before the New Age."

"We'll keep the peace," Alex said, raising his hands.

"You do that. And I'll do my part."

There was a pause. Alex glanced down.

"I'm still sorry, you know? Your parents should be here with you."

Brian softened. "Look, nobody blames you, Alex. It was their dream. They chose to go. We miss them, but we carry their memory. They left a holographic message; the three of us play it often when we're together. They're always with us."

Alex's voice cracked. "I could've done better. They'd be proud of you. You three remind me of what I lost, too." Alex's voice dropped, and he looked slightly away. "Still, eight other families don't feel the same."

"You can't blame yourself…"

Before Brian could finish, the screen door creaked open. Art, Rose, Grayle, Tash, and Will emerged. They gathered for goodbyes as Will and Tash prepared to leave.

"Family Dinner," Rose said with authority. "One month from now. Sunday, six p.m. That means you, too, Alex. Don't be late!"

"Ooooof course!" Tash teased. "Italy, here I come! Maybe I'll find a handsome Italian?"

"Mind your P's and Q's," Art warned, though his voice carried affection.

"Will, keep her safe," Rose added.

"Don't worry. I may be older," Will said, side-eyeing Alex, "but I'm not… reckless."

"You just couldn't help yourself," Alex muttered.

"Enough from you two," Rose snapped.

With that, Will and Tash gathered her things and boarded the sleek aircraft. The others watched from below as it lifted off.

"Using autopilot, Uncle Butch?" Tash asked in the cockpit.

"Nah. I'll pilot us myself."

Tash looked out the window and waved. She'd be back in the fall, but it felt different this time. More permanent.

Back on the ground, Art watched with a soft smile. "How fun to be that young."

Grayle crossed her arms tightly. She didn't want anyone to see how much she would miss her sister.

As the aircraft disappeared, Brian cleared his throat. "I've got to get back. Things are ramping up."

"Where to?" Art asked.

"California. Briefing. More patrols. I'll be out a lot."

"Be careful. Don't be a hero," Grayle said in a sisterly voice.

"Never," Brian replied. He hugged them each and left.

With Brian gone, Rose and Art lingered.

"They're all grown up," Rose said quietly, slipping her hand into Art's.

"We've taught them well," he replied, giving it a gentle squeeze.

"I just wish Brian weren't a Defender. It's dangerous."

"We won't go back, Rose. Our civilization has come too far."

"Let's hope so," she whispered.

Grayle turned to Alex. "Come on. Let's sit on the patio and catch up."

"Sure. Let me grab a coffee first," Alex said, turning back toward the house. Grayle followed, and when they made their way to the patio, they both took in the mountain view, which stretched endlessly. Flowers lined the perimeter, swaying in the breeze.

Grayle exhaled deeply as she dropped into a chair. "I'm going to miss this."

Alex sat beside her with a steaming mug and lit a cigarette.

"That's gross," Grayle said, wrinkling her nose.

"It calms my nerves."

"That's not true, dipshit," she replied, grinning.

"Maybe not. But it justifies my bad habits."

There was a quiet pause before Alex looked at her.

"Why don't you work here, out of Wyoming?"

Grayle shook her head, her eyes distant.

"I can't stay hidden forever. I'm thankful we were raised here, but it's time to carve out my own space in the world."

"Understood," Alex replied, sipping his coffee. The warmth settled in his chest, though it did little to calm the sting of her words. "Still, you'll always be linked to the past."

"Yes, because people like you continue to bring it up," she said, slightly scolding him. "We don't want that to be our identity. All of us. All of the families. We're tired of being the poster children of tragedy. You don't have the right to keep talking about it."

Grayle's tone stayed composed, but her eyes gave her away. The simmering frustration had been building for years, and now it slipped out in the form of a carefully aimed jab.

"I'm sorry," Alex's reply died on his tongue. He stared at the mountains instead.

Grayle shot him a sideways glance. "All apologies, all the time."

Alex cleared his throat, searching for a way out of the tension. "So... you excited for your interview in Florida?"

Grayle let out a breath, her shoulders sagging. "I'm... I'm excited for an interview, just not that one. Look, it's eventually going to come out, so I'll tell you about it now. I'm heading to Philly. I'm going to meet and interview with Phil Wells next week."

Alex blinked, surprised. He shook his head, disbelief in his voice. "Ugh, Grayle. That's a waste of time." He looked at her, disappointment shadowing his face.

"Huh," she replied coolly. "I figured you'd say that." Her smile was faint, tinged with sarcasm as she shrugged. "Richard thought it was a good idea when I briefly mentioned it to him."

"He would," Alex muttered under his breath. "He probably was thinking the same as me, he just..."

Grayle smirked. "He just wouldn't be an asshole about it."

Alex chuckled softly, eyes rolling skyward. "Right. Well, I wasn't going to phrase it like that, but..."

She patted his arm gently, a gesture of peace. "Relax. It's just an inquiry. I don't even know if I'll like it or Wells, for that matter. I'm just curious." Her voice softened, inviting calm back into the space between them.

"I'm surprised none of you wanted to become an Explorer," Alex said, tilting his head.

"Well, I finished decently in school, just not the top one percent. And exploring quantum mechanics and physics sounds utterly fucking boring," she laughed, her expression brightening.

Alex grinned. "Yeah, to tell the truth, your mother was never over the Moon about it either. She just liked the adventure."

A brief silence fell. The air grew still between them. Then Alex gently pivoted the conversation.

"So, are we... good?" he asked hesitantly.

"Oh, you mean you missing my graduation?" she replied, eyebrow raised.

"Yeah. That," he admitted, visibly uneasy.

"Fuck no! Not even close! You owe me. Big time," Grayle fired back with her signature blend of irritation and charm. Even in her anger, she couldn't help the slight lift at the corner of her lips. "That was a shitty thing to do to me. And you're not forgiven. You need to make it up to me."

"I'll try," he said sheepishly.

"No promises. Just results." She nodded with finality, though her smirk hinted at forgiveness waiting in the wings. "I'm just glad you didn't bring Tim with you."

Alex burst into laughter. "Oh, I at least know better than that! I'll never understand the hate you have for him. He's never been anything but nice to you. I remember when you were barely a year old. You sat on your mother's lap, staring a hole right through him. Didn't take your eyes off him. You looked like you wanted to kill him!"

"It's... I guess it's his aura," Grayle replied, her voice dipping into something more enigmatic. "There's just something about him that I really can't put my finger on, and it makes me not want to be anywhere near him. Besides, he's always saying weird shit! He's always talking about different scenarios where he's died in some horrific manner. You know that's not normal, right?" She leaned in closer, eyes narrowing slightly. "You do understand that, right?"

She waited for him to respond, but his silence lingered, prompting her to continue, softer this time, but more unsettling. "I don't know what kind of weird experimental shit you two are into, but it's very off-putting. And also… have you looked in a mirror lately?"

Alex took a long pause, his jaw tense as he chose his words carefully. "I… I wish I could say, Grayle. I really do." He offered a small smile and a subtle nod. "Maybe someday."

"Well, in other news," she said, eager to redirect. "I've had a few successful dates with this guy, Matt. He just took me to dinner last week…"

"Wait, what did you eat?" Alex interjected with sudden enthusiasm.

"Oh my God! Why do you always ask that?" Grayle laughed, her voice rising with amusement.

Alex chuckled, raising his hands in surrender. "Sorry. Go ahead. Tell me more. How's that going?"

Grayle rolled her eyes but smiled. "Good! He's very nice and very sweet."

"What's he look like?" Alex asked, leaning in.

Grayle pulled out her small comm device, tapped the screen, and a soft bluish hologram glowed to life above it, an image of her and Matt, smiling in front of what looked like a trendy street café.

"He's rather unspectacular looking. Nerdy, even. Too skinny," Alex judged, squinting at the projection.

"Oh, whatever. He's great, something you'll never amount to," she teased. "He just graduated, too. Majored in architecture. And…" Her eyes flicked to the time on her device. "Oh, shit - he's going to be here shortly. We're grabbing a late lunch and hanging out for a bit, so I've got to get moving."

Grayle stood quickly and wrapped her arms around Alex's shoulders in a brief, tight hug. "I still love you, you unreliable asshole," she said with a grin, disappearing into the house.

"I'll see myself out. I'm just gonna sit here for a minute," Alex called after her, waving and smiling.

He remained for a while, quietly watching the wind shift through the nearby trees, the mountains stoic in the background. Eventually, he stood and walked back into the house. Rose was knitting in her usual chair, half-watching a program on the television, while Art sat nearby with a worn book open in his hands.

"I'm going to head out," Alex said.

Rose stood to greet him, embracing him warmly. She stepped back and placed her hands on his shoulders, steadying herself as much as him.

"Remember! A month from now. Sunday dinner. Six p.m. Don't be late."

Alex smiled. "I'll see you then. Six sharp. I'll bring that wine you like."

"You better," she replied, dabbing quickly at a tear on her cheek. "Sorry. Just missing the old days. Dumb nostalgia."

Alex gently patted her shoulder before turning to Art. "Art, I'll see you."

Art lifted his hand without looking up from his book and laughed. "Don't be late!"

"Never!" Alex replied, chuckling as he walked toward the door.

Outside, the soft hum of a transport approaching drew his attention. A young man stepped out, casually dressed and carrying a nervous energy. He looked up and waved toward the upper story of the house.

Alex turned and saw Grayle at the window, waving back.

He smiled and approached the transport, keeping his expression light. "Hello, Matt. I just heard about you a little while ago."

"Hello, Mr. Belle," Matt replied, extending his hand with practiced politeness.

Alex shook it and leaned in slightly, his eyes returning to the window where Grayle had just disappeared.

"Smile a little, will ya? I want her to think our first meeting was cordial."

Matt grinned on cue, even offering a comically exaggerated laugh, bowing slightly as if in a play.

"Grayle just informed me she's heading to Philly to interview with the Paranormal Department. Did she ever mention that to you?" Alex asked, lightly patting Matt's shoulder as he kept up the charade.

Matt kept his fake smile wide. "No. She never did."

"Well, keep an eye on her," Alex said quietly, his tone darkening just enough to shift the mood.

"How do you want me to handle this?" Matt asked, watching as Alex stepped away.

"Don't do anything. Just keep an eye out," Alex replied, his voice light again, masking the weight behind the words. "We'll talk later."

Chapter 15: Waste

Monday morning finally showed itself, and Grayle was in Philadelphia on her way to her interview with Phil Wells. She was having a hard time containing her excitement. She was eager to talk to Phil, so much so that she barely slept the night before. She tried to nap on the Metro, but her excitement made it impossible. She was finally here.

Making her way into Center City, Grayle took her time despite her grogginess. She wanted to take a leisurely walk through the city so she could take it all in. Phil's office was on the outskirts, just beyond the refurbished skyscrapers that retained the look and feel of the city's rich history. The Liberty Bell, still perfectly preserved in its original home at Independence Park, remained a popular destination; the disgusting litter and homelessness that once surrounded it - now memories. Grayle stopped and stared at the landmark, amazed that such a treasure could still be so preserved.

Continuing her walk through the city, Grayle finally reached her destination. She had to check the address a few times before heading in, because she was in a residential neighborhood. While it was a very nice house with a rustic aesthetic that paid homage to the history of the city, it was still just a house, not the business she had expected.

Standing on the sidewalk in front of the door, Grayle muttered to herself, "Well, this is a little uninspiring. Let's hope the opportunity is more rewarding." She sighed and then stepped toward the building. "Okay! Let's do this." She was nervous. This would either lead her down a path of enlightenment she'd been seeking since childhood, the start to uncovering answers to the burning, lingering questions about the woman in her dreams, her parents, and all the other supernatural and otherworldly things she'd experienced — or it would be a bust, a big disappointment, a waste of time; just as she had often been warned.

She slowly made her way to the door and raised her hand, but before she even got the chance to knock, a man opened it and smiled down at her. "Hi! I'm David. Are you Grayle?"

"Yes, I am," she nodded, still a bit taken aback.

"Great! You're early," he said with a smile. "Phil's office is down that hallway to the left, just past the kitchen. Go ahead in. I'll be back in a bit. I'm running an errand for him."

"Sure. O…kay," she replied, unsure why he felt the need to explain what he was doing, but still finding him friendly and unthreatening.

When David left, Grayle entered the home, appreciating how well-kept and spotless it was. Yet, for all of its cleanliness, the decor was very bland. Nothing but white walls with hardwood floors. She noticed some furniture and a desk in the front room, but nothing impressive. To her left, the living and dining rooms served as the main sitting area, and down the hall to her right, a small kitchen housed a refrigerator and minor appliances. Beyond that was a single door, which turned out to be nothing more than a bathroom. A privy. Bland.

Continuing, Grayle noticed that nothing adorned the walls. No art, no décor, nothing. Everything was completely bare. She had to say that she wasn't impressed by the amenities, but at least the place seemed nice.

Finally, after walking through the halls of bland, Grayle reached the end and peeked around the corner into a room from which light crept across the floor and spilled into the hallway. Phil was at a filing cabinet, reviewing a file folder. Grayle smiled. He was still in great shape and sharply dressed, not a wrinkle or crease on his suit. Grayle gave a subtle knock on the door, and Phil turned around and greeted her with a gesture of his hand.

"Hello, Grayle! How are you today? Please, come in and grab a seat." Phil waited for Grayle to sit, then placed the folder down and took a sip of water from the glass on his desk. Remembering his manners, he gestured toward the glass. "Can I get you anything?" he asked. "Water?"

"Um, sure. Some water would be great, thanks," Grayle responded, realizing that her face felt flushed.

"Great. I'll be right back," he said, turning and heading into the kitchen. A second later, he returned with a bottle of water.

"Here you go," he said, handing it to her.

"Thank you!" she replied, opening the top. "Quick question, if you don't mind?"

"Yeah, sure," Phil replied as he returned to the desk and sat down.

"Why are you using a filing cabinet and paper documents? Don't you have any computer equipment, AI, or anything like that?"

"I do," Phil chuckled, sitting back. "I know it's uncommon to use paper, but I prefer it. Call me a bit old-fashioned."

Grayle smiled, but then looked down at the nameplate on his desk. It read: Phil "Waste" Wells.

"Waste?" she asked, a bit surprised. "What's with that nickname?"

Phil made a sheepish face. "Yeah, well, when I tell people I'm a paranormal expert, they just look at me and say, 'Oh...' and usually add, 'Isn't that a waste of time, that occupation?' So David had this made for me."

Grayle wrinkled her brow. "How many people do you have working here, exactly?"

Phil, now looking a little disappointed, replied, "Oh, it's just David and me. Everyone else who's been with us transferred to other occupations. I know that's not super reassuring, but we take this work seriously. In fact, I've encouraged people to leave because their level of commitment didn't meet my standards or expectations. I cleaned house." Phil's demeanor changed slightly. He became a bit more tense. "I'm not afraid to work alone, Grayle. If you're not committed to this, then this is the wrong place. I'm not trying to be standoffish or mean, I just don't want to waste your time or mine."

Grayle shook her head ambitiously. "No, I get it. So, you're the only one doing this in the U.S.?" she asked.

"Yep, just me. There are other departments around the world continuing the work. I coordinate a lot with other countries and frequently travel abroad to help when needed. They're shorthanded too, but we try to do the best we can."

"I'm sorry, I feel like I'm interviewing you," Grayle chuckled, her face flushing again. "I don't mean to be so forward."

Phil smiled and waved his hand. "That's fine! I like it." He folded his hands together and set them against his lips. "I've been watching you for a long time, Grayle."

Grayle blushed and stammered slightly. "Did... did you mean to make that sound creepy?"

Phil quickly put up his hands defensively. "No, what I meant was, a long time ago, your parents contacted me about you. Do you remember?"

"I do," she said. "That's one of the reasons I came here."

"A bit of a recap," Phil began, "Your parents said you were always sad and occasionally dreamed of a woman. At the time, I didn't think much of it. You see, when we're reborn, sometimes we take remnants of a previous life with us to the next. I think that may have something to do with it. It's more common than people realize. Anyway, I thought a dream catcher would do the trick, and it did. For a time, anyway."

Grayle appeared lost in her memories. "I remember asking my parents why they had to die before they left for the test run on the Intervention," Grayle said, her voice cracking and her demeanor sliding to sadness.

"I knew about that," Phil replied gently. "Your parents contacted me when they were on their way to the Cape. They were concerned. After the accident, I tried to see you. Your grandparents denied me access, which I totally understood; they were trying to protect you, and when they took you out West, I kept track of you through them from time to time. Did they ever tell you?"

"No! They never mentioned it." Grayle's sadness quickly turned into anger. "I wish they had."

Phil shook his head. "It's okay, Grayle. Don't be mad at them. They were just doing what they thought they should. I'm sure they're fine with everything now that you're here?" He asked the question hopefully.

Grayle shook her head. "They don't know I'm here. Very few people do. I didn't want to make a thing out of this, so I didn't tell many people."

"Don't you think you should tell them?" Phil looked concerned.

"No." Her reply was cold, and Phil just raised his eyebrows and sighed.

"Anyway, I've been wanting to have this conversation with you for a while. Do you still see the woman in your dreams?"

Grayle replied, "The woman with the flowing, gorgeous red hair? Yes, still. I don't know who she is, but I still dream about her. Over the years, it's getting harder to see her and hear her, but I feel her presence. Always."

"Interesting," Phil replied, eager to proceed with passing on his knowledge. "When you're young, it's easier to remember. Your mind is fresh and full of awe and wonder, not clouded by years of new experience, new memories."

"I understand," Grayle replied. "How much do you know about the afterlife?" she asked.

"A lot, and very little at the same time," Phil replied. "There's no way of knowing for sure how accurate we are with the information we have. It's all still such a mystery. We have a Reverie Halo that could unlock so many mysteries, so many possibilities, and answers that continue to elude us, but we can't get anywhere near it. It's been deemed too dangerous to use." He sat back in sheer and utter disappointment, staring off into space as if dreaming out loud. "It's sad, but the thing that would take all my research over the top is something I know I'll never be able to touch. No pun intended, but that Halo is my Holy Grail."

Grayle smirked. "Yeah. They used to call me that in school. Holy Grail. I hated it! It had so many different connotations."

"You do have an interesting name. Where'd it come from?"

"G-R-A-Y-L-E," she said. "I was named after my mother's parents, who passed away in a tragic AI accident. An AI was transporting them in a car when it malfunctioned and crashed. Their names were Ray and Gayle."

"Ugh. I'm sorry to hear that. Your other grandparents. I had no idea."

"I wish I had gotten to know them," she said sadly, then shook her head. "But, enough about my name. Do you think you can help me figure out who she is?"

"Maybe. No promises. I never make them," Phil said curtly. "Okay, now I'm sure I don't have to ask if you believe in all of this; I know you do. So why else would you want to become a paranormal investigator?"

"That's the main catalyst, sure. But I also think I can make a difference. This isn't just a fascination for me. I've been quietly working and researching the paranormal for years. I've always known that this is where I belong. Still, I can't tell anyone about it because, you know..."

"They'll look at you like you're crazy," Phil interjected with a knowing smirk.

"Yes! That! I don't know why this subject gets discredited like it does."

"The Halo and other things. Simple as that," Phil gestured. "Once that program failed and ended in controversy, people stopped caring. You know, I'm sure, that even since the days of YouTube, a couple of hundred years ago, paranormal investigations have been faked. So, now, when people look back at the archives, they think that's what I'm doing; fake, phony, staged research. The bad part is that most of them know it's real! It's like the existence of extraterrestrials was before the arrival of the Norn."

"Just like anything else, they're just afraid of the unknown. Afraid of what it might mean if it were proven real," Grayle added.

Phil looked down and paused. "Yeah. They'd rather not know. And they'll do anything to ignore it."

There was an awkward silence as the reality hung heavy in the air. Grayle broke the silence with a bit of laughter. "So, do I have the job?"

Phil smiled, snapping out of a funk he had fallen into. "I'm sorry. This hasn't been much of an interview."

"When's the last time you interviewed someone?" she asked.

"Five years ago. I'll tell you what," he closed her file and set it aside on his desk. "I've got a case I'm working on. Tomorrow night I'm heading to Virginia. I should be able to wrap that one up quickly, so come back next Monday and we'll go over everything you'll need to know: equipment, EMFs, etc. I'll send you some reading material and…"

Grayle interrupted. "Oh, c'mon. Screw that! Let's start now! I'll go with you tomorrow night."

Her eagerness caught his attention, and Phil raised an eyebrow toward her.

"There are things you should know first," he spoke cautiously.

Grayle's excitement and pressure continued. "Look, Phil, there's no better experience than learning on the job. And let's face it, I'm overqualified for this position. I have some combat training, and I can handle a stun gun. So I'm technically proficient. And nobody's knocking down your door to take this gig."

"Be that as it may, none of those things will help you with this," Phil said.

"All the more reason to go with you."

Phil leaned back and considered. He rolled his chair to face the window and stared out while he mulled it over.

"Hmm," he muttered. "I generally don't take inexperienced people with me," he started. "But since you're insistent and this should be a quick and easy case to handle, I'll make an exception." He appeared to go on the defensive then. "I want you to just sit back and observe, okay? Just watch." His hands were up in a warning gesture.

"You got it!" Grayle said enthusiastically. Maybe a bit too enthusiastically, but she had a hard time containing herself. "Just watch. Yes, sir. Simple enough. So what's the case?"

"Pretty run-of-the-mill, mundane stuff."

Phil reached across his desk and grabbed another file. He handed it to Grayle.

"This is Mark and Liana Wilks. They have a daughter, Stephanie, six years old, who claims to have an invisible friend of the same age. According to the little girl, a boy named Ethan hangs out with her and plays. The family just moved into that house about five months ago from Oklahoma to Virginia, and right away bought this old Victorian home. At first, the parents thought nothing of it because she was an only child and they had just moved there. The daughter had no friends yet, so it seemed inevitable that the girl would drum up an imaginary one. Lots of kids do that. Where it gets weird is, they caught footage of some of the toys moving by themselves in their daughter's room. Actual video footage! And, at night, while they're trying to sleep, they can hear a small child running through the hallway upstairs, laughing, playing around, and calling for their mother. And it's not their daughter. It sounds like a little boy."

"I don't know. That seems kind of... harmless," Grayle replied.

"At first blush, it sounds that way. It doesn't appear to be a mischievous spirit. The daughter, Stephanie, is unharmed. No reports of trauma or abuse of any sort. But here's where it gets interesting. I looked up the history of this house, and ninety-five years ago, there was a fire at that house that destroyed the right corner of the dwelling. The fire started because an AI model number VNG723, a second-generation cleaning bot, that was stored in the closet of the home, short-circuited and caught fire. A little boy, aged six, named Ethan, was the only casualty of the fire. His bedroom was right above that closet. He had two older siblings home watching him that night, but the fire started and spread so quickly that they had no time to react."

"Oh my God," Grayle was drawn in by the story now. "Those bots... my brother hates those things. Says they're nefarious. There's something... 'off' about them."

"Well, they ruled the fire an accident, so there isn't any proof the bot had anything to do with it, except a short-circuit, but it gets worse. The mother was heartbroken and inconsolable. She wound up taking her own life in that house about two weeks later. At the time of her passing, she was holding onto a music box she had made for him. When her husband found her, she was already gone, the music from that box playing. As you can imagine, the father took the other two children and moved after that. He couldn't take the horrible nightmares he was having." Phil stopped and then sat back in his chair to release the tension. "Ever since then, there have been numerous reports by other families who tried to live there, all experiencing the same thing. They heard a child running around calling for his mother. I believe what's keeping him attached to the home is his mother's spirit, which is tied to that music box. So that's our mission. I think if we're able to find that box, we can set them free."

Phil waited for Grayle's response, which was a little slow in coming. "Why do you think the box is still there?" Grayle asked. "I mean, it could be anything that's the tether."

Phil shook his head. "No, that's the only thing the father didn't take with him when he left. According to the lore, that is. And, judging by the fact that several families who briefly took up residence there have all reported the same thing, I've been able to rule out everything else."

"Hmm, do you have a description of the box?" Grayle asked, her adrenaline up, her heartbeat racing in her chest.

"I do," Phil replied and then shook his head sadly. "It's been ninety-five years, however, so if it's there, it's unlikely to look anything like the description."

"Well, we can get to that later. Any theory about where it could be?" Grayle asked curiously.

"Not really," Phil conceded. "I'm going to start with the backyard. I'll run a scan around the house first. With any luck, the music box is buried in the yard somewhere, and we can find it and dig it up. If it's not outside, then we move indoors and search the house."

"Sounds simple enough, but what do we do if... when... we find it?" Grayle asked.

"We say a prayer, burn it, and hope that it sets that family free," Phil replied. "That's the plan anyway."

Grayle nodded and glanced at a clock on Phil's desk. "So, what time do we leave?"

"I suppose that depends on how fast you want to get there," Phil replied.

"Alright! Let's do some good old-fashioned driving. I think that sounds like fun." Grayle was halfway out of her chair and ready to go.

Phil wrinkled his nose. "That'll take about five and a half hours, Grayle," Phil interjected. "You sure you want to do that?"

"Absolutely!" There appeared to be no end to Grayle's enthusiasm. "We can do the second half of my interview on the way and get to know each other some more."

Phil shrugged. "Okay. I'll notify the Wilks family and inform them that we'll be there no later than seven p.m. We'll leave at noon, get there, and check all of our equipment beforehand."

"Is the family typically around when you work?" Grayle inquired.

"No, not traditionally," Phil replied. "I usually request that they leave the premises so as not to interfere and possibly skew our research. Most times, even trying to be bystanders, they just get in the way. It can be fifty questions if I let them stay. I'll just notify them when I'm done."

"Alright! Sounds good," Grayle's enthusiasm had reached a fevered pitch. "Wanna hand me those reading materials? I'll get started right now!"

Phil did as she asked, her enthusiasm bubbling over onto him. "Okay!" He handed over the material, hoping that his new partnership would turn into a winning opportunity.

Chapter 16: Lullaby

It had been a rough night for Grayle, cooped up in her hotel room waiting for dawn to arrive... and then noon. The silence of the room only made the hours longer. The clock on the wall ticked steadily but not audibly, yet watching it slowly move around its face, she could hear her brain tick off the seconds. It was almost mocking her anticipation, and she silently cursed Seth Thomas, which apparently never closed its manufacturing doors since its inception in 1813.

Finally leaving the confines of her room, Grayle spent the morning at the hotel gym, where the hum of treadmills and clank of weights did little to ease her nerves as she whiled away a couple of miles on the treadmill. Following that, she visited the coffee shop downstairs, grabbing a cappuccino and a flaky, almond-glazed Danish. The warm steam from the coffee briefly relaxed her, but as she returned to her room and flicked on the television, nothing could eliminate her excitement. Her thoughts kept racing forward. The morning dragged on, the news a blur, until it was finally time to go to the lobby and meet up with Phil.

When he arrived, she was able to let go of what had built up inside her, the tension leaving her shoulders in a rush. She climbed into the transport before Phil could even get out and courteously open the door for her.

She smiled. She loved the modern-day transports. They were a marvel of design and indulgent convenience. Self-driving if you wanted them to be, fully manual if you wanted to reminisce and pretend that you actually had control of what was generally automated. The interior often felt more like a lounge than a vehicle; airbags in every direction, all-wheel drive, climate-controlled to perfection, ambient lighting for those inclined to nap, and overdrive for the thrill-seekers. They were a modern feast for the eyes and senses, and Phil's transport matched and even surpassed anything Grayle had ever seen.

Huge and boxy, not very aerodynamic, his transport was flat black and otherwise nondescript. Its appearance gave no hint of the high-end tech it carried inside. It had two seats in the front, two in the back, and the cargo space had been modified to hold all of the equipment that could ever be needed for a job like... chasing ghosts.

"I would have come out and opened the door," Phil said, closing his door as Grayle entered.

"I'm not much for chivalry," Grayle replied as she adjusted herself in the seat, running her hand along the smooth interface panel at her side.

"Alright then," Phil replied. "Are you ready?"

"Sure am. Let's hit it!" Grayle hoped her enthusiasm would be contagious. What she had seen so far from Phil was dry and predictable. Something she expected from a man who had been doing the same job for as long as he had.

"Alright. Let's get to it," Phil pushed a button, and the automation screen in the dashboard slowly made its way upward. The screen glowed to life with a soft pulse. Without hesitation, he typed in the coordinates, set the cruise control, and they were underway.

Phil then swung his driver's seat to the right and faced Grayle, who was looking on with a combination of dismay and surprise. "What? Not going to drive yourself? I thought we said yesterday that we..."

"No. If you remember correctly, you said you wanted to do some old-fashioned driving. I said that would take too long. I haven't physically driven a vehicle in fifteen years," Phil replied.

Grayle scrunched her eyebrows in disappointment, a slight frown curling at the edge of her lips, but Phil kept talking, effectively putting a damper on Grayle's conversational ramblings.

"Let's get down to business, Grayle. I'll give you a quick rundown on what to expect on this investigation." He adjusted his chair again, turning to face the back of the vehicle. On his right side, embedded into the B-pillar, was a control panel with softly lit buttons. He pushed a few of them, and the back seats folded down with mechanical precision, and a viewing screen slowly rose from a compartment behind the seats. The windows dimmed, becoming tinted to allow for optimal video viewing, and they began reviewing footage from the home's security system.

Grayle was pleased, but a bit surprised that things started so quickly.

"As you can see in these frames, Grayle, Stephanie appears to be running around and playing with someone. She's laughing, and it looks like she's having a conversation with someone who isn't visible," Phil said.

Grayle responded matter-of-factly. "Right. Think little girl. Active imagination."

"Correct. That's what most people would want to believe. That's what I believed," Phil replied. "Until...," he pointed toward the screen. "...this."

Stephanie rolled the ball to the middle of the floor, where it stopped dead in its tracks as expected. Then... it rolled back to her.

"Oh shit!" Grayle said, adjusting herself in her chair. "Oh my God!"

"I took it to several specialists to see if the footage had been tampered with," Phil continued, "and it always came back completely unaltered and unedited."

"Can you catch an apparition on video?" Grayle asked.

"No. Contrary to popular belief, apparitions don't appear in any kind of physical form or manifestation. Some people say they see orbs, some say tendrils of light like an angel, but usually, there's nothing. That makes the job of an investigator even harder. When you enter a smart home, you see a wide array of recording equipment, infrared scanners, and video feeds. That way, if you or another member of your family is having a serious situation like a heart attack or stroke, the system notifies emergency services immediately. That's what it's designed to do. Consequently, that's where skeptics come in. They say that with all of this advanced equipment, one would think a camera would catch something. Unfortunately, that's where they're wrong. What they don't understand is that an apparition isn't physically part of this world. A spirit walks between both worlds, the living and the dead."

"Check this out." Phil reached into his bag and pulled out a cube, the size of a Rubik's Cube. He seemed eager to show it off. The cube was sleek, with softly glowing seams and metallic edges that hummed faintly with energy. "This is the latest piece of tech from an archaeologist friend of mine. Officially, it's called the SCX-1 Spectral Cartography Unit, but out in the field, everyone just calls it the Echo Cube or the Spectra Cube. Let's stick with Echo Cube because that's what it does. It finds the echoes of what has been." Phil glanced at Grayle who seemed entranced by the tech.

"Amazing. How does it work?"

He held it out to her and she took it carefully, afraid to touch something as amazing as the tech entrusted to her. "You set it in the middle of a room, and it can scan through walls, floors - anything. All you have to do is program it for what you're looking for. If that music box is in the home, this cube, the Echo Cube, will find it."

"Unbelievable," Grayle handed the cube back to Phil, glad to have it out of her possession. Her fingers still tingled slightly. "What will I be doing?" she asked.

"I'll have you stationed in the hallway with a touchscreen. We'll connect to the smart home system, and you'll be able to monitor me anywhere inside and out," Phil explained.

"Okay. Easy enough," she shrugged.

"Yes. Like I said yesterday, this is a pretty simple investigation. I'm not sure we'll find anything. About eighty-five percent of my cases come back inconclusive. Not a high success rate," Phil sighed in what appeared to be defeat.

"Do you feel you overly critique your work?" Grayle asked, trying to redirect his self-doubt.

"I have to," Phil replied. "Sometimes I second-guess myself too much, but if I don't, I leave myself open to criticism. So many people want to invalidate what I do, so I have no margin for error."

"Understood," Grayle replied, effectively beginning a silence that grew uncomfortable. The hum of the vehicle filled the pause between them. She tried to undermine it. "So... you know a little about me. But what about you? What led *you* down this path?" she asked.

Phil sat back and took a quick breath. "When I was fifteen, I had an experience. It was a summer night. I was sitting in my room, watching something, I can't remember what, but I couldn't sleep. I went upstairs to use the bathroom. While washing my hands, I splashed cold water on my face and looked in the mirror. That's when I heard a faint whisper call my name... 'Phil'... and felt a hand touch my left shoulder. I'm not afraid to tell you that it scared the shit out of me. I began to try and dismiss it, but then I felt a piercing sensation through my back, like something exploding out of my chest. I screamed in agony, at the top of my voice, but my parents claimed they never heard a thing."

"Wow. That's nuts. I presume you looked into it further," Grayle asked.

Phil nodded. "Yep. It was explained to me later that something had moved through me. I wouldn't have believed it if someone else told me, but I was talking to a paranormal expert, so I figured he knew what he was talking about. Since that night, I've had this burning desire to find out more about the paranormal. It started consuming me until it became all I wanted to do."

"In all of your experience, you've never seen anything? You never saw what touched you, called your name, passed through you?"

"No. Nothing," Phil held out his hands in a negative gesture. "I was looking in the mirror, and there was nothing behind me."

"Did you ever tell anyone?"

"Of course!" Phil laughed. "In hindsight, I don't know if that was the correct thing to do because I told everyone... and I'm not sure anyone believed me."

"That's crazy how people can deny so quickly when they weren't even there. Everyone is quick to cast doubt."

"No kidding," Phil replied.

Grayle didn't let the conversation stop. "You were top percentile in your class. An All-Star football player. You probably could have gone pro. Why didn't you do that or something else besides the paranormal?"

Phil smiled. "Because after that," Phil gestured behind him, in the past, "it was always this," he gestured toward the truck. "Don't get me wrong, I loved playing ball, I loved architecture, even thought about becoming a Director someday. But this? This was my one true love. I couldn't put it away."

"How did your parents feel about you joining the P.D.?"

"Less than thrilled. The Paranormal Department doesn't quite have the prestige of the other fields. To say they were embarrassed by me would be a monumental understatement," Phil said, laughing.

Grayle laughed, too. "So that's what I have to look forward to, huh? Ridicule and scorn?"

"Yeah, pretty much. Sorry," Phil grinned.

The conversation waned and sometimes flowed again, and even though it wasn't five hours as Phil had predicted it would be if they were manually driving, it was still a few hours before they reached the Virginia residence. The trees along the roadside began to thin, revealing rows of orderly homes and an expansive sky overhead. As requested, the Wilks family wasn't present.

When they exited the transport and approached the house, Phil entered the security code they'd been given, and the two let themselves in.

The interior of the 3,000-square-foot home was welcoming. The air held a faint trace of lavender and wood polish. The master staircase led up to the hall, where four bedrooms waited as if in invitation. To the right, a spacious living room was connected to the dining room. Straight ahead was the kitchen, and to the left, a sitting room and bathroom.

Slowly progressing through the house, the pair made their way to the kitchen, where they located the basement door, directly under the massive staircase.

From their location, Phil could see the dining room, and he quickly headed in that direction, specifically, the left corner. "Right here is where that bot caught fire. Check this out."

He pulled out his touchscreen and retrieved the Echo Cube from his satchel. He placed it on the table. With practiced dexterity, he touched the cube in a few places, and a beam of light flared out from the top, projecting a 3D overlay throughout the room. The projection shimmered like static fog, giving shape to moments now long past.

"RIGHT HERE!" he shouted, pointing. "THIS IS WHERE THE BOT WAS POSITIONED!" Catching himself, Phil exhaled and quickly lowered his voice. "Sorry."

Grayle smiled, ignoring his excitement. She walked around the room, amazed. "This *is* exciting! I can understand why you would get caught up in all of it."

Calmer now, Phil pointed upward. "Up there is where Ethan's room would have been." There was no longer any fire damage — that had long since been repaired — but it seemed as if Phil could still feel the event as it had occurred so many years ago. He broke the trance they had both fallen into. "Alright, let's go upstairs."

As they made their way up the massive, wooden staircase, the steps creaked softly underfoot. Phil handed Grayle a small earpiece.

"Go ahead and put this in. The cube is programmed with what we speculate the music box looks like. The touchscreen is linked to the home system, so you'll be able to monitor me in every room. Once upstairs, we'll do a sound check to make sure we can hear each other. I'm starting outside, checking the grounds."

"Okay. I'll be watching," Grayle replied, caught up in the blend of excitement and suspense. Her pulse was steady, but the anticipation made her skin feel charged, like electricity waiting to arc.

For forty minutes, Phil walked the grounds surrounding the house. Grayle was so eager and caught up in the moment that time seemed to have no meaning as it hastened by. She had barely noticed his absence. The soft hum of the house's systems, the subtle creak of the wooden floor beneath her as she paced now and then, and the occasional chirp from the touchscreen kept her company — a quiet orchestra of tension.

His search turned up empty, and finally, he called it quits. "Nothing outside. I'm going to make my way inside and start scanning rooms."

"Very good," Grayle replied as prim and proper as an apprentice on her first day might. "I'm hanging out in the upstairs bathroom. It's all so exciting here." She leaned against the counter, glancing at the mirror with a slight grin, her reflection sharing her anticipation.

"Yeah. Nice house, isn't it?"

Grayle spoke nonchalantly. "I wouldn't mind calling it home," she began to walk into the master bedroom. The plush carpet muffled her steps as she passed through the doorway. "It's pretty cozy."

Phil continued the tedium of clearing each room. "Upstairs is clear. Living room, clear. Dining room, clear. Kitchen..."

Grayle yawned. The excitement had begun to give way to a lull, the ebb of a high tide. "Let me guess, clear."

Phil chuckled. "Was that a yawn I heard?"

"Only a little yawn. I have to admit that I didn't sleep great. I was too excited."

"And... this job will put you to sleep," Phil joked. "As you can see, a lot of it is just moving from room to room, hoping to catch a glimpse of something. Anything! More often than not, you leave..."

"Inconclusive!" Grayle finished his sentence.

Phil laughed. "Yep. You guessed it."

He scanned the sitting room. Nothing. The flicker of ambient lighting reflected off untouched surfaces. No movement. No temperature fluctuation. Just the hollow stillness of a house holding its breath.

"Well, down to the basement I go. After that, let's get something to eat. I'm starting to get a little hungry."

"Me too," Grayle replied. She had changed her location and was perched near a window now, watching a breeze ripple the trees. "Just how do you not get disheartened doing this?" she asked.

"Eh, I've learned to live with it. There was one time, though," he turned the conversation in a hopeful direction as he descended into the basement. The echo of his steps softened into the distance. "A colleague and I almost found a portal to another dimension."

"You're kidding me!" Grayle perked back up, her whole posture straightening as she heard what Phil was telling her.

"True story. At least *we* think so. We had the right coordinates, just the wrong time. We plan to revisit it in five years. His name's Ronnie. I hope you get to meet him if you stick with this long enough."

"Tell me more over dinner," Grayle replied eagerly. "I want to hear more about it."

Phil's comm was quiet as he set the Echo Cube down in the basement. A moment passed where only faint static could be heard, and then the soft beep of the cube's activation.

He pressed the controls, and it began scanning. "Let me scan this basement and then we can get..."

A second later, the cube began to beep, the sound growing louder with each intonation, and marked a red X in the right rear corner of the house. A laser traced the mark with unwavering precision, its beam dancing softly against the concrete wall.

"What's that noise?" Grayle's ears perked up along with her once drowsy disposition. She leaned toward the monitor, her fingers brushing the edge of the screen.

"I'm not sure... Yes, I am! I think we found the music box," Phil announced.

Grayle turned her attention to her monitor. A glowing readout pulsed slowly in soft red hues. "The readout says it's just one foot down."

"I'll be right back, Grayle. I'm going back to the transport so I can grab the excavator bot. Stay where you are, please."

"Got it. I'm here. Going nowhere. I loooove being stuck in the bathroom."

In a surprisingly short amount of time, Phil returned with the bot, its compact form whirring to life as it unfolded beside him. He set it where the X was displayed by the laser from the Echo Cube and activated it. The mechanical arms moved with precision, scooping earth and material quickly. The scent of disturbed soil mingled with the old air of the basement.

When the bot finished and mechanically backed away, Phil reached down, pulled out a bag, loosened the drawstrings, and retrieved the music box. It was in terrible condition from its long burial, damp and a bit moldy, but he still managed to gently turn the key. The mechanism groaned, but the gears gave way.

Softly and with gentle encouragement from Phil, the box remembered its tune. Both he and Grayle raptly listened as the box slowly came back to life. Its melody was warbled, each note like a forgotten whisper returning to the world.

"Wow! I can't believe we found it! And that it still plays," he said softly and a bit gleefully.

"What are you going to do with it?" Grayle asked from her location, still at the monitor in the bathroom. Her voice had quieted, as if she feared breaking the spell.

"Take it outside, say a prayer, bless it with holy water, and burn it."

Grayle swallowed hard and spoke softly. "What's that song that's playing?"

"Too-ra-loo, ra-loo-ral.' From a long time ago. Forgotten era. It achieved prominence when the popular crooner, Bing Crosby sang it, but it was written by James Royce Shannon," he replied. There was some sentimental silence, and then Phil softly spoke again. "I'm heading outside now."

As Phil stepped outside to perform the ritual, Grayle tapped the touchscreen, queuing up the song on one of the more popular video-sharing sites. The gentle melody of "Too-ra-loo, ra-loo-ral" spilled softly through her earpiece, laced with the crackle of age, like it had traveled through time just to be heard again. The tune floated through the silence like a lullaby meant for the soul.

Too-ra-loo, ra-loo-ral, Too-ra-loo, ra-li

In her other ear, Phil's voice came through the comm, steady and low, his tone hushed with reverence. "Spirit of the child, wanderer of time, by this fire and in this light, be released from your waiting."

Too-ra-loo, ra-loo-ral, Hush now, don't you cry

Grayle sat still, transfixed. The melody wrapped around her like a memory she had never lived but somehow remembered. The sound of Phil unscrewing the holy water came faintly through the comm. "To the mother who weeps, your love has lingered long. May this flame carry your grief away."

Too-ra-loo, ra-loo-ral, Too-ra-loo, ra-li

The box lit with the small flame of a careful fire, and Grayle could hear the gentle hiss as the holy water touched it. The music continued to drift between the spaces of Phil's words. "Let this vessel return to ash. Let memory return to peace. Let soul find soul once more."

Too-ra-loo, ra-loo-ral, That's an Irish lullaby

Grayle's eyes began to sting with tears. She blinked hard to drive them away. Then, as the final chord of the lullaby played, the hallway before her grew brighter. Not from the house lights. From something else.

She looked up and headed out of the room.

Standing at the other end of the hallway was a woman in white. A blinding light flared around her. Grayle couldn't see her face clearly from the luminescence, but she could still see her outline, and goosebumps made their way up and down her body. Another figure appeared, a small boy, and Grayle gasped.

"Mommy! Mommy! Mommy," the boy cried with an excitement that had been ages in the making. He ran to the woman.

Within seconds, the boy reached his mother, and she picked him up and held him tightly. Their reunion was complete.

The woman looked at Grayle, smiled, and winked. Then, with a flicker, both of them disappeared.

Grayle remained frozen in awe and disbelief long after they departed, returning to herself only when Phil came back inside.

"Welp, I think we can call it a night," he announced plainly, then noticed her shocked expression. "Grayle... Grayle! Are you alright?" His concern for her was paramount.

Slowly, as if weighing every word, Grayle told him everything she'd seen, trying hard to keep her composure.

Frantic, Phil pulled up the pad in front of the monitor, replayed the footage from the hallway camera, and hoped beyond hope that something, anything would be there. Still... nothing. Just light flickering across the floor from a distant source outside.

"I swear I saw what I saw!" Grayle insisted, jumping from her seat and pointing at the monitor. "Run it again! I..."

"I believe you," Phil said calmly, placing his hand on her shoulder in a reassuring manner. He was smiling, trying to put her at ease.

Grayle struggled to speak. "It... was... beautiful," she whispered, tears in her eyes. "We did it. We reunited a mother and her child."

"We just solved our first case together," Phil said proudly.

Methodically, they began to gather up their things in silence. For Phil, the cleanup was routine. Just a day's work.

For Grayle, it was something far more.

Once everything was packed up, the pair headed out.

"I don't know how I saw that," Grayle said, still stunned.

Phil looked in her direction, not sure how to answer her except with the most reassurance he could muster. "Yeah, we're going to look into that."

Chapter 17: You Shouldn't Follow Me

Flying over the Pacific Ocean on a crisp, clear, and picturesque afternoon, Alex headed to China in his jet to help the Chinese Space Explorers with a minor problem on their space station. The clouds wafted by as they had done through the centuries, slow and serene, as if dragging time behind them. Even in the afternoon, the Moon and Sun were both visible, the whisper of clouds floating by the glow of the satellite. In ancient cultures, this phenomenon was viewed as a balance, and Alex hoped that this was a good sign. Maybe there would be balance in his life for at least one day.

The engines hummed beneath him, a soft purr barely audible within the luxury of the cabin. It was then that he chose to call Matt and check in on Grayle's exploits. He hoped that planting Matt into the situation would yield good results. Within seconds, Matt answered the call and appeared on Alex's digital screen.

He had caught Matt mid-sentence in whatever dense material he had been absorbed in. Books and data sheets filled the space around him like a wall of solitude.

"Alex. What can I do for you?" Matt asked, his tone sharp, his eyes never leaving the page. His irritation was palpable; the balance between personal boundaries and obligation was clearly disrupted.

Alex flinched at the tone. "That's no way to answer me," he replied, his irritation rising like steam. Whatever balance he had was now evaporating fast.

"Yeah, well, I'm in the middle of something, so let's make this quick," Matt replied flatly. Still, he didn't glance up. His eyes remained pinned to whatever document or screen had his attention, as if Alex were just background noise.

There was a pause, just enough for Alex to reel his temper back in. He exhaled slowly before asking, "How's Grayle?" His voice had cooled to a brittle edge, not friendly, not neutral, just hard.

"Fine. Her first assignment with Wells in Virginia a couple of days ago went well... I guess? She didn't say much more than that," Matt muttered, sounding more like a guy checking a box than a man concerned.

Alex's jaw tensed. "And where is she now?"

"How should I know? I'm not her keeper," Matt snapped, still flipping through pages. His refusal to make eye contact was deliberate now, a power play.

Alex leaned forward, narrowing his eyes. "Look, are you going to do what I told you?"

That did it. Matt slammed the material shut and finally locked eyes with the camera. His face was tight with fury. "I don't fucking work for you, Belle! Got it?" he shouted. "I'm done spying on her. Do your own dirty work. I'm out. Goodbye."

The screen went dark before Alex could even reply.

Alex let out a long, deliberate sigh and leaned back in his seat, closing his eyes for a brief moment. Frustration lingered in the air like smoke. The tension clung to his chest as he sat still, eyes closed, listening to the hum of the aircraft and the faint whir of cabin systems.

After a beat, he turned his gaze to the window, where the Moon was still partially veiled by gathering clouds. Even through the shifting haze, it remained steady. Quiet, graceful... balanced.

Yet where was *his* balance? That was the word that had been haunting him, that was the emotion that was eluding him. After a minute of reflection, Alex reached for his comm and called Tim. The line connected just as quickly as it had with Matt. He silently hoped this call would yield better results.

Balance, he thought again.

Tim appeared on screen, walking the streets of a sprawling city. Based on the crowded skyline and flickering neon, Alex guessed he was in New York.

"'Sup, Alex?" Tim asked, casually, as if they'd just bumped into each other on a sidewalk.

"Tim, how's it going? Did you find the other team members?"

"Nothing yet," Tim replied. He ducked into an alley and came to a stop beneath a dim security lamp, shadows dancing across his face. "They've done a great job covering their tracks. Exactly how I trained them. I'm totally impressed right now." He smirked, clearly expecting a compliment, a verbal trophy for his genius. After a long, quiet pause, Tim raised an eyebrow. "What? Nothing? You're not impressed?"

Alex took the bait, but his tone was far from warm. His mind was still elsewhere. "Sure. Good job, whatever."

Tim's smirk faltered for a moment. The underwhelming response didn't land the way he had wanted it to, but instead of pushing it, he pivoted. "Alright, well, I have a slight, and I do mean slight, problem."

"Go on," Alex said, finally tuning in.

"Stan Collins is following me."

Alex's eyebrow arched. "What?" he asked, followed by a short, amused chuckle.

"Yep. He's on me right now. He's an amateur and was pretty easy to spot. So, I'm guessing Richard wants eyes on me." Tim paced deeper into the alleyway, boots echoing against the pavement. "I think I'm going to send him a message."

Alex's grin curled slowly. "Good. Send him an old-fashioned message. One that Richard will understand."

"Will do," Tim said, his voice low and confident. "Consider it done."

The call ended with a soft tone, leaving Alex once again in silence, with only the hum of the engines and the whisper of clouds outside to keep him company.

Balance. He flew on, hoping to achieve just that.

As Alex and Tim were discussing his future, Stan Collins reached out to Richard on his comm. "Hey, Rich. Just checking in."

Richard, working in his office at home, quickly responded as if he were awaiting hopeful news. "Hey, hey, Stan. How's it going out there? You find him?"

"Roger that. I'm following Stevens on foot. I'm about... two blocks away from him. He seems to be just wandering around aimlessly. I can't pinpoint any destination or motive, so I'm just about ready to call it a day. I have my transport on autopilot picking me up around the corner."

"Good work," Richard replied. After a brief moment, he added, "Stan, I'm checking the tracking screen now, and... did you say he was two blocks away from you? Do you see him at all? Because from what I see, he got into a vehicle and is heading in your direction."

"Hmm. Yeah, I... I picked that up here as well," Collins replied as he studied his tracking device. The digital map blinked softly, a small marker drifting toward his location.

Just as he was looking at his tracker, Tim cruised by and Stan tried to look inconspicuous as he took cover in a nearby alley. The smell of oil and city grit filled the narrow space as he watched Tim go by.

"I'm not sure if he saw me. I'm going to get in my transport and follow for a bit," Stan said.

"Nah," Richard replied nonchalantly. "Call it a day. Just let sleeping..."

"No. Screw it!" Stan replied, a bit stronger than he wanted to. "My wife's already out with her sister, grabbing an early dinner. I might as well see where he's going."

Richard sighed, then gave Stan a stern order. "Alright. But not too much longer."

"No, it's fine," Stan said. "I'll get back to you when I know more."

Walking back to the main street, Stan rounded the corner where his transport was waiting for him. Touching his palm to the reader on the door, he got in and began to follow Tim. As they left the city, Stan wrinkled his brow in confusion.

"NOVA?" he addressed his AI (Navigation and Observation Virtual Assistant).

"Master Stan," came the refined reply in a crisp British accent. The tone was ever-so-slightly theatrical as if NOVA delighted in being summoned. This made Stan smile. Talking to NOVA always gave him a lift.

"NOVA, I am following the transport in front of me out of the city. Can you give me an estimate as to where we might end up?"

There was a brief silence as the progress indicator on NOVA's display swirled like a gentleman pondering a chess move. Finally, the smooth voice broke through with calculated cheer.

"Based on the current velocity, heading, and fuel reserves of the vehicle ahead, I would surmise, quite confidently, if I may be so bold, that the gentleman in question is en route to New Buffalo, sir."

Stan frowned. "Thank you, NOVA. New Buffalo? Why are we heading in this direction?"

NOVA replied without hesitation, his tone ever deferential. "Ah, I do wish I could provide insight into human intention, Master Stan. Alas, I remain but a humble assistant. However, should you desire, I can prepare a dossier on New Buffalo's recent activity and architectural developments."

Stan cut him off quickly, studying the darkening skies as the sun began to set. The sky turned a warm shade of gold, with hints of magenta brushing the clouds. "No, thank you, NOVA. You've been a huge help as always."

"You are most gracious, sir. Should you require anything further, a soothing playlist, perhaps, I remain at your disposal."

As the transport glided along the shoreline highway, the outer edges of New Buffalo came into view. A tapestry of scaffolding, synthetic glass, and the soft pulse of construction drones lit up the late-afternoon haze. The water on the horizon reflected the sky like a still mirror, broken only by the occasional glint of a passing ship.

Stan narrowed his eyes and sat forward. "NOVA," he said, half-curious, half-cautious, "what do we know about this place? It looks so… different."

The screen on the dash flickered to life with a polite chime. "Ah, New Buffalo, Master Stan. A bold undertaking in urban reinvention. Formerly a graveyard of rusted steel and crumbling concrete, the city has undergone what one might poetically term a resurrection."

Stan raised an eyebrow.

"In the last thirty days," NOVA continued, "over ninety-seven percent of the original infrastructure has been systematically dismantled. In its stead, gleaming modular constructs rise. They have been fabricated off-site and assembled by autonomous rigging systems with an efficiency that makes your average ant colony appear disorganized."

Stan chuckled. "Well put, NOVA. And the landmarks?"

"Preserved where feasible, recreated where not," NOVA replied with pride. "The old meets the new, sir. A curated past embedded within a crystalline future. All of it encased, soon enough, beneath a fully climate-regulated dome. Once deemed entirely unnecessary, the city has changed its thinking and supported the construction of the dome, given the rather unforgiving temperament of Lake Michigan winters."

Stan leaned back, watching the emerging skyline through the windshield. "I gotta admit, NOVA, that's impressive."

"Indeed," NOVA said warmly. "A fine blend of nostalgia and next-gen pragmatism. If cities had souls, sir, this one might just be finding its own."

Stan was smiling at NOVA's oft-welcome banter when Richard videoed back in, breaking up the reverie.

"Update. I see you both stopped in District A, just off the shoreline. What do you see?"

Stan shook his head to get back to the task at hand. Scanning his display and the view in front of him, he replied, "I'm still in my vehicle. It appears Stevens stopped about five blocks up. He got out and walked one block back, then entered a building under construction."

He glanced at the structure again. "Give me one minute for drone surveillance."

Stan tapped a button on the screen to activate a drone housed in his transport, then pointed it in the direction of the target. A soft hum filled the vehicle as the drone launched skyward.

"From the drone, it looks as if he has a bag of some sort. According to his timestamp, he's been in there for about fifteen minutes. He made much better time than I did. Anyway, the building he is in is six stories high and appears to be a… new living complex. Expensive apartments, I guess. From what I can tell, he's on the top floor and hasn't moved since he got there. There's no one else in the building."

"Okay, Stan," Richard intervened. "I want you to call it a day and head back home. It's four fifteen anyway. Almost evening."

The room was quiet except for the soft hum of electronics. A faint reddish hue from the setting sun poured through the office windows, casting long shadows across Richard's desk.

Stan was confused. "I don't get it. What about Stevens?"

"I'll monitor him from here. No worries."

Stan continued his questioning, still not sure he understood what was going on. "I don't get it. And why are you working out of your home office today?"

"No particular reason," Richard shrugged. "I have a ton of stuff to review, and I'm on standby in case the Chinese Director reaches out a little later. They say that their space station should be fully operational by the end of their day, which is just getting started, so it made more sense to work from home." Richard dropped his voice slightly, almost mumbling to himself rather than to Stan. "Which, by the way, I'll be doing a lot more of in the coming months."

"How do you mean?" Stan was fully engaged in the conversation, forgetting about Tim and the bag he had been carrying.

"Come see me at home," Richard teased him with a large, inviting wave. "I'll tell you in person."

"No, no," Stan laughed. "You know I hate cliffhangers. What's going on?"

"Come over," Richard said a little more vehemently, now sporting a huge smile.

Stan started to sigh heavily but then noticed activity on the drone following Tim. The room's mood instantly shifted. "Wait! Stevens is on the move. He's coming down now. He just exited the building, Rich. And without that bag he was carrying," Stan said, eyes narrowed as he leaned in toward the display.

"Interesting," Richard replied, adjusting his seat with a pensive look.

"I'm going to hold that drone here for a bit longer. I'll mark the bag's coordinates and release Tim. I want to see if anyone comes and retrieves it. It could be one of the people they're working with. They're all offline, so maybe we'll get lucky. Find another team member of Belle's team this way."

"Alright, just be careful," Richard replied despite his reservations.

There was a long silence, and then Richard chimed back in cautiously. "Are you still there, Stan?"

Stan let out a laugh. "So about that thing you're going to tell me."

"The hell with you! I thought something happened. Ugh. Okay. I'm stepping down as Director within the next couple of months. It's your time, Stan. You're ready! I have a ninety-five-year-old bottle of Scotch that I've been saving for the day I name my successor. Today's that day… if you ever get here. I wanted to wait until I saw you in person, but you're out there refusing my orders, so… just to stick a pin in your bubble… I already told your wife."

Stan almost choked on his words. "Jessica knows?" He couldn't stop smiling.

"She does," Richard replied. He seemed proud of himself as if he had just made one of the most momentous decisions in his life.

Stan sighed. "Okay, fine. I'll tell you what, I'm going to camp out here for another hour or so. Keep a lookout. Then I'll come right over. I'm not that far away."

"I'll stay on comms with you until you arrive. Maybe I'll open the Scotch without you. See how far I can get." Richard replied with a chuckle that hinted at relief.

"Fair enough," Stan replied. "Why do we need eyes on Stevens anyway? We know where he is. What's the deal?"

Richard took a breath and looked away from his screen, then looked back. He seemed distant for a moment. "I believe he and Belle can turn their trackers off and also register in other locations. For instance, if his signature pings him in Columbus, but you physically see him in New York, then there's a problem. He has the means to be anywhere he wants."

"And that would prove your theory," Stan inquired.

"Correct. I know you don't agree with me about Belle and Stevens, but your loyalty has never wavered, and that means a lot."

"It's not that I don't agree with you necessarily, Richard. It's that we've never found a shred of evidence linking Belle and Stevens to the Intervention explosion. No matter what we want to think, in the end... It's just a tragic accident."

"So why stay with me all these years?"

"Because that's the job," Stan replied confidently. "That's what we do. We keep everything safe on the ground and prepare for unsavory aliens who might try to harm us. And while I don't necessarily agree with everything you say, you leave no stone unturned. And that, my friend, makes you the absolute best person to do this."

"Thanks," Richard nodded, touched by the affirmation.

"So, that poses the question, why retire?"

Richard offered a partial shrug. "Mostly because I want to track those two assholes and catch them. I can't keep the Earth safe and track them twenty-four seven. It's not fair to the people I serve. It's not fair to you. This is my thing now, and I need to do it."

"Fair enough," Stan replied. "Can you tell me what happened between you and Belle?"

Richard's eyebrows raised as if he were passing on a large secret. "Truth, Stan? I never really liked him," Richard laughed. "Deep-space at ungodly speeds. That's just not possible, and he knows it. It might take another two or three centuries to achieve that. And that's if we're lucky. It's physically impossible. The human race wasn't designed for that. Still, he'll push past that and blaze past all of the people he swore to help. And he'll do it all for glory."

"Sounds about right," Stan interjected.

"Well, enough is enough. His glory has driven him mad, and I need to check him before he gets anyone else hurt or dead."

Stan nodded at his video screen and subsequently at Richard. "That's why it's been an honor working with you, sir."

"Thank you again, Stan."

Silence once more. An hour passed. Neither man spoke, and nobody showed up. Nothing happened. Zero. Zilch. Nada. The tension in the air had dulled into a quiet ache, like a held breath that never released. Finally, Richard relented and asked Stan to return.

"Might as well call it, Stan. Come back in," Richard commanded, his voice clipped and tired.

"No," Stan replied slowly. "My curiosity is getting the better of me. I want to know what's up with that bag. I need to know if anything's inside it."

"For the love of... Stan! While we've been sitting here listening to each other breathe. I've tapped into the CCTV all over that area. We have a drone or two in the sky, and so far, nothing. If anyone comes in or out, I'll see them and act accordingly. Believe me."

Somehow, that was the trigger, and Stan opened the door to his transport. The hiss of the pressurized seal breaking echoed faintly in the empty air. "I'm going in..." In a flash, he exited his vehicle and put in his earpiece to communicate with Richard.

"Stan!" Richard barked into his ear, his voice sharp and laced with growing frustration, but Stan ignored him as he made his way to the building.

The sky above had darkened with the thick haze of early evening, casting a dusky glow over the cracked pavement. He immediately headed through the lobby to the far wall.

"I'm taking the elevator," he said as he pushed the button, the mechanical chime breaking the stillness.

Again, Richard barked his name.

"Going in." Stan knew that he'd be out of communication for a minute or so, but he pushed on anyway, heading directly to the sixth floor.

When he reached his destination, Stan walked out of the elevator and drew his weapon, anticipating what? Resistance? A trap? He wasn't sure, but his weapon was a stun gun with burst rounds capable of incapacitating any human or non-human alive. Stan walked with his breath and his weapon drawn as he carefully surveyed the scene. Dust motes danced in the air where shafts of fading sunlight pierced through unfinished windows.

Richard's panicked voice pierced his comm. "I'm blind up there, Stan. No cameras installed yet. Where's your body cam and gear?"

"In the car. Didn't think I'd need it. There's nobody here anyway. Do you see anything? Anyone come near the building?"

"Negative," Richard replied with a sigh that barely masked his concern.

With methodical steps, Stan walked to the center of the vacant room. The walls loomed like silent witnesses. He looked around and offered up a sigh of relief. "Found it, Richard. The bag. It's in the right corner. I'm gonna take a look inside."

"Will you please be care… oh for God's sake, Stan."

Stan got to the bag, reached in, and pulled out a piece of paper. It was a note, and it read: **YOU SHOULDN'T FOLLOW ME.**

He laughed, the sound dry and nervous in the stillness. "Cute. He's on to me. What an asshole that guy is. It's just a note." Stan read it back to Richard.

"Alright, alright. Was there anything else in there?" Richard asked, obviously becoming agitated.

"Nope. Just that note," Stan replied, lifting the bag and giving it a shake. He then took a look out the window and walked over, the note in hand. He placed his hands on the glass. "Great view from here," he added, almost wistfully.

"Wonderful. Whoever moves in will be happy. Now pack it in and get over here," Richard said.

"On my way," Stan replied, his comm cutting off abruptly.

The cutoff from Stan was so abrupt that it made Richard sit upright in his chair. "Damn fool," he muttered. He kept an eye on surveillance, still waiting for word from Stan. Two minutes, nothing. Three minutes, no pedestrians in sight. Four minutes and his heart began to race. All was quiet and still. Too quiet and still. Five minutes, and he desperately tried to break the comm silence. "What's taking so damn long, Stan? Did you take the stairs?" Richard laughed nervously. Suddenly, not only did it not sound right, it didn't feel right.

Richard clicked on a CCTV feed that was facing the front of the building, and he realized then that he had been set up. A body fell like a grand piano from the top floor and smacked the pavement with a thud he could hear in his mind, even though he wasn't there. In shock, Richard leaped to his feet, trying to catch his breath. "No! No! No!" He adjusted the controls on the CCTV unit and zoomed in.

Stan.

Richard pushed away from the monitor, shaking and beginning to weep. He frantically called the Emergency & Defense Departments and dispatched them to the location as shock began to course its way through his body. When he reached his transport and started it, he immediately called the emergency crews he knew would be on their way or already there. "Don't touch anything! Cordon off the area! I'm en route and will be there momentarily!"

Even as fast as his transport could travel, Richard thought it had been too long. By the time he arrived, there was already a gathering of onlookers, and the situation couldn't be contained. Mass panic was sweeping through the crowd. With the murder of Owen Stipe still fresh on everyone's minds, the concern only deepened with Stan's death. No one would feel safe any longer.

As Richard tried to make his way through the crowd, Captain Rogers of the New Buffalo Defenders approached Richard and spoke to him as professionally as he dared. "Sir! We've done as you asked. We've taped off the area and left the body undisturbed."

"Very good, Captain. Thank you. I'll take it from here," Richard dismissed him hastily.

Seeing the panicked faces in the crowd, the spectators, and the Defenders themselves, Richard knew he was on the clock. He needed to settle this bitter feud once and for all, or risk losing the confidence and peace the Norn had instilled in the world.

Lifting the tape when he approached it, he walked underneath and began surveying the scene. Approaching Stan's body, he motioned to Captain Rogers.

The Captain walked over, already filling Richard in on the details that had been ascertained so far. "Director, we've reviewed the security footage and found no trace of anyone in or around the scene. We've cleared all six floors. On the sixth floor, there was blood splatter across the floor, right by the window," the captain proclaimed as he pointed upward toward the building.

"Did you find anything else on the sixth floor?" Richard asked, following the Captain's upward glance.

"No, sir," the captain shook his head. "What exactly is going on here? Can you tell me?"

Richard cleared his throat, trying to maintain his composure as he inspected his friend's body. He took several minutes, looking over Stan's corpse. Richard grimaced as he replied, ignoring the previous question. "His throat was slit."

"What? Why would somebody do that? Why would someone throw AD Collins' body out the window like that after he's already dead?" The captain asked, stunned and beginning to tremble with anger. He looked as if he needed to sit down or at least stand against something for support.

"To send a message," Richard muttered.

"What did you say, sir? I couldn't hear you," the captain asked, trying to clear the cobwebs in his head.

"Nothing," Richard dismissed him. "Take me to the sixth floor."

"Yes, sir," The Captain was grateful to get out of the crime scene, and he started toward the building, calling, "Make way!"

On the sixth floor, Richard began to walk around the scene. Missing were the note and the bag that had carried it.

"This is exactly how you found everything, correct?" Richard asked.

"Yes, sir. All six floors were empty. We contacted the Infrastructure Department, and they informed us that this building wasn't going to be completed for another couple of days. Hence the vacancy."

Richard nodded. "Did you scan the floor for any footprints?"

"Yes, sir," the Captain answered as if a dog awaiting a treat for a job well done. "The assailant, or assailants, left no trace. No footprints, no fingerprints — nothing. It's like a ghost was in here."

"Okay," Richard nodded and walked over to the blood on the floor. "This was massive blood loss. Look at all this. He bled out here, approximately four and a half feet from the window." He knelt and pointed to the spot. "The carotid arteries were severed. Just takes a few minutes to bleed out with that kind of wound. From there, whoever did this was strong enough to lift Stan's body over their head and toss him through the window. Not an easy feat, considering this newer, tempered glass."

"So we're looking for something otherworldly?" Captain Rogers asked in a troubled and frightened voice.

Richard stood up straight and looked at the captain blankly. There was nothing he could think of at that moment that would be reassuring, and his pain made him numb. He simply responded, "I wish I knew." He paused for a few seconds, his mind tossing with the questions. "Captain," Richard added, "I'm going to have to ask you for a favor."

"What is it, sir?" the captain responded.

"We need to officially rule this an accident," Richard replied.

The captain stared at Richard in shock and disbelief. "How could you ask that of me? A man was murdered here in my jurisdiction. He was tossed out of a window, and I'm supposed to just look the..."

"It's simple, Captain," Richard interrupted. "We're nowhere near solving the homicide of Owen Stipe, and nowhere near solving the probable homicide of Michael Wilson, the reporter. Everyone's already on edge with these recent events. We don't need mass panic and hysteria. I'm not thrilled about this either, but we can't let this get completely out of control. The world's watching us."

"I'm not comfortable lying to the public," The Captain shook his head, his anger rising. "That's what they did in the Dark Ages, sir. We're better than that!" He watched Richard, hoping for a change of instruction, but none was coming. The captain stood his ground. "You want it done that way, *you* make the official statement to the press, DIRECTOR!" He turned and stormed out of the room.

Richard turned away and stared blankly out the window as if looking for Stan one last time. "I'm sorry, friend."

Chapter 18: Exorcise

Summertime approached, and with it, the promise of fireworks, barbecues, and sunburns. Independence Day loomed just days away. In Philadelphia, the heat had already begun to settle in like a heavy coat no one could take off. It was late June, and the air was hot and sticky, pressing itself against windows and sidewalks... and the people of that fine city. The sky above shimmered with humidity, and even the pigeons looked as if they were reconsidering their life choices.

Currently not affected by the heat, Grayle sat inside the Paranormal Department's modest Philadelphia office, grateful for the hum of the air conditioning. It pushed a steady breeze across the room, lifting the corner of a forgotten memo on her desk. She glanced out the window at the passersby fanning themselves with whatever they had available: folders, laptop cases, even their hands. The smarter ones yielded an umbrella, and she smiled and silently congratulated them whenever they appeared, small champions against the tyranny of summer.

Enjoying the gentle breeze of the air conditioner, she waited for Phil Wells to return from a follow-up case with another family. The office smelled faintly of old books and copier toner, a scent she had come to associate with this new chapter of her life.

As she lounged in one of the padded chairs near her desk, her comm buzzed to life. She glanced at the screen and lit up when she saw the name. She righted herself, smoothing her shirt. She didn't want to look lazy, even if it was just an audio call.

"Hey, Gram," she answered, grinning wildly.

"Hey, love. How are you doing?" Rose's warm voice on the other end of the comm made Grayle smile. She always loved to hear from her grandmother. There was something in that voice, a kind of softness wrapped in quiet strength, that always seemed to steady her.

Grayle leaned back, looking up at the ceiling. "All good. Just waiting on Phil to get back from a meeting. What's up? How are you and Grandpa?"

"He's good. Always underfoot, but still good," she chuckled. "Listen, the reason I called… I know we've been putting off having a get-together, but I think it's time for a Family Dinner." Her tone was both firm and gentle, as if she were suggesting something that was already a certainty.

Grayle smiled at the thought. The idea of everyone gathered around the table, voices overlapping, stories retold. "I agree," she replied wholeheartedly. "When were you thinking?"

"In about three weeks? What do you think? That should be plenty of time to see who's available."

Grayle's voice softened. "Sounds good! I miss you, Gram. I can't wait."

"Me too," Rose replied. "Are you okay, love? How's everything going?"

Grayle smiled, a genuine contentment in her tone. "It's good. I love what I'm doing so far. It's been better than I expected." She paused, allowing the words to settle, almost surprised at how true they felt.

From the hallway, David's voice echoed into the room as he approached. His footsteps marked his impending arrival. "Hey, Grayle. Phil should be here in a minute." A moment later, his head popped around the corner. He cringed with embarrassment. "Oh, I'm sorry! I didn't know you were on a call."

Grayle waved him off with a smile and gestured for him to take a seat. He complied as she wrapped up her call. "Gram, I have to go. I'll call you later when I get finished today, okay? We'll go over more details. Love you!"

"I love you too, dear. Be safe out there," Rose replied warmly.

Neither Grayle nor David could get a word out before Phil strolled in, looking relaxed and slightly amused. His shirt was unbuttoned at the collar, and the heat hadn't seemed to faze him. "Hey! Good morning! How are the two of you?"

"You look chipper," David observed, raising an eyebrow with suspicion. He lifted a folder off the desk and started thumbing through it. The tab read BURTON in hand-scrawled letters. "Do we have a successful case with the Burton family? That's one old Civil War-era house, but I'm not convinced about the creaky floorboards and shadows on the wall. Could be a hoax."

"I concur," Phil laughed, setting his bag down and loosening his collar. "I'm classifying this one as an elaborate hoax."

Grayle and David exchanged a glance, eyebrows raised.

"Then what are you so happy about?" Grayle asked with mock suspicion.

Phil leaned against his desk, clearly in a good mood. "Well, I had a feeling going in that the Burton family's teenage sons were behind it. And I was right. Just a couple of pranksters trying to spook their parents. Hidden wires and weakened wood on the steps. Can't be too careful with teenage boys trying to get out of mowing the lawn or something else they don't want to do."

Grayle and David both chuckled. David closed the folder and tossed it back on the desk. "Okay, so why the jovial mood?"

Phil smiled even brighter than before. "I heard from an old friend last night. Father Vince."

David perked up instantly, practically beaming. "Father Vincent!"

Grayle chuckled at David's outburst. "Who's he?"

Phil grinned. "A rather... let's say... mercurial priest who specializes in exorcisms. He believes he has a case here in the States, - Norman, Oklahoma, to be exact. He's flying in from Ireland today. We'll be meeting him tomorrow." He looked at Grayle with excitement in his eyes. "How do you feel about seeing your first possible exorcism, Grayle?"

Grayle's eyes widened. "Um, ah, yeah! Do you even have to ask?"

"Great! We'll make preparations for the jaunt tomorrow," Phil smiled at her enthusiasm, already mentally reviewing the checklist.

"What do we need?"

Phil smiled. "Some religious icons and holy water. I'll have to go to church."

Grayle tilted her head, bypassing Phil's church comment with a smirk. She was more focused on the timing. "Why did he contact you on such short notice?"

Phil leaned forward, the seriousness returning to his expression. The mood in the room shifted subtly, lighter tones giving way to a weightier current. "When I spoke to Father Vince last night, he wasn't sure he was even going to pursue this. The man in question hadn't shown the usual signs: no convulsions, no speaking in tongues, just an overwhelming sense of sadness and foreboding."

He paused to let the oddity of that settle in.

"Medically, he's clean. CAT scans, MRIs, and full evaluations. The hospital chalked it up to clinical depression, which is incredibly rare these days since the arrival of the Norn. The post-Norn society has brought changes in many ways — some good, some bad — but one of the good ones is that societal shifts have gone one hundred and eighty degrees from people feeling sad and unworthy to being more positive, more… accepting of the human race."

He paced slightly, thinking aloud now.

"Anyone who even remotely shows signs of clinical depression is treated before the illness can go any further and become debilitating. That's what raised Vince's suspicion. He told the possessed man's brother to keep an eye out for anything weird."

Grayle waited, her curiosity now visibly piqued. Her eyes were focused, her brow just barely creased. "And?"

Phil gave a short exhale, like he was about to tell a ghost story around a campfire. "And the brother recorded him. At first, it sounded like nonsense. But Vince ran it through some old translation software. The man was speaking Latin, Spanish, Italian, German, and Russian. All at once. Complete sentences."

Grayle blinked. "How is that possible?" she asked with a suspicious tone, trying to balance skepticism with an open mind.

Phil sighed. "When you've been in this business as long as I have, Grayle, you learn not to ask too many questions. Strange things happen, things that don't make sense on the surface. A man speaking five languages at once? That's a perfect example."

He leaned forward slightly, voice low but steady.

"Father Vincent told me it sounded like pure gibberish at first, but there were fragments, little clues. So he took the recording to a local studio. With some advanced filtering, they were able to isolate different frequencies… and what they found was impossible. The languages weren't spoken sequentially; they were layered. All five at the same time. Latin, Spanish, Italian, German, and Russian. Like a… a chord instead of a melody. I know how it sounds. Completely absurd. But I've worked with Father Vincent long enough to know; if he says it's real, it's real."

Phil paused, studying Grayle's face, watching for a twitch of disbelief. But there was none.

She simply nodded, taking everything Phil said at face value. He was certain she would struggle with it later, but for now, she showed no cracks.

So he continued. "Once the languages were separated and translated, they all said the same thing: 'Bring on the end already. I'm ready for it.'"

Phil stood and began pacing slightly, a habit he had when recounting details that lived too large in his head. The worn carpet under his shoes muffled the sound, but his movement charged the room with a quiet urgency.

"That got Vince digging deeper. Turns out the house is built on what used to be a small family cemetery from the eighteen hundreds. It was preserved but forgotten after the chaos of the twenty-thirty-two Norn invasion. Vince overlaid historical maps with current satellite data. They match exactly. He just made the discovery a few days ago and decided to fly out. He would've called earlier, but he was closing a case in Ireland."

Phil stopped pacing and looked directly at David. His voice was steady now, almost reverent. "I don't have to tell you, David, whenever Father Vince calls… I come running."

Grayle folded her arms thoughtfully as if she were in her own line of reasoning. Her mind ran through possibilities, connecting the dots like a detective on a cold case. "What are the brothers' names?"

"Jake and Bob Dumphrey. Bob is the one possibly possessed."

"Okay. What would you like me to do?" Grayle rearranged herself in her seat and almost begged to get started. Her fingers drummed softly on her knee.

Phil smiled at her. "Hang back, observe, and record. Only an ordained priest can carry out an exorcism."

Grayle looked at David, a bit dejected. "What about you? What's your role?"

David laughed, shaking his head. "Not be there. I sit these things out. Not my cup of tea."

Grayle turned back to Phil with a slight shrug. "So just the two of us?"

Phil nodded. "Yes. David had a… unique experience once. He'd rather not repeat it."

Grayle raised an eyebrow, curiosity reawakened. "I'd like to hear about that sometime, David."

David pointed a finger and shook his head, albeit only semi-seriously. "Nope. You'll have to read about it in my memoir. I'm never talking about it again."

Grayle laughed and nodded. "Fair enough."

Phil interrupted. "Okay, gang. We ship out to Norman early tomorrow."

"Alright. Can't wait!" Grayle replied, practically glowing with anticipation.

The following day – Norman, Oklahoma, 2:03 p.m.

Grayle and Phil pulled into the Historic Campus District. Their transport hummed to a quiet, electric stop in front of a quaint brick building bearing the name *The Old School Pub* in faded, hand-painted letters. Though the signage had been restored, it had been done with care to preserve its original charm, as if the past still breathed quietly beneath the surface.

The Old School Pub was the only bar in the city that still operated without an AI staff. There were no automated bartenders and no touchscreens at any of the tables, just human hands, human voices, and the comfortable buzz of lived-in imperfection. The place stood as a throwback, an ode to a slower time. The floors had been revarnished, the booths reupholstered, but the bones of the place remained rooted in a bygone era. It was something more fitting for the 2020s than the sterilized sophistication of modern establishments of the day.

"What are we doing here?" Grayle asked as she stepped out of the vehicle, stretching her legs beneath the heavy Oklahoma sun. Her boots hit the pavement with a soft scuff as heat rose from the sidewalk in lazy waves.

"Stopping in for a quick drink," Phil replied casually, adjusting his sunglasses with one hand and tugging open the car door with the other, his face unreadable behind the tinted lenses.

"When and where do we meet Father Vince?" she asked, squinting slightly at the brightness, her arm instinctively raising to her forehead in an attempt to block the sun's glare. The air was thick with late-afternoon heat, and sweat was already threatening to form at the small of her back.

"In town, and soon enough," Phil answered with a sly, knowing smile. "We can't always work, Grayle. Sometimes we need to relax and take in our surroundings. Perks of the job." He gallantly held the tavern door open for her and gave a half-bow. "After you."

Grayle smiled and stepped inside, the heavy door creaking softly on its hinges. Phil marked her footsteps behind.

Inside the establishment, the air was comfortably cool, a welcome contrast to the thick warmth outside. Grayle scanned the space instinctively, always observing, always... working. Phil's advice about slowing down wasn't lost on her; she just had a hard time following it.

To the left stretched a forty-foot-long bar complete with ornately carved trim, the lacquer slightly worn from years of activity and spilled drinks. Beyond that, a straight path led to the back, where dimly lit hallways broke off toward restrooms and a small kitchen. To the right were tables and chairs adorned with traditional Irish flair. Edison bulbs hung from their cords like old-world chandeliers, casting a warm, amber luminescence over the weathered wood. With the rays of the afternoon sun coming in the front windows, dust motes floated lazily over the establishment like tiny stars caught in daylight.

"Grab a seat. I'm going to use the restroom real quick," Phil said, giving her a nod before disappearing down the hallway.

Grayle made her way to the corner of the bar where it curved to the back wall and took a seat on a high stool. The wood beneath her fingers was cool and worn smooth with time. A middle-aged bartender in a flannel shirt gave her a nod. "I'll be right with you!"

"Okay," Grayle replied politely, crossing one leg over the other. She felt oddly out of place, like a puzzle piece wedged into the wrong box.

A moment later, a younger-looking man approached and nodded toward the empty stool beside her. "Is this seat taken?"

"No," she said, shifting slightly, a bit unnerved that of all the empty seats in the bar, he should want to sit next to her. "All yours." Perv.

The man sat with a grunt. He was short and stocky, with shoulder-length brown hair and round glasses that slightly magnified his dark eyes. His voice was unusual, guttural, yet oddly high-pitched, and it put Grayle slightly on edge, though she kept her posture relaxed despite her growing concern. In the back of her mind, she was beginning to scream, *Phil! Where the hell are you?*

The bartender finally arrived, wiping his hands on a towel. "What can I get you?"

"Ladies first," the man said, gesturing grandly toward Grayle.

"Just a seltzer water, thank you," she replied, feeling a hitch in her throat as she tried to keep her voice steady. His chivalry in allowing her to go first was a point in his favor, but still, she was on edge.

"And for you, sir?"

"Shots of whiskey. Give me three."

The bartender left and quickly filled the order. He returned and set up his patrons. Without hesitation, the man next to Grayle slammed the first one back and exhaled sharply, his shoulders relaxing with theatrical flair.

"Ahh! Heats you up and cools you down at the same time," he said, smacking his lips. He glanced around, then turned to the bartender again. "Where's the betty's at?"

The bartender gave a weary smile and a shrug, clearly used to eccentric regulars.

Grayle instinctively turned her head away from the man and focused on an old spot on the wall, hoping to discourage further conversation. *Phil,* she mentally screamed again. She didn't have the patience today for barroom banter with strangers.

The man leaned toward her slightly, and it set Grayle's already frazzled nerves on edge even further. "I'm pretty good at reading faces, Grayle, so let me just tell you that you don't have anything to worry about. I'm here on business."

Her head snapped back toward him, eyes narrowing. She hadn't introduced herself. How did he know...

Just then, Phil returned from the restroom. He lit up when he saw the man seated next to Grayle. "Father! Good to see you!" he said, giving the man a warm embrace as he stood.

"You're Father Vince?" Grayle asked, stunned, a smile of relief now coming over her face. She tried to disguise her relief.

"Yes. Father Vincent Rich. At your service," the man replied, offering a short bow that was equal parts humorous and sincere.

Grayle tilted her head. "Oh, my goodness. You had me in a panic there. I was trying to figure out how to get rid of you while mentally begging Phil to return."

Phil and Father Vince both laughed, and then she spoke again. "Just how old are you?"

"Thirty," Vince answered without missing a beat.

"Well, let me tell you, you're not what I was expecting," she said with a chuckle, trying to reconcile his appearance with her assumptions.

"Yeah, well, they'll let anybody in these days," Vince replied, flashing a grin and raising his second shot glass.

"So, how have you been, Vince?" Phil asked, settling onto the stool next to him.

Father Vincent shrugged. "Who knows? Better. Worse. Whatever. Took a shot, now I'm recharged." He slid one of the remaining shots over to Phil. "Here. Have one of these with me."

Both men lifted their glasses, clinked them together, and Phil said, "Sláinte." He lifted his glass and they drank. "Whew! Always burns," he blinked hard as it went down.

"Yeah. Speaking of burning, you ready for this shit?" Vince asked, voice dropping slightly, his mood shifting to something more serious.

"Yes, let's go," Phil replied with a nod.

"Great! Let's get down to business," Vince said, smacking the bar with his hand and rolling his neck slightly as if preparing for a fight.

Grayle leaned in, elbows on the bar, listening carefully, trying to will herself into the conversation, eager to learn how the process worked.

"Alright," Vince began. "So, I arrived yesterday and dug in right away. Here's what I found at the historic documents building. That family cemetery from the 1800s that I thought the house was sitting on? Turns out it was moved, seven miles southwest of that plot. Moved in 2067, during one of the relocation efforts after the Norn invasion. I had the records updated, so whatever's going on in that house - it's not connected to that old cemetery."

He took a deep breath, the edge of cynicism softening just a little as he leaned back in his seat. His fingers traced the rim of his glass absentmindedly, as if grounding himself through touch.

"I also reviewed Bob's medical charts again. Still nothing out of the ordinary. Physically, he's fine. Honestly, I'm not even sure this qualifies as a possession. I have my doubts. But we're here, so screw it. We'll see what happens." Father Vincent shrugged. "I just hope I'm not wasting both your time."

"No, no. Happy to assist, Vince," Phil said reassuringly with a slight wave. The whiskey was already fading from his system as the gravity of the job came into sharper focus.

"Good. 'Cause I hate doing this stuff alone," Vince said with a lopsided grin. The humor was there, but the undertone was genuine... he meant it.

"Why *are* you alone?" Grayle asked. "I'm not trying to be contrary, I'm genuinely just curious."

"Well, here's how it works," Vince explained, slipping effortlessly into teacher mode. "The local clergy are alerted to suspicious activity, unusual behavior, that sort of thing. They do a preliminary investigation. If it's credible, then they notify the Vatican. Once that occurs, the Vatican then contacts me. I'm the specialist, the Exorcist."

His tone was matter-of-fact, but not without a trace of weariness. You could hear in his voice the years spent doing something few truly understood - and fewer wanted to.

"I coordinate with paranormal investigators around the world. Which... there's not a ton of those left, to be honest," he added with a sigh, as if bearing the weight of that dying profession. "But we try to do the best we can." He paused and studied Grayle's face for a brief second. "You look eager to get started, Grayle."

"I am, even though I feel like I shouldn't be," she admitted, suppressing a grin, trying to hide her excitement. Her fingers twitched slightly on the bartop, betraying her energy.

"Hey, I don't blame you," Vince chuckled. "I remember when I was in training. The first couple of years? Nothing. Dead silence. I wondered if I'd made a mistake choosing this path.

Honestly, I didn't believe. I still had faith in God, don't get me wrong, just not in evil. Not in *that* kind of evil. Human evil, that goes without saying. That's everywhere. People killing people, people suffering and dying for no good reason. But… demons?"

He leaned forward, eyes twinkling with memory.

"That all changed when one day I went with Father John on a case. I wouldn't have believed it had I not seen it, but I witnessed a woman climb a wall. Backwards. No wires, no tricks. She just crawled up the damn thing like a spider. We expelled a demon that day, let me tell you, and… Father John retired that same night." Vince let out a belly laugh. "'You're ready to be on your own,' he told me, pale as any ghost I've ever seen from that day on. I never heard from him again." Father Vincent laughed. "Can't say as I blame him."

Even Phil had to laugh at that. Grayle just stared, wide-eyed, unsure if she wanted to believe it, but still completely absorbed. Her eyebrows were raised, her mind struggling to find a rational place to land.

Then Vince's laughter tapered, replaced by something quieter, more solemn. His shoulders lowered slightly, and the glint in his eye faded into something darker.

"I wish people took this seriously," he said with a shake of his head. "We've accepted aliens as fact, but we still can't fathom that there are otherworldly forces of a different kind. Spirits. Demons. Things that exist between the folds of what we know. It's crazy, but… not everybody gets a visit from a demon. We've all been visited by an alien. For better or worse."

He placed a ten-dollar bill on the bar and slid his chair back with a soft scrape of wood on tile. Phil and Grayle followed suit, and they left the pub. When they stepped outside, the late afternoon sun cast long shadows across the sidewalk. The air had shifted, drier now, with a hint of cooling evening breeze beginning to stir.

They walked toward their vehicles.

"Vince, you want to ride with us?" Phil asked, tilting his head toward the transport.

"Nah, I'll take my Subaru," Vince replied, patting his keys in his pocket and then pointing toward Phil's old automobile. "I know those things are cleaner and quieter and fancier, but I'm old school. I'll take the beater. You've got the address, I'll see you there."

"Always full of surprises," Phil chuckled. "See you there."

As they drove through the outskirts of town, the buildings began to thin out, replaced by low grasses, distant silos, and the quiet rhythm of a summer breeze. The sky was wide and open, painted in watercolor blues and dusty whites.

"Mercurial, eh?" Grayle said with a laugh.

"Yes, he's something," Phil agreed, grinning at the road ahead. "Don't let the looks and age fool you, he's one of the best exorcists working today."

"I read about his exploits before we came. I guess I just expected someone older, more... weathered. And what's with the glasses? On top of that, shouldn't he be wearing the collar?"

"The glasses? Just a fashion thing," Phil replied with a shrug. "And the church? Totally relaxed about dress codes these days. It's not like the old days. These guys blend in better that way. Who wants an exorcist strolling around their neighborhood?"

It wasn't long before they pulled up to the Dumphrey residence. It was an isolated, high-tech modular home sitting squarely in the middle of three acres of flat, grassy land. The sun's light bounced off its sleek paneling, giving it a slightly surreal sheen. The property felt untouched by time, or people, for that matter. No neighbors in sight. Just the house, the wind, and the wide open quiet.

It was hard to miss.

A young man stepped out of the front door to greet them. He was in his early twenties, dark-haired, clean-cut, but visibly tired. A cautious hope lingered behind his polite smile.

"Hello. Thank y'all for coming today. Much appreciated," he said with a slow nod. "Name's Jake."

"Hello, Jake," Phil replied warmly, putting out his hand for a shake that didn't appear to be happening. He wanted to wait for Father Vincent to arrive, but his driving that Subaru... who knew how long something like that would take? He dove right in. "I'm Phil Wells, and this is my partner, Grayle Mackey. I should probably wait for Father Vincent, but..."

Jake exhaled, bypassing the formalities and charging ahead. "You want to know how long Bob's been acting strange? About a month ago," he said. "He just started sitting out back in a chair, staring into the woods for hours at a time. Always at night. Not that we didn't sit outside before, but he's been doing it for hours at a time. And..."

"What does he say he's looking at?" Grayle asked, a bit sorry that she had interrupted, but she was studying Jake carefully for any cracks in his story.

In the distance, the sound of an old automobile could be heard approaching, and everyone presumed it was Father Vince, but Jake pressed on. "He doesn't say much, Ma'am. Says he's just relaxing. It doesn't make much sense," Jake said, rubbing the back of his neck. "During the week we work, and he's almost not present. It's like he's halfway somewhere else."

"What do you do during the weekend?" Phil asked, keeping his tone even.

"We like to go out with friends. We attend Mass every Sunday," Jake replied, his voice softening, as if that detail might serve as some sort of protective charm.

Just then, Father Vince appeared. He had been pacing the perimeter of the modular home. He was brushing a trace of red clay from his hands.

"So, Jake," Vince said, sizing up the surroundings and taking over the conversation. "I understand the two of you work for the Infrastructure Department?"

"That's correct, Father," Jake answered automatically.

"Call me Vince," he replied with a quick smile. "Tell me, whenever you're out and working on roads, buildings, that sort of thing, have you ever come across any... relics? Something you found that looked cool, brought home with you?"

Jake looked startled. "No, Fath... I mean, Vince," he corrected himself quickly. "We were raised right. We don't touch anything that doesn't belong to us."

"I believe you," Vince said with a nod, seemingly satisfied. He clapped his hands together once, sharply. "Alright. Take us to your brother. Let's get a look at Bob."

Jake held out his hand in a gesture toward the mobile home. Grayle and Phil grabbed their equipment from their transport, and the four of them headed in that direction. Once inside, the air sat heavy, the only circulation from a free-standing fan that oscillated in the corner of the main living area. The interior of the home was tight and somewhat cramped. It was almost too quiet.

Bob sat in the center of his room, sunk deep into a lounge chair that faced a wide, curtainless window. His gaze appeared to be fixed on nothing... or maybe something that only he could see. His face was slack. His eyes didn't track them as they entered. He was there, but not present.

The bed had been folded away into the wall, leaving a wide-open space that felt both deliberate and strangely ceremonial.

"Jake, do you want to be present?" Vince asked gently.

"No." Jake's voice cracked, and his eyes welled. His voice hitched in his chest. "Just... please help him."

Vince placed a hand on the young man's shoulder as he was turning to leave. "Don't worry. Everything's going to be okay. I promise."

Jake nodded and backed out of the room, closing the door gently behind him. Heavy sobbing could be heard drifting away outside.

Once they were alone, Vince turned to the others. "Alright, gang. Go ahead and set up the recording devices. Once you're ready, let me know."

Phil nodded, already pulling out the equipment from a slim black case. He worked quickly, like a man who had done this many times. The handheld recorder was no larger than an old-school cellphone, and the four pin-sized cameras adhered easily to the corners of the room. The operation was a model of efficiency. Once active, their faint green lights pulsed softly.

"We're set," Phil said after a few minutes. "Time and date already logged."

"Good. Start recording now," Vince instructed, voice steady.

"Recording," Phil confirmed.

Vince stepped behind Bob and began in a clear, steady voice, projecting authority without aggression. "I am Father Vincent Rich, conducting Special Assignment number 9265, located in Norman, Oklahoma. We are at the residence of Jake and Bob Dumphrey. The subject under observation is Bob Dumphrey, currently exhibiting signs of potential possession or unexplained affliction. His brother, Jake Dumphrey, is present on the premises but has chosen to remain outside during the examination." He paused, glancing down at Bob, then back toward the wall-mounted cameras. "According to initial testimony, the family reports no known contact with demonic arti-facts or cursed objects. Both brothers are regular attendees of Mass and maintain consistent religious practice." He gave Phil and Grayle a quick, ironic smile.

Then his tone shifted. The real work was about to begin.

"Bob. Bob. Bob." Vince called his name softly, waving his right hand in front of Bob's blank, unblinking face.

Nothing.

There wasn't even a flicker behind the eyes. The man might as well have been made of wax.

Vince sighed, stepped back, and turned to Phil with a subtle tilt of his hand. He whispered, "Hand me the holy water, would you?"

Phil reached into his kit and retrieved a small, stoppered bottle. The water inside shimmered faintly in the light as if it knew what it was meant for. He passed it to Vince, who uncapped it and offered a quiet blessing under his breath.

"In nomine Patris, et Filii, et Spiritus Sancti, amen," Vince said firmly. He made the sign of the cross, then flicked the water in a crisp arc toward Bob.

Grayle, watching intently, tilted her head slightly, her curiosity clear.

Noticing, Vince gave a brief nod and murmured just loud enough for her to hear, "It's Latin. Means, 'In the name of the Father, and of the Son, and of the Holy Spirit.' It's the foundation of our authority. Everything we do here is by God's permission, not our own."

The droplets landed on the man's skin and shirt.

Still nothing.

Not a blink. Not a twitch.

Vince's frown deepened. The silence pressing against the room grew heavier. He reached into his coat and pulled out a set of rosaries, worn from countless prayers, each bead smoothed by time and petition. They clinked softly in his hand, the sound strangely out of place in the stillness. Lowering them gently onto Bob's lap, Vince placed them with reverence, like a sacred offering.

Still no response.

It was the kind of silence that felt heavier than noise; unnatural, dense, and brimming with invisible tension.

Turning toward Phil now, brows furrowed, Vince asked, "Do you have the holy ashes on you?"

Phil nodded, already reaching into the supply case. "Yes."

"Give them to me," Vince said with more urgency than before.

Phil handed over the small container, and Vince knelt quickly. He worked with the precision of ritual, drawing a thick circle around the chair using the fine, dark ash. Each line was careful and exact, as though sealing something ancient and unseen.

"Nothing to worry about," Vince said, standing again and dusting off his hands. "Just being cautious. If there's something demonic happening, that spirit's trapped in that circle."

Grayle stared at the ash-ringed chair, her stomach tightening. The air felt different now, slightly thicker, like something unseen had been summoned to attention.

"But... he was unresponsive. That means we're in the clear, right?" Phil asked, though his voice had lost its confident edge.

"Not... necessarily," Vince said, slower now, more deliberate. "I encountered a situation once where I thought I was in the clear, only to realize that I was wrong."

He paused and grinned unexpectedly.

"This demon, Mert..." Vince shook his head, a dry, humorless laugh slipping out. "I've been chasing that bastard for six years. Slippery son of a bitch has learned how to hide. He barely reacts to anything holy anymore. Icons, blessings, rituals - you name it, he shrugs it off. Makes him a damn nightmare to track."

He paced a slow half-circle behind Bob's chair, his tone growing more serious.

"That's why I use the ash now. It's the only thing left that might trap something if it's there. You never know when you're going to run into that stubborn prick again."

Grayle blinked, caught between amusement and concern. The casual profanity, mixed with religious solemnity, was both disarming and somehow oddly comforting. But everything about this still felt... off. The air. The silence. Bob.

"You look a little uneasy, Grayle," Vince said, catching her expression. "You okay?"

"I'm fine," she replied quietly, though even she wasn't sure if she meant it.

"Just because we're at an exorcism doesn't mean it can't be fun!" Vince declared, throwing his hands up like he was hosting a celebration instead of walking the fault line between worlds.

Grayle watched him carefully. Maybe this was his release, comic antics to ease the strain of being so close to whatever lurked beyond the veil.

"Okay. Let me get back to it," he said, his tone sharpening again.

Phil asked, "What should we do next?"

"Nothing."

The voice did not belong to Vince. Or Phil. Or Grayle.

They all froze.

It had come from Bob.

"I'm sorry, what?" Vince snapped his head around, eyes locking on the man still sitting in the chair.

"Nothing," Bob repeated, softer this time. A smooth, low murmur. It was almost hypnotic, soothing, melodic, and eerily unfamiliar.

"Bob... how are you feeling?" Vince asked, his voice steady, but lined with caution. Wary.

Bob didn't answer right away. His eyes remained fixed on the window, as though watching something move in a realm just beyond their understanding. Slowly, almost reverently, he lifted his arms heavenward, like one waking from a long, sacred dream. The chair beneath him pivoted with a soft groan, its legs creaking against the floor. Sunlight behind him swelled, casting him in a warm, almost holy halo.

"I feel fine," he said at last, the words drifting out like a whispered benediction.

But it wasn't Bob's voice. It was softer. Purer. Refined. And it sent a chill through the room.

Vince leaned closer to Phil and Grayle, his whisper urgent. "I've heard Bob on a video Jake provided. Bob's normal voice has a deep Southern accent. This... is not him."

"He's right," Bob said plainly. The words landed with weight, like stones in a still pond. "I'm not."

Then his eyes, clear, calm, and impossibly knowing, found Grayle.

"You never get him," he said, with a certainty that pierced the very air.

Time itself seemed to slow. Even the atmosphere felt suspended, like the universe was listening in.

The three stood frozen, hearts clenched by a sudden, unknown awe.

"Get who?" Grayle asked, barely above a whisper.

"Him. Not in any life. You never catch him. Remember that," Bob replied.

Vince narrowed his gaze, keeping his tone reverent. "Who are you?" he asked. "And why are you here? Is Bob safe?"

"He is safe," the voice said through Bob, the tone gentle as a lullaby. "When he awakens, he will never have felt better."

Vince leaned toward Phil again. "I'm going to begin the prayer to Saint Michael," he whispered, conviction in every syllable.

But Bob's voice, still glowing with radiant calm, cut through. "That won't be necessary. I'm not from there."

Then, with a tranquility that defied the gravity of the moment, Bob stood. He moved with the grace of someone recently returned from a long, celestial journey. He crossed the ash circle without even the faintest disruption. Whatever it was meant to contain had no power over him.

"What do we do?!" Phil whispered, panic rising.

"Wait," Vince said, raising a calming hand. "I don't think we're in danger."

"You're not in danger, friends," the figure said warmly, the words a balm to their frayed nerves. "I mean no harm. I am simply here to bask in the blessings of God."

"Are you… an angel of the Lord?" Vince asked, voice cracking with awe.

Bob, or whatever was within him, stepped forward and gently handed Vince back the rosaries. As he smiled, the sunlight seemed to swell around him, painting the room in a brilliance that felt like the breath of heaven itself.

He placed a hand on Vince's shoulder; the touch was light, but charged with power. Vince's face lit up with joy. "Keep up the great work, brother," he said.

Then he turned to Phil. The smile remained, glowing with something eternal.

"You will find the answers you seek."

Lastly, he faced Grayle. His voice grew even softer, rich with sorrow and compassion.

"Bridgette. She waits. She won't move on without you. Choose between your love or your vengeance. You cannot have both. Let go."

His words clung to the room like incense. Lingering. Heavy. Sacred.

Then, without another word, he returned to the recliner. He sank into it with a long, final breath, folding his hands over his chest as if preparing for a journey beyond their world.

"I must be on my way," he said, voice already fading. "I have stayed too long."

"Wait!" Vince cried, stepping forward, the reverence cracking under urgency. "What did you mean when you said, 'Bring on the end already'?"

Bob opened his eyes one last time, his face illuminated with the last glimmer of divine light. A soft, knowing smile played at his lips.

"Beware of false prophets," he said.

Then he closed his eyes and was gone.

Moments passed. The air shifted. Warmer now, both in temperature and feeling. The weight had lifted. Bob stirred. His fingers twitched. His chest rose and fell with renewed rhythm. Slowly, his eyes opened. They blinked in confusion before settling on the three strangers.

Startled, he sat upright. "Who are y'all? What are you doing here?!"

He scanned the room, eyes searching for something familiar. "Where's my brother?!"

Vince stepped forward, his voice calm and composed. "Relax. I'm Father Vincent Rich, and these are my associates. Do you know where you are?"

Bob looked around, still dazed. "Yeah... my room," he said. His voice was back — deep, Southern, familiar. Earthy. Real.

Just then, the hallway thundered with running steps. Jake burst in, eyes wide with disbelief. He didn't hesitate. He crossed the room in three long strides and threw his arms around his brother.

"Are you alright, man?" Jake's voice cracked, thick with emotion.

Bob smiled and returned the hug with genuine warmth. "Hey, I'm fine, little brother. Never better." His arms wrapped around Jake with the kind of tenderness that only years of shared history can create. He scanned the unfamiliar faces and equipment in the room, his eyes narrowing slightly, and leaned into Jake, lowering his voice. "Exactly what the hell is going on?"

Vince stepped closer, his expression calm and composed. His tone was gentle as he kneeled beside Bob and carefully recounted the events, the strange encounter, the observation, and everything they had witnessed. The words came softly, woven with reverence, as if describing something sacred rather than supernatural.

Bob shook his head, his brows knitting as he tried to make sense of it all. "All I remember was sitting in church a while back… I don't remember when exactly. But I looked up at the cross while we were praying and felt a presence. Something beautiful. Sweet, even. I felt this… touch. And then I woke up here." He rubbed his eyes, the gesture almost childlike, as if trying to scrub away a dream and anchor himself back in reality. "How long was I out of it?"

"It's been a minute," Vince replied with a quiet, knowing smile, a faint twinkle in his eye that belied the intensity of what had just transpired.

Bob's stomach gave an audible growl. He chuckled, patting it as though it had spoken out of turn. "I'm hungry. Anyone else?"

"Sure," Vince said, his simple reply landing with the finality of a sacred confirmation, as if the question had settled something deeper than appetite.

The five of them ended up around the kitchen table that evening. The lights in the Dumphrey house glowed golden against the deepening dusk outside, casting long shadows and a warm glow that made the moment feel suspended in time. The air smelled faintly of coffee and old wood. Conversation flowed slowly at first, tentative like tiptoeing into a cold lake, but soon laughter broke through the unease.

Vince, Phil, and Grayle took turns asking questions, casually observing and recording Bob's awareness. They probed his memory with gentle curiosity, threading through his responses for anything that felt out of place. But everything about him felt right, more than right, as if the strange encounter had never happened at all.

By the time the last rays of sunlight had dipped below the horizon, painting the sky in bruised purples and fading gold, they were satisfied: Bob was whole.

As they prepared to leave, Jake stepped outside with them. The porch light glowed behind him, silhouetting his frame. His face was flushed with lingering emotion, but his smile beamed with a quiet, honest gratitude.

"I can't thank you folks enough! I appreciate you!" he said, pulling each of them into a tight hug, holding on a little longer with each embrace as though imprinting his thanks into their bones.

Vince grinned, brushing off the praise with his usual humility. "We didn't do that much, but you're welcome. I'll be in town for the next couple of days, so I'll be by tomorrow to check on you two. Okay?"

"Okay, sir. Thank you. Thank you!" Jake called, his voice trailing behind him as he turned back inside, still riding the emotional high of his brother's return.

The evening air was cooler now, brushing gently against their skin like a blessing. It carried with it the scent of earth, grass, and something softer… something holy.

Vince turned to the others.

"Let's go back to that joint we were at earlier. Get a nightcap. What do you say?"

Phil and Grayle nodded without a word.

Back at The Old School Pub, the place was quieter now. The crowd had thinned. The jukebox had fallen silent. Only the low murmur of distant conversation and the occasional clink of glasses filled the space. They found a booth tucked away in the corner and sat together, the weight of the day sitting with them like a fourth companion. It pressed lightly, but lingering like smoke from a burned-out candle. For a while, they just sipped their drinks in silence, each one locked in their own spiraling thoughts.

Vince finally broke it. "This was a first for me," he said, grinning, though disbelief still clung to the edges of his expression.

Grayle gave a soft smile. "Everything's new to me."

Phil glanced at her, noting how composed she looked despite everything. "You've had one hell of a first couple of months."

She leaned back in the booth, eyes distant and thoughtful. "Okay… what Bob said to me? I'm trying not to freak out about it, but I'd love to know what he meant."

The men exchanged a glance. For once, neither had an answer.

"I don't know, Grayle," Phil said at last, his voice low and even. He offered up a slight shrug, helpless in the face of the unknown.

"I need to go in a minute," Vince said, rubbing his eyes and letting a long yawn escape instead of more conversation. "I need some sleep."

Phil turned toward him. "What's next for you?"

"I'm going to stay here another couple of days," Vince replied, downing the last of his drink in a slow, thoughtful swallow. "Then haul ass back to the Vatican. I need to talk about what we saw." He gave a lazy swirl with his finger in the air. "You know. Process, closure."

Grayle stood, stretching her legs. "I'm going to use the restroom, so I'll say goodbye now." She leaned in and hugged Vince, holding it a moment longer than expected before disappearing into the back hallway.

Vince watched her go, then turned to Phil.

"Keep an eye on that girl," he said softly. "She's special. There's a presence with her. Something… tied to the tragic events with her parents. And that awful day."

Phil nodded slowly, his face shadowed with memory. "I know. I'm going to help her any way I can." He paused, then added with quiet weight, "But I keep wondering… what Bob… or not Bob, said to me. He said I'd find the answers I seek. What did he mean?"

Vince opened his mouth, then closed it again. The silence stretched. For once, the ever-confident exorcist seemed uncertain, as if the question itself had pulled him into deeper waters than expected. "I… I'm not sure, friend."

Phil stood and embraced him. He placed a steady hand on Vince's shoulder, and their eyes met — no words, just a firm nod. Their usual way of saying: I'll see you again.

Vince turned and walked toward the door.

"Hey!" Phil called after him.

Vince turned back, brow raised.

"When Bob… whoever… touched you," Phil asked, "you looked euphoric. What did you feel?"

Vince paused. The question lingered, heavy and fragrant like incense in a cathedral. He let the silence breathe between them before answering, his voice soft, almost reverent.

"Peace."

Chapter 19: Help!

It was 9:00 a.m. on the Fourth of July.

Since the Norn intervention, the holiday slowly began to carry a different weight. A global community had become the norm, and although each country still celebrated its foundation, the celebrations weren't as vigorous as they once were. Fireworks still lit the skies, but the explosions carried undertones of history, of unity, and sometimes of loss.

Inside the Philadelphia office, Phil, Grayle, and David were lingering over coffee, not much work being done. The lights were low, the room quiet, except for the hum of distant street traffic. They were waiting for Father Vincent's call, an update on the Dumphrey brothers from two days earlier, but once the call came, they planned to officially break for the upcoming weekend festivities.

"So, what do you two have planned for the weekend?" David asked, leaning back in his chair with his mug resting lazily in his hands.

"Me? Nothing," Phil replied with a slight grin. "I'm going to review some case files. I'm never not working."

"No family? Dates? Nothing? You don't do anything except work?" Grayle asked, surprised. "Booring."

Phil shrugged, his eyes focused somewhere beyond the room. "I mean, I'll head to Michigan at some point. But honestly, I don't socialize much these days."

"Why is that?" Grayle pressed, her voice softening with empathy.

Phil paused, weighing how much to say. "Let's just say... not many people in my family understand why I chose the path I did," he said at last. "Rather than sit around defending my life choices, I'd rather work."

Grayle smiled and changed the subject, her hands spreading out slightly in invitation. "Well, now's a good time to bring up 'Family

Dinner' then," she said, laughing lightly. "You're both invited. It's in three weeks."

"Family Dinner?" David asked, intrigued.

"Yeah," Grayle said, settling back in her chair with a nostalgic warmth in her eyes. "My family. We get together four times a year, kind of a quarterly tradition. My grandparents, siblings, Commander Will, and a lot of others who worked with my parents, you know, Explorers. When my grandparents moved us to Wyoming, they kept it going to honor my parents' memory." She studied the two men for their reactions. "So if you're free?"

"What the hell, why not?" Phil replied with a small smile that seemed to grow into something bigger the longer he considered it.

"I'm in!" David said enthusiastically.

"I'll be there too!"

The three turned, startled. The fourth voice had come from behind them, completely unsuspected.

Grayle spun around. "Richard!" She jumped up to greet him, pulling him into a hug. "I'm surprised to see you! What's going on?"

"I'm sorry to startle you," Richard said, smiling faintly. "Hope you don't mind that I let myself in."

"Not at all, Director," Phil replied, rising and shaking Richard's hand.

"Could I steal Grayle away for a moment?" Richard asked.

"Yeah, sure," Grayle said, curiosity flashing across her face.

Before they could step away, Phil's comm buzzed. He glanced at the screen. "Ah, Father Vincent," he said, stepping aside. He nodded in Grayle's direction. "I'll catch up with you later, Grayle."

Before she could reply, Richard gave a nod toward the door. "Let's step outside. Get some air."

They moved out to the front porch. The morning was warm, the early summer sun already heavy in the sky. The scent of early, distant barbecue prep and cut grass hung faintly in the breeze. It was then that Grayle turned serious.

"I haven't heard much from you since Stan's funeral. I left messages, but you never replied. What gives?"

Richard sighed, a sound weighted with weariness. "I'm sorry. I've been busy trying to find a replacement for Stan. I've been vetting people... and working on something else. Something important. That's actually why I'm here today."

Grayle raised an eyebrow, confused and slightly irritated. "Okay...?"

"I'll get straight to the point," Richard said. "There's something I need help with. And I was wondering about Mr. Wells. Tell me, what kind of investigator is he?"

"Phil? He's great," Grayle said immediately. "Very thorough. When he takes a case, he almost immediately tries to debunk it."

"Interesting," Richard said. "Why that approach?"

"In this line of work, he knows he has to be perfect," Grayle explained. "There are too many frauds out there. If the Paranormal Department is ever going to be taken seriously, that's what it takes." Grayle paused. "Why the interest? Can you tell me?"

Richard nodded as if confirming something to himself. "Well, I'll get straight to the point. It involves you, too. Are you free tonight?"

"I am," Grayle said, though she felt a ripple of uncertainty.

Just then, Phil stepped back outside. "All good with Father Vincent, Grayle," he said. "He's heading out of town. The Dumphrey brothers are fine."

Phil turned to Richard with a nod. "To what do we owe the honor of this visit, Director?"

Richard smiled tightly. "I was just telling Grayle, I'm working on something privately. I was wondering if you two are available this evening. I need you to come to my home in upstate New York."

Phil shrugged slightly. "Sure. If you need us, we're available."

"I'm sorry I didn't call ahead," Richard said, genuinely apologetic. "I'm trying to keep this quiet. That's why I came in person."

"Can you give us any details about what this is?" Grayle asked.

"I'm afraid not," Richard said. "Not yet."

"What time?" Phil asked, glancing at his watch as he spoke.

"Be at my place at 9:00 p.m.," Richard replied mysteriously.

"Alright," Phil said, drawing out his words almost in a question of confusion. "See you then."

Richard offered a quick wave goodbye and left as quietly as he had come.

Once he was gone, Grayle turned to Phil, still processing what had just happened. "Okay... I don't know what that was all about, but my curiosity is piqued," she said.

"He didn't give you any information?" Phil asked.

"Nothing. And that's not like him. He's usually closed off, sure, but this feels... different somehow. I don't know what it could be." Grayle's voice trailed off with her thoughts.

Phil nodded, giving a slight shrug. "I'll head home and get ready. Is flying okay with you? I can set up my private jet."

"Flying's fine," Grayle said. "Actually... would you mind if I rode with you? I think it would just save some time."

"Yeah, why not?" Phil said with a grin. "I have to go home first, so don't expect anything special."

"Alright. I'll be ready in a few minutes. Just let me make a phone call," Grayle said, pulling her cell phone from her pocket.

"Alright," Phil replied. "Don't linger."

Grayle smiled, gave a quick wave, then stepped onto the sidewalk. She took a few nervous steps before dialing Matt's number. He answered almost immediately. His voice was upbeat, and her heart skipped a beat. She didn't have time to ready herself.

"Hey! I was hoping I'd hear back from you," Matt said. "I messaged you last week. You said you'd get back to me, but you never responded."

"Yeah... sorry about that," Grayle said, pressing a hand to her forehead. She felt as if she were letting Matt down, but her work was... was it more important? "Something's come up."

"Everything alright?" Matt asked, concern edging into his voice.

"Everything's fine," Grayle replied, shaking her head, perplexed. "It's Richard," she sighed. "He stopped by and wants Phil and me to come by his place tonight. He didn't say much else, but it sounded important."

"I see," Matt said, the line growing quiet for a moment. Grayle didn't know exactly what that meant, but she could guess it wasn't good. Matt finally spoke. "Well... does that mean you're still coming to Florida for the Fourth of July weekend?"

"I think I can come by tomorrow," Grayle offered. "If you'll still have me?"

"Yeah, of course!" Matt said quickly. Maybe he wasn't as upset as she had originally thought. "Absolutely."

"Oh, good. I was afraid...," she cut off her own words. "So, I'll see you soon. Tomorrow!" Grayle said, ending the call with a sigh and a faint smile.

"To tomorrow," Matt replied happily.

She slipped the phone back into her pocket and headed inside to rejoin Phil.

In Florida, Matt leaned back in his chair, staring out his window with a heavy expression. Sunlight filtered through half-drawn blinds, casting slanted lines across his face and the polished floor. Something gnawed at him, an uncase he couldn't shake. After a long breath, he tapped his comm and placed another call. The screen flickered to life, its glow cutting through the room's late-morning stillness.

Alex answered, a smirk pulling at his mouth when he saw who it was. "Didn't think I'd be hearing from you again, hotshot," Alex said, amused before his tone turned cold. "Just what do you need, Matt?"

Matt hesitated. He didn't want to be making this call, but something inside him insisted. His fingers drummed briefly against the desk. "It's about Grayle," he said quietly.

Alex's smile faded instantly. "Go on," he said, his voice sharpening, his fear increasing.

"Director Douglas just paid her a visit," Matt explained. "She and Wells are meeting with him later tonight at his place before she comes here tomorrow. I don't know what it's about... but I thought you should know. I'll ask her about it when she gets here."

Alex's eyes narrowed, gears visibly turning in his mind. His posture stiffened as if bracing for news he didn't want to hear. "And... then you let me know," Alex replied tersely. "Thank you, Matt. Keep me posted."

The video feed cut out abruptly, the room falling into silence once more.

Alex turned toward Tim, who had been standing silently nearby, watching the exchange with an unreadable expression.

"Apparently, there's a secret meeting going on tonight with Richard, Grayle, and Wells," Alex said, his voice cold, edged with suspicion.

Tim's face darkened, the muscles in his jaw tightening. A shadow passed across his features, and for a long moment, he said nothing.

"I think it's time," Alex said, slamming a fist lightly into his palm. The sound echoed in the room like a final decision. "Time to end this nonsense. How do you want to approach it?"

Tim sat down slowly, leaning back in his chair and lacing his fingers behind his head. His eyes stared at the ceiling, lost in calculation, as if the answer might be written there.

"I don't know..." he said quietly, the words measured and slow. When he looked back down, his expression had hardened into resolve. "I want you to camp out near Dick's place. As soon as Grayle and Wells leave, let me know. I'll pay Wells a little visit. We'll find out what he learned."

"Very good," Alex said, already turning away to begin his preparations, his movements quick and mechanical.

Later that evening, Phil and Grayle approached Richard's secluded home on the Lower South Bay of Oneida Lake in upstate New York. The last light of sunset lingered along the horizon, casting long shadows across the wind-churned waters. The shoreline stretched wide and empty, with no neighbors within a mile on either side. The lake shimmered under the fading sun, its surface dancing with ripples as a breeze skimmed across.

A half-hour before their scheduled time, they touched down near a special landing pad Richard had installed, an open patch of shoreline about fifty yards from the house. The wind whipped across the water, sending waves slapping against the rocks with a rhythmic roar that echoed in the quiet.

The house was modest and unpretentious, a one-story ranch-style home Richard had built himself. From a distance, it seemed ordinary, almost deliberately plain, as if trying not to draw attention. As Grayle and Phil made their way up the drive, a figure stood waiting for them in the golden wash of porch light.

Grayle's heart leaped. She knew that figure anywhere. "Brian," she called out, breaking into a jog.

Her brother smiled and caught her in a tight embrace, his arms wrapping around her with the comfort of home.

"Hey, babe," B.J. said, his voice warm, like a familiar song on a tough day.

Grayle pulled back and laughed, surprised. "What are you doing here?"

"Same as you," B.J. replied, glancing toward the house. "Richard asked me to come. Said he had something important to tell us. Wouldn't say more."

He frowned slightly, his tone shifting to concern. "I don't know what's going on, but we'll find out soon enough."

Grayle turned to Phil, gesturing with a smile and a quick wave of her hand. "This is Phil Wells, my partner and the lead investigator for the Paranormal Department."

"Mr. Wells," B.J. said, offering his hand with a steady grip. "Nice to meet you, sir."

Phil shook it firmly. "Pleasure to meet you, Brian."

Before they could exchange more, Richard's voice called from the porch.

"All three of you are early! I love punctuality," he said, waving them toward the house. "C'mon in."

The trio made their way up to him, exchanging greetings before stepping inside. The screen door creaked slightly as it swung shut behind them.

Once inside, Richard shut the door with a quiet finality.

Phil took a quick, instinctive sweep of the interior. The house was open and uncluttered, with a small living room in the center, a simple dining table behind it, and a compact kitchen along the back wall. The walls gleamed with vibrant white paint, and the hardwood floors echoed lightly beneath their steps. Phil decided it was an odd look given the amount of space afforded him, but it was Richard's place, so what did he care?

A black leather couch and two matching chairs sat five feet from a neat, eight-chair dining table. Behind that stood a minimalist kitchen island, a few appliances, and cabinets pressed neatly against the back wall. To the left of the kitchen was a hallway that led to the bathroom and three bedrooms. Another door stood just beyond the hallway, but it was hard to discern what that was or where it led.

"Impressed with the layout, Mr. Wells?" Richard asked.

Phil grinned and nodded his manly approval. "Very basic. Just the way I like it."

Grayle laughed softly. "There's a little more to this place," she teased. "His den in the back is immaculate."

"Den?" Phil raised an eyebrow.

"Yes," Richard said, smiling faintly. "And there's a lot more to it, which I'm about to show you."

B.J. crossed his arms. "Been holding out on us, huh?"

"Follow me," Richard said, leading them toward the back.

Passing through a second door, they entered the den. It was a sprawling, windowless space nearly two thousand square feet in size.

The atmosphere shifted immediately: where the front of the house was bright and open, the den felt closed and deliberate. Paneled walls of rich, light-brown wood gave the room a warm, grounded feeling, almost like the inside of an old lodge or library.

A massive area rug stretched across the center, anchoring the space. To the right, a towering bookshelf lined the wall, crammed with old books, records, and artifacts. Centered against the far wall was a heavy executive desk, flanked by two guest chairs and a large, commanding chair behind it. Off to the right, a grand fireplace framed by two deep armchairs invited quiet conversations and reflection.

Phil's jaw tightened in surprise. "This is... quite the room," he said, awestruck.

For Grayle and B.J., the den was familiar, the hidden heart of Richard's home, a place of memories and family counsel. For Phil, however, it was the first glimpse behind Richard's polished public image.

B.J. shifted uncomfortably. "Alright," he said. "Why are we here, Richard?"

Richard took a long breath as if steadying himself. "There's something you two need to know," he said quietly. "Phil, you're here because I need an experienced investigator. I need help."

He paused, weighing his next words.

"I've been working on something —and I can't do it alone anymore. It concerns Alex and Tim. What I'm about to tell you and show you won't be easy to hear. But it's time you learned the truth."

Without waiting for a response, Richard walked to the far end of the den, where the area rug met the polished floor. Kneeling, he folded the rug back about four feet, revealing a concealed metal hatch set flush with the floorboards. Bending low, he pressed a hidden button on the frame.

With a soft, mechanical hiss, the door lifted, revealing a spiral staircase descending into the unknown.

Grayle and B.J. stared, thunderstruck. They had spent countless hours in this house growing up, and never once had they suspected this secret chamber existed.

Phil, by contrast, watched with keen interest, impressed by the craftsmanship and the clear layers of secrecy.

Richard turned back to them, his face grim. "Follow me," he said.

One by one, they made their way down the winding steps. The air grew cooler, the scent of concrete and cold steel replacing the warm wood of the house above.

At the bottom of the stairs, they stepped into a sprawling, stark underground bunker that looked very clean and clinical. The floors were bare concrete; the walls were reinforced, and bright white lights gleamed above. To the right stood an old-style interrogation room, windowless and ominous, and just beyond that, another heavy door led to an emergency exit, presumably opening onto the beach.

"Grab a seat," Richard said, pointing toward a row of chairs against the far wall.

"You're going to want to be sitting for this." His voice was so dark and somber that the weight of tension settled over them like a physical force.

"What's this all about?" B.J. demanded, his voice rising sharply as his impatience grew. He snapped and then quickly appeared to regret it. "What the hell is going on, Richard?"

Richard didn't flinch. He walked to a metal table near the center of the room, opened a nearby drawer, and pulled out a small, weathered box.

"I have reason to believe," Richard said carefully, "that Alex and Tim sabotaged the Intervention... killing all ten of its passengers. Including your parents. Back in 2206."

Silence crushed the room.

Grayle and B.J. looked at each other, stunned into paralysis. The breath seemed to leave their bodies all at once.

"I'm sorry for being blunt," Richard continued, sitting across from them, his voice heavy with regret. "I don't know any other way to say it. I've imagined this conversation for years... and none of the versions ever got easier."

Richard sat across from them and opened the box. "There was something off about Alex and Tim before that day; I could never put my finger on it. I thought they were losing their minds." Richard reached into the box and lifted out an object that seemed to shimmer faintly in the fluorescent light.

It was the Reverie Halo. He gently placed it on a nearby table.

Phil's eyes widened. He leaned forward slightly, captivated, an unspoken hunger glinting in his gaze.

"I have reason to believe," Richard said, placing his hand on the Halo and rubbing it gently like a relic, "that Alex and Tim experimented with this technology."

B.J. immediately shook his head. "That's impossible. They would never do that. They know the risks. Everyone does. No way they were that stupid."

"I thought the same thing," Richard said softly. "But Alex gave this to me a long time ago. Asked me to keep it safe because he knew I wanted nothing to do with it. I didn't think much of it at the time... but soon after, I started noticing changes. Subtle at first. Then undeniable."

Richard lifted the device, stared at it for a haunting second, then returned it to the table. "They..." he waved his hand as if searching for the proper word. "They became unstable. Paranoid. Violent."

Grayle finally found her voice. "I have to say I'm with B.J.. Why? Why would they even mess with something like that?"

Richard leaned back, choosing his words carefully. "After the failed test launch of the Elevation, when Alex's dream of achieving mass acceleration collapsed, he spiraled. Badly. He became despondent."

"I remember that day," Phil said, frowning. "Tiny puncture in the hull. It could've happened to anyone. Small piece of debris..." his voice fell off.

Richard nodded. "True. But Alex couldn't accept it. Especially when Britain upgraded their shuttle designs based on his research. It wasn't about exploration anymore. It was about pride. About being first." He looked down for a moment, then added, "That kind of pride blinds you. Makes you do things you never thought possible. I remember him repeatedly saying that it 'needs to be him,' and 'they're going to beat me to it.'"

Richard shook his head sadly. "I think that Alex saw this as a competition. A competition that flew in the face of everything the Norn had taught us. Unity. Togetherness. That was their mantra. We can achieve everything together." Richard shook his head in disgust. "I don't think it was good enough for Alex. He couldn't be outdone. His obsession started to take hold. And that's where the Reverie Halo comes into play." He gestured again to the device on the table. "I believe he used it, hoping to amplify his abilities. Hoping to outpace everyone else. But instead, it consumed him."

Phil leaned forward in his chair, the glint of professional curiosity sharp in his eyes.

"And Tim?"

Richard exhaled slowly. "Tim's always been a follower. Loyal to a fault. Especially to Alex. Whatever Alex wants, Tim will back him without question."

B.J. shook his head in disbelief. "Wait, wait, wait. None of this is making any sense."

"I know," Richard said. His voice was grim. "But it's the truth." Richard grimly continued, "I'm aware that they went on to develop that liquid metal. They claimed it was to help the Intervention achieve acceleration and structural stability during takeoff." He looked at each of them. "But what do I really think? I think they made it to contain the blast." He reached for the console and added, "If you'll allow it, I'd like to show you the footage from that day."

Grayle glanced around the room and then gave a hesitant nod. "Go on."

Her voice was soft, reluctant. The last thing she wanted was to relive the trauma of the explosion, but she needed to know what was hidden in those final moments. What they'd missed. What they were never meant to see.

Richard pushed a few buttons. The lights in the room dimmed, and a hidden screen descended from the ceiling with a low mechanical hum. The footage began, grainy at first, then sharpened as it stabilized.

"Alright," Richard narrated. "This is right before takeoff. Here, Alex is passing the checkpoint. Nothing suspicious. He boards the ship." The screen showed Alex greeting several crew members, then pausing to speak with Grayle and Brian's parents. The image was bittersweet, a mundane moment now laced with a heavy sense of finality. "He turns to leave," Richard continued. "But then, watch this... he stops."

The video showed Alex pausing mid-step, glancing toward a corridor.

"He turns toward the propulsion room," Richard said, his voice tightening. "He disappears out of frame for twenty-seven seconds. Then he re-emerges and walks off the ship."

Richard hit pause.

"We couldn't get any footage from inside the propulsion room. Our cameras never worked around those engines, too much magnetic interference. But Alex was the last person seen near them before the explosion."

He didn't need to say what came next. The three of them already knew.

"I'm not going to replay that part," Richard said quietly. "You've both seen it enough."

The screen faded to black, and silence filled the room.

"The explosion originated in the propulsion room," Richard said, his voice low and haunted. "The very same one Alex walked into. And I stood next to him and Tim when the Intervention exploded. I saw their faces. Not a single ounce of remorse." His sadness twisted into something sharper - anger barely held in check. "They didn't even flinch."

He turned back to them, more resolute now. "That day wasn't just a tragedy. It was calculated. And it didn't end there."

Richard stepped to a nearby terminal and tapped through several files. "Twenty-one people have disappeared over the last seventeen years," he said. "Twenty of them were on-site that day. Ground crew, tower staff, security. All vanished. Quietly. Without a trace."

Grayle gave a short, sharp gasp and then tensed.

"My belief is this," Richard continued. "Those people either worked with Alex and Tim, or they knew something. Something they weren't supposed to. And Alex made sure they were silenced." He brought up another file. "And then, shortly after the Intervention catastrophe, Alex assembled a private team, eight individuals handpicked to 'continue the mission.'"

He let out a bitter laugh.

"The global community had already suspended deep-space trials. Or so Alex was told. In reality, the NU and the Space Explorers had voted to remove him entirely. They didn't trust his leadership or his judgment. So, they told him the program was on indefinite hiatus. It was their way of quietly cutting him out... under the guise of letting him save face while keeping the world safe."

Richard turned off the screen and let the weight of his words settle.

"But he didn't step back. He doubled down. And everything that followed... traces back to that choice and the Reverie Halo." Richard walked over to a secure cabinet, opened it, and pulled out another device; sleek, black, no larger than a foot long and a quarter inch thick. It resembled an ancient computer tablet, yet it emitted a hum that held an eerie alien quality.

"This," Richard said, holding it up, "was given to me by the Norn. Right before they left Earth to deal with... whatever crisis summoned them away. It's a data reader. Designed to interact with the Halo."

"The Norn?" Phil asked, eyebrows raising high. "You've been in contact with them?"

"Briefly," Richard said. "They realized, albeit too late, that they might have introduced something dangerous by leaving the Halo behind. Before they departed, they gave me this and taught me how to use it."

He set the device carefully on the table, its surface sleek and black against the gray concrete.

"I'll put it in layman's terms. The Halo records data... but it doesn't play back memories like a movie. It stores... experiences. This device transcribes them. Converts them into readable information."

Phil's eyes practically gleamed. His mind was spinning with thoughts of how he might use this opportunity to access unfiltered, undeniable proof of the paranormal.

Brian and Grayle, on the other hand, clung to each other, their hands tightly intertwined. Both looked on, half dreading, half desperate to know what would be revealed.

Richard placed the Halo flat atop the alien device. There was a soft mechanical chime, and then a side panel slid open with an audible hiss, revealing alien symbols scrolling in rapid succession.

"I can't read any of this," Richard muttered. "They only showed me how to turn it on and off." He offered a hollow chuckle, but nobody in the room was laughing. They wanted answers. Finally, he continued. "Alright," he said, pressing another button. "I'll..."

A soft blue light pulsed from the device's core, forming flickering words that hung in midair like a shimmering hologram.

"Here's what it pulled from Alex."

The glowing letters shifted and organized into English. Richard read them out loud as they appeared in a column of data.

Alex Belle Data:

- Lawman — Died on the Oregon Trail, 1800s.
- Scientist — Worked with J. Robert Oppenheimer during the Manhattan Project.
- Astronaut— Died during the Challenger disaster.

"This..." Richard barked, slapping the table lightly. "This right here! I think this is where he got the idea for the Intervention."

Grayle and B.J. sat stiffly, absorbing every word.

"The rest of his incarnations? Honestly? Pretty unspectacular," Richard continued. "Tim, however? Tim, you need to worry about."

The light shifted again.

Tim Stevens' Data:

- Marshall — Killed in a gunfight in the 1800s.
- Soldier — Fought in both World Wars and Vietnam.
- Expert marksman.
- Serial killer — Rob Anthony

Richard hesitated before reading the final line. "But here's where it gets dark." He steadied himself before speaking. "Serial killer, Rob Anthony." He faced the group with a heavy gaze. "In the 2010s, Tim lived as Rob Anthony, a prolific serial killer. He was never caught and probably would never have been identified... except... he died in a car crash while disposing of his last victim."

Richard paused to gauge their reactions. The air seemed heavier now. Dense with the horror creeping into the room.

"He had this sick habit," Richard said, voice low. "He would call the victims' families... play a song on the phone... then hang up. That was the last connection they'd ever have with their loved one, and it was hardly pleasant." He cleared his throat roughly, pushing through the weight of the memory. "Rob Anthony died when a tractor-trailer hit his car. He was most likely transporting the last body. The police investigated for a long time, thinking that was the case, but sadly, there was no evidence. Just speculation. They did DNA analysis, but nothing could link Rob Anthony to the other victim in the car. Her name was..."

Grayle leaned in and squinted toward the bottom of the holographic screen, where more information had begun to form. "Hold on," she said, pointing. "That name. At the bottom."

With a quick spread of his thumb and forefinger, Richard enlarged the image. The letters glowed larger, more distinct:

Bridgette O'Hanlon.

The room went ice-cold. Phil looked at Grayle.

Grayle's breath caught in her chest. A tingling sensation washed over her skin as if her very soul had been stirred. She remembered what that angelic... whatever it was had said, "Bridgette. She waits. She won't move on without you. Choose between your love or your vengeance. You cannot have both. Let go."

She gave the slightest shake of her head. Half denial, half disbelief encompassed her. Making eye contact with Phil, she barely managed to whisper, "Nah."

Richard, sensing the overwhelming shift in mood, quietly turned the lights back on to dim, keeping the atmosphere subdued.

"You get the idea now," he said grimly. "Tim... he's the real danger. Alex? He's just a man consumed by ambition. But Tim? Tim is something else entirely."

A soft click echoed down the spiral staircase. Already on edge with heightened emotion, all three heads turned and spun around as a woman slowly descended into the hidden room. She moved with caution, but also with a weary sort of grace, as if each step carried the burden of long-held secrets.

Richard stepped toward her. "You can come down now."

The woman reached the floor and stood before them, offering a faint but steady smile.

"Hello. I'm Addison Heinz," she said, her voice calm but marked by exhaustion. Grayle, B.J., and Phil nodded in acknowledgment, though no one quite knew what to expect next.

"I worked with Alex and Tim," Addison continued, her eyes flickering to Grayle and B.J. "I was one of the eight."

Tension crackled in the air. Grayle and B.J. immediately stiffened, instinctively moving closer together, protective and wary.

Richard caught the shift and quickly interjected, his voice gentle. "Go on, Addison. It's alright. You're among friends now."

But Addison didn't miss the skeptical glances from the siblings. She turned to face them fully. "I don't trust them," she said plainly, giving a slight nod in Grayle and B.J.'s direction.

"Hey," B.J. said, his voice hardening as his hands lifted in calm protest. "We're just hearing this for the first time. I'm a Defender. I've sworn to protect this planet and the people in it against whoever it might be. No matter what. If Alex and Tim are doing something... something nefarious... I'll put a stop to it."

Grayle nodded firmly beside her brother, sitting tall and unflinching.

Richard gave a faint, approving smile. "That's exactly why you're here, young man," he said.

Addison relaxed just slightly at the response, then leaned back against the wall as though steadying herself. The light in her eyes dimmed, shadowed by whatever she was about to share.

"There's a lot you need to know," she said. "And not all of it is easy to tell."

"Look," Grayle replied. "We need to know if those two are responsible for the death of our parents and the other eight crew members."

Addison took a deep breath, bracing herself. "Okay. There's not much I can tell you about what we did when we were with them. Even though we were supposed to be a team, they kept everything compartmentalized. We ran flight simulators, did analysis, and assembled equipment... but we were never told what it was really for. Pieces. Fragments. Nothing ever added up. And we were all off the grid. It was all covert." She sighed. "Looking back... that's probably the way they wanted it, fragmented so no one saw the entire picture."

"What got you involved with them in the first place?" Phil asked, interrupting her gently.

She shook her head slowly, as if still trying to make sense of it herself. "It felt... exciting at first. Important. They said it was a top-secret mission, that the Norn had entrusted them with something revolutionary, and we were their conduits."

Phil's expression tightened. His mind was racing ahead, already lining up questions.

"You said you were off the grid. How did you manage that?" he asked.

Addison folded her arms tightly across her chest, her jaw rigid. "They had the tech for that, too. The Norn gave it to them. We could disable the tracking implants that everyone had. At first, it felt freeing, not being constantly monitored by AI, not having our every move cataloged." She paused, her gaze drifting toward the floor. "In hindsight... it would've been better if we had been trackable. Maybe someone would've noticed sooner if something went wrong."

Phil leaned in a little closer, sensing Addison's guilt. "So why come forward now?" he asked softly.

Addison's voice grew even quieter, almost hollow. "Owen Stipe. Paul Lamb. Scott Sims. Michael Wilson, the reporter. All dead. One single night. And it was likely Alex and Tim who did it."

Phil's eyebrows lifted slightly. "Likely?" he echoed.

Addison nodded grimly. "Owen had gotten into trouble with them. He broke ranks and visited family. His mother, specifically. Someone snapped a photo. Michael Wilson picked up the story. Once it hit the airwaves, Owen's cover was blown. We were supposed to be OTG — off the grid." She closed her eyes for a moment before continuing. "Alex and Tim were furious. They called us all together and threatened us. They told us that if we jeopardized the mission, there would be consequences, not just with them, but with the Norn as well. No one understood how far they'd go... until Owen was murdered. Then Scott and Paul disappeared on the island."

The room fell into a tense silence. Even Richard stood stiffly now, his face unreadable.

Phil broke the moment. "Why the extreme measures? Why kill their own team?"

Addison shrugged helplessly. "I don't know. I honestly don't. They talked about the importance of secrecy all the time, but it felt like... something more. Paranoia. Fear. Maybe even pleasure."

She looked down at her hands, her knuckles white from clenching. "I should have seen it coming."

Phil pressed further, his voice steady but urgent. "Did you ever try to leave?"

Addison gave a short, bitter laugh. "They told us we could leave anytime. 'No questions asked,' they said. It was a lie. We were free to travel, free to live like kings, but the second Owen stepped outside their little world... he was dead within days."

"And you?" Phil asked. "You stayed."

Her next words came out in a whisper. "I stayed because... I was in a relationship with Tim."

That admission sent a ripple through the room.

Phil sat forward, his voice softening. "How serious was it?" he asked.

Addison exhaled slowly, steadying herself before answering. "I loved him," she said simply. "Or... I thought I did. In the beginning, he was charming and magnetic. He made me feel like I was part of something bigger than any of us." Her voice hardened. "But the longer it went on, the more it changed. He started to scare the hell out of me."

Phil frowned, concerned. "How?" he continued, his tone careful.

Addison glanced at Richard, then back at the group, as if weighing how much to say.

"He would talk about death like it was an old friend. Casual. Almost nostalgic. He'd recount the ways he died in past lives – always violently. Always proudly. He described combat deaths, executions, even... killings he committed himself." She paused. "Even when he killed women. He would just blurt these things out. It felt like I was living with a paranoid schizophrenic half the time. On other days, he was sweet and attentive. Normal. It was like flipping a coin. You never knew which Tim you were going to get."

She paused, then added with a dry laugh, "In school, I used to wonder how people got sucked into cults. I took classes in it, psychology, and history. I thought I was immune to that kind of manipulation. Then one day I woke up and realized... maybe I wasn't."

The confession hung in the room like smoke, thick and hard to breathe.

Phil spoke carefully. "Where are the others now? The rest of the team?"

Addison shook her head. "I don't know exactly. They're somewhere safe. Off the grid for real this time. The less I know, the better... for all of us."

Richard cut in, his tone emphatic. "And for their protection, that's how it needs to stay."

Phil nodded, understanding the weight of what he was hearing. "Fine. I agree. As long as you're safe."

Addison gave a small, tired smile. "For now, we are. But we're not taking any more chances. Once we walk away tonight, we're gone. For good."

Phil leaned back in his chair, rubbing his chin thoughtfully. "Let's put it all together," he said slowly, glancing between Grayle, Brian, and Addison. He stood and began to pace, gathering the threads aloud. "Alex failed in his attempt with the Intervention test flight. Instead of seeing it for what it was, a minor setback, he internalized it as a personal failure. His obsession with achievement... it grew into something dangerous." He stopped and looked at Richard. "He and Tim, desperate to regain an edge, experimented with the Halo. Knowing full well the risks – the psychotic breaks, the distortion of mind and spirit – they still went ahead. Believing, maybe, that they could somehow control it. Use it to outsmart the rest of the world."

Richard nodded grimly. "Exactly."

Phil continued, the words gaining momentum now. "Their jealousy and ambition twisted into something darker. On the day of the

Intervention launch, they sabotaged the ship and murdered all ten crew members, including Grayle and Brian's parents. Then, to cover their tracks, they orchestrated the quiet disappearance of anyone who might've known or suspected too much."

Richard crossed his arms tightly. "And if anyone tried to leave their circle... well, we know what happened to Owen, Paul, and Scott."

"And Michael Wilson," Grayle added softly, anger sharpening her voice.

Phil nodded heavily. "Yes. And Michael."

Richard jumped back in. "I had Stan Collins following Tim. Even though they couldn't find any evidence to support it, I firmly believe that Tim killed Stan and then threw him from that five-story window."

The room fell into a moment of heavy silence. Only the hum of the hidden equipment filled the void. Richard weighed their lack of response and then continued. "Alex and Tim are dangerous. They're not just misguided, they're lethal."

Grayle's fists clenched. "So why don't we just arrest them? Bring them in?"

Richard and Phil exchanged a long, knowing look, then Richard nodded at him. "You're an experienced investigator. What's your professional take, Mr. Wells?"

Phil answered slowly, measuring each word. "Conjecture," he said bluntly. "That's all we have. Suspicion. Circumstantial evidence. Compelling, yes, but not enough. Not legally. In court, it would fall apart. Worse," he looked at Grayle seriously, "it would make us look unstable. Reckless. We could lose everything. Our positions, our credibility. Maybe even our freedom."

He ticked off the points with his fingers: "Alex cleared security checkpoints before boarding the shuttle. Nothing suspicious about him. The sabotage, if it happened, left no direct evidence. No smoking gun. Owen Stipe's murder? Long-range shot, no fingerprints, no weapon found. The incident at Beaver Island that Addison brought up? No bodies. No proof. Buffalo? No forensic evidence tying Tim to

Stan's murder." Phil shook his head in frustration and shrugged. "We have a theory. A strong one. But without hard evidence," he spread his hands helplessly, "we have nothing."

Richard nodded grimly. "That's why I brought you here. That's why I need help. I can't do this alone anymore."

It was just past 1 a.m. when Richard walked his guests to the door. The night air was still. The lake behind the house stretched out in calm, glassy silence, catching reflections of the stars like a mirror to the sky. A light breeze rustled the trees, but otherwise, everything was quiet.

Richard exhaled and turned to face them, his shoulders hunched under the weight of what he'd just shared. "Thank you all for coming," he said. His voice was low and worn. "I know I just unloaded a lot on you tonight. Four hours straight... Geeze. I'm sorry. I wish there were a better way to do it."

None of them responded right away. It wasn't necessary. The fatigue on his face said more than his words. His posture was sagging, his eyes heavy; not from lack of sleep, but from the burden he'd been carrying for far too long.

Brian stepped forward, answering first. His tone was steady and full of quiet conviction. "You can count on me."

"Me too," Grayle said, offering a faint smile. She gave Richard a quick hug, her hand resting briefly on his shoulder before pulling back. "I always hated Tim anyway."

Richard turned to Phil, who had been standing silently through the exchange.

"What do you say, Mr. Wells?"

Phil met his eyes, calm but resolute. "Everyone already thinks I'm crazy, so let's do the right thing. Let's rein these two in."

Richard let out a slow breath, visibly relieved. His shoulders loosened just slightly.

"Very good. Thank you. Get some rest over the weekend. Come back in a couple of days, and we'll strategize. We'll come up with a plan."

Brian glanced up with a nod toward the house. "What about Addison?"

"She's staying here tonight," Richard replied. "She'll lie low tomorrow, then leave. After that, you won't see her until this is all over. Now, if you'll excuse me... I'm going to jump on my boat and cruise for a bit."

He gave them a nod, then turned toward the dock that stretched out into the lake, his figure soon swallowed by the shadows along the water's edge.

The three of them turned toward their transports parked out front. The night felt colder, as if the air had shifted just slightly.

Grayle glanced sideways at the two men. "Either of you hungry?"

"Sure, I could eat," Brian said, rubbing his hands together and giving a half-shrug.

"I'm good," Phil replied, already stepping toward his vehicle. "But I could use a stiff drink. Let's head back to my place. There's an all-night diner right around the corner. You two can grab something to eat there and then come over."

"Sounds good," Grayle replied. "I'll ride with my brother and then catch up with you later." Grayle gave Phil a small wave.

"See you in a bit," Phil called over his shoulder as he made his way to his shuttle. He waved as he taxied away and then took off, lifting silently into the air and vanishing into the dark.

Grayle and Brian climbed into the Osprey-like transport that Brian had arrived in, and their vehicle followed, coasting low over the tree-tops.

Grayle gave a whistle of approval when she climbed in. "Nice ride, brother!"

B.J. just smiled. "Yeah, perks of the job. I convinced them to let me borrow it for the evening."

Once they were airborne, Grayle turned in her seat to look at him. "Well? What do you think, B.J.?"

Brian shook his head, eyes fixed on the horizon ahead. "I don't know what to make of it. It's a lot, and he can't hide how troubled and confused it's made him. I don't want to jump to conclusions, not without proof, real proof, but this all feels like a conspiracy within the Space Explorers, grudges, rivalries… old ghosts."

Grayle nodded slowly, processing the same thoughts. "Well, if they're as skilled as Richard says, we might be in over our heads."

Brian gave a quiet, dry chuckle. "That's for sure."

They lapsed into silence. The hum of the craft was the only sound as the sky began to lighten faintly along the edges. The soft glow on the horizon hinted at morning's approach, though night still clung stubbornly to the world below.

After a few minutes, Brian spoke again. "We need to leave Tash out of this. She's not cut out for it."

"I agree," Grayle said. "But if we find something? We'll have to tell her eventually. She deserves to know. If Alex and Tim are really that dangerous, she could be in trouble, too."

"Uncle Will's always watching out for her, so there's comfort in knowing that she's safe with him," Brian said.

Grayle gave him a doubtful glance. "Yeah, but is she? I mean, safe?"

Brian didn't answer. He just exhaled and gave a slow, tired shrug.

After more silent flying, they were landing in front of a small, all-night diner tucked just off the main road near Phil's neighborhood. The place looked like it hadn't changed in decades – neon signs buzzing, chrome accents still glinting under dim lighting, and a faint hum from an old refrigeration unit leaking out the back. The only thing that screamed modernism was the vehicles, the high-end transports, and the shuttles parked along the streets and parking areas. All very sleek, they outclassed the cars of days gone by. Or at least their owners thought so. Grayle and Brian exited their shuttle, walked to the entrance, and went inside. The chime above the door rang softly as they entered.

The air inside smelled like coffee, grease, and nostalgia. A soft jazz track played in the background as they slid into a corner booth beneath a hanging light that flickered faintly. The place was mostly empty except for a lone trucker seated at the counter and an old couple sharing a piece of pie two booths down.

For several long minutes, neither spoke. Finally, the AI waiter approached them and gave a friendly nod as it projected a glowing menu into the space between them.

They just sat there, tired, heavy, scrolling through the menu options more out of habit than hunger, when a soft *bing* occurred on Grayle's comm. She lifted her wrist to look at the message. Grayle finally broke the silence. "Phil's already home. I just got a message. He's into the bourbon."

The two of them touched their orders on the menu, and it quickly disappeared.

Brian smiled faintly. "He's a good man, isn't he?"

"He is," she agreed.

He looked at her for a moment before adding, "And you're doing the right thing. Even if people don't understand."

Grayle offered him a grateful smile. "I'm no closer to figuring anything out. The dreams, the experiences — it's all still a mystery. But it's real. There's more to this world than we're allowed to see."

"I believe you," Brian said without hesitation and a positive shrug.

"Yeah, well, you're one of the few," Grayle muttered, glancing away.

Brian leaned forward, folding his hands. "You remember when Grandma and Grandpa used to sit with you during your nightmares?"

Grayle nodded faintly. "Vaguely."

"One night, I overheard them in the kitchen. I was sneaking around when I wasn't supposed to be up. They said they swore they saw something. They didn't say what, but they were freaked out for days after. The point is, I think you're right where you're supposed to be. Mom and Dad always said our paths would come to us. I think this is yours."

Her eyes softened. The warmth in her chest had nothing to do with the booth's heater. "Thank you. That means a lot."

The AI waiter returned with their orders, and Grayle took that moment to stand and give a half-hearted smile. "Bathroom break."

As she left, Brian nodded and sipped his coffee, watching her disappear down the hallway. The music shifted to a slower tune, something old and smoky. He closed his eyes for a second, just to reset.

When Grayle returned, they lingered for a few more minutes and picked at their food. She teased Brian about a girl he'd been dating – light banter, the kind only a sister could get away with – and Brian deflected as best he could, grinning despite himself.

Eventually, Grayle glanced at her watch. "We should head to Phil's. We've been here almost forty minutes."

"Yeah," Brian said, sliding out of the booth. "Let's go." He touched the comm device on his wrist to a small kiosk on the table that read PAY HERE, and when it confirmed his purchase, they got up and left.

They stepped out into the cool night air. The sky had darkened again, cloud cover creeping in. The streets were still and quiet as they made their way back to the shuttle.

Grayle's wrist buzzed.

She glanced down casually.

She froze.

Her body stiffened.

Her eyes went wide.

"What?" Brian offered up the concerned query.

She turned her wrist so he could see the screen.

A single message glowed: **WE'RE IN DANGER! DON'T COME BACK HERE! GET TO A SAFE PLACE!**

Grayle's breath caught, and she spoke softly, but with urgency, "Oh my God. B.J.! Phil's in trouble! What do we do?!"

Brian's voice was already hardened. "We go help him!"

They ran to the shuttle and jumped in, the engines igniting with a sharp whir before Grayle could even pull her door shut. Within seconds, they launched into the air, heading full speed toward Phil's home, unaware of what awaited them in the night.

"What kind of weapons do you have onboard?" Grayle asked, scanning the compartment for options.

"Three stun guns with a seventy-five-yard range," Brian replied, reaching behind the seat and tossing her one.

"That'll do," she nodded.

"It's going to have to," Brian muttered, eyes narrowing on the nav display. "I didn't anticipate being in a spot like this."

Within a few minutes, they approached a quiet street nestled in a pocket of old, middle-class suburbia. The noise and the wind current that the transport brought with it were enough to rattle the windows, but they landed in a field two streets over, hoping for some discretion, but certain that there wasn't time for that.

Quickly scanning a live satellite overlay of the surrounding blocks, Brian pointed to the route to Phil's neighborhood.

Lined with modest, single-family homes and aging trees that cast wide shadows under the streetlights, Phil's house sat at the center of a cul-de-sac. It was a pale, weathered structure with a low roof and ivy creeping across the brick façade. A second street ran behind the lot, offering a rear exit. His driveway and garage were tucked along the left side.

"Okay, we're here on the next block over. I'm sure our arrival announced us to everyone, but if we're careful, we can make our way through the back. Do you remember your training?" he asked, looking over at his sister as if she were a cadet just out of school. Which, compared to him, she was.

"I do," Grayle said without hesitation.

Brian killed the engine of the shuttle, and they stepped out into the night. The sound of the doors closing seemed too loud, but what could be louder than their arrival? Brian motioned toward a group of trees, and Grayle soon followed. If anyone was looking for them, maybe they could evade them here first.

After a quick scan of their surroundings, Brian motioned for Grayle to follow him. Every motion from then on was precise and deliberate. They kept to the shadows, slipping through a neighbor's yard, cutting across damp grass and low shrubs that clung to their legs. The night had grown heavier, more oppressive, as if it sensed what was about to unfold.

Phil's house glowed ahead like a beacon, every light inside blazing unnaturally bright against the stillness of the neighborhood. It looked less like someone had left the lights on and more like someone had turned them on intentionally — as if to say, *"Look here."*

They crouched behind a thick maple tree in the yard behind his, the bark rough against their backs.

Brian kneeled, and Grayle followed suit, both low to the ground. He leaned in, voice hushed and tense. "We're roughly thirty yards from that back door. You go up the right side, I'll take the left. We meet in front."

Grayle gave a single nod. Her heart pounded against her ribs. Adrenaline coursed through her veins, buzzing in her ears, making every sound sharper, every breath louder. But before either of them could move, the rear door to Phil's house opened.

A figure emerged. Cloaked in black, face hidden behind a sleek tactical mask, the stranger looked like something out of a covert war zone. The figure stepped out carefully, shutting the door behind them with near-silent precision. Then, as if sensing something behind them, the head tilted ever so slightly.

The movement was chilling in its deliberateness.

Without a word or warning, the figure broke into a sprint, veering hard to the left, fast and smooth like a shadow caught in motion.

"How the hell?" Brian barked, startled by the sudden flight. "I'm going to pursue! Clear the house!"

He was gone in an instant, vanishing into the dark after the suspect with a fluid urgency that showed his training.

Grayle gritted her teeth, steadied her nerves, and focused her breathing. She wasn't comfortable with her brother leaving her alone, not in a situation like this, but she shoved the fear down. Her fingers tightened around the grip of the stun gun. She turned toward the back door, jaw set, heart hammering.

Each footstep was measured and silent as she opened the door once more and slipped through the threshold, gun drawn, senses sharpened to a knife's edge.

The kitchen was dim and eerily still. A faint hum from the refrigerator was the only sound. Something was off. The silence wasn't natural; it was *constructed*. Intentional.

She moved like a shadow, sweeping the space with methodical care. Every corner held weight. A narrow hallway opened to her right, leading to the living room. Another branched left, lined with closed doors. Bedrooms.

Grayle paused at the corner, heart pounding so hard she feared it would give her away. She crouched low, steadied her weapon, and turned sharply into the living room, ready to fire...

Phil was there.

Slumped on the couch.

A dark bloom soaked through his shirt, glistening, spreading like ink across the fabric. It flowed freely from a wound in his chest, vivid and final.

Her breath caught.

He had already bled out.

She froze, just for a moment, paralyzed by the sight. Then she backed hard against the wall, mouth open, fighting back the rising bile in her throat. Her stomach turned in knots. The shot had been recent, minutes old. Whoever killed him had done it just before she arrived.

The fleeing figure... they had just missed him.

"NO!" she shouted, a strangled cry of grief and horror, but quickly clamped her hand over her mouth. She still had to clear the rest of the house. She couldn't afford to break, not now.

One by one, she opened doors with agonizing caution.

First, the bathroom on the right... empty. Tiled and still.

Then, the bedroom to the left... clear. Bed untouched. Nothing disturbed.

Finally, the last door. She peeked in, heart thudding.

Nothing.

The house was empty.

She returned to the living room, feet heavy, and stood in silence, staring at the scene. The blood had soaked through the fabric and pooled on the hardwood floor beneath the couch. The shot had gone straight through the heart. There was no chance of survival, no time for painkillers or farewells. It was swift. Cold.

A crash split the silence.

The front door burst inward, slamming against the wall.

Grayle screamed and dropped to a crouch, weapon raised and shaking.

"It's me!" Brian shouted, breathless, backing up with his hands raised.

He stepped forward, his face collapsing as soon as he saw Phil's body. His expression crumpled in a way that made him look ten years older in an instant.

"No... no..." he muttered, hands going to his head as he hunched forward in anguish. "Oh no..."

Grayle's voice cracked as she shouted, "What happened to the guy with the mask?"

"He got away!" Brian said, gasping. "I lost track of whoever it was. Too quick, too fast. They must've had a transport waiting nearby. They vanished like smoke!"

Grayle began sobbing. The full weight of the moment crashed in all at once. The adrenaline turned to helpless grief. Brian dropped to the floor with her, wrapping his arms around her as she shook with sobs.

"We need to call Richard!" she cried. "Right now!"

Brian nodded and pulled up his comm device, his hands trembling.

Richard answered on the first ring. "Hey, Brian. What's up?"

"We need you at Phil Wells's house, right now. He's been murdered!" Brian shouted, voice breaking under the weight of what he'd just said.

There was silence on the line, long enough to feel like a vacuum.

"Oh. My. God," Richard finally replied. "Alright. Ping your location. I'll be there as fast as I can. I'm alerting the Defenders in that area now. I'll have them there right away!"

Grayle buried her face into her brother's shoulder and cried a million horrible tears. It wasn't just sorrow; it was injustice. Fear. Rage.

Brian disconnected the call and held her tighter.

***

Within moments, Defender units began to arrive. Black armored vehicles pulled into the cul-de-sac like a swarm of hornets, engines growling. If the neighbors weren't alerted by Brian and Grayle's arrival, they were now. The ruckus was monumental, lights flashing, sirens low but persistent.

Neighbors poured out onto their porches, drawn by the chaos. Richard's transport screeched to a halt across the lawn, its headlights slicing through the dark. Residents from all directions emerged, approaching Phil's yard like zombies from a B-movie, hair disheveled, faces blank, clad in robes and pajama pants. Except now, in a distinctly modern twist, they held up their phones to film instead of merely watching.

"Secure the fucking perimeter," Richard barked to his men, waving his hand with sharp urgency. "Get these people back and off this lawn. C'mon, you monsters!"

He didn't wait for an answer. He stormed toward the house.

Inside, the Philadelphia field commander was already coordinating.

"You're Captain Olm, correct?" Richard asked, stepping into the room.

"Yes, Director."

"What've you discovered so far?"

"The S-3 security cams were offline. The home AI was completely dismantled. We've got nothing inside. We're gathering footage from neighboring houses and speaking to the residents. So far, we've captured the Mackeys approaching from the rear and another figure exiting after them. No tracking device. The person just vanished. No sign where he went."

Olm gestured toward the front window, where a small, round hole shattered the glass, spiderwebbing outward.

"Also, our preliminary review of the body shows that he took one shot, not close range, but maybe about fifty-five yards out." Captain Olm pointed in the direction of the broken window where the shot had originated, then back to Phil. "Poor guy got it straight through the heart."

"Sniper shot," Richard said grimly, eyes narrowing.

"We believe the shooter took the shot from the front, then entered the house. Possibly to search for something. But there's no sign that anything was taken. After that, they exited through the rear just before running into your agents. Then poof. Gone. I don't know what else to say, sir. Whoever it was must have had more than one escape route. I just don't know what to say."

"No signs of an accomplice?" Richard asked, his tone cold and analytical, though his mind seemed elsewhere, processing, calculating.

"None so far. We'll see what the neighbor cams tell us."

Richard placed a hand on the captain's shoulder. "Good work, Captain. Let me know if anything else comes up."

After leaving the Captain, Richard stepped back outside into the chaos. The lights from squad cars painted the trees in flashing reds and blues. Grayle and Brian sat side by side on the front lawn, too shaken to speak. Their faces were pale and distant.

"I want you both to get out of here," Richard said quietly, voice heavy with emotion.

"I have my shuttle nearby," Brian replied, tone flat. "We'll be safe." He swallowed hard, then his voice rose suddenly, his face contorting with grief and rage. "Just what the fuck did you get us into, Richard?"

A single tear slipped down Richard's cheek. He turned his face away, shame bleeding into his silence. "I'm sorry."

Grayle stared at him. Her voice came out low and cold, drained of all warmth.

"Phil deserved better than apologies."

Miles away, deep in the woods, far from the chaos and noise, a sleek airborne vehicle touched down on a bed of dead leaves. The forest was silent. The craft hissed softly as it shut down, exhaling like some predator curling into rest.

The side door opened.

The masked assailant stepped out.

He pulled the mask off.

Tim.

His jaw clenched, muscles twitching. His eyes darted in every direction, wide with adrenaline and fury. His hands were shaking. Not from fear, but from the high of what he'd done.

His comm device crackled.

Alex's voice came through, calm and icy.

"Did you learn anything?"

"Yes!" Tim snapped angrily. "Fucking Addison is at Richard's house right now!"

"Calm yourself," Alex replied smoothly. "I'm about eight miles from the house, just hanging out. I'll keep an eye out."

"Do that. I'm on my way to you."

"And Wells?" Alex asked, his tone emotionless.

"Dead," Tim said simply.

"See you soon," Alex replied.

The line went dead.

Chapter 21: Brutality

It was just after 8 a.m. when Richard returned home. The door shut behind him with a quiet click that echoed too loudly in the silence of the empty house. The sound lingered, bouncing off the walls like a memory. He stood there momentarily, still wearing last night's suit, its collar loose and wrinkled, his hair disheveled from wind, stress, and grief. He looked like a man who had crossed some invisible threshold and left a piece of himself behind.

Moving without thinking, he headed into the kitchen as if on autopilot. The scent of stale coffee clung to the air, bitter and faint. Sunlight filtered weakly through the blinds, casting pale bars of gold across the table like prison slats. He pulled out a chair and sat down slowly as if the weight of his body was suddenly too much for his legs to bear. His heavy sigh spoke volumes, and he leaned forward, bracing his elbows on the table. He rubbed his eyes with the palms of his hands, but nothing helped. Nothing could eliminate the pressure, the stress, the exhaustion. Something inside was breaking.

Footsteps creaked softly on the hardwood floor behind him, and Addison appeared in the doorway, still in the clothes she'd worn the night before. Her face was pale, her lips drawn, but her eyes held concern. She stepped forward and sat across from him, her voice barely above a whisper.

"Richard… are you okay?"

He looked up slowly. His face was slack, the corners of his eyes drawn in as if he were trying to focus on something miles away. His mind wanted to just give a heavy sigh and relax, but that seemed like an impossible task. "No, my dear. I'm not," he said. There was no anger in his voice, just bewilderment, raw and hollow.

Addison hesitated. "Do you think it was them? Alex? Tim?"

He nodded faintly, his gaze dropping to the table. "I believe so. But again, I have no proof. The security feeds were blocked. Just for a minute or so. A perfect window, just long enough to get in, do the job, and disappear. Always a perfect window. Nothing clear enough for an ID." He gave a brief, eyes-widening glint of hope, then quickly dashed it. "Grayle and Brian saw someone… but not well enough to describe."

She swallowed hard. "Where are they now?"

"Safe. Secure," Richard replied quietly, nodding slightly as if hoping they would remain that way. He sighed again. "I need to get some rest. We'll pick this up later, okay?" Reaching across the table, he touched her hand gently, then stood and walked away, each step dragging just a little. The weight of everything seemed to weigh on him, and he appeared to physically sag. When he reached the bedroom, he went inside, and the door clicked shut behind him.

Addison remained still for a moment, watching the door. The moment he was out of sight, her posture changed. Her back straightened. Her jaw tightened. She stood, walked to the back of the house, and slid open the glass door that led to the deck. Outside, the air was crisp and clear. The lake shimmered under the morning sun, the water still and bright like a sheet of silver. The pier stretched out from the deck, wood weathered smooth by years of sun and rain. At the end of the pier, one of Richard's boats bobbed quietly, tied and waiting.

Addison walked to the edge of the pier where the boat bumped softly against the wood and pulled her comm device from her coat. She dialed.

After only one ring, she spoke. "Quentin. It's me."

There was a sharp intake of breath on the other end of the line, followed by a long, exhausted exhale. "Damn, Addison. It's been four days since we've heard from you. What the hell's going on over there?"

"Nothing good," she said. "I don't think Richard can help us. I think he's in over his head."

She glanced back toward the house, toward the door she'd just walked through, as if anticipating something to interrupt her. "I don't trust the Mackeys. There's something strange about those two. And the fact that they're brother and sister makes me even more leery.

They have a strong bond." She paused, looking back at the lake again. The other man, Phil Wells, was killed last night. Shot. Right after he left here."

There was a pause on the line.

"We're aware," Quentin said quietly.

Addison didn't show any sign of surprise. She was long past surprises. "I'm going to wait a few more minutes, then get out of here. I'll meet you at the campsite."

"Good. It's time we left. Get back here, we'll pack up and move tonight. Are you telling Richard you're leaving?"

"Hell no," Addison snapped. "If I tell him, he'll try to talk me into staying. The five of us are better off on our own. My bag's packed already. I'm crossing the lake now, and I have a car stashed at Bernhards Bay. I'll see you soon."

"See you soon, Add," Quentin said. Then, softly, "Be careful. Please."

Addison ended the call.

She waited on the pier for twenty minutes, studying the water, the early morning sun, and the loons as they floated on the lake. Every second made her more sure of her decision. More sure that if she stayed, she wouldn't survive. None of them would. Finally, she headed into the house.

She left a handwritten note on the table by the door:

I've left. Don't try to find me. Your boat's across the lake. I'm sorry. - Addison

Grabbing her bag and slipping back out of the house, she hurried down the length of the pier once again, climbed into the boat, untied the moorings, and fired the engine. It roared to life beneath her, and she began gliding across the quiet morning water.

Three miles away, on a hill above Billington Bay, Alex knelt beside a surveillance case nestled in the brush. He peered through a long-range scope, watching the boat slip across the lake like a dart of white over blue glass.

"There you are," he whispered. "Got you."

He tapped a control panel. Eight bumblebee-sized drones launched from the side of the case and zipped into the sky. They were silent, fast, invisible, and very efficient.

He opened his comm.

"I've got her," he said. "She's crossing the lake now."

"Great!" Tim's voice snarled over the line. "Don't let her get away!"

"Dude… relax," Alex snapped back. "I'm trailing her. I've deployed the B-drones. What's your ETA?"

"I'm twenty-five minutes out. Coming in from the east."

"Copy that. I'll keep you updated."

Alex continued to watch, his eyes locked on the boat as it skimmed toward Bernhards Bay.

And the drones kept pace, silently hunting her through the sky.

***

Addison pulled the boat toward the rickety dock at Bernhards Bay, its boards creaking as the hull bumped gently against them. Once whitewashed and pristine, the pier was now worn and mold-streaked. She didn't bother tying it off properly; she just looped the rope around the first cleat she saw, gave it a hard yank, and climbed the metal ladder two rungs at a time. The instant her boots hit the wood, she was already scanning the shore. Tim and Alex were masterminds at camouflage, and she had no intention of being their next victim.

The quiet here was different from that on Richard's lake. Here it was less serene, more ominous. The trees that framed the water seemed too still. It was like they were holding their breath. Or hiding in the shadows.

She spotted the overgrown hedgerow she'd hidden the car behind, and her heart gave a painful thump of relief when she saw it was still there. It appeared to be untouched, exactly where she'd left it days ago, so she took off in a jog in its direction, ducking low out of habit.

When she reached the car, Addison made a quick sweep beneath the frame and around the tires. No wires. No blinking lights. No unfamiliar footprints on the soft earth. All seemed clear. With a deep breath and a wince of pain, she began to open the driver's door. She had it about halfway open when a voice cut through the air and startled her, forcing her knees to buckle.

"Excuse me, miss! Is that your vehicle?"

Addison spun, her breath catching. "Dear God, man. What the actual fu…" She looked across the road where a man stood on his porch in a bathrobe, coffee in hand, eyes squinting against the morning glare.

"Y… yes! Thank you!" she called back, trying to sound casual, but her knees were knocking and the tension was evident in her tone.

"Oh, okay," the man said slowly. "Just curious. It's been sitting there a while."

"Who are you?" she blurted, alarmed by such a disturbance.

He raised both hands, startled. "Whoa! I'm sorry! I live just over there. Didn't mean anything by it."

Addison didn't have time to listen. She was already in the car, door slammed shut, engine roaring to life. Gravel sprayed behind her as she peeled out, the wheels grabbing the dirt road in a frantic escape.

***

High above, the B-drones were tracking her, flitting from tree to tree, their visual cloaks rendering them nearly invisible to the naked eye. A silent swarm that never blinked.

Inside the car, Addison finally exhaled, shallow and shaky. She switched to autonomous mode and leaned back, pressing her hands against her forehead. Her skin felt clammy. Her thoughts were scattered, adrenaline still flooding her veins. Phil was dead. Murdered.

She closed her eyes for just a second, and the image flashed, his name in Richard's voice. *'Phil Wells is dead.'* The words had rung out like a sentence. No trial. No second chance.

She rubbed her eyes, then looked down at her shaking hands. She clenched them, trying to stop the tremor.

She felt like she was unraveling, while above her, the B-drones continued to track her.

Three miles behind, nestled along the treeline, Alex coasted in his own transport, staying just outside radar range. The B-drones pulsed updates into his console, mapping her every turn.

He tapped the comm again. "Tim. Addison's heading northeast. Fast. B-drones are starting to fall back in this terrain, but they've still got a lock."

"Copy," Tim said. "I see it. She's cutting between the Buck and Blue Mountains. Smart move. If she follows the ridges, she'll try to shake you before cresting Tirrell."

Alex grunted. "Whatever. I'm hanging back. Let me know if she shifts course."

Addison stopped again.

She'd pulled off near Wolf Pond and left the vehicle half-concealed beneath a thicket of pine, hoping whoever, if anyone, was watching her, tracking her, they'd be thrown off course. There was no hesitation this time. She opened the back, slung her gear over one shoulder, and set out on foot.

The woods closed in around her. The terrain was thick and wild, branches clawing at her sleeves as she pushed deeper. With every step, the sound of her boots on damp leaves seemed to echo louder than it should.

Two miles in, the woods broke. A field opened before her, wide and quiet. The late afternoon sun burned low behind the clouds, washing everything in a pale amber hue, and she paused at the edge, crouching low.

Silence.

She took one last look around, then stepped forward...

And vanished.

An hour later, Tim met Alex near the edge of a high ridge, overlooking the clearing where Addison had disappeared. A chill breeze moved through the trees, brushing their jackets with whispering fingers. Alex didn't turn as Tim approached, just gestured down with a nod.

"Took ya long enough." He didn't give Tim enough time to tell him to 'suck it' or offer some other snarky comeback. He simply continued, "The drones tracked her there. She's inside."

Tim studied the open field, his eyes narrowing with a flicker of satisfaction. "Perfect spot. Just like I taught them. They're using mirror screens."

Mirror screens had been designed years ago for campers who wanted privacy, an outdoor illusion of invisibility. The system projected a seamless 3D holographic image of the natural surroundings, hiding anything behind it. A perfect camouflage. A clever tool, once innocent, was now a shield for fugitives.

"They'll wait until nightfall," Tim murmured, his voice laced with calculation. "That's when they'll start packing up. I guarantee they've got sensors out. Probably a four-point field. I'll wait until they trigger movement before making my approach."

"You need backup?" Alex asked without much enthusiasm, his voice distant.

"No," Tim said flatly. "I'll take it from here."

Alex finally turned, his face cool and remote, eyes detached. "Fine. Just don't drag this out. Once you're done, get back to Dayton. We owe them."

Tim didn't look at him. "Not with Addison. I won't make it quick. It's personal."

Alex scoffed, his tone dismissive. "Fine. Take your time with her. Just make it quick with the rest."

Without another word, Alex vanished into the trees, swallowed by the dense forest, leaving Tim alone with the dying light and the weight of his obsession.

The last golden rays of sunlight bled away behind the trees, casting the camp into a dusky hush. Shadows stretched long and thin across the clearing. Inside the perimeter, all was calm. Too calm.

Quentin stood by the center table, checking over a hand-drawn map, double-checking their route. The paper rustled faintly in the soft wind. The others moved quietly around him, packing essentials, extinguishing lamps, and coiling gear with quiet urgency. There was an unspoken agreement in the air: this was it.

Rachel sat on a blanket by the fire pit, rubbing her temples with tired fingers. Roland knelt behind her, wrapping his arms around her gently, resting his chin on her shoulder. The firelight flickered against her hair, the strands catching copper like a halo, casting their faces in a soft orange glow.

"Is she asleep?" Rachel asked softly.

"Yes," Quentin said. "She's had enough for one day. I'll wake her around eight. We'll move under full darkness. If all goes well, we'll be out of here before midnight."

"Agreed," Roland nodded, his hand rubbing slow circles on Rachel's arm.

Eddie stirred a pot on the camp stove, the aroma of simmering broth barely covering the tension in the air. "One of our last nights together," he said, his voice trailing off with quiet sadness. "It's going to be…"

He was going to expound on the sentiment, but Quentin interrupted his thought.

"I know," he replied, his eyes fixed on the fire, watching the flames dance. "But it's for the best. If we split up, we make it harder for them."

There was a long silence, filled only by the subtle crackling of the fire. Then Roland cleared his throat.

"Rachel and I... we have something to tell you." Rachel reached for his hand, squeezing it gently.

"I know this is terrible timing," she said, her voice soft but clear, "but... I'm pregnant." Her quiet and solemn mood was deflated by her smile, a rare and fragile joy surfacing.

Eddie blinked, then smiled. Quentin raised his eyebrows, caught off guard.

"Well, hell," Roland said with a soft chuckle. "At least something good came out of all this."

"You'll always be our family, you two," Quentin said. "In a couple of years, when it's safe again... we'll find each other. Somewhere quiet. Somewhere new."

Rachel tried to smile, but her eyes shimmered with tears, and her smile began to wilt. "I just wish Owen, Scott, and Paul were still with us."

"They deserved better," Eddie agreed. His voice tightened. "It's up to us now. We make sure their story is told. That they don't get away with this."

Quentin nodded, the fire reflecting in his eyes. "We will. I swear it." He stood, stretching out the tension in his shoulders, his breath catching slightly. "For the rest of the day, however, let's relax. We move soon."

They nodded, the weight of his words sinking like stones dropped into water.

A short while later, as the fire dimmed to glowing embers, Eddie approached Quentin, his hands in his pockets.

"Can I talk to you?" he asked. Quentin stood, and the two men stepped away from the others, walking toward the shadows beyond the firelight. The trees loomed. Silent sentinels.

"What's up?" Quentin asked, his eyes scanning the woods even now, alert and cautious.

"I don't like this," Eddie said. "Rachel and Roland having a child… it makes things riskier. They'll have to turn themselves in eventually. This isn't sustainable."

Quentin stopped, folding his arms across his chest.

"They know that," he said evenly.

"You don't seem worried."

Quentin exhaled, slow and steady. "When Alex pulled Rachel out of school, she was seventeen. She was the smartest of us all. She was supposed to be an Explorer. They robbed her of that. She deserves a little happiness, wouldn't you agree?"

Eddie frowned, shoulders tense. "I don't need a history lesson, Q. None of us were forced into this. She made her choice like we all did. I'm just saying, this changes things. Do you really want to risk getting caught? Banished to North Dakota? Living out your life in the middle of nowhere?"

"No," Quentin said sharply. "We could end up like Owen, Scott, and Paul, and I like that alternative less."

Eddie shook his head and scoffed. "Whatever." He walked off angry, muttering to himself, easily the most paranoid of the group.

From across the camp, Rachel and Roland had been watching.

"What do you think they're talking about?" Roland asked.

Rachel didn't answer. She just smirked, her eyes following the two figures.

Roland chuckled and pulled her close. "Probably just how dumb we are. Or how paranoid he is. Honestly, I don't know what he has against North Dakota. It's beautiful country."

"It is," Rachel whispered. "I can't wait to get out of here. Live normally. Make new friends. Raise our child."

"I love you, Rachel," Roland said, his excitement increasing like a fire catching wind. "You know what? Let's just go. Now."

Rachel leaned into him. "No. Let's have one last dinner. Say our goodbyes. It's the right thing to do. We… we won't see them again."

Roland nodded. He kissed her temple, brushing his hand through her long, straight brown hair. He kissed her gently on the cheek, calming, loving. Their relationship hadn't been planned. That's why it worked.

Sometimes, love just finds you.

The sun had now fully set. Shadows had deepened into black, swallowing the clearing.

Addison emerged from her tent, a little pale but steady. Her posture was tight, but her movements were sure. She was packing her remaining gear when Quentin showed up.

"Hey. How are you feeling?"

"Good. Fine. Hungry," she answered quickly, brushing hair out of her face, her tone clipped.

"You want to talk about last night?" he asked gently.

"No, I do not," Addison replied firmly. "Phil was assassinated. I shouldn't have contacted Richard. I was wrong. I nearly exposed all of us. I'm done. I want out."

Quentin nodded quietly. "Understood."

Addison's voice quickly softened. "Q… I'm sorry. I'm trying to keep it together. It's just hard."

"I know," he said, giving her a soft pat on the shoulder. "Dinner's ready. Come join us. One last meal. Then we move."

"I'll be right there," Addison replied with a half-hearted smile.

"I'll make it right," Quentin said as he left her.

Eddie was already seated at the table, arms crossed, scanning the trees with eyes sharp as glass. "How's she doing?" he asked.

"Traumatized," Quentin replied. "And Ed… don't ask a thousand questions."

Eddie just raised his hands and nodded. "Understood."

Everyone gathered. Their final supper. The mood was solemn at first, the clinking of utensils the only sound. But then Quentin stood, raising a glass.

"To the five of us," he began. "The places we've seen. The things we've survived. Thank you." He glanced at each of them. "As we get ready to leave this place, let's remember the good times and our friends. And Owen, Scott, and Paul, I swear to you all... Alex and Tim will face justice. Then, one day, we'll be free again. Together. No hiding. No running."

The moment broke the tension. They began talking, reminiscing, even laughing.

Eddie leaned in. "Hey, does anyone want to hear my latest theo..."

"No!" Quentin said with a grin.

Laughter.

For a moment, they forgot the danger.

But not far off, Tim was already moving.

Night fell hard.

The mirror screens were taken down, revealing the surrounding woods. Tents stood empty. The camp was being broken down. Their vehicles were stashed roughly a mile from the camp, tucked away beneath a thicket of brush on the far side of the woods. The final departure was drawing near.

As part of their security protocol, the team had established a four-point perimeter, fifty yards wide in each direction, surrounding the camp in a precise square. Each corner of the perimeter was marked by a camouflaged sensor, carefully concealed in the undergrowth, and monitored by a corresponding display inside each tent.

The camp itself had been positioned with purpose. All five tents stood clustered on the western edge, near the field's opening. The eastern side backed against dense forest; an intentional design, giving them cover as they exited into the trees.

The sensors created a nearly invisible detection field, sensitive enough to register movement as small as a passing insect. If anything crossed the barrier, it would register across all five monitors, alerting them immediately.

But now, the time had come.

Once the sensors were shut down, they would depart as a group and begin the mile-long journey through the woods; silent, fast, and hopefully unnoticed.

Quentin gathered them. "I'm deactivating the sensors and rounding them up. I'm taking them with me."

"Just leave them," Eddie muttered.

"I'll need them," Quentin replied.

"Where are you going?" Rachel asked.

"It's better you don't know," he replied.

"I'll help," Addison said.

"Me too," Eddie added.

"I'll grab one," Roland said.

Quentin sighed. "Fine. Roland, Eddie, west side. Add, the east side. You take the one on the right. I'll take the left. Once we regroup, we head out."

They split up.

Eddie reached the outer edge of the west side. The trees were thicker here, their tall trunks rising like silent sentinels under the cloak of night. The forest was quiet, unnervingly still. Even the insects seemed to have taken shelter. He spotted his sensor nestled beneath a mound of leaves and pine needles.

"There you are, you bugger," he muttered.

He crouched, brushing debris aside with impatient hands. "Damn thing's really in there..." The stake wouldn't come easily. Roots clung to it like tiny fingers, reluctant to let go. He wrestled it free with a grunt. "God, I can't see shit out here," he added with annoyance. "Why does he even want this stuff..." Clicking on a small utility light, Eddie cast a soft circle across the damp forest floor. It glinted off the wet earth and reflected faintly in a nearby patch of moss.

"Ugh. Damn it. I've got to piss again. Every damn time..." he grumbled, turning away toward a nearby tree.

Finished with the bodily function, he zipped up with a sigh, picked up his light, and turned...

A hand, cold and firm, wrapped around his forehead and yanked him backward with brutal force. His body jerked, instinctively trying to twist away, but it was too late. A blade whispered through the air and sliced across his throat in one clean, practiced stroke. Deep. Fast. Perfect.

His body convulsed silently. Blood sprayed in wide arcs across the pine needles, dark and steaming in the night air.

The figure knelt beside him with eerie calm, lowering Eddie's body gently to the ground. He took the light, extinguished it, and vanished into the shadows, as if swallowed by the forest itself.

Quentin was at his sensor, crouching low in the grass. The air had grown colder now, and a faint mist had begun to creep along the ground.

He bent down to pull the stake...

A blur rushed in.

One slash.

His head rolled to the side. His body collapsed in the opposite direction.

No sound. No warning.

It was surgical. Clean. Unfeeling.

Completely unaware of what was happening around them, Rachel and Roland approached from opposite ends of the clearing.

"Where's Eddie?" Roland asked, glancing around with a puzzled look.

"He's probably off peeing again," Rachel replied with a faint roll of her eyes. "Let's just get this to Quentin." She pointed ahead. "There's Addison. Let's meet up."

"Wait. Look," Roland said, peering into the trees. "I see Quentin's light. I'm going to check on him real quick."

"I'm right behind you," Rachel said, adjusting her pack.

Ten feet away, Quentin's body lay crumpled in the shadows, his headless form partially obscured by underbrush.

Roland stopped.

"Q...?" His voice wavered.

He stepped closer, sweeping the light slowly upward from Quentin's boots, then to the crimson pool spreading through the leaves... then to the clean-cut edge of the neck... and the absence above it.

His eyes went wide, horror blooming like fire behind them.

"Rachel? Sweetheart?" he called out, spinning in her direction, panic rising.

She froze mid-step. "Babe?"

Turning on her light, she swept it across the clearing. Behind her, the attacker stood tall, motionless, sword drawn. A strong hand dropped onto her shoulder.

"Please... don't," Roland begged, voice cracking, breath short.

In the distance, Addison saw what was happening. Her eyes locked on the scene, breath catching in her throat. She immediately cut her light and melted back into the shadows.

Rachel froze. "Tim... is that you?" she whispered, her voice trembling. "I'm pregnant. Please... Please just let us go. No one will say anything..."

Tears slipped silently down her face, trailing along her cheeks, glistening in the faint light.

The attacker didn't speak. He only moved her backward slowly, step by step, away from Roland.

Roland edged forward, fists clenched. "You touch her and I swear I'll..."

"I love you, Roland!" Rachel cried, her voice suddenly raw and desperate.

Roland began to sob uncontrollably, his breath hitching, the horror of the moment rendering him helpless. "I love you!"

The blade plunged through her back.

Roland screamed and charged, unthinking, no longer caring about his safety. He had to stop this... revenge, fury, grief all merged into a single instinctual surge.

But the attacker spun, caught him mid-run, and drove the sword into Roland's heart with brutal precision. Roland's momentum carried him forward a step more before his knees gave out.

On the ground, her face wet with tears and dust, Rachel watched through blurred vision as the figure stepped forward and drove the blade into her chest with a final, merciful thrust.

He dragged Roland's body beside hers.

Knelt.

Ran a hand gently through Rachel's hair, smoothing it back from her face with almost tender care.

Across the field, Addison had seen everything. The lights that had been dropped during the attack still glowed faintly, casting terrible clarity on the scene. She dropped flat to the earth, hidden, pressing a trembling hand over her mouth to suppress the hyperventilating breaths that threatened to give her away. Her entire body shook violently.

The attacker grabbed both lights, lifted them, and saw nothing.

Tilting his head ever so slightly, he extinguished them both.

Darkness.

Complete suffocating darkness fell, thick as velvet.

Addison bolted into the trees.

Heart hammering, lungs burning, she tore through branches and underbrush, letting them slash at her arms. She didn't care. She needed to move, to survive. She had to reach the vehicles. Somewhere. Anywhere safe.

She ran blindly on pure adrenaline, dodging trees, stumbling over roots.

Behind her, nothing. No sound. No footfalls. But she didn't trust the silence.

She ran harder.

In her mind, she tried to count the steps, calculate the distance, and orient herself to the hidden vehicles. But she dared not use her light. Not yet. She needed the cloak of darkness a little longer.

She hit a path. Gravel crunched beneath her shoes.

She ran faster now, weaving between trees, then finally, she reached a clearing.

Breath heaving, she raised her light and aimed it low, the beam trembling in her unsteady hands. She scanned left. Then right.

Nothing.

She had overrun the vehicles.

Cursing under her breath, she turned off the light and dropped to one knee, hands shaking violently.

Then, a hand.

Tim's voice was cold and quiet. "Addison," he whispered.

A stun gun was pressed against her back. There was a soft click. A sudden *szzzz*. And then... darkness.

Tim began to drag her limp body into the night.

Chapter 22: The Impossible Odds

The following day, as dusk settled across the horizon, Grayle and Brian returned to Richard's house. The air felt heavier than usual, like a humid fog that refused to lift. Grief sat in the corners of every room, unspoken but undeniable, pressing down on everything with a quiet weight. Phil Wells was gone, and the loss felt like a deep ache they couldn't shake; it hadn't settled into something they could process yet.

The three of them sat in Richard's hidden room. Once a place meant for planning, the space was now thick with uncertainty. The warm light from a single lamp cast long shadows across the walls, but no one spoke. The stillness hung like cobwebs.

"So… Addison Heinz left yesterday morning," Brian said at last, his voice dry and hoarse from fatigue. "Has she reached out to you?"

Richard shook his head slowly. "No. Nothing. Wherever she and her team are now, they've gone dark again. This time for good. And honestly — it's probably for the better. We can't protect any of them anymore." He looked over at Grayle, his eyes reddened and tired. "How are you holding up?"

Grayle didn't answer at first. She sat slouched in her chair, arms crossed, staring blankly at the wall. Her jaw clenched tightly. Then she closed her eyes, drew in a shallow breath, and turned to him. "I don't know what you've gotten us into…" she said quietly. Her voice then climbed, edged with fury. "But you need to fix this. You need to make this right."

She stood, her tone rising as if shaking the walls themselves. "Whatever it takes, Richard. You make it right!"

Richard looked down, the guilt that was already etched into his face deepening with each new chastisement. His shoulders sagged as if her words added weight to his very bones. "I'm sorry. I should never have involved either of you. I regret it."

But sympathy wasn't what they needed. Not now.

Brian stood abruptly and began pacing the room, fists clenched. He had taken Grayle's charge, and he, too, had turned on Richard. "How many more people have to die before you get the courage to do what's necessary?" he shouted.

"What are you suggesting?" Richard snapped, standing as well. "That I break laws? I have nothing on them. And even if I did, they've always had the advantage. Ten-to-one. And Tim alone…" He shook his head, eyes wide. "He's as dangerous as they come."

Brian stopped pacing. He closed his eyes and inhaled deeply, trying to rein himself in. "Look, I'm sorry," he said. "You've been doing this alone for a long time. I just…"

"It's fine. I get it. I dropped a lot on you both," Richard said quietly. "It wasn't fair. Or right."

"For the love of all that is good, will the two of you quit apologizing?" Grayle interrupted sharply. "This isn't a love fest. What do we do next?" She raised her arms in question but continued with her angst. "Because the longer we sit here saying we're sorry, the further ahead they get."

"She's right," Brian said. "They already know we're with you. They're likely plotting their next move right now. So…" He glared at Richard, his eyes like daggers digging for an answer. "What's ours?"

Richard sat down again, rubbing his hands together. He was thinking, retracing their steps. "They had to be watching us," he said. "How else would they know where to go? Following you to Phil's house, waiting for the right moment…"

"And if they followed us, they could've followed Addison too," Brian added.

Richard nodded grimly. "Yes… I'm afraid so." That realization landed with force. He had dragged all of them into the crosshairs, only he had no clear path forward.

Richard stood, crossed the room, and opened a small, locked case. From inside, he removed the Reverie Halo. Its sleek, alien-looking exterior shimmered faintly under the lamp's glow, its curves smooth and almost organic in appearance. Grayle and Brian's gaze snapped toward it.

"I need your help," he said.

Grayle sat forward, eyes narrowing. "Wait. What is that? Is that..."

Richard held it up gently, reverently. "This is the Halo. Stan used to help me with it... back when I first tried working with it."

Brian leaned in, curiosity overtaking his hesitation. "What... Just how can that help us?"

"It has... unique capabilities," Richard replied. "Applications we never publicly disclosed. It can access the minds of those who've worn it before. Because Alex and Tim used this at different times, I can..." He waved his hand in a slow, searching circle. "I can sort of get inside their heads."

Grayle and Brian exchanged a glance.

Richard continued, "There's a reason we kept this hidden. Through testing, we found you can only wear it for two minutes. That's it. No more. Go past that, and it begins pulling you deeper. Not just into their minds, but into your own. Past lives. Future probabilities. It's not just a memory experience; it's a soul-level experience. A dangerous soul-level experience."

"Why would the Norn give us something like this?" Brian asked, his brow furrowed with confusion.

Richard turned toward the window, then back again. "Free will. When they came, they said that they would give us the tools to achieve greatness, to show us how vast the universe really is, and how far behind we are. How far behind in knowledge, technology, even compassion, and... peace. But, they didn't give this to us to figure out in a day. This is a final exam. A challenge to be mastered over centuries. Until then, it's dangerous. It's what those two represent: danger, death, and destruction. Their selfishness and their desire for power — it's out of control."

Grayle looked confused. "I'm lost. You said you've used it before... and got nothing."

Richard gave a slight nod. "I wasn't ready then, but now, I think it's the only way to find something useful. I've thought about it, strategized it over and over again in my head, and I have a plan. You see, Tim doesn't think like a modern man. He's a soldier from old wars. And like soldiers from old wars, he might be predictable. I'm hoping to find a pattern to his tactics. Something that will let me anticipate his moves."

Brian raised an eyebrow. "It's still a gamble."

"It's all we've got. Besides," Richard opened a bottle of small white pills and set it on the table. "I wasn't asking your permission."

Brian's face looked as if he had just been smacked, not just verbally. He couldn't respond, but Grayle pointed at the pills. "What are those?"

"They help stabilize the system after use. Coming out of the Halo creates confusion. You experience chemical spikes: dopamine, serotonin, etcetera. This counteracts that. Without it, the brain can spiral. And the chip inside each of us, our personal tracker, interfaces with the Halo. That's why the two-minute limit is critical. Past that, the chip reboots. And once it starts recording everything, you can't undo it."

"Okay. While you're in... how do we communicate with you?" Grayle asked.

"I'll still be present here. With you. So I can hear you, and I can respond. You're just watching me on the outside while I'm inside a type of virtual space. It'll be like I'm traveling inside a computer." He lowered his eyes. "But listen carefully to what I'm saying now. You cannot touch me while I'm wearing the Halo. If you do, the feedback could fry both our minds."

Grayle and Brian nodded.

Richard took one of the pills, swallowed it dry, and sat down.

"Ready?"

"We're ready," they said in a crazy sibling unison.

He placed the Halo on his head. As it settled, it adjusted itself, shrinking slightly to fit. A pale white glow surrounded the rim, and Richard's eyes rolled back, turning completely white.

"Two minutes," he said. "And when you get to one minute forty-five, I want a fifteen-second countdown."

Brian started the timer. "Gotcha. Man, the control panel on that thing is something else."

Richard sat perfectly still, jaw slack, eyes glowing. "Yes, it allows me to view the information imprinted on the device from both Alex and Tim's minds."

"One minute, thirty seconds," Brian said aloud.

"I can hear you. No need to shout," Richard replied calmly.

Time passed with extreme anticipation.

"Fifteen seconds," Brian called out. "Ten... nine... eight..."

Before he could hit six, Richard pulled the Halo off himself with a gasp.

"Whoa... Woooo!" He laughed. "Stuck the landing."

Grayle rushed to him. "Are you okay? What did you discover?"

"I'm fine," Richard said, still catching his breath. "I don't know what their ultimate goal is, but I think... I think they're eliminating threats. Anyone who could expose them. I think the Intervention bombing was born out of pettiness, but once they realized what they'd done, they started covering their tracks. That's why the abducted never came back. That's why Owen was killed. Stan, Phil..."

"It makes no sense," Brian said grimly. "Our society is structured so that no one could ever have total power like that again."

Richard nodded. "Yeah, but... This is how old regimes used to operate: secret purges and disinformation. They're using history as a blueprint. They aren't thinking in terms of a new society, Brian. They're thinking like the past."

Grayle leaned forward. "What else did you see?"

"Well, it's quite obvious that they're skilled with long-range weapons. They've mastered being killers from a distance. If we have any chance of neutralizing them, I think we'll need to draw them in. Close quarters."

"We'll need help with that," Brian said.

"I was going to reach out to Commander Phillips," Richard said, setting the Halo down.

"Our uncle?" Brian blinked. "Why?"

"He hates Alex. Still blames him for the Intervention. And he still feels guilty for not being on that shuttle. He loves you both. He'd fight to protect you."

"He's retired," Grayle said. "You'll be putting him in danger. I don't think there's any need to put him in harm's way."

"You may be right, but we're already there," Richard said bluntly. "This way, four on two gives us a chance." There was a silence before Richard spoke again, this time solemnly. "You do realize that this is the end of the line, right?"

"No shit," Brian muttered. "We noticed."

Richard ignored the jab. "Brian, I want you to try the Halo next."

"Why?" Brian's eyes lit up with a quick jolt of fear.

"I want you to go back two nights. To Phil's house. See if there's anything you missed during the chase."

Brian hesitated. "I couldn't catch him."

"I know. But maybe you saw something. You can slow it down. Rewatch it. I'll show you." He pointed to a small button on the Halo's control panel. "You focus on the moment. You'll drop into your memory, fully immersive. But two minutes only, Brian. I'm serious."

Brian paced, his anxiety rising. "What if I don't want to go? And what happens if I go past the two minutes?"

"Look, I'm not making you go. You go on your own accord. But if you do and you go past two minutes, you slide further into your past. Your chip reboots. And then… the past starts recording into your present. If you push past five minutes, you lose yourself."

Brian began pacing the room, and Grayle tried to calm him. "Look, Bri. If you don't want…"

Brian took her arms and looked her in the eyes. He gave a large sigh to try to settle himself. "No, no. I…I can do this," Brian said. "Let's go."

Grayle tried again, this time a bit harder. "We can figure something else out, Bri. You don't need to…"

Brian looked away, grabbed a pill, swallowed it, and braced himself. He sat. And waited.

Richard gently set the Reverie Halo on Brian's head. His eyes turned white. The glow returned.

"He'd better be okay, Richard, or Tim and Alex will be the least of your worries."

"Shh," Richard snapped at Grayle. "He'll be fine. Watch."

"Oh my God…" Brian whispered. "This is… unbelievable…" He paused, his eyes wide and unfocused as if waking from a vivid dream. "Wait, wait. Focus. I need to focus."

They watched the timer, the seconds ticking down with a soft pulse from the Halo's console, each beep like a heartbeat counting toward the end of Brian's journey.

"Fifteen seconds," Richard called out, his voice tense.

Brian waited a few seconds longer, then yanked the device from his head. His face was soaked with sweat, and his breathing came fast and shallow. He looked like he'd run a mile.

"I saw it. I saw everything again. Wow! That was incred… Oh man, that guy was so fast. He obviously had the escape route planned. But I… I stopped time. I don't even know how to explain it. I just… paused it. Moved around. Watched."

Grayle's eyes widened with awe and a flicker of envy. "That's incredible."

"It was like a movie… I could rewind, fast-forward, and pause. All in real time." Brian exhaled sharply, dragging both hands down his face. "Ugh, but I didn't learn much. He's elusive. We'll need more help. He's too good."

Richard nodded solemnly, his jaw tightening. "That's what I was afraid of."

"I'll go now," Grayle said suddenly, her voice cutting through the room. The words came fast, filled with urgency and defiance.

"Oh no," Richard replied, firm and immediate.

"Why not?" she asked, holding out her hand for the device, her palm steady.

"Your brother chased him. You didn't. You had the same view as him, and I won't let you relive Phil's death. You don't need that."

"You don't think I can handle it, isn't that right? You think I'm weak. You think I can't..."

"I need to use the bathroom," Brian said faintly, still dazed, wobbling on his feet.

"C'mon. I'll take you back." Richard helped him up, keeping a hand under his arm as they made their way toward the hall.

When they returned, Grayle was already seated in the chair. The Halo sat in her lap — a crown waiting for its queen. Her fingers were wrapped around it, her posture upright, her gaze fixed and steely.

"Grayle, no!" Richard shouted. "Don't!"

"You'd better start counting," she said coolly, already raising the Halo to her head. "I already popped the pill." She pressed the center button, and the inner light burst to life with a brilliant pulse.

In the distance, she could hear Richard and Brian shouting to her, their voices hollow and distorted. "No! Grayle, no!" But it was already too late.

She was back in the living room. The air felt thick and unreal, like walking through a dream. Phil sat slumped on the couch, lifeless, his blood stark against the fabric. It looked too fresh. Too red.

"Phil..." she whispered, leaning in and blowing him a kiss. "I hope you found what you were looking for."

"One minute thirty, Grayle!" Richard's voice rang faintly in the distance. "Time to take it off!"

"Wait. I see something. I need to look around."

"No! Ten seconds!" Richard called out again, louder, more urgent.

Brian moved to help, stepping forward to grab the Halo, but Richard flung out an arm, stopping him. "No! Don't touch her!" He turned to Grayle, shouting now. "Grayle! Five... four... three... two... one..."

Nothing happened.

"Shit," Richard hissed, eyes wide. "She's slipping!"

She was falling deeper, spiraling through her own mind. Images bled into each other. Past and present collided. She started to shake her head as if trying to force the vision to clear, but then... she stopped.

A woman appeared before her, glowing softly. She wore white, and her long red hair flowed gently around her shoulders like flame.

"Bridgette?" Grayle whispered.

The woman smiled faintly. "Yes." Her eyes were calm, but carried the weight of something terrible. "Don't go further. There's only pain," Bridgette said gently.

"I have to," Grayle said, her voice breaking as tears spilled freely.

Bridgette's face fell into sorrow. "I'll be back. We only have one more chance." Her form shimmered, then disappeared like mist in sunlight.

"Who's she talking to?!" Brian asked, his voice filled with confusion.

Richard stood motionless, stunned. "I don't know," he admitted, shaking his head. He turned back to the clock. "Three minutes. Damn it, Grayle!"

But she didn't hear him. Or maybe she just didn't care.

Ahead, a tunnel had opened - narrow, glowing with an ethereal light. As she stepped closer, a wave of raw emotion hit her. Rage. Grief. The memory of the Intervention exploding swept around her like a storm, but she pressed on, drawn by the pull of something beyond.

And there, at the tunnel's end, stood a mirror.

Grayle approached cautiously. The surface rippled like water, and as she gazed into it, the face staring back wasn't hers.

It was Paul O'Hanlon. Her former self.

A husband. A brother. A man in love.

2017

Memories flooded in and took over, leaving Grayle shaken, a tide of forgotten warmth rushing through her, catching her breath and holding her still. She was Paul again. The world around her felt textured and real. The sights, the smells, the very weight of the air pulled her deeper.

"Paul!"

The voice echoed from above, vibrant and impatient.

"Get your ass out here! You're gonna miss kickoff!"

"I'm coming! Will you give it a rest already?" Paul shouted back with a laugh, setting down his phone on the counter and grabbing a fresh beer from the fridge. The amber bottle was slick with condensation, the hiss of the cap releasing its seal, grounding him in the moment.

He made his way from the kitchen into the finished basement, its walls a shrine to Ohio State football. Framed jerseys, signed photos, old ticket stubs, all preserved under glass and pride. His two older brothers, Mark and Roy, were already sprawled across the L-shaped sectional, their drinks in hand. Their father, Pat, sat in the leather recliner, nursing a small tumbler of Jameson, eyes locked on the pregame broadcast.

On the far side of the room, two of Paul's oldest friends, Oliver and Jimmy, circled the snack table like vultures. Wings, sliders, and nachos covered every flat surface, the scent of melted cheese and barbecue hanging heavy in the air.

"Big Ten Title Game, baby! Go Bucks!" Roy bellowed, raising his beer high as the room let out a cheer.

A fire crackled in the stone fireplace behind them, casting flickering shadows that danced across the walls. The massive 85-inch flat screen glowed with scarlet and gray, flashing player stats and game predictions. It was the perfect setup, just like the rest of Paul's life.

A promotion at work. A new house, bought that September. And most importantly, Bridgette, his wife of just one week. They had married on Thanksgiving Day, surrounded by family, laughter, and snow. Life felt full.

Paul was just about to plop down and join the chaos when his phone buzzed again. Bridgette. He stepped into the hallway, away from the noise, for a little privacy.

"Hey, sweetheart. Whatcha up to?"

Her voice cut through the static of the moment, sharp and clearly annoyed. "I'm coming home tonight."

Paul straightened. "Everything alright?"

"It's fine. I just…" She sighed hard into the receiver. "My sister is pissing me off royally."

"What happened?"

"I asked why she didn't come to the wedding. You know what she said? Nothing. Just silence. Then my mom started defending her like she was ten years old. She's thirty-six, Paul. It's so damn cringy."

Paul rubbed his forehead with his free hand. "I'm sorry, baby. How's your dad doing?"

"He's resting. Doctors say it's probably just a food allergy. No heart trouble. He's gonna be okay."

"You sure you don't want to just stay the night? Come back tomorrow?"

"No. I'm wired from all the caffeine and pissed off enough to drive through a snowstorm. I've had it. I just want to come home and be with you." She paused, and then her tone lightened. "Besides, I'm freezing my ass off out here. With any luck, I'll get back before the game's over."

"Not with that bladder," Paul teased gently.

"Ha. Ha. I love you!" she shot back.

Paul smiled and closed his eyes for a second. Even in the quiet darkness of the hallway, he could see her face, see the playful smile tugging at the corners of her mouth. Her eyes, so full of light and intelligence.

"I love you, too. Be careful, okay?"

They hung up.

He stood there a moment, phone still in hand, then headed back to the den. The room erupted again as he entered: shouts, laughter, beer bottles clinking. But over it all, Pat gave him a once-over with a father's eye.

"How's Bridgette's dad?"

"Doing okay," Paul said as he dropped onto the couch. "Apparently, it was just a reaction to something he ate."

"And where's she now?"

"Driving back. Should be here by eleven."

Jimmy looked up from a handful of chips. "Bridge is on her way?"

"Yep."

"How long a drive is that?" he asked.

"About three hours from Kentucky."

Mark and Roy both perked up.

"She find out what was up her sister's ass?" Mark asked.

"Yeah, what was that shit about? Why be a cunt like that?" Roy added with a crude snort.

"Hey!" Pat snapped, his glare sharp. "Watch your damn mouths."

The three brothers had always been different. Mark and Roy were all brawn and beer, big laughs and bigger mouths. Paul was the quiet one. The calm. He simply shrugged.

Oliver leaned over from the snack table. "Seriously, man. What's the deal with them?"

Paul hesitated. "Honestly... I don't know. Her sister's always been kind of a gypsy. Free spirit. Bridgette looked up to her when they were kids. Still loves her, but Bridge moved on. Career, marriage. Her sister... kind of faded out. I think that hurt her."

He lowered his gaze. He could have said more, but didn't.

Roy laughed and elbowed Paul. "I was hoping she'd show. I mean, I'd hit it. She's hot!" He took a long sip from his beer, then added with a grin, "She doesn't have hairy armpits or something, does she?"

"Roy!" Pat barked again.

"Dad," Mark chuckled, "why you actin' like Mom's here and gonna dock you points?"

"You guys are idiots," Paul muttered, though a sly smile twitched at the edge of his lips.

"Let's watch the damn game, you idiots," Pat grumbled, lifting his glass. "And pass the Irish whiskey."

The night stretched on. They cheered. They cursed. They told old stories and roared with laughter. It was the kind of evening you didn't want to end.

At 10:00 p.m., Paul's phone buzzed. A text from Bridgette: *Almost there. Just one last pee stop. Love you.*

He grinned as he read it. The others caught the look and fell quiet for a moment. As rough as they were, every one of them respected Paul. He was the one who made things work, who stayed steady, who got the girl and kept her.

By 11:30, the game was winding down. Still no Bridgette.

Paul wasn't worried. Not yet. She'd probably stopped again. Maybe grabbed a coffee.

By midnight, he hovered over his phone. Called. No answer.

Called again. Still nothing.

The room fell silent. The loud, raucous atmosphere was gone. Now, everyone watched Paul. No one left. They stayed because something was off.

At 12:30 a.m., Paul stepped outside. The night air bit at his skin. He lit a cigarette and stared down the snow-dusted street.

"Fuck this," he muttered. "I'm getting in the car. I know which way she comes. Maybe she broke down."

He flicked the cigarette away, grabbed his coat and keys.

"We're coming with," Roy and Mark said without hesitation.

"Jimmy and I'll hit the side roads," Oliver added. "Split up, cover more ground."

"Dad, stay here," Paul said firmly. "In case she makes it back."

Pat nodded slowly. "Okay, boys. Be careful."

Paul drove for nearly an hour, his headlights carving twin blades of light through the cold, lonely darkness. Snow clung to the shoulders of the road, and the occasional flicker of a road sign was the only thing breaking the monotony. He reached the rest areas where Bridgette sometimes stopped, the ones she always mentioned when talking about long drives or needing coffee. But tonight, they were deserted. Not a single trace of her car. Not even a tire track out of place.

His heart sank a little lower with every passing mile. Each rotation of the tires felt like it was grinding away at his hope. The silence in the car was thick, pressing in on him. Roy sat next to him in the passenger seat, scanning the road ahead. Mark was quiet in the back, watching through fogged windows. The hum of the engine was the only sound for long stretches, punctuated now and then by Paul's deep, weary sighs.

Finally, with nowhere left to check and exhaustion washing over him, Paul slowed and made a wide U-turn beneath a green highway overpass. The snow was just beginning to fall again, soft and slow like ashes drifting from the sky.

"No sign of the Civic," he said quietly, eyes still sweeping the roadside like they might catch something he missed.

"Maybe a little further?" Roy offered, his voice low, uncertain.

Paul nodded and pressed the gas. The car surged forward again.

It was nearly 2:00 a.m. when Paul's phone lit up on the dashboard and began to ring. His heart jolted. Bridgette's name.

He hit the answer button with trembling fingers, barely able to hold the phone in place. "Babe? Bridgette? Are you okay? Where are you? Are you..."

But on the other end... nothing. A deep, eerie silence. No breath. No voice. Just dead air.

The kind of silence that empties you in an instant.

Roy and Mark both turned toward him, their expressions tightening, fear rising behind their eyes.

Then… music.

From the car's speakers came a soulful oldie, The Drifters. A slow, aching voice slid into the cabin like a ghost. "There she goes," the man sang, "wonder where she is bound…" The song trailed off with a soft static crackle. The call ended.

Paul stared at the screen, his mouth open slightly. He redialed. Straight to voicemail.

Again. Voicemail.

Again.

Only silence.

Far away, back in the present, Richard's voice barked from the edge of panic. "Grayle! TWENTY SECONDS LEFT! Take the Halo off!"

Grayle gasped sharply and yanked the Halo from her head. Her body collapsed to the floor like a dropped marionette.

Brian caught her before she hit the tiles.

"What happened to Bridgette?!" she cried out, breathless and wild, the pain in her voice cracking the air.

Hours passed. The adrenaline faded, replaced by a crushing stillness. Grayle lay curled on a couch, a blanket over her, her eyes closed but not asleep. Finally, her body stirred. She sat up slowly, shoulders slumped, as if the memories still weighed on her like stones.

"Tell me," she whispered, her voice barely audible.

Richard sat across from her, arms folded, his brow drawn tight. He reached into his coat pocket and pulled out a small white capsule. "First, take this. It'll take the edge off." His tone was quiet, almost fatherly.

Grayle took the pill without hesitation, her fingers trembling slightly as she brought it to her lips.

She swallowed, then blinked back the rising sting of tears. "What about the girl?" she asked. Her voice was hoarse, scraped raw from emotion.

"We can talk about it later, Grayle. You need…"

"No! Please!" Her hand shot out and latched onto Richard's arm. Her grip was firm. Desperate.

Richard shifted in his seat, visibly uncomfortable. His eyes drifted toward the floor as he gathered the words. When he finally spoke, his voice had lost all detachment. It sounded pained. Human.

"A little over three years later," he began, "a man named Rob Anthony was found dead in his home in West Virginia. When local law enforcement entered the property, they uncovered... a nightmare." He paused and rubbed the bridge of his nose. "The garage contained a green Honda Civic, Bridgette's exact make and model. Her wedding ring was found inside, along with... an unsettling collection of women's clothing and jewelry. Dozens of pieces."

The room held still.

"Investigators realized they'd stumbled upon the man they'd been hunting for years. A suspected serial killer whose identity had always eluded them."

Grayle's breath was shallow. She didn't blink.

"In the backyard," Richard continued, "they found human remains. Sixteen bodies in total, all buried in shallow graves. DNA matched several missing women from surrounding states." He hesitated, then spoke even softer. "But none of them was Bridgette O'Hanlon. Her body was never found."

Silence fell over the room again until Grayle spoke.

"And Paul? What happened to me?"

Richard looked away. The pause stretched too long.

"Died in 2030," he said finally. "Drank himself to death. On their wedding anniversary. He had been drinking since the day she vanished, and cirrhosis of the liver caught up to him."

Grayle sat stiffly, as if bracing herself for the next blow.

"Rob Anthony..." she muttered.

Richard looked at Brian, let out a long, hollow sigh, then turned back to Grayle.

"That was one of Tim's other lives," he said. "He was the one who took her."

Grayle's voice broke. The words barely made it out. "...Impossible."

Chapter 23: Family Dinner

The weekend approached slowly, but with a mounting tension no one could quite name. It had been two weeks since Grayle wore the Halo. She was still reeling from the aftermath; emotionally bruised and chemically unsettled, her thoughts often jumbled like static. At Richard's urging, she and Brian had remained at his home in upstate New York, tucked away along the lake in a fragile pocket of calm, where only the wind and water dared disturb the silence.

Richard had advised against attending the family gathering in Wyoming, not wanting to risk exposing them again. But neither sibling was having it. "We're going," Grayle said firmly; her voice absolute, sharp as stone. "We can't stay here forever, you know?"

Richard stood at the window, watching Brian Jr. pace along the shore, his figure silhouetted against the pale shimmer of lake water. He turned toward her, frowning. "I know. You're not prisoners. You can come and go as you please. I'm just concerned you'll see them. Alex and Tim will be there. You're going to come face-to-face with Tim. How are you going to react? Can you keep it together?"

"I'm fine," she said, half-distracted as she moved about, packing with a slightly trembling hand. "Still a little dizzy... but it's better."

"That's not what I meant." Richard's voice was low, weary. "Physically, you'll recover. You're young. But emotionally?"

Grayle paused, unable to find words. She looked up, eyes conflicted and clouded with a weight she couldn't define. "I don't understand how we ended up in the same place, interacting across centuries. I've analyzed my past lives using the Norn equipment. Tim and I... we've crossed paths three times before." Her voice suddenly surged with intensity. "Why do our lives keep intersecting?!"

"Maybe... it has to be you who stops him," Richard said softly. A single tear slid down his face, glinting briefly in the dim light. He didn't try to hide it.

"I will stop him," Grayle said. "I'm going to fucking kill him. Then maybe Bridgette can finally be free." Her voice broke as she spoke, cracking under the burden of loss. "God, I wish Phil were here. He'd know what to do. This is the most..." she waved her arms in exasperation, "...paranormal thing ever."

Richard reached out and hugged her, apologizing again. His arms wrapped around her with surprising tenderness, like someone clinging to what little hope remained.

Brian stepped back inside the room and saw them. "You two need a minute?" he asked, eyebrows raised gently.

"No, we're good," Grayle replied quickly, breaking off the embrace and wiping at the tears that were now on her face. She sighed, a little more exhausted now, as if even moments of comfort required strength she didn't have.

"I tried reaching out to David, Phil's assistant," Brian said. "He doesn't want to talk. I don't blame him."

"They were close," Grayle murmured. "And I ruined it."

"You did nothing of the sort," Richard said firmly. "Tim did. Don't own what isn't yours."

He drew a breath and straightened his tone. "Since you both insist on going to Wyoming, here's the plan. We'll stay the weekend at your grandparents', then leave the morning after the party. I believe we'll be safe. They won't reveal themselves in front of everyone. But be careful. They'll try to rattle you. Don't give them an opening."

He looked directly at Grayle, his eyes sharp. "You have the advantage. He doesn't know what you know. Keep it that way."

Grayle nodded. "Okay."

"I'll be fine too," Brian added.

"Good," Richard said. "We leave at noon."

The morning passed uneventfully. They boarded Richard's shuttle, bound for Wyoming. The vehicle hummed with quiet efficiency as it lifted from the platform and angled toward the horizon. Grayle paused before climbing in, drawing in a long breath. The morning sun warmed her cheeks, but it couldn't soften the tension in her chest. Her thoughts still felt fractured, scattered like windblown ash. Brian could see it in her eyes, the way they lingered without focus, the shadows tucked beneath them, but he hoped the comfort of home might help her heal.

As they descended over Cody, the mountains rolled below them like an old dream. Familiar. Grounding. The rugged terrain spread out in soft blues and browns, painted in memory.

When they landed, the shuttle doors opened with a hiss, and Grayle was the first to step out. A gust of prairie wind lifted the hem of her coat as she scanned the quiet runway. Her grandparents, Rose and Arthur, stood nearby, bundled in light jackets against the cool breeze. They were already waiting.

"Hi, honey!" Rose smiled warmly and opened her arms. Her voice, tender and inviting, carried a hint of emotion.

Grayle said nothing. She walked directly to her and buried her face in her grandmother's shoulder. The embrace was long, silent, and deeply needed.

Rose held her close, her wrinkled hands gentle on Grayle's back. She was aware of Phil Wells' death but unaware of the deeper trauma Grayle had endured, the kind that left no visible wounds.

As Arthur walked past them, he touched Grayle's shoulder gently, a brief but intentional gesture of reassurance. Then he approached Brian with the same steadiness he always had. "How are you, young man?" he asked, his arms opening for an embrace.

"I'm fine, Grandpa. It's great to be home." Brian slung his bag over his shoulder, already feeling the warmth of familiarity settle over him. He nodded toward Richard.

"Richard," Arthur said, extending his hand with a firm grip. "Mind if we take a walk?"

"Of course," Richard said, his voice calm but guarded.

They strolled down the long gravel driveway, the stones crunching beneath their shoes. A gentle breeze rustled the cottonwoods as the two men walked away from the others.

"What's going on?" Arthur asked, his tone growing stern. "What happened with Phil? And how are my grandkids involved?"

Richard sighed and briefly looked away, his eyes scanning the distant hills as if searching for easier answers. "We're working on it," Richard replied. "That's why they're with me. I swear, Art, I'll protect them."

Arthur studied him for a moment, his eyebrows lowering as he considered the weight of Richard's words. Then, with a slow nod, he relented. "I believe you. You and Will have always looked out for them, and I trust you will now, too."

Richard exhaled, relieved that the inquisition appeared to be over for now. He tried to switch the direction of the conversation, gesturing toward the barn in the distance. "Tomorrow's party should be… eventful."

"That it should," Arthur said. "It's gonna be more intimate this year. Only about eighty are coming. Most everyone else is out on assignment."

"What about Alex and Tim?" Richard asked cautiously, his voice tightening just slightly.

"They'll be here," Arthur said dryly, rolling his eyes for effect. "We'll be regaled with Alex's tall tales, I'm sure."

"Yeah," Richard muttered. "He's usually full of shit."

They both chuckled, the sound easing some of the tension. Arthur turned toward the house and began walking. Richard took the cue and followed closely behind, their footsteps soft on the gravel path.

That evening passed quietly. The five of them lounged on the back deck, enjoying each other's company and the wind as it swept through the trees and over the plains. The setting sun cast long amber streaks across the grass, and the air smelled of pine and cooling earth. The rhythmic creak of an old porch swing joined the occasional clink of glasses as soft laughter rose and fell between them. It was the kind of night that might've felt perfect, if not for the heaviness Grayle carried.

Later, when the sun dropped below the horizon and they all called it quits for the night, Rose and Arthur retired to their room. A floor lamp bathed the space in soft gold as Rose slipped off her earrings and began undressing.

"Something's off with Grayle," she said as she slipped into her nightclothes, the fabric whispering against her skin.

"She went through something violent. Of course, she's off," Arthur replied, undressing in the corner and flipping through hangers in his closet with a slow, methodical rhythm.

"No, I mean… deeper than that." Rose looked thoughtful as she folded her blouse neatly on the dresser. "Something is missing in her eyes. Like she's not entirely here. It's like she's a different person."

Arthur paused what he was doing in the closet and turned to face his wife. The lines in his face deepened as he considered her words. "Maybe she should stay here. She needs space. Time to get away from all this."

Rose lay down in her bed, smoothing the comforter with her hand. "She won't walk away," she said gently. "She's too much like both her parents."

Arthur laughed as he turned off the closet light. "No kidding! Strong. Smart. Stubborn. Yep. She's got it all." He shook his head with a smile, then climbed into bed beside her.

* * *

Across the hallway, Grayle sat on the edge of her bed, her body tense, her hands clenched in her lap. The soft light of the bedside lamp gave the room a peaceful glow, but inside her, there was only turbulence. She was trying to calm herself without Richard's pills, but the battle in her mind was loud and constant. Her hands trembled slightly, and she fidgeted until she couldn't take it anymore. Her thoughts were all noise, rising and crashing like waves in a storm.

Reaching out for her comm, she tried to call Tash. No answer. She left a message. "Shit, Tash. It's 6:30 there. I don't know why I thought you'd be up. Call me when you can. Love you, sweetness."

Eventually, she gave in and took one of the pills. She swallowed it dry, the bitterness lingering on her tongue. As she waited for it to kick in, Brian slowly cracked the door and peeked in, his voice soft and concerned.

"You okay?" he asked gently.

She glanced at him and smiled slightly. "Yeah, I'm okay. For now."

"Alright. I'll check in later."

"Thanks, B.J."

Their bond had always seen them through. But this, this was different. Her soul was fraying. The ache was deeper than pain... it was disconnection.

At 12:05 a.m., her comm buzzed. It was Tash. Grayle answered.

"Hey," Tash mumbled groggily. "What's going on, babe?"

Grayle couldn't stop the tears. They welled up and spilled over before she could speak. She broke into sobs immediately, not able to form the words she needed.

Tash's voice was panicked. "Grayle? Grayle! What's wrong? You're scaring me!"

"I'm sorry. I'm okay. I'm just... sad. I miss you. I wish you were coming in today."

"I'm sorry, I have a lot going on. But I'm coming next week, and I'll spend all the time you need, okay?" She paused and tried to erase the sadness as only she could do. "Hey... I might've met a sweet Italian boy."

Grayle sniffed, perking up slightly. "Go on."

"He's kind, funny, very cute, and... studying architecture. He's taking me to Spain tonight. Romantic little date." Tash's voice, always smooth and comforting, had a calming effect on Grayle.

"Mmm... that sounds nice."

"He's probably brought other girls there before," Tash giggled. "At least, that's what Uncle Will said. You know how overprotective he can be."

Grayle smiled for the first time in hours, her voice growing tired. "Tash?"

"Yep?"

"Listen. I'm gonna try and rest now. I love you very much, Tashy."

"Love you too. Call me if you need anything."

Tash ended the call. As Grayle turned in for the night and finally calmed down, the weight in her chest began to lift just slightly. The pill was working, but it was the voice of her sister that truly softened the edge of her pain. Across the globe, Tash's day got started.

By the next afternoon, the gathering had begun. Friends, colleagues, and old associates flowed in through the wide gate of the ranch, their vehicles crunching across the gravel and kicking up soft puffs of dust in the dry Wyoming air. The ranch's back pavilion had been transformed, glowing gently beneath strung lights that swayed in the afternoon breeze. Tables draped in crisp white linen stood in neat rows. At the center of each one sat ten red roses, each bloom a silent tribute to the lost crew of the *Intervention*, surrounded by rings of wildflowers, hand-picked from the surrounding fields, in remembrance of those who had perished on the ground.

As guests arrived, Art and Rose stood at the entrance to the gathering space, offering warm embraces, gentle handshakes, and heartfelt words to each person who approached. The air was thick with nostalgia and reverence, but also the cautious cheer of old friends reunited under difficult circumstances.

Inside the house, Richard, Brian, and Grayle prepared to join the crowd. Grayle adjusted the cuff of her sleeve without looking up, her expression unreadable.

"Okay," Richard said quietly, his tone low and direct. "Alex and Tim will be here soon. You two... no scenes. And don't be alone with either of them. Understood?"

"No shit," Grayle muttered. She walked out without another word, her head down and shaking slowly from side to side, her boots scuffing faintly against the hardwood floor.

Richard sighed and turned to Brian. "Watch her, will you? Don't let her near Tim."

"I won't. What about you? What are you going to do?"

"I'll do my best," Richard said. "Let's go."

Outside, the guests mingled beneath the soft lighting of the pavilion. The hum of conversation floated through the late-day air, blending with the occasional chime of silverware on china and the quiet laughter of someone recalling better days. Glasses of wine clinked softly. Plates of food were passed around. The scent of grilled meats and herbs drifted from the nearby buffet. But even in this comfortable setting, a low hum of anticipation hung just beneath the surface, unspoken and taut.

Richard was immediately pulled into conversations. A group of guests gathered near the center table, asking him about the investigations into Owen Stipe, Stan Collins, and Phil Wells. Their faces were pinched with concern. No one had seen a string of deaths like this in nearly two centuries, and Richard, as always, carried the weight of their questions with calm and poise.

Unlike Alex and Tim.

The two men moved through the crowd like shadows, silent and deliberate. They stood a few feet behind Richard, lingering just at the edge of the gathering. The moment Richard felt their presence, a cold ripple went down his back. He turned.

"Alex. Tim," he said, nodding in greeting. "Good to see you."

To the other guests, it appeared to be nothing more than old friends catching up at a memorial. But behind their tight smiles, the air between them was electric. Richard's fists itched to strike. Tim's jaw flexed with restraint. Alex's smile was hollow, rehearsed.

Alex was the first to speak, placing his hand on Richard's shoulder and waving a fake smile to others across the room. "Good to see you too, old friend. Haven't seen you in a while."

Tim interrupted with a cold smirk. "Not since that rather shocking little visit in Dayton."

Alex chuckled, glancing toward the dessert table. "Yes. That. I didn't get a chance to say it in person, but I was sorry to hear about Stan Collins."

Tim stepped forward and embraced Richard with a sudden, false hug. As his arms tightened briefly, he leaned in close and whispered in a voice so low only Richard could hear, "He was always a bit clumsy, wasn't he, Dick?" Just as quickly, he pulled back and walked off, his smirk trailing behind him.

Richard didn't move. Didn't flinch. His eyes followed Tim for a moment, his body motionless but rigid with tension.

Alex followed Tim, pausing just long enough to get closer to Richard and murmur under his breath, "Sorry. He can't help himself."

Elsewhere, Commander Will Phillips arrived, stepping out of a dusty transport with a confident stride. His arrival brought a breath of something familiar. He was warmly greeted by Rose, Art, and the siblings. They caught up briefly near the entrance to the pavilion, their smiles real, their laughter unforced. For a moment, it felt like a real family gathering, like the good ol' days before tragedy had taken root.

"How's everyone doing?" Will asked, hugging Brian firmly and giving Grayle a kiss on the forehead.

"All good here. How's Tash doing?" Rose asked.

"She's charming some Italian boy, I think," Will replied flatly, with a half-smile that carried both affection and caution. "I think that's why she chose not to come."

"She told me about him," Grayle added with a laugh. "Sounds like she's having a good time."

"She's always up to something," Brian added as he shrugged his shoulders and shook his head.

"I'm glad you're keeping an eye on her, Will," Art chimed in briefly, patting Will's back.

As the pleasantries continued, Grayle's smile faded. She turned slightly and scanned the crowd. Faces moved past her in a blur, but one figure remained locked in focus.

She saw Tim.

As their eyes met, something inside her cracked. Bright flashes, like camera flashes, flickered behind her eyes. Her head swam with a sickening rush of disorientation. She pressed her fingers to her temple.

Brian noticed immediately and rushed to her. "Whoa, now," he said, gently guiding her to a table. "Let's sit down for a minute."

The suddenness of her weakness had alarmed him. Her skin looked pale under the ambient lights, and her steps faltered as though her balance had simply evaporated.

"Is she okay?" Will asked quickly, his face etched with concern. He hovered, uncertain whether to step forward or give her space.

"I don't know," Rose replied, her worry mounting. Her brows furrowed, and she reached instinctively toward Grayle, her hand brushing her shoulder.

Grayle took a slow sip of water Brian had handed her. The glass trembled slightly in her hand. "I'm okay. Just... a dizzy spell. I'll be fine."

"If it happens again, I'm pulling you out of here," Brian said, scanning her face for signs of worsening.

She nodded, steadying herself, though her fingers clutched the edge of the table. "Maybe... maybe I just need food."

Brian looked across the room to where the bots were rolling in with trays of food of every kind imaginable. Gleaming silver platters shimmered under the overhead lights, releasing the warm aroma of home-cooked meals. Guests began to form lines like kids at a carnival buffet.

Alex's voice carried through the air. "Chicken Parmigiana! My heart! Ravioli! Oh yes, come to Papa!" he announced dramatically, arms raised in theatrical joy.

Will took that moment of interruption to step in behind him.

"Hello," he said with the warmth of a dead fish, his tone flat and devoid of emotion.

Alex glanced back and tried to register a fake smile. It wasn't working. His lips curled, but his eyes were icy. "Oh, hey. Didn't see you, Commander."

"Let's cut the small talk," Will said. "I don't know why you continue to come to these dinners. You're the reason we're all gathered like this in the first place."

Alex's smile vanished like a snuffed candle. "Fuck you, you smug asshole," he said under his breath, not wanting to draw any attention.

Will just shrugged and smiled. "Coming from you? That's almost a compliment."

"Look, old man. We'll never like each other again, and that's fine by me. So, why don't you quit acting like a jerk?"

"Well, if people knew who you really were, they'd feel the same. You can't hide forever." Will moved away quickly, his shoulders squared with restrained fury.

Alex muttered, "Fucking child," as Will walked away, stabbing at his food with annoyance.

Behind Will, Rose sidled up to Alex. She had heard it all. "Are you two finished?" she asked, stepping in with the sharp tone of a mother who'd had enough. "Because I swear to God, if I have to supervise you like toddlers, I'll throw you both out."

"I'm good," Alex said quickly, flashing a fake smile like a mask. "Promise I'll behave. I won't take the focus off where it needs to be tonight."

"Oh, give me a break, Alex. You've never kept a promise in your life," Rose snapped, then walked off, her heels clipping hard against the tile in direct counter to what she had just warned him about.

Alex shook his head and then finished getting his food. He went back and sat next to Tim. "Let's eat, have a drink, and get the hell out of here. I'm over these sanctimonious pricks."

"Agreed," Tim replied, his voice low and gravelly.

As they ate, Tim's eyes drifted across the room straight to Richard. Their eyes locked in a cold, silent confrontation. Tim slowly raised a butter knife, held it just high enough for Richard to see, and then dragged it across his throat in a slashing motion. He smiled with an evil smile, slow and deliberate, but Richard didn't react.

Grayle, however, saw it all. Her heart jumped. She gritted her teeth. Rage surged through her, white-hot and uncontrollable.

Brian sensed it instantly, and he slid back his chair with a quiet scrape. "Whoa now, sis. Hey. Let's take a walk. Cool down a bit."

But she wouldn't move. She was locked in. Her eyes had become like glass: cold, reflective, distant.

Brian walked over to Richard. "She's going to snap."

Richard nodded, already heading toward them, but was quickly intercepted by more guests trying to speak with him. He waved them off politely, murmuring quick apologies, and tried to make his way through.

Alex got up from his seat and made his way to the bar. He ordered a drink and took a sip when it arrived, his fingers tapping the glass nervously. Seeing Grayle nearby, he spoke smoothly, his voice laced with charm. "What's a pretty girl like you doing in a joint like this?"

Grayle didn't blink. Her stare was fixed, her posture frozen like a statue ready to break.

"I… I didn't see you come in," he continued. "Been hiding? Hey. You okay?"

She didn't answer. Her eyes were fixed beyond him. On Tim. Seeing her raging at him, Tim joined them a moment later, waving a hand in front of her face. "Hey, Grayle."

Still nothing.

Then… finally… she spoke.

"How are you doing, General Smith? Captain Burns? Tim Stevens? Or should I say… Rob Anthony?"

Tim froze. Alex's face went pale, the blood draining from it like water through a sieve. "Excuse me?" Tim said, completely thrown off.

"Rob it is, then," Grayle said coldly.

Tim backed off slightly, regaining some composure. He held up his hands with mock calm. "Careful there, Grayle."

"She's been ringed," Alex muttered, barely moving his lips.

"Clearly," Tim replied.

Across the room, Richard and Brian saw what was happening. They tried to cut through the crowd, but again were held up by bodies and polite interruptions.

Grayle leaned forward, her voice barely audible.

"Do you even remember her?" she whispered. "Bridgette? Or any of the women you killed? Any of the lives you destroyed?"

Tim smiled slowly, his cold, arrogant confidence resurfacing. "Are you still wondering where she's bound?"

Tears spilled from Grayle's eyes. She trembled like a live wire. "I want to fucking kill you," she said through clenched teeth.

Alex sat forward. "Grayle. No trouble tonight. We can work this out."

"You should listen to him," Tim added, still smirking.

Art walked by just in time. Seeing his granddaughter in distress, he stepped in with gentle urgency. "Grayle, what do you say the two of us… I don't know, take a walk?"

She wiped her face, her hands shaking, and left with her grandfather, glancing back at Tim with vitriol in her blood. Her gaze burned into him.

Rose followed her husband, glaring daggers at the two men. "What did you do?" she demanded.

"Nothing," Alex said. "She's upset. That's all. I'm not sure why."

Rose glared at him for a few seconds longer before quickly following after Grayle.

Alex and Tim retreated to a quiet corner. "How the fuck do you two have any history?" Alex hissed.

"I don't know! Holy shit!" Tim hissed back.

"Keep your voice down," Alex snapped. "We need to leave. We need to rethink everything."

"Richard let her use the Halo," Tim said. "That's very obvious."

"No shit. We need to end this."

"I agree."

They turned to go, but Richard blocked their path in a sudden wall of authority.

"Go to your sister," he told Brian, who was right behind. "I'll handle this."

Brian nodded and slipped away.

Richard approached Alex and Tim. They stood in a tense triangle, a foot apart. Their bodies were taut, breaths short and controlled.

"What did you do?" Alex asked, seething.

"What did *you* do?" Richard shot back. "Let's tally it all up."

Tim stared him down, unmoving, and Richard stared back, the tension growing to a fevered pitch. Their silence crackled with impending violence.

"We're ending this," Alex said, his voice tight.

Tim added, "And it won't be quick. Or humane like the others."

Alex grabbed his arm. "Stop. We don't need to tell him any…"

Richard narrowed his eyes. "I fucked Addison."

Tim smirked. "Yeah, well, she's met her end."

"Shut the fuck up, Tim," Alex snapped, dragging Tim away. "We're leaving! Now!"

They stormed off toward their transport.

When they reached their transport, Alex and Tim slammed the doors with a force that echoed off the hills. Inside, the tension boiled over.

"Fuck. Fuck. Fuck. Fuck!" Alex snapped, fists clenched around the steering wheel. "Tim, it's time we take Richard out."

"I agree," Tim muttered, dropping back into the passenger seat. His voice was tight, low. Dangerous.

Alex continued. "We need to get the Mackeys out of the way. All of them."

Tim exhaled hard. "Alright. Just give me a minute to think."

Neither said another word.

Finally, the engine roared to life, and the transport tore away from the ranch, gravel spitting under its wheels as they vanished into the dark.

"Where do you think they're heading?" Brian asked as they watched them leave.

"I don't know," Richard said. "But we're not safe. We'll stay the night, but tomorrow, we're gone. I'm pulling Tash out whether she likes it or not. Your grandparents are coming with us, too."

He looked away, jaw tight with a knot of emotion.

"I got my answer about Addison," he said quietly. "Tim killed her. And the rest of them."

He turned back to Brian.

"No one is safe now."

Chapter 24: Psychosis

Five days had passed since the confrontation at the family gathering in Wyoming. In their empty warehouse hideout on the outskirts of Dayton, Alex and Tim regrouped. The building was vast and silent, filled with broken crates and discarded tech parts. Shafts of muted sunlight cut through dusty, cracked windows. They were alone, volatile, and increasingly unhinged.

"Stop pacing," Alex muttered, seated at an old desk in the center of his abandoned office. His fingers tapped absently on the scarred wood, each click echoing through the high-ceilinged room like a warning.

"I can't believe we're linked together like this!" Tim shouted into the echoing space, his footsteps pounding a rhythm into the concrete floor. His fists clenched, and his voice cracked at the edge of disbelief.

"The odds...," Alex murmured, eyes locked on nothing, "are astronomical." He finally looked up, his expression a mask of irritation and disbelief. "Who would've guessed this would get in our way?"

Tim turned, frustration burning behind his eyes. "It's like the Norn said, there are forces at work beyond anything we understand. Scientific, mystical, maybe even divine."

"Guess they weren't fucking kidding," Alex replied, almost bitterly. He looked at Tim in continued disbelief, uncertain what to do next. The silence pressed in on them like a weight.

Tim stopped pacing. His tone shifted. Calculated. Cold. He answered Alex's unasked query. "Here's what we do. Tash is coming in within the next twenty-four hours. I'll intercept her." He hesitated, letting the weight of the plan settle over him like a slow, creeping fog. "I know how to lure Grayle. I'll bring her here... and I'll end it. Then you and I take out Richard together."

"No," Alex interrupted, calm but firm, shaking his head slowly, but emphatically. His voice was quiet, but resolute. "I'll face Richard myself."

"What? Why?" Tim shot back, his hands out in disbelief. "We're better off together. You know that!"

"Because it's what I want," Alex said, eyes narrowing. "It'll be less volatile without you. He always underestimates me."

Tim frowned. "Then you'll need to be armed. You're no match for him in a physical confrontation."

Alex stood and started away from the desk. His footsteps were slow and deliberate. "Okay, what do you have?"

Tim gestured toward a duffel near the wall. "Mesh suit under your clothes. It'll absorb the stun gadgets. Glock nineteen with hollow point rounds. And a thirty-eight Special."

"A thirty-eight?" Alex raised an eyebrow.

"Close-range. Just… don't get too close." Tim added with a warning in his voice, "You know he's going to kill you, right?"

Alex's reply was dry. "Hey, thanks for the vote of confidence, asshole."

"You should wait for me," Tim tried again.

"We know what we need to do," Alex said. "Let's just fucking do it."

He turned and stormed out of the warehouse, the metal door slamming behind him with a sharp clang that echoed long after he had vanished, leaving Tim in silence.

At Richard's estate, Brian and Grayle lingered. The estate's towering walls and manicured gardens stood in stark contrast to the chaos they had fled. Grayle was still struggling with flashes of euphoria and disorientation. Her steps were slow, her gaze unfocused.

Richard pulled Brian aside. "How's she doing?"

Brian shot him a sharp glance. "How do you think?"

Richard looked away from the glare and spoke coldly. "You're eventually going to have to get over being mad at me," Richard replied. "We've got bigger problems."

"She's restless. I'm taking her back to the ranch tomorrow. Tash is flying in. We'll lay low."

"It's not safe there. Have Tash come here."

"We're going to Wyoming and that's that," Brian's tone was sharp and cold, almost bitter.

Richard nodded, accepting the boundary. He patted Brian on the shoulder and walked away. "Fair enough, B.J. Fair enough."

The next day, despite Richard's final protest, the siblings departed in Brian's shuttle. The sleek craft rose silently into the sky, cutting through thin cloud layers. There wasn't much conversation left between the three of them, but they did reach out to Will to check in on Tash as they flew.

"Uncle Will, how's the flight?"

Will's voice came through clearly. "All good, amigos. Halfway across the Atlantic. Clear skies."

Brian smiled. "Hey, baby, sis. How are you doing?"

Tash chimed in over some light static. "Still hate flying." She chuckled and they all joined her.

"It'll be over before you know it," Grayle said, smiling.

"I miss you guys," Tash added. "Can't wait to be home."

"Should be back around sunset," Will spoke matter-of-factly.

"Great. See you soon," Brian said.

"Love you both," Tash replied before cutting the connection.

Grayle leaned back, and Brian watched her closely. Her smile had returned, but the weight never left her eyes. "I know. I'm still freaked out, too," she admitted. "I keep thinking about Phil. I wish David would talk to me again." She turned toward Brian. "When we get to Wyoming, I need you to reach out to someone. Father Vincent Rich. He's at the Vatican. He can help. He knows who to call."

"I'll do it," Brian promised. "What's the worst part? The feeling?"

"I don't feel like myself," Grayle said quietly. "I drift between memories that feel familiar, but I know they're not mine. It's like someone else is piloting me. I'm... sorry I touched that thing." She buried her face in her hands in an exasperated manner, looking out her window. "I wish I'd *never* touched that thing."

Brian exhaled. "That's probably your chip trying to hold onto fractured memories. And yeah, I wish you hadn't also. But, it's done." He paused. "Look. I have something I need to say. I'm done with all of this. Let's grab our grandparents, Tash, and Uncle Will, and let's leave. Let Richard, Tim, and Alex handle their mess. It's their fight, not ours. All we are is collateral damage to them."

Grayle smiled. "You know, I'd actually like that."

"Good. It's set. We'll talk to them as soon as we land," Brian said.

"Where do you want to go?" Grayle continued to focus out the window in a daydreaming state.

"I don't care. Italy, maybe? Anywhere but here."

"Father Vince is at the Vatican," Grayle noted softly.

"Perfect."

As they crossed into Wyoming, their home came into view. Rolling hills, golden fields, the comforting sprawl of the ranch. It was like a warm blanket on a cold day. Even though they were there just a week ago, they both realized they should have stayed. The long dirt drive and wooden fences looked as familiar as ever, peaceful and still.

"I'll land behind the house," Brian said, adjusting the shuttle's controls.

"Good," Grayle grinned. "Grandma hates it when you park this contraption in the driveway."

The shuttle descended gently, the landing pads kicking up dry grass and dust. Brian began to shut it down, fingers dancing across the console with routine precision, then…

BOOM!

A massive explosion erupted from the house.

The shockwave struck like a monstrous fist, lifting the shuttle from the ground and flinging it sideways as if it weighed nothing. A deep metallic groan filled the air. Metal screamed under the pressure.

Brian and Grayle were thrown violently to the floor, limbs tangled, their heads smacking against the console and floor with jarring force.

A raw, primal scream tore from Brian's throat. Not from pain. Not even fear. But helplessness. The kind of cry that ripped straight from the soul.

"No!" Brian shouted. He jumped to his feet, grabbed a portable scanner from the storage unit, and bolted outside in a combination of fear and Defender training. His boots hit the ground hard, every instinct firing. "Wait here! I'm going to go take a quick scan!"

Grayle watched him in stunned silence, too shaken to move. Her ears rang. Her body trembled. Smoke billowed in the distance, dark and rising.

Her comm lit up as did her eyes. It was her grandfather.

"Oh my God, yes! Where are you?" she answered breathlessly, hope flooding her voice.

"We're okay!" Art shouted. "We're a mile out! We were visiting friends and we heard the explosion from their house. We're on our way back!"

Grayle ran to the shuttle's doorway and waved Brian back, calling to him. "They're safe!" she called out. "They weren't home!"

Brian sprinted back inside. His face was ashen, but there was relief in his eyes. He threw himself into the pilot seat and immediately flipped on the comm, reaching out to Will and Tash.

"Uncle Will! Don't land! The ranch is gone, but Gram and Gramps are okay. Still, the location is not safe! Take Tash somewhere secure!"

There was shock on the other end of the line, and then finally, Will spoke. "Dear Lord, when will they ever stop?" He sighed. "Okay, copy that. We're diverting now."

"Tash!" Grayle cried. "Call me when you're safe!"

"I will," she replied in a voice that could only be described as frightened and shattered.

Brian killed the call and immediately hailed Richard. When he answered, Brian screamed into the comm. "There's been an explosion at the ranch!" Brian shouted. "I set the emergency beacon, so I'm presuming that emergency crews are en route!"

"Your grandparents?" Richard demanded.

"They're okay," Brian said, breathless. "They weren't home."

"Thank God. Come back... now."

Brian programmed the shuttle for return. He turned to Grayle, his hands still shaking slightly. "Autopilot's on. I'm sending you to Richard."

Her eyes widened. "Wait. What about you?"

"I'm getting them to safety. When I get everything settled, I'll join you. I love you."

He kissed her forehead and ran out. The shuttle lifted into the sky, rising fast through the smoke-veiled air.

A couple of hours later, the transport touched down at Richard's estate. He was waiting at the pad, arms crossed, face grim. As the transport powered down, Grayle climbed out. She barely made it out of the hatch before collapsing in Richard's arms.

When Grayle awoke, she was on his couch. The soft cushions pressed against her back, and a light blanket had been draped over her. Her head throbbed, and her breathing was shallow, her chest rising and falling with effort.

"You're okay," Richard said gently, offering a calm presence from the armchair beside her. He gave her a faint smile, his eyes tired. "You were out about ninety minutes." He held out a small white pill in one hand and a glass of water in the other. "Here, take this. It'll help take the edge off."

She took the pill from his hand and swallowed hard, the water cool against her dry throat. "What time is it?"

"Almost eight," he replied, glancing at a sleek wall-mounted screen nearby.

"Brian?" Her voice cracked as she asked.

"He's safe. He dropped off your grandparents with the Defenders and is en route back here."

Sitting up slowly, Grayle held her head in one hand and squinted in pain. Her temples throbbed with each pulse of her heart. "I need to get hold of Tash." She fumbled for her communicator on the table next to the couch and tried to reach her sister. The call didn't go through. She stared at the blank screen for a moment, then left a message. "Let me know where you are. I love you."

She set the communicator down with a shaky breath and turned to Richard. "What now?"

"Now… we regroup," he replied, his voice steady.

Grayle shook her head, each movement sharper than the last. Her eyes began to well up, her frustration boiling over. "No. That's not good enough. They blew up our home, Richard. That can't go unanswered."

"We wait," he said calmly, raising his hand to slow her down. "Your heart rate is spiking. That pill should help, and I need to think, so I'm going to my study. You just relax for a bit."

He started to leave the room, but her voice followed him.

"I don't know how you can say that, 'we wait.' If it were your home, you'd feel…"

"I'm not doing this now, Grayle," he interrupted, his tone suddenly sharp. "We're going to regroup, and that's all there is to it." He turned fully, his eyes flashing. "I need to think, so I'll be in there." He spun around angrily and disappeared down the hall, leaving Grayle alone in the silence, her hands clenched in her lap, her jaw set tight. Outside the window, the stars blinked indifferently overhead.

Watching Richard leave, Grayle sank deeper into the couch, the sedative washing over her like a warm tide. Her limbs grew heavy as the cushions embraced her, and her thoughts began to drift. Sleep crept in slowly, like a curtain being drawn over the day. Soon she was floating, weightless, beneath a velvet sky dusted with stars.

***

A familiar presence stirred beside her, so gentle and unmistakable that she knew who it was before she turned to look. A radiant red-haired woman in gleaming white stood quietly beside her. Bridgette.

Grayle turned to her, the sound of her voice catching in her throat. "Bridgette..." she called, reaching out.

But Bridgette wouldn't meet her eyes. She turned away in silence and walked off into the darkness, her figure fading like mist into the night.

"Wait!" Grayle whispered, her voice cracking. "Don't go..."

A tear welled in the corner of her eye, the ache of loss pressing hard against her chest.

Suddenly, her communicator buzzed, vibrating against the table with a mechanical urgency that yanked her from the dream. She blinked and sat up, groggy. The screen flashed. **8:47 p.m.** Tash's name illuminated the display.

"Sweetness?" she asked softly, rubbing the sleep from her eyes. "Where are you?"

No answer came.

Only a song. Faint. Haunting.

There she goes... wonder where she is bound...

Grayle froze. Her blood ran cold. A sickening fear flooded her, as if every nerve had been dunked in ice water.

Then came a voice. Calm. Unfeeling.

"Still there, Grayle? Paul? Come to Dayton. Our warehouse. See you soon."

Click.

Tim ended the call and turned to Alex.

"She's coming. Go and make your way to Richard's. She'll be here soon."

Alex gave a grim nod and stepped away, his face a mask of determination.

Back at Richard's estate, Grayle stormed into the study, breath ragged and heart pounding.

"I just received a call from Tim," she blurted. "Richard, I think they're coming for us. I have to get my things…"

"Divide and conquer," Richard muttered under his breath, already thinking ahead.

"Look, I need to go to Dayton. Alone!"

"Absolutely not," Richard snapped, his voice rising in fury. "No. You are not!"

"I can do this," Grayle insisted, her voice rising to match his. Her eyes blazed with intensity.

"No, you can't!" Richard shot back. "He'll kill you, Grayle! Sure, you've had a little training, but you're completely outmatched against someone like Tim. He'll kill you in the blink of an eye. Do you understand me?" His voice was harsh, his words like slaps.

"Then arm me!" she shouted. "Give me something! You have an entire arsenal at your disposal. I need to get him. For Bridgette, my parents, Phil… Addison. Anyone else he's killed! I need this!"

Richard stared at her. Then he began pacing furiously, one hand pressed to his temple. "Shh. Stop. I'm thinking."

Finally, he turned toward her, eyes locked. "Look. I have something. Something they won't be able to detect. But it's a one-way ticket. If you do this, there's no coming back from it."

"Okay. Show me," she said, steady and resolute.

Richard walked into an adjacent room, the doorway still in view. Grayle watched as he touched his hand to a bookcase. With a soft mechanical click, the bookcase swung open, revealing a hidden room beyond. He vanished into the dark for several minutes, then returned, holding a gun-like injector and three small capsules.

Grayle's eyes widened. "What is that?"

"This first capsule is the bomb. I'm going to implant it into your right shoulder. This will hurt."

She gritted her teeth. "Do it. I'm not changing my mind."

Thwip.

"Aaaargh!"

She cried out, gripping the arm of the couch as the injector pierced her skin.

"This one's the detonator," Richard explained. "It goes into the center of your chest. Your heartbeat is the timer. The more you panic, the faster it counts down. You'll have about three hours."

Grayle was already sweating. "Yeah, yeah. I fucking get it. Do it."

Thwip. Another searing jab of pain.

"I'm going to measure your heart rate now…" He pressed two fingers to her wrist, old school, and counted. "Now I'm going to set the bomb." He touched a few places on his comm. Three, two, one. Time. Now, it'll take you thirty minutes to get to Dayton. I want you to go straight there."

Grayle nodded. Richard handed her a thin wrist cuff. "This will display your heart rate. Keep it low if you want more time."

She took it and strapped it on.

"I'll go down and get your shuttle ready. Stay here until I return. Don't waste heartbeats."

"Thank you, Richard," she said sincerely.

He nodded, turned, and rushed out of the room.

Minutes later, Richard pulled the shuttle around and came to the doorway. As he stepped out, he embraced her tightly.

"Go. Now. Don't be late."

Grayle kissed his cheek. "Thank you, Richard. I'm going to get this son-of-a-bitch and end this once and for all."

She jumped into the shuttle, glanced up at the night sky, and spotted another ship approaching.

She groaned.

"Alex," Richard muttered under his breath. He turned to Grayle, eyes sharp. "Go!"

Grayle ascended.

Richard took a deep breath and walked back toward the house, his steps even and composed, readying himself for whatever came next.

As Grayle raced through the sky, her comm lit up and Brian's voice burst through, taut with worry.

"Grayle?! What's happening? I see my shuttle's been activated for Dayton!"

Grayle gave a soft, bittersweet smile. "They blew up our home. I'm blowing up theirs. I love you, B.J."

She cut the feed without waiting for a reply.

Back at Richard's, Alex approached the house slowly. The lights inside were all on. Every step brought a fresh layer of tension. His fingers flexed near his sidearm, his breath controlled but shallow. He waited for Tim's go-ahead before breaching.

Meanwhile, Grayle reached the warehouse. Without hesitation, she disembarked and marched toward the front entrance, each step echoing with purpose. Her heart rate was rising, the digital display on her wrist flashing red. She noticed, but didn't care.

Inside, Tim opened a comm line to Alex. "She's here. Go ahead and breach."

"Copy that."

At the front door, Grayle paused, closed her eyes, and inhaled slowly. The moment of stillness was brief, but necessary. She reached for the doorknob, surprised it was unlocked, and slipped inside.

The warehouse was fully lit. Everything was quiet. Nothing moved. Her senses were tuned to every creak and flicker.

"Tim! Rob! Whoever the hell you are, come out and face me!"

Tim stepped out from a side room, his hands raised in a non-threatening gesture.

"Grayle..."

She shook her head sharply. "No. No, we're not doing that. It's over now. But I don't want to hurt you."

Tim nodded. "You're right. It is over. It's done. Alex is at Richard's house right now. He's putting an end to all of this."

Again, he raised his hands. "Look, we don't have to fight. It's okay." He glanced left toward a small corner office and motioned. "Come on out."

Grayle frowned, her brow furrowing in confusion. "Who are you talking to?"

From the shadowed doorway, Tash, Will, and Addison stepped out cautiously.

Grayle's breath caught in her throat. Her vision blurred. Her knees bent slightly, and she rested her hands on them for support.

"What the hell?" she whispered.

"That's right, Grayle," Tim said quietly. "They're all here. Safe. We need to talk."

Tash shouted, voice trembling. "Listen to him!" She started toward her sister, but Grayle held up her hand.

"Stop!"

Tash froze mid-step. Will stepped beside her, voice firm but gentle. "Grayle... let's slow this down here. We love you."

Grayle gave a confused smile. "What is this? Some kind of intervention?"

Back at Richard's, Alex crept inside. The place was eerily calm, every light blazing as if to lure him in. He moved silently, cautious with every footstep.

On the counter, he noticed a handwritten note.

I'm in the den. Security's off. Come in.

Alex made his way toward the open doorway. The light from within glowed warmly.

Inside, Richard stood by the fireplace, one hand shielding a match as he lit a thick cigar.

"Jesus Christ," Richard muttered without turning. "Would you hurry the fuck up? I haven't got all night."

"I'll stay right here if it's all the same to you," Alex replied from the threshold, his tone guarded.

Richard finally turned and met his eyes. "You don't need that gun, Alex," he said smoothly. "Come sit. Let's talk like civilized men."

He waved a hand toward the chair opposite him.

Then, moving with unhurried calm, Richard grabbed a fire poker, adjusted a burning log, and placed the poker back in its stand. He sank into his chair with a sigh, the flickering fire casting long shadows across the room.

"So," he said between cigar drags, "when did you know it was me behind all of this?"

Chapter 25: A Drink

The Warehouse

Two confrontations occurred simultaneously, two rooms—two endings written at the same time.

At the warehouse, Grayle stood face-to-face with Tim in the open space. Overhead, the fluorescent lights hummed faintly, casting a pale, sterile glow that deepened every shadow. The vast, empty building amplified every footstep, every breath, every heartbeat.

"You're here with me right now," Tim said evenly. His hands hovered just above waist level, palms open in a pacifying gesture. His voice was low, almost careful. "And Alex is with Richard. But none of this has to end badly. We can still fix this."

Grayle's eyes were wide, burning with fury. Her chest rose and fell in sharp, ragged bursts. She looked like she hadn't slept in days. "Did you give Bridgette that same choice?"

Tim exhaled slowly and closed his eyes for a moment, as if some weight were pressing inward. He gave his head a gentle shake, almost mournful. When he looked back at her, he gestured toward Commander Phillips, who stood off to the side like a protective wall, shielding Tash and Addison behind him.

"Get them out of here," Tim said.

Will didn't argue. He took Addison gently by the hand and guided her back — she was shaken but no longer bound; whatever leverage Tim had used to draw them here, he'd dropped it the moment Grayle walked in. Tash resisted, twisting in his grip.

"Grayle, stop!" she cried. But Grayle didn't respond, didn't move, didn't even seem to hear. Her world had narrowed down to a single target. Her stare was locked on Tim like a hunter tracking prey.

Tim didn't move either.

"How long?" he asked softly, keeping his eyes on hers. "How long did you have the Halo on, Grayle?"

"Long enough," she growled. Her voice was gravelly. Her muscles were coiled. "Long enough to see what a fucking monster you are."

Tim didn't flinch at the words. He tilted his head slightly, as if trying to see her more clearly. "C'mon. How long?"

Grayle's hands balled into fists. "Just under five minutes."

Tim's mouth drew into a thin line. "Shiiiiiit," he breathed out slowly, dragging the word like the hiss of a leaking tire. "That explains it."

Grayle stood like a statue carved from rage.

"What you're experiencing right now..." Tim continued, "...we call it HPS. Halo Psychosis Syndrome."

"HPS?" she sneered. "Now that's a cute acronym, dickhead."

He ignored the jab. "Alex and I came up with it. We saw it in all twenty-one people we tested. The confusion. The emotional swings. The illusion of clarity. You think you're seeing the truth, but the Halo's burned a new reality into your brain."

Grayle's teeth clenched tighter.

"That's how he got to you," Tim said. "Richard. He's using you. The Halo scrambled your wiring, and now he's guiding you right where he wants you."

"I'm done talking," she said.

And she lunged.

Her body launched across the concrete floor, her face wild, mouth open in a cry that was part scream, part grief. She threw a haymaker, full-force, full of every wound she'd carried, but Tim moved like smoke. He sidestepped, letting her momentum carry her past him.

She hit the ground hard, knees and palms smacking into the floor.

And then... she laughed. Low. Gut-deep. Mad.

She rolled and sprang to her feet in a single, fluid motion, an animal uncaged. She charged again, delivering a furious series of strikes: jabs, knees, elbows. It was messy, primal, and emotional.

Tim never raised a hand.

He slipped through her assault like wind through branches, flowing from one evasion to the next. Nothing connected.

Her pulse surged in her ears. She could feel it hammering in her chest. The embedded capsule beneath her skin ticked down, hungry for adrenaline. She was shaving seconds off her life with every heartbeat.

Tim sighed. "Enough, Grayle."

She threw another wild punch.

He countered with a single jab, controlled, clinical, and it clipped her just beneath the chin. Her body sagged, strength leaving her all at once. She dropped to her knees, muttering a curse through clenched teeth.

Tim gently lowered her onto her side and reached into his coat. From it, he pulled a jet injector. He placed it against her neck and depressed the plunger. "I'm not here to hurt you, Grayle."

A soft hiss.

A blink of breath.

Then stillness.

Tim knelt beside her, his own chest rising and falling quickly now. Her long, sweat-damp hair fanned around her face like a halo. He brushed it back gently.

"How did we get here?" he whispered. "We're going to work this out, Grayle. I promise."

Richard's Study

At the same time, Alex stood just inside Richard's study, gun still raised. The room was dim and warm, firelight flickering off the antique wood-paneled walls. Opposite him, Richard reclined in a worn leather chair, completely at ease. The cigar smoldered between his fingers. He didn't look up.

"Sit," Richard said, waving lazily with his other hand. "Have a drink with me. We don't have much time."

Alex frowned. "Why? You got somewhere to be?"

"Yeah," Richard said with a chuckle. "Dead."

Alex blinked.

"I took a capsule before you came in," Richard continued. "Cyanide. Slow-dissolve. Custom blend. Should hit me in about... I don't know. Maybe twenty minutes?"

"You're insane," Alex said, but his hand lowered an inch.

Richard pointed to the gun. "Keep it up if you like. Doesn't matter to me. If I wanted to take it from you, I would. But we're beyond all that now. So, last offer: brandy and a cigar?"

Alex hesitated, then stepped forward. He didn't holster the gun, but the muzzle dipped slightly. "Brandy."

Richard rose and moved to a cabinet. He poured two snifters of glowing amber, the scent of oak and vanilla filling the air. He handed one to Alex, who took it without a word and sat down across from him.

The fire crackled between them.

Richard gestured toward the flame. "We've got time. Let's talk. You start."

Alex stared into the drink. "What's going on? Why are you doing this?"

Richard leaned back, exhaling a plume of smoke. "Simple. Well... not really. When the Norn started grooming you, I got a visit. From someone else. A woman. Alien. Beautiful. Scary as hell. She made me an offer."

Alex's brow furrowed. "What kind of offer?"

"A choice," Richard said. "Keep playing by Earth's rules... or change the game."

"You changed the game," Alex muttered.

Richard raised his glass in salute.

"She wanted me to sabotage your efforts. I agreed. The first thing we did was kill the Elevation test."

Alex blinked. "That wasn't human error," he asked in stunned disbelief.

Richard laughed. "She put a hole in it the size of a penny. You thought it was a glitch."

Alex shook his head. "And I believed it. Mother fuc..."

Richard poured more brandy into his own glass and interrupted. "You were too busy chasing the stars to notice the cracks under your feet."

"And the Halo?" Alex asked.

Richard grew still. "You used it. Didn't you?"

"Yes," Alex said. "Tim and I wore it for ten minutes. It rewired everything. We were sharper. Stronger. Faster."

"And hooked," Richard said softly.

Alex's eyes narrowed. "You used it too."

Richard pulled a black bag from beside his chair and unzipped it. Inside, gleaming like something sacred, was the Halo.

"I got my own," he said, lifting it slightly. He turned an inquisitive eye toward Alex. "But you gave me yours first. Why?"

Alex looked down. "Because we didn't trust anyone else with it."

"No," Richard said. "Not entirely. You aren't that… noble."

Alex sighed. "Fine. Because I wanted to keep it for myself. For Tim and me. We thought we could control it. We thought we could be the first to achieve interstellar travel. I wanted that legacy."

Richard leaned forward. "So why'd you kill Stan?"

Alex froze. "I didn't."

Richard's face twisted, in a very real contortion of confusion. "What? He wasn't part of this, you know. He was a good man."

Alex shrugged. "We were playing games with him, toying with him. I don't know, maybe he got scared. Maybe he tripped. All I know is I didn't kill him."

Richard looked away, eyes dark. "He tripped after his throat was slit? Through tempered glass?" Richard shook his head and sighed in disbelief. It was a long time before he could speak again. His words were deliberate and calculating. "Someone else is in this. If you're telling me the truth… someone else…"

A beat passed between them, heavy as they weighed the evidence.

Then, Alex spoke again, voice sharp, passing on Richard's reasoning on a third party.

"My turn," he said. "How, and why, did you take down the Intervention?"

"How?" Richard returned his attention to the conversation. He leaned back, almost casually, as if they were old friends chatting over trivial matters. The firelight flickered across his face, casting half of it in a golden glow and the other half in a creeping shadow.

"I seeded a bomb inside one of the crew members," he said bluntly. "The same one you checked on when you were leaving the ship after your little powwow with Lisa and Brian Sr."

Alex's stomach dropped. The blood drained from his face, and he swallowed hard, the brandy suddenly bitter on his tongue.

"Oh, yeah," Richard added, grinning darkly now, lips curling like a predator's. He pointed his cigar hand in Alex's direction. "The same kind of bomb I put in Grayle."

Alex froze. His eyes went wide with horror. A pulse beat hard at his temple. "No! Why?"

"Never mind that for now. We'll come back to it." Richard's tone was icy and amused, a chilling mix of detachment and glee. "Like I said before, part of my assignment was making sure you didn't achieve your goal. And let's be honest, you wouldn't have anyway. That liquid metal fantasy was never going to hold up. You put people in danger, and you knew it. So don't act innocent. I just made sure your failure was... definitive."

He paused to take a long pull from his glass, then exhaled slowly, savoring both the flavor and the confession. "Truth is, you should have taken the hint with your first failure... the Elevation! But... no. You had to keep pressing. It's what triggered you to mess with the Halo in the first place, am I right?"

Alex's jaw clenched. He didn't like where this conversation was heading. There was a weight in his chest now, heavy and hard. "Yes. That did push me."

"Exactly," Richard said, leaning forward slightly, his voice dipping lower. "And you kept pushing. One thing I'm not sure of is what about the Norn? Why did they leave before the launch?"

"They warned us we were in danger," Alex said, his tone shifting to something more somber. "Said they had to leave and contact... a friend. Someone who would help. They weren't specific. They just warned us to be cautious in our decisions, but... we didn't listen. I realized a long time ago how grave that mistake was."

Richard nodded slowly, swirling his brandy in thought. "So... when I... she... blew up the Intervention, I stood nearby. Watched you. You didn't show an ounce of emotion. What were you thinking?"

"We were panicking," Alex admitted. "We knew everyone around us could be a suspect. We knew how wrong we'd been and how dangerous this had become. That's when we decided to form a small task force. Eight specialists, each from a different discipline, to help uncover the truth from that day."

"See? That's the problem." Richard shook his head. "Still thinking small. The Intervention was just one piece. You never saw the whole picture." He leaned forward now, his voice sharpening, laced with arrogance. "Tell me about that and how you selected your team."

"We chose people who had no families," Alex said quietly. "No spouses. No children. All single. All looking for something different. We used my reputation to convince them and gave them an off-the-grid opportunity. The Norn gave us a device to switch off their tracking signals. They felt free. They *were* free. And they were willing. We compartmentalized the tasks to protect them. Tim and I did all the heavy lifting. We kept them safe."

Richard laughed, his arrogance growing with each word. "Safe? That's laughable, Alex."

"The first person we grabbed was a security guard," Alex continued. "We held him for several days. He was lucid... coherent... but something was off. We ran tests. We saw signs, subtle but undeniable, that he had used the Halo. So we created a retina scanner." Alex gestured toward his own eye. "Overexposure leaves a ring around the pupil. We called it being 'ringed.' Once we confirmed it, we suspected you of the Intervention explosion because, at that time, we thought there was only one Halo. Yours. We hoped it wasn't you. I didn't want to believe it was, but in time, we couldn't come to any other conclusion."

Richard clapped his hands slowly, mock applause echoing softly in the study. "Bravo. I noticed you were taking my people. I figured it out pretty quickly, I might add. And honestly? It was hilarious. I kept helping *her* while you ran in circles, spinning your wheels." He leaned in, voice still condescending. "You weren't a threat. Until now." Richard lowered his eyes, letting his words linger. "That's when she said: it's time. Time to eliminate your team. And Tim."

Alex swallowed hard. "Why not me?"

Richard grinned. "You'll find out."

"Why not just tell me?"

"Because," Richard said, rising slightly from his chair. He began to pace the room, fingers trailing the edge of the desk. "Let's keep it moving. Time's wasting."

He walked over to his display, tapped a few icons, and scrolled through a file. The screen lit his face with a sterile blue glow.

"Owen Stipe. Kansas City. Florida. Dropping Michael Wilson's chip in a swamp. What the fuck was that about?"

"We used Michael," Alex admitted. "He was one of the ringed. We..."

Richard cut him off. "Real quick. What did you do with those twenty-one people again? *My* people?"

Alex's voice cracked. "Fear tactics. At first. But they weren't responsive. They were brain-dead, essentially. We... we euthanized them. We thought it was humane. The only choice we had."

"Okay," Richard said flatly, almost as if logging the confession for later. "Go on."

"You used Michael to publish the story about Owen, so it blew Owen's cover. Once he was exposed, we had to move him. We tried to bait you. We knew you were at Grayle's graduation party, so we put Owen on a train to Seattle. I was hoping to lure you out. I planned to follow you while Tim doubled back. But... you shot him. How the hell did you stay completely undetected?"

Richard chuckled and waved dismissively. "I have toys—black suit, hood? Completely invisible to satellites, radar, sonar—you name it. Same with my vehicles. Cloaked. Real Star Trek shit." He laughed, a maniacal laugh. "Oh my God, I can finally say Star Trek and someone gets the reference."

As Richard laughed at himself, Alex said nothing.

"You see, Alex, I have advanced tech paired with good old-fashioned weaponry. Sniper rifles. Swords. Bows and arrows." He laughed. "I'm like James Bond when it comes to weaponry. And you want to know the best part? Everything you tried… It all backfired on you, didn't it?"

"Yeah," Alex muttered. "Owen wasn't even supposed to be involved. He came in late. The original team member dropped out."

"By the way," Richard added with a wink, "that guy who walked up to Owen? One of mine. I just needed him to stay put long enough for a clean shot. And boy… did I get it."

Alex's eyes slowly closed. When he opened them, the pain and guilt were etched deeply across his face. His posture sagged with the weight of it all.

Richard continued, pressing the advantage. "Then I went to Dayton," he said. "Confronted you. Provoked you. I watched you lead me straight to Beaver Island. Such a great, remote little place. I would have loved to have vacationed there back in the day."

"You were there?" Alex whispered, his voice hollow with realization. He took a sip of his brandy, trying to calm the trembling in his hands.

"I wanted to confront you, but then changed my mind. I cloaked my shuttle, waited, and watched for you to do something stupid, and you didn't disappoint."

"Fuck you," Alex spat.

"I got Paul Lamb and Scott Sims after that. Bow and arrow." Richard chuckled and returned to his chair. He sat with a heavy sigh, like a man recounting fond memories. "You know, I was ten feet from you and Scott while you were talking. I was wondering, Alex, after Scott left, you told Tim to 'end it here.' What did you mean by that?"

Alex sighed. "We were going to let them go. We thought they'd be safer without us. Tim burned the safe houses and covered our tracks. We didn't want anything left. After you got Owen, we knew the others were in danger."

"And they were." Richard's smirk returned, smug and merciless.

Alex's voice trembled. "Why Phil Wells? Why Grayle?"

"Ah… Grayle was long-term planning," Richard said. "An asset years in the making."

"How?" Alex asked. "Why her?"

Richard leaned forward, and for the first time, his voice dropped into something deeper. A shadow passed over his expression.

"Because you don't have a fucking clue what the Halo actually does. I've got all your data. Your movements. Your memories. But there's so much more…"

He tapped his temple.

"And I'll tell you two things about it…"

The conversation turned darker. "One," Richard said, holding up a finger with exaggerated showmanship, drawing out the word like a magician beginning his final trick, "if you're touching another person before you activate the Halo, just a simple hand on the shoulder, skin to skin, you can connect to them. Not just their current thoughts or feelings. Their past. Their experiences. You can see it all."

Alex blinked, confused and unnerved. A slow chill climbed the back of his neck.

"And the best part?" Richard's grin widened into something almost inhuman. "No side effects. You remain completely yourself. Just a silent passenger… watching someone else's nightmares."

He leaned forward, elbows resting on his knees, lowering his voice to a reverent hush. The shadows from the fire flickered across his face, highlighting every furrow and scar as he continued. "When Grayle was a kid, I used to take her and her siblings on little adventures. You know, back when things were still sweet. I always wondered about those dreams she'd have. The redheaded woman in white. Always showing up. Always whispering things."

He paused, then chuckled softly to himself, like he was savoring a secret. "So... I tested it. While she slept, I crept in. Placed a hand on her arm. Put the Halo on." His eyes lit up with a manic glint, as though reliving the thrill. "And wow. You wouldn't believe what I saw. The torment. The pain. That little girl suffered more than anyone should. And it all traced back to that woman. The one in white."

Alex watched him closely, mesmerized and horrified, the fire throwing strange dancing lights across the room.

Richard continued, more animated now, hands gesturing freely. "It took me a second to piece it together, but when I figured it out, I was like, holy shit! I asked my friend, you know, the one you still don't get, and she explained it all. The soul. It's layers. The meaning behind those visions. It was earthshaking, Alex. Completely earthshaking. I wanted to call you right then and there. Share it. Talk about it like we used to. But I couldn't." He sat back, exhaling with something like nostalgia. "I had to wait. Play the long game. And man, what an ace card I had up my sleeve."

Richard tapped his temple with a smirk, then let his hand drop to his lap.

"But to get to Tim... I needed Grayle going in the right direction. So... Addison came along. I knew I could finish it off. That was it. That was my in. I put a tracker on Addison, and the rest is history, so to speak. Through her, I was able to find the rest of your little off-grid team. No sweat."

His tone hardened, and he pressed on.

"I knew if I took Phil out, Grayle would spiral exactly how I needed her to. Easy manipulation, really. And once I had her? It was over. I planted the bomb in her. I knew Tim would never see it coming."

Richard glanced sideways, his voice suddenly light again. "By the way? Props to Tim for getting to Addison before I could. Amazing what people will do when they think someone's dead. I hope they had a moment. Something sweet. Maybe even said something poetic to each other. Because they won't get many more."

"You didn't have to kill the rest of them!" Alex shouted suddenly, the pain in his voice cracking through like a thunderclap. He leapt from his chair, knocking it over with a clatter as he stood. The fire behind him flared, like echoing his rage. "You could've left them alone!"

Richard tilted his head and let out a short, sharp laugh. "Leave no stone unturned, my friend. That night at the camp, I wasn't even sure Tim was there. I was hoping he was. God, I wanted that one-on-one. But I had to go big. Take out as many as I could. Make sure none of them came crawling back. Where was he?"

Alex turned away, panting, hands clenched into fists at his sides. He walked toward the fire, his shoulders stiff. He no longer wanted to be here, to have this conversation, but he needed it done. He needed to finish it for the others. His voice dropped low, worn with grief. "He was by the escape vehicles. Waiting. He was going to give them safe coordinates. But he was too far away to help."

"Shame," Richard said, almost cheerfully. "Addison ran. I let her. Pretty little thing. Good energy. Good… well, let's just say it's a shame to waste it. Who knows, maybe she and Tim can die together. Romantic, right?" His grin twisted at the edges. "Besides, chasing her into the woods would've given Tim a tactical edge. I'm no idiot. So I bounced."

Alex's jaw tightened, teeth grinding against the helplessness welling up inside him.

"Oh!" Richard snapped his fingers, triumphant. "Right. You asked about the second use of the Halo."

Alex didn't answer. His frame was slumped, his posture hollow, and all the fire had gone from his eyes. But Richard pressed on, delighted anyway.

"Once you've used the Halo," he said, tapping the side of his neck where the device usually sat, "there's this little button here. You activate it and boom, you can track a soul. If that soul ever finds a new life, if it reincarnates, if it transfers, you can find it."

He paused then, and when he continued, his voice softened, almost gentle. His expression changed into something strangely sincere as he looked at Alex. "I just thought you'd want to know that. Maybe in all this chaos... that brings you a sliver of comfort. Maybe you'll find the people you lost."

Richard's eyes held Alex's gaze, and in that moment, something deeper passed between them, something haunted and unsaid.

The fire between them hissed, and a single ember leapt into the air before vanishing into the dark.

Alex stood there absorbing every word like poison. His brandy remained untouched on the table. "Why?" he finally asked. "All of this... hate? Spite?"

Richard exhaled slowly, his complexion beginning to pale further under the firelight. He rose again, slowly, and wandered over to where Alex stood. The movement looked effortful now, his limbs heavier than before. But his tone held reverence.

"I know you won't believe me, but I love you as a friend, Alex. One of the reasons I pulled away from you, kept my distance, was because I wouldn't have been able to do what was needed if I remained close."

Alex spun on him and shouted, his voice raw and torn. "Why won't you just tell me everything else? I don't understand..."

Richard held up a hand. "Can't. Sorry." He gave a weary smile. "You see, I, too, wanted to be remembered. True story, Alex," he said, holding a finger to his lips, almost conspiratorially, and began to pace again. "Once, I was a sniper named Josh Fabijanic. Germany, 1930s. But you've never heard of me, have you? World War Two broke out, and I couldn't care less. You see, there were two kinds of soldiers in the army - those who believed in what that idiot, Hitler, was spewing, and those who were scared. Me? I wasn't scared, but I wasn't following the nonsense either."

Richard turned and fixed his eyes on Alex, pausing.

"Then came Operation Valkyrie. They asked me to take part and I agreed. I said I'd take the shot on Hitler. Of course, the plan failed. I would have killed that fucker, too. They'd still be talking about me, centuries later! I lost my chance to be remembered." He smiled, wide and unhinged. "Now? I have another chance. Not in history books. In the stars. I have recaptured my stolen glory!"

"You're insane," Alex said, recoiling. "You've operated in total secrecy. How will anyone ever…"

Richard waved him off, furious now. "Again, small-minded. Fuck the world, Alex! I'll be remembered by the universe!"

His eyes burned with delusion, and Alex reeled from the sheer manic energy. Richard's skin was nearly gray now, the blood draining from him like color from a fading photograph.

He glanced at his wristband and checked his vitals. The display pulsed softly, numbers dropping. His heart rate was steadily declining.

"You got any more questions, Alex?" Richard asked, his voice thin and fading. "Because I don't have much time left."

Alex looked away. The firelight glinted off the glass nearby, illuminating the hollows under his eyes. "Just a second ago, you said, 'If the soul finds a new life.' What did you mean by *if*?"

Richard nodded solemnly, as if he had expected that question all along. "That's a good one to leave off on," he said softly. "There's so much more to all this… supernatural, paranormal stuff than people know. You, me, and Tim, we've seen pieces of it. More than most. But not everything."

He took a breath, staggered to the hearth for balance, and looked to the ceiling as if peering into the beyond.

"Do you remember what happens after you die?"

Alex shook his head. "No. Not really."

"Well, you do leave your body. It's real. It starts with a kind of darkness. Not pitch black, just… shadowy. Like twilight. It's quite beautiful, actually. It's like you're gazing up at the stars. But stars so bright that they light up the sky."

He swept his arm across an invisible constellation, painting the air with unseen galaxies. He continued, speaking not to Alex anymore, but to something greater.

"If you're ready, you can enter a portal, and that will take you to your new destination." He looked back at Alex with sudden intensity. "You go back to where you came from, Alex. Or close by. Not exact, but close."

Richard returned to the chair, visibly swaying. He collapsed into it, breathing hard. "I need to sit or I'm gonna fall." He shut his eyes briefly, then reached for his brandy glass. It trembled in his hand. He coughed into his sleeve, then took a heavy gulp, the warmth steadying him slightly.

"You return somewhere that resonates with who you were, Alex. A place, a memory, maybe even people you once knew." His voice softened to a whisper. "You ever look at a place... a town... a landmark... and feel like you've been there before, but can't remember when?"

Alex gave the faintest nod.

"That's the soul remembering," Richard said. "We don't forget as easily as we think. You know that déjà vu feeling? Like you've been somewhere before? It's because you have. And when you're young, you still remember. Until time washes it away."

He looked at Alex, vision fogged and wavering.

"Leee me 'splain," he slurred, then tried again. "Let me explain the *if*. When someone dies by suicide, for example... the soul can get stuck. It's too broken to move on. That's what happened with Grayle's first case. The mother couldn't leave. Her child had died, and she wouldn't move on without him. And if a soul is too weighed down by grief, it can latch onto objects. That music box? Probably kept the mother from reaching the child."

He laughed faintly, then coughed hard into his arm.

"Not... not every...thing's clear. I don't know why exactly. But I guess I'll find out soon."

"What's that have to do with any of this?" Alex pressed, voice strained.

Richard's coughing subsided. He looked up at Alex with eyes rimmed red.

"In Grayle's case, there's a soul, Bridgette, that's still tethered to her. Waiting on the other side. But Grayle's drive for vengeance is stronger than her ability to hear her. Bridgette warned her about her parents. That's how she knew they were going to die. She's been trying to reach her since childhood."

Alex's jaw clenched. He stepped forward. "You're stalling."

Richard raised one brow, barely. "Maybe."

"You put a bomb in her," Alex growled. "She'd be taking her own life. You're trapping her, dooming her to repeat it. You bastard. If you weren't already dying, I'd kill you myself."

Richard gave a cracked smirk. "Small potatoes. Grayle's just one tragedy among many... unless someone stops what's coming."

Alex turned away, trembling. "I'm done here."

"Wait." Richard held up both hands. Blood had begun forming at the corners of his lips, bubbling with each breath. "One last question. Then we're square."

Alex paused, reluctantly.

"How did you find those twenty-one people I programmed to serve me?"

Alex sighed and shrugged. "Not that it matters, you self-absorbed prick, but someone left the list. Just a pile of names. Handwritten. No explanation, just a note at the bottom that said, 'Look into them and you'll find answers.' Once we picked up the first one and ran our tests, we knew the Halo had been used. You became our prime suspect. But we couldn't reach you. You were the Director. So we turned to the next best option: put them out of their misery. They were suffering, and you know it. All that time with the Halo had fried their brains."

Richard gave a cold, slow smile. "Yeah... I know." He leaned back again, the weight of his own fading life starting to settle in. The blood on his lips had thickened, drying at the corners of his mouth. His breath rasped slightly as he wiped at the crimson smear on his chin, an oddly graceful gesture despite the tremor in his hand. His skin had paled to a ghostly hue, and the golden firelight did little to bring warmth to his expression.

He sighed and closed his eyes. "All right then," he said quietly. "We're finished here."

Alex looked at him for a long moment, a last bit of compassion entering his body. The tension in his posture softened ever so slightly. "You want me to stay?"

Richard gave a weak laugh, more breath than voice. "I'm sure you'd love to watch me die, but no. I'd rather be alone. I'm going to put my favorite record on, finish this brandy, and call it a day."

"You might get, you know… stuck, killing yourself," Alex said flatly.

"May…ee," Richard admitted. His voice was thinning now, each syllable trailing slightly. "Still worth it."

Alex stood, turned, and walked toward the door. The room felt heavy behind him, laden with smoke and shadow.

"Goodbye."

Richard opened his eyes, lifting his brandy glass with the last of his strength. The liquid sloshed, splashing over his trembling fingers and onto the chair's armrest. He offered a crooked smile. Through blood-choked words, he bid adieu.

"Betr… Be…r… I'll try… do… better next time."

Alex didn't look back. He just walked out, leaving the past and Richard to burn quietly in the dying light.

As he heard the door latch behind him, Alex wondered if perhaps Richard was able to see the unattended flames in the fireplace beginning to die, and him walking to his transport from a vantage point above. He smiled as he lifted his middle finger upward.

Chapter 26: I'm Sorry for Everything

After his sign off with Richard, Alex realized, with sudden horror, that he had left Grayle alone with Tim - and vice versa. His pulse spiked. Adrenaline surged through his chest as he tore out of the house and sprinted toward his shuttle. The night air was cool and damp, brushing past his cheeks as he slammed the shuttle door shut behind him. He immediately opened a comm channel, the console lights flickering as he keyed in the frequency.

"Tim! Tim! You there?"

"I'm here," came Tim's steady voice, calm and unchanged.

Alex exhaled sharply, a strained breath of relief escaping as he tried to regain composure. He leaned forward, resting his forearm against the control panel, but Tim didn't allow space for hesitation.

"Did you take Richard out?"

"He took himself out," Alex said, his voice suddenly quieter, the edge replaced by something more reflective. "Listen..."

A beat of silence stretched between them; Tim could tell Alex had more to say.

"Go on."

"Grayle... What did you do with her?" Alex asked.

"I knocked her out and gave her a mild sedative. She should be out for another hour. I called Will — he moved Tash and Addison to a safe place. We'll catch up later." A deep silence lingered on the line before Tim spoke again. His voice dipped slightly. "Why, what's up?"

Alex gritted his teeth, trying to hold back the panic rising in his throat. His knuckles were white on the console edge. "I'm coming to you. Stay there."

Tim's reply was casual, too casual. Alex could almost picture him shrugging. "All right, well, get here."

The shuttle flight didn't seem nearly as long as it was. Every minute that ticked by felt compressed, folded into the urgency of his thoughts. He sat at the controls, watching the horizon blur into a silver streak of movement as the stars outside hung silently overhead.

Minutes later, he touched down near the Dayton warehouse, its descent rougher than usual. The instant the doors cracked open, Alex was already sprinting across the concrete, the bay lights illuminating his frantic form. He called out loudly. "Tim!"

His voice echoed inside the half-lit building. His anxiety had reached a fevered pitch by the time he reached the front.

He wasn't fifty feet from the building when Tim stepped out of the shadows and waved him over, casually holding open the door with his right hand.

Alex rushed inside, chest heaving, his eyes darting. "Where is she?"

"I moved her to the corner office. What the hell's the matter with you?"

Alex made his way to the small room and peered inside. The lighting was dim, a flickering bulb casting shadows over the space. Grayle was passed out on an old leather couch in the corner, her body still and peaceful in a way that felt unnatural.

"How much longer will she be out?" Alex was still breathless from his sprint.

"You seriously need to get in better shape," Tim said, one eyebrow raised.

"Asshole," Alex snapped, clapping his hands together with urgency. "Be serious. How long?"

Tim shrugged again. "I don't know, thirty minutes? Give or take."

Alex leaned down, resting a hand on his knee, trying to slow his breathing. The weight of what he had to say pressed against his chest. His voice was flat. "She has a bomb inside her." He gestured toward Grayle; his hand trembled.

Tim's eyes widened. The humor vanished from his face. "Well, then what the fuck are you doing here?"

"Because I need to talk to her," Alex said, his voice weighed down by grief. "I can't let her go out like this."

"Meaning? What the hell did Richard tell you?" Tim asked.

Alex recounted everything: the pills, the afterlife, the confession, and the devastating truth about Grayle's fate. As he spoke, Tim stood motionless, listening in disbelief.

"Oh my God," he whispered. "Fuck!"

"What are you thinking?" Alex asked.

Tim's expression grew darker. He stared down at the concrete. "Beaver Island. I knew I wasn't alone that night. I should've double-checked. I should have made sure that Scott and the team got away. I should've checked Addison, too. Richard must've tagged her somehow. Tracking, maybe. So many errors..."

"We were outclassed," Alex said, his eyes dull and tired.

Tim nodded grimly. "Remember all the crap we gave Michael Wilson? About being superior? Richard was savvy, but we thought we were gods. Now look at us." He laughed, but it was a sharp, bitter sound. "We were gonna drag the human race forward! Ha!" He ran both hands through his tangled hair. "Seems pretty stupid now."

The warehouse fell quiet again. The silence wasn't peace; it was defeat.

"We lost," Alex said quietly.

Tim nodded once more, slower this time. Then he took a breath and tried to push forward. "So... what do we do with her?"

Alex looked toward the corner office, at the woman who had risked everything. "Try to do something right."

He walked over, grabbed a chair, and planted it by the couch. The metal legs scraped softly across the concrete. He sat, heavy with regret. "We wait."

Tim looked down at Grayle. Then, without a word, he disappeared for a moment and returned with his own chair. He placed it beside Alex, and together... they waited.

Grayle stirred first, just a twitch, then a groggy flutter of the eyes. Her lashes trembled slightly as she blinked herself into consciousness. The air around her felt heavier, humid with tension. They sat her up slowly, her body sluggish from the sedative, her hands still restrained tightly behind her back. Tim gently brought a plastic cup to her lips, giving her a small sip of water.

"Grayle," Alex said softly, leaning in, his voice barely above a whisper. "Can you understand me?"

Her eyelids lifted further, revealing tired, defiant eyes. "Fuck you," she murmured.

Alex didn't flinch. He just nodded gently. "Please listen," he said, his tone still calm and sincere. "This is important. How long do we have before the bomb goes off?"

"You bought yourself a minute or two," she replied, her voice coated in sarcasm.

"Do you know how long, exactly?" Alex pressed.

"My heartbeat is the timer," she said with a twisted smile, eyes narrowing. "Why don't you let me take a jog and see?"

Her gaze shifted suddenly, locking onto Tim's. A new venom flooded her voice. "You're coming with me, motherfucker."

Tim leaned in, grabbing Alex's arm and pulling him gently back. His whisper was fast and sharp. "Here are our options: we euthanize her and stop the bomb — I think. Or we leave. Or I stay with her. I'm the one she wants."

Alex shook his head slowly, as if the words themselves stung. "I can't kill her," he said. "And you can't either. If Richard was right about the afterlife, killing her would damn her. And I won't leave you. If you go, I go, brother."

Tim dropped his gaze. A long silence passed between them. "Maybe that's it, then. I'm tired."

Alex exhaled, his shoulders slumping under the weight of everything. "Me too."

The warehouse seemed colder now. The light overhead buzzed faintly as it flickered.

After a few minutes of contemplation, Tim finally spoke up, his voice more resolved. "Go," he said firmly. "Take Addison somewhere safe. That other island safehouse. Retire. Get some rest."

Alex nodded, his eyes heavy with sorrow. He turned to Grayle and knelt beside her, placing a hand gently on her knee.

"Listen to me, love. You need to let go. Okay?"

Grayle's eyes searched his, her expression softening just slightly. "What did you say?"

"You need to let go. Let go of the anger. Move forward."

Her lips trembled, and her eyes welled. "I think I under—"

BANG!

A single gunshot cracked. Sound exploded in the warehouse, metal and concrete answering it. Alex and Tim spun. Tim drew his weapon in a flash, dropping to his knees and scanning the space for the threat.

Brian Jr. stood just inside the warehouse door, his hand still raised, the gun gripped tightly, smoke curling from the barrel. Tears streamed freely down his cheeks, illuminated in the pale overhead light. His face contorted as the weight of what he'd done landed. He dropped the weapon and clutched his head, wailing.

"I'm sorry, baby! I'm so... sorry!"

"B.J.!" Alex shouted, rushing toward him. "What did you do?"

They turned back to Grayle. Blood poured in thick, hot ribbons from a wound at her neck, spreading across her shoulder and down her side.

"Oh my God," Tim cried. "She was hit in the carotid! I can't stop it!" He pressed both hands against the wound, desperately trying to stem the flow, but it was too much. The color was already draining from her face. He looked into her eyes, and for a moment, time stood still. "Grayle! I'm sorry! For EVERYTHING!"

Alex stood frozen, devastated, watching as the life faded from her body.

The world fell silent.

A thin, expectant hush hung... then nothing. No detonation. Tim glanced at Alex—confused, then grim.

"Heartbeat trigger," Tim said, swallowing.

Grayle opened her eyes again, only now, everything was different.

There was no sound, only stillness. A serene, weightless hush surrounded her, as if the very air had been replaced by starlight. She looked down and saw her body lying motionless. Tim and Alex clutched her hands. Alex stroked her hair with infinite tenderness. Nearby, Brian Jr. had curled into a fetal position, his cries broken and raw, his body shuddering beneath the grief.

Grayle turned her gaze to her own hands and feet. They shimmered faintly, growing translucent, the edges of her form blending with the light. Her breath caught in awe as she realized: she was no longer inside her body.

The warehouse faded like mist, replaced by a night sky woven from gold and indigo. Above her, stars blinked in quiet reverence. She stood in a realm between realms, poised in luminous suspension. One path led to a distant, glowing white light pulsing softly on the horizon. Another opened to her left, a simple doorway, quietly waiting.

Behind her, Alex, Tim, and B.J. dissolved into memory, like photographs curling at the edges of a fire. "You got away again," she whispered toward the pair, but then turned her stare toward the horizon and the glowing white light. "Bridgette?"

She turned toward the doorway, then back at the white figure ahead, indecisive. Her voice echoed faintly in the vastness: "Let go… Let go…" She looked up at the stars, longing and fear mingling in her eyes.

A voice interrupted the silence.

"Hey."

She turned to see Phil Wells standing nearby. He was calm, illuminated in the same golden hue that bathed the stars, his smile warm and welcoming.

"Phil?"

"I've been waiting for you," he said with a lightness in his voice. "Didn't want to go back until I saw you."

They touched hands, the contact full of peace. Grayle laughed softly, tears in her eyes. "How do we still look like this?"

"This is your last form," he said. "You move on from here."

Grayle studied her hands again, half-expecting them to melt or shift, but they remained as they were, perfect echoes of her earthly self. "Why are you here?"

Phil gestured toward the soft glow ahead. "That's Bridgette. She waits for you every time. But you have to choose. You can end the suffering. You can find peace. Do you want that?"

"Yes," Grayle said, her voice breaking. A smile crossed her lips, lit by the anticipation of something eternal.

Phil stepped aside. "Then go. Don't keep a lady waiting."

He turned to walk toward the doorway, but Grayle's voice called him back.

"Wait! Are you going to be okay?"

Phil paused and nodded. "Yes."

Grayle tilted her head, thoughtful. "One more thing... I vaguely remember being here before. I remember... rules. No interference. What you're doing now... isn't this breaking that rule?"

Phil's smile widened. "Yes. The Creator allowed it this time."

Grayle replied, "The Creator?" Her soul radiating. She finally found the peace she had been yearning for.

Phil winked, eyes twinkling with divine mischief. "Always sharp as a tack, Grayle." Then he turned and stepped through the door, vanishing into the light.

Grayle turned toward the brilliant horizon, and with steadiness, she walked forward, fading gently into the stars.

Back in the warehouse, the aftermath was chaos. The air still held the acrid scent of gunpowder, mingled with the metallic sting of blood. Alex and Tim were crouched beside Brian Jr., who sat collapsed against a stack of crates, trembling with grief. His clothes were stained with tears and blood.

Commander Phillips burst in, his boots echoing sharply across the concrete. He took one look at the scene and froze, his mouth opening as if to speak, but unable to find words. When he finally did, they came out as a broken demand. "Grayle! What the... what the hell happened?!"

His eyes darted wildly from the pool of blood to Brian, to Alex, then to Tim. "What did you do to...?"

Before Alex could respond, Will's fist flew through the air and connected with Alex's jaw, sending him stumbling backward.

Tim rushed forward and wedged himself between them. "Will! Listen!" he shouted.

But the commander was inconsolable, fury blazing in his eyes. He shoved past Tim, grabbed Brian by the arm, and started pulling him toward the exit.

Brian stumbled upright, staggering like a drunk. His voice cracked. "Can you - can you just get me out of here? I'm exhausted and broken and - I need to leave."

Will stopped just long enough to nod. "I'll take him. But this isn't over."

He turned back to Tim, his voice shaking with rage. "You two owe me an explanation. And you'd better pray I don't kill you myself."

He cast one last glance at Grayle's lifeless body. His hand trembled as he pointed at her. "I'm taking her with me. Stay out of my way."

No one moved.

Everyone watched in stunned silence as Will gently gathered Grayle's body, eyes dark with sorrow. Without another word, he loaded her into the shuttle and left, the sound of the engine rising into the hollow night.

Alex and Tim walked outside together, staring upward as the shuttle disappeared into the sky.

"Hey," Tim said quietly.

"Huh?" Alex answered, still dazed.

"You got a heater?"

Alex passed one over and struck the lighter. The orange flame flickered in the breeze.

"What do you say we give him some time before we try to talk to him?" Tim asked, blowing out a long stream of smoke.

Alex nodded, the smoke curling around his face like fog. "Yeah, no shit."

They stood in silence, sharing the cold and the ash, when footsteps approached from behind.

The Norn emerged from the shadows - N1 and N2.

Alex turned slightly, not surprised. "Can I help you?" he asked, his tone laced with mild sarcasm. It was as if he'd expected them all along.

N2 stepped forward. "We know things have been - difficult."

Tim scoffed, laughing bitterly. "That's putting it mildly. Just about as fucking mild as possible."

For the first time in a long while, N1 spoke. His voice was deep and crisp, like ancient stone being moved. "I understand your frustration. I'm sorry we couldn't help more. We've been… away."

Tim muttered under his breath, leaning toward Alex. "So he… can talk?"

"Shhh," Alex replied, eyes still on the Norn.

N1 continued. "We went to get help. He's here now."

From the darkness, a tall figure stepped forward. His frame was broad and upright, his suit a sleek black-gray that shimmered slightly in the low light. Silver hair fell across his brow, and a well-kept beard framed a face that looked almost human. That is, until he spoke.

"Sjjcuhebhg kkfbbvwvvsghj. Oh, sorry. You can't understand me," the man said, the smirk on his face barely concealed. "My people are the Daig. Rhymes with Craig."

Tim raised an eyebrow and leaned toward Alex. "This mother-fucker looks like Sean Connery on steroids. And why would he add that, 'rhymes with Craig thing?' Does he think we don't understand?

The stranger gave a polite, condescending smile. "The alien whom your friend has been helping has been giving us problems of late. I'm here to remedy that. You've done fine work helping us, but your services are no longer required. I'll handle the rest."

"A — he wasn't my… well, at one point he was, but lately, he wasn't — my friend," Alex said, squinting slightly. "And two, do you have a name?"

The alien paused as if downloading a file from the void. "Ah, television sitcom reference, not incorrect grammar. You call me Jim. That should be simple enough for you - well, men of your species, to remember."

Without waiting for a reply, Jim gave a short nod to the Norn. And then, just like that, they vanished.

Tim blinked. "What a condescending prick. So… are we done?"

Alex stared at the space they had occupied. "Fuck yeah, we are. It's clear that we're in over our heads, right? I mean, that's what Jim says." He lifted his fingers to make exaggerated air quotes.

"Richard's mystery alien buddy, now Jim. It's quite clear that we've lost. It's a power struggle now, bigger than us. I mean, we can keep an eye on things, but there's already been enough damage and death, don't you think? I feel like… in this moment, we know even less than we did before."

"I agree," Tim said.

"I don't want to be a space explorer anymore."

"Me neither."

Tim grinned. "Let's find the reincarnated Beatles and get them back together."

Alex laughed. "Actually — that gives me an idea."

"What?" Tim asked, still chuckling.

Alex shook his head. "No, no. Not yet. First… we have something else to do."

Epilogue: Three Weeks Later – Cincinnati, Ohio

Two nurses sat in the break room of Christ Hospital, the quiet hum of the vending machine underscoring the low volume of the television. "Jenn, turn this up," Marcy said.

ON-SCREEN:
The screen lit up with the face of Wes Waters, seated behind the anchor desk.

WES WATERS:
"Tonight, a new figure enters the spotlight: Jim, the new spokesperson for the Norn. Alex Belle has stepped down, and Jim assures us: peace is coming."

ON-SCREEN:
Jim is standing at a podium, looking impeccably composed, his voice smooth with performative charm.

JIM:
"Greetings, friends. I'll keep this brief, and I'll be taking questions from your journalists shortly, but for right now, let me brief you on why I am here. The tragic murders of Owen Stipe, Stan Collins, and Phil Wells were the work of one of ours. A rogue acting with malicious intent. I'm here to ensure justice and help restore a peaceful society. You have nothing to fear. I guarantee that."

WES WATERS:
"Jim promises to keep the peace. After everything revealed about Alex Belle and the events around him, many will feel safer with Jim and the Norn's return. Wes tapped his tablet. *"Speaking of Alex Belle, the scientific community and the world are still stunned by his announcement four days*

Jenn shook her head. "That's a lot."

Marcy giggled, twirling her hair. "That Jim's kind of a hot alien."

"Marcy," Jenn laughed, smacking her playfully on the shoulder.

Meanwhile, down the hall, Alex quietly slipped through a side door. A doctor spotted him.

"Mr. Belle?"

Alex smiled. "Hi. I'm just saying hi to a friend."

"Will you be making a statement soon about the Paranormal Department?" the doctor asked, then blushed. "I'm sorry. I'd be remiss if I didn't ask."

Alex chuckled. "Yes. Very shortly." He gave the doctor's shoulder a light pat and walked away.

Outside, Tim leaned against the vehicle, arms crossed. Alex approached, calm and clear-eyed.

"Grayle?" Tim asked. "Bridgette, too?"

Alex placed his hand over his heart and nodded.

They both smiled, wide, genuine, and free.

Inside the hospital nursery, soft music played as nurses moved from crib to crib. Two newborns lay side by side in matching blankets. The doctor peered over the charts and smiled.

"These two have been here a little over a day," Jenn said. "Born three minutes apart. They smile every time they're together. It's like they know each other."

The doctor looked at them thoughtfully as they cooed.

Two souls, beginning again.

Lovers again.

THE END

Thank you for reading <u>The Conspiracy Within</u>

Make sure to follow Phillips & Dunn Publishing on social media
for more information on the sequel to this book

<u>The Conspiracy Within – Lost Souls</u>

and other exciting new releases!

About the Author:

Sean Mackie has always been drawn to stories that ask, "What if?" His debut novel, a mix of sci-fi, fantasy, and murder mystery, marks his first step into the world of fiction writing. What started as an idea scribbled in a notebook became a full-fledged story that combines imagination, suspense, and the thrill of discovery.

This is Sean's very first book, but it certainly won't be his last.

www.ingramcontent.com/pod-product-compliance
Lightning Source LLC
Chambersburg PA
CBHW071743110726
47908CB00006B/1684